The Montfort Prescription

The TransAmerica Pyramid

The Montfort Prescription

A Novel

John Sutherland

ISBN: 979-8-9853929-1-3 (Paperback)
ISBN: 979-8-9853929-2-0 (Hardcover)

This is a work of fiction. Any references to historical events, real people, or real places are used fictitiously. Other names, characters, places and events are products of the author's imagination, and any resemblances to actual events or places or persons, living or dead, is entirely coincidental.

Cover: The Fountain of the Turtles

Campbell Park
10645 N 10th Place
Phoenix, AZ 85020

www.themontfortprescription.com

for Maria and Gordon

"A country rapidly passed through under favourable auspices may leave upon us a unity of impression that would only be disturbed and dissipated if we stayed longer. Clear vision goes with the quick foot. Things fall for us into a sort of natural perspective when we see them for a moment in going by; we generalise boldly and simply, and are gone before the sun is overcast, before the rain falls, before the season can steal like a dial-hand from his figure, before the lights and shadows, shifting round towards nightfall, can show us the other side of things, and belie what they showed us in the morning."

Robert Louis Stevenson
An Autumn Effect

"At this second stage of development, the conscience exhibits a peculiarity which was absent from the first stage and which is no longer easy to account for. For the more virtuous a man is, the more severe and distrustful is its behaviour, so that ultimately it is precisely those people who have carried saintliness the furthest who reproach themselves with the worst sinfulness."

Sigmund Freud
Civilization and its Discontents

On January 25, 2004, I told my grandfather that I had been accepted into the San Francisco Police Academy. The priest had told us that morning that January 25 is the Feast of the Conversion of Saint Paul the Apostle, patron of authors and tent-makers. The patron saint of police officers (and sailors and grocers) is St. Michael Archangel, but his feast day wasn't until September.

After a roadside IED brought my military career to a premature end, I'd decided that passing the police Physical Ability Test and psych exam would be one way to show myself I wasn't damaged goods. I hadn't stopped to ask what would happen when I proved myself right.

I don't know what response I had expected. I'd lived with my grandparents since my mother died, and Granddad had been proud when I joined up to fight the Taliban after 9/11. But the police were another matter. Gardena wasn't Watts, but we'd still had The Talk one Saturday when I was 10 and my grandmother was visiting her sisters. "Being only a quarter black doesn't mean you're a white boy. Don't you go telling yourself otherwise."

Now he was leaning back in his chair, the Sunday paper abandoned on his lap. "Dragon's teeth."

"Dragon's teeth?"

He nodded. "Yeah. Remember the book of Greek myths you had as a kid, the one with all the pictures?"

"Uh-huh. There was a man scattering dragon's teeth, and the teeth turned into soldiers." It had been one of my favorites, a muscular young man striding forward with his cloak blowing in the wind under against a sky filled with storm clouds.

He nodded again. "He thought he was going to build an army to protect his country, but he ended up with a bunch of loose cannons and killers instead."

"And you think that's going to happen to me at the Academy?"

"I'm saying you ought to know enough to tell boys' stories from the real world. You want to go be a cop, save everybody, change the system from inside? Just watch out it don't change you so you end up sowing dragon's teeth."

"Somebody has to protect people."

He shook his head. "Yeah, I know; somebody's got to be entrusted with the power. Trouble is, nobody can be trusted with power. Nobody."

We were silent for a bit.

"Cadmus," I said finally. "His name was Cadmus."

PURGATION

ONE

The call from Lombard Street comes in just after 5:30 in the morning. The 911 call taker contacts radio dispatch a couple of minutes later, and the sky is still dark when Franklin Washborne's phone rings. "Hey, they need you at Lombard and Hyde."

"Got something for me?"

"'Someone, Sergeant. A dead someone."

Traffic on the 101 isn't as bad on a Saturday, but a crowd of onlookers already blocks the Powell-Hyde cable car tracks by the time Franklin arrives. Crime scene tape stretches across Lombard Street at both Hyde and Leavenworth. He heads toward the uniforms at the end of the first switchback. A couple of photographers from the Medical Examiner's office are snapping shots of some guy lying on the sidewalk; everybody else is just standing around.

Franklin recognizes two of the unis. "So, what's the story?"

"Uh, it's a nice morning and we thought we'd play tourist. Visit the Crookedest Street in the World, and then maybe a trip to Golden Gate Park."

"Sorry, I thought this was a homicide scene."

"Yeah, there's a dead guy over there. Looks like somebody just missed a step. Ortega and Loeffler have already been here. If somebody tripped over this guy in the Tenderloin ..." He shrugs.

"You're right. If this guy died in the Tenderloin, no one would give a damn. What the hell, maybe I should just go home. What do you think?"

The Lombard Street Steps

"Hey, c'mon Sarge, you know what I'm saying. It's this neighborhood. You see those gawkers? I almost had to arrest a bunch of them because they won't stay behind the tape. Poor bastard falls down the steps, and they treat it like it's part of a show we're putting on for them."

Franklin relents. "I hear you; all this may be overkill. You weren't on the force back when the murder clearance rate was 25%. But City Hall still remembers, so now we over-investigate everything."

"Yeah, departmental policy. I'm just saying that somebody dead on a street loaded with million-dollar homes and a couple of million tourists a year is gonna get special treatment, no matter how it happened."

A second cop joins in. "And the people here are something else. You know how many calls we get about the traffic jams and boomboxes and blocked driveways? And littering, and people taking selfies on somebody's front porch. Last week I got a call from a guy in the 900 block who wanted me to stop his neighbor from modifying Scottie Ferguson's house."

Franklin frowns. "Scottie Ferguson?

"Yeah, the detective in Hitchcock's *Vertigo*. Jimmie Stewart?"

"Planning a new career as a movie critic, officer?" Sergeant Miguel Ortega is the lead detective on this case, and his patented "go to hell" glare is enough to end the conversation. "Nice you could join us, Inspector Washborne."

"Morning, Mike. You think you need all four of us?"

"What I think doesn't matter; policy is policy, even if this guy was just some drunk frat boy who took a header. I wanted Loeffler here because he's still learning the ropes, but I figured this case also needed a decorated Afghanistan War veteran. You do a better job acting like you give a shit about the Very Rich than I do." He glances toward the sidewalk. "The stiff's in front of 1079."

"Somebody in the third-floor front efficiency noticed something on the sidewalk but didn't dial 911 until he figured out it looked an awful lot like a human being who wasn't moving." Kevin Loeffler glances down at the sheeted figure lying in front of him. He wears his red hair in short spikes, which gives him a look of perpetual mild alarm.

"Did the guy come down to look?"

"Hell no; just made the call. We had trouble getting him to admit even that much; only thing he's sure of is that he doesn't know anything."

Franklin stares at the sheet. "That seem a little avoidant to you?"

"Yeah, but I don't take it personally. I'm used to people trying to avoid cops and dead bodies. If I was paying three thou a month for six hundred square feet in a 1909 house in SanFranLand Theme Park, I think I'd want everybody just to go away and let me get back to making the rent too."

The medical examiner's crew has finished taking pictures. Franklin pulls back the sheet. The deceased is a sinewy bearded man in his late twenties, wearing business casual. "Was he like this when they found him?"

"No, he was face down. Mike and I checked his pockets and then rolled him over for the examiner's guys. He had a backpack, but nothing else with him. Based on body temperature, they think he died somewhere between midnight and 2 AM."

A pool of congealed blood has formed next to the railing between a basement entry and a set of carriage-style garage doors. A short set of stairs leads up to a driveway and five steps that abut the house's main entryway. Past this, the walkway divides into two flights of narrow steps, flanked by iron railings that continue up to Hyde Street.

Kevin frowns. " I suppose he could have just tripped and lost his balance if he didn't know the neighborhood. There was some fog last night. This area could be tough to negotiate in the dark."

Franklin shakes his head. "The fog was patchy, and the moon was full two nights ago. There are plenty of railings here. And why would someone try to walk down 200 steps when he could have used the road? There wouldn't have been any traffic at that hour. Or at least use the stairs on the other side."

Kevin glance at the broad brick stairs marching down from Hyde Street. "Somebody's lawyer must have told the owners on that side about personal injury lawsuits. Guess the folks over here didn't get the message. Suppose Ortega's right and the guy was just wasted?"

Franklin climbs ten feet up the hill and looks back. "Standing here, I can't see the blood stain by the doorway. How did a guy coming down these steps end up wedged against that railing?"

"He wouldn't have unless he was running."

"And?"

"And he wouldn't be running in the dark here except on a dare. Or unless someone was chasing him."

"Or unless someone placed his body there." Franklin hasn't worked with Kevin before, but he's heard about him. He's a newly minted Inspector, supposed to be smart and sarcastic and very gay. *I can see that two of those things are true, and I'll bet the part about you being pretty sharp is also on target.*

Mike Ortega is strutting down the first hairpin, waving on the Medical Examiner's van. "They're ready to transport. I guess we can start closing out the Case of the Clumsy Yuppie who got himself killed on one of our historically decrepit sidewalks. You can wrap it up here, Loeffler." He nods to Franklin. "Washborne, check if anyone else has turned up who knows anything. People might be home on a Saturday and up by now—not that anyone could have missed this." He turns without waiting for a response.

Kevin runs his hand through his spikes. "So that's it? Case closed?"

"Mike has a short attention span. We still have no idea who this guy is. You said he had no ID?"

Kevin shakes his head. "No wallet. And no cell phone. I guess I'll head back and have another look at that backpack."

"OK. I'll canvas the patrolmen to see what else they've heard."

"Cool. Later."

Franklin spends another hour at the 1000 block of Lombard Street, but this must be a neighborhood of sound sleepers. Other than a joy rider with a death wish negotiating the hairpins around 3:30 AM, the locals didn't see or hear anything. So after explaining to some concerned homeowners that the Homicide Division can't issue a summons to any of the onlookers for trespass, he starts back to the Central Station. *I just hope this case can be closed before the Lombard Hill Improvement Association Open House next month.*

TWO

Franklin is crossing Union Street when the flickering at the edges of his visual field begins. He fumbles for the container of Advil Migraine. *Not now. Not again.*

The bottle is almost empty. *But still—lucky; I've been damn lucky.* The headaches started in rehab but had been gone for years. He'd been just a kid playing football for Junipero Serra High School when the Twin Towers came down and he signed up. Three years later they'd been driving through the lunar desolation of the Spin Boldak district when he'd found himself on the ground, surrounded by smoke and confusion. He remembers trying to get to his feet and the second explosion.

Recovery from a closed head injury is always unpredictable, but his progress had satisfied the doctors. They said the vivid dreams and headaches would gradually dissipate. There would always be things he couldn't remember; some retrograde amnesia was to be expected. It could have been a lot worse. All he needed to do was take his meds and avoid stress.

And they had been right. He can't remember much about the carnage after the explosion. His share was the end of his military career and his engagement to a high school sweetheart—and a straight shot at the SFPD's Veteran's Preference program. As Ortega said, the city liked the window dressing that someone like Investigative Division Sergeant and war veteran Franklin Washborne provided.

They need a sign on Lombard Hill. "WARNING: This neighborhood contains citizens known to the State of California to cause severe head discomfort." Because the headaches have come back, but now they're different. Instead of flashing lights, he sees shapes and figures standing just out of sight. When he turns to look, they're gone. *Stand still, dammit, so I can see you. This isn't supposed to be happening.*

8

He concentrates on driving, hoping that the stuff in his peripheral field is only in his head and not in the real world. The headaches distort his vision and sometimes his thinking. They fade rapidly, but they leave a nagging uncertainty about what might lie behind them. He hadn't questioned the doctors' assessment until now. Part of him doesn't want to think about the other shoe that could be waiting to drop. *Because medicine isn't an exact science and doctors can be wrong. And one thing I've learned in Homicide is that what you don't know can kill you.*

The backpack sits ignored on Kevin's desk along with a pile of papers; he's concentrating on something on his workstation monitor.

Franklin pulls up a chair. "Anything new?"

"This FBI briefing just came in. It's an update about what could be a mass poisoning in Colorado Springs. Could be a street drug laced with something weird, but they're also worried about a potential terrorist attack."

"Given all the defense industry contractors and high-tech stuff around there, and Fort Carson and the USAF Academy right next door, that could be a possibility, even if it's not one I want to think about."

Kevin looks serious for a moment, but it doesn't last. "I like some of the other suggestions I've seen online. A local religious group is calling it a judgment from God, though who or what is being judged isn't clear. And somebody else wants to blame it on the space aliens in Area 51."

"And aliens in Nevada are poisoning people in Colorado because?"

"The FBI isn't saying. But then they wouldn't, being part of the whole Area 51 cover-up and all."

Franklin takes a deep breath. "Tell me something. Have you always been like this?"

"Like what? I've known I was gay since I was ten."

"That's not what I meant."

"Oh. Well, it's all related; I always believe in looking at the big picture. Remember, I grew up in Reno and started out earning money by giving blow jobs to truckers and out-of-town businessmen. After I figured out that was a career path with limited advancement opportunities, I got a job working casino security, watching grifters and working girls on closed-circuit TV. Then I applied to the Criminal Justice program at UNR because I figured it was a field I knew a lot about. After that, I moved here and applied to the SFPD. I figured my knowledge of the habits of the morally challenged would be pretty good credentials."

Franklin puts up a hand.

"What, TMI?"

"No. But why San Francisco?"

"Because Reno still isn't a gay-positive city. The mob might have been OK with me; they're an equal opportunity employer. But their glory days in Reno are long gone. Given how out I am, San Francisco seemed like a good bet."

Franklin takes a moment to catch his breath. "OK. So this morning's case; is this the stuff from the guy's backpack?"

"Yeah." Kevin points to a booklet on the desk: *Computer Poker and Imperfect Information: Papers from the 2014 AAAI Workshop.* "Some of it is this computer stuff. And there is also some poetry." He holds up *The Testimony of the Suns* by one George Sterling and a typed sheet entitled *Jack London's Credo.*

> *I would rather be ashes than dust!*
> *I would rather that my spark should burn out in a brilliant*
> * blaze than it should be stifled by dry rot.*
> *I would rather be a superb meteor, every atom of me in*
> * magnificent glow, than a sleepy and permanent planet.*
> *The function of man is to live, not to exist.*
> *I shall not waste my days in trying to prolong them.*
> *I shall use my time.*

At the bottom of the sheet someone had written, "To Matt—when I read this, I thought of you."

"So the guy on the stairs is Matt?"

"Seems more likely than that he's Henry Qu; that's the name on the book's flyleaf. I checked the DMV; a Henry Qu lives on Dixon in Hayward. He's about the same age as our victim; could be a friend or roommate. And he's home; I just called."

"What did you tell him?"

"'Sorry, wrong number'. I didn't want to break the news over the phone."

"So you and Ortega going to drop in on him?"

"The Great Man is too busy at the moment. Feel like a drive to the East Bay?"

THREE

"Wow, this must be as close to open spaces as the East Bay gets."

The Mission-Garin neighborhood is on the east side of Hayward and overlooks the rolling hills of the East Bay Regional Parks. Kevin is still looking around when Henry Qu opens the door. Henry's about six feet tall and in his late twenties. It's the frames of his glasses that pull Kevin's attention away from the landscape. "Are that real redwood?"

"No, just wood-grain. Vint and York."

The thing Franklin notices first is that though he's at home and it's Saturday, Henry is carefully dressed; dark olive needle cords, an open tea collar polo, and Bass Weejuns. He looks relaxed; alert and a little curious, but not apprehensive. *Henry isn't a man whom the police have visited often. Like an animal who's never encountered humans, he doesn't know enough to be afraid.*

"First off, please excuse my ignorance, but could you tell us how you pronounce your name?"

"Sure. The Q sounds like both 'ch' and 'sh'." Henry's mouth makes a sound Franklin knows he'll never be able to reproduce.

"Oh, sort of like 'shoe'?" Kevin asks hopefully.

Henry smiles. "Please, just call me Henry."

"Henry, do you know anyone named Matt?"

"Matt Glover is my roommate." He stiffens. "Has something happened?"

Franklin ignores the question. "Is he home right now?"

"No. I haven't seen him since last night."

"Last night. Can you tell me about what time?"

"Around eleven, I guess. A bunch of us went to the Black Magic Voodoo Lounge after work. Matt arrived late and was there a couple of hours."

"And then he left?"

"I guess. I don't remember seeing him leave; I just noticed at some point that he wasn't around."

Kevin puts on a sympathetic but puzzled face. "This 'Voodoo Lounge'—that's a bar?"

"It's a dive bar on Lombard; we have a bunch of Saints fans at work. The decor is hokey—lots of Mardi gras beads and voodoo dolls hanging from the ceiling—but it's friendly and the drinks are cheap."

Lombard Street. "After he left, what did you do?"

"I stayed at the bar until about one; then I came home."

"And Matt hasn't shown up yet?" Franklin tries to make it sound like a neutral question.

"No. I just assumed he'd gone to Myra's for the night."

"Myra?"

"Myra Johannsen. They've been going together for almost a year." The puzzlement on Henry's face is intensifying, and there's an edge of annoyance in his voice. "Can you tell me what this is about?"

His confusion sounds genuine. Franklin hands him one of the ME's photographs. "Do you recognize this person?"

Because it's hard-wired into our brains, grief must feel the same to all of us, but its outward manifestations reflect the different worlds in which we live. The initial wave of shock that crosses Henry's face fades quickly and is replaced by what Franklin senses is a stoicism that comes from someplace deep inside. "There's no easy way to do this; we're very sorry for your loss."

"But this makes no sense. How did it happen?" Henry takes off his glasses to wipe them.

"They found him early this morning on Lombard. It looks like he died from a fall; the steps are especially steep right there. You said the Voodoo Lounge is also on Lombard?"

"Lombard and Van Ness. But why would he climb Russian Hill and walk down the stairs? He'd left the bar by eleven; he couldn't have been lying in the street for hours without someone noticing."

Franklin sees Kevin wince. "It's still very early in the investigation. We're here because we needed someone to identify Matt. It would help if you could tell us a little about him? How did you two meet?"

"We work together; we're both software engineers at Janus Health."

"And before that? You were classmates?"

"No. Matt's a Rensselaer grad from Albany; I'm UC Berkeley. They hired us at the same time. Janus was on an expansion binge and was hiring software engineers *en masse*. We'd both made it through the references and background checks and came here for interviews."

Kevin has been listening intently. "So what do they do at a Janus interview, other than check what color you are?"

Is this an interrogation technique or a statement of kinship among victims of prejudice? Whichever it is, it works; Franklin can see Henry visibly relax.

"Besides checking on stuff they're not allowed to ask on applications, they're watching during the interview to see how you respond to hypotheticals."

"Like what?"

"There are a dozen eggs in a carton. Twelve people each take one egg, but there's still one left in the carton. How do you explain this?"

Kevin gives Henry his best WTF look.

"Eleven people take an egg; the twelfth guy grabs the box with the egg still in it."

Kevin looks pained. "And the point of this is?"

"It's supposed to test your ability to 'think outside the box'—get it? They throw oddball stuff at you because they can. It's a way to remind everyone that Janus Health is part of Grandview Corp, a big player in Silicon Valley. A sort of shock and awe thing to remind us we're in the major leagues now."

So Kevin's uncovered a subterranean current of rebelliousness in this buttoned-down engineer? Perhaps there's more intuitiveness beneath that outer layer of flamboyance than first meets the eye.

Kevin smiles. "Sounds like a high octane testosterone event. How did Matt react?"

"That's one of the first things I noticed. He had an openness, almost a naivete, that made him stand out among the rest of the hyper-competitive types. This was all new to him, and it didn't occur to him to hide it."

Franklin nods. "And you appreciated that. Were you a little worried about him?" *For a techie roommate, Henry seems observant, even insightful. If that's true, it could be a gift to the investigation.*

"Not really. Matt wasn't good at hiding things, but he was hardworking and very bright. I thought he'd be able to hold his own and could be a potential ally. He was new to San Francisco, I had a lead on this apartment, and we ended up roommates."

"All spur-of-the-moment?"

"Pretty much. Matt liked this area. He'd been a big hiker back in New York—someplace called the Silver Lake Wilderness? I've never been to Albany, but I gather it's not San Francisco. At least in Hayward there's a little open space nearby."

"So everything was simpatico. Did you work together?"

13

Henry shakes his head. "Different divisions. We both worked long hours, so we didn't see that much of each other during the day."

"And after work?"

"After work, we'd come home and talk about work. Until he met Myra."

Kevin looks up from his note-taking. "OK, so tell us about Myra."

FOUR

"We were at this Artificial Intelligence symposium at the Hyatt Regency. It's sort of an interesting place. There's a big central atrium with a giant geodesic sculpture in the middle that's illuminated by colored lights. We were at the bar when Matt noticed a woman circling the sculpture, dancing with the changing lights. That's how he met Myra."

Kevin almost grins. "And here I thought first meetings like that only happened in Julia Roberts movies."

"Myra wanted to be an actress, and she has a sense of theater. She majored in it in Chicago."

"So why come to San Francisco and not New York?"

"Her boyfriend took a job with a dot-com startup here, and she came with to find people interested in writing plays and acting. The dot-com and the boyfriend didn't pan out, so she moved into some sort of writer's commune."

Kevin looks at Franklin. "Who said the 70s were dead?" Then to Henry: "Was Matt interested in writing? We found a book of poetry in his backpack."

"Not really. That was mine; I loaned it to him because its author was also going to be a character in Myra's play."

"Did Matt and Myra have a lot in common?"

"Myra likes techies, and I guess Matt was nicer than her last boyfriend. And Matt liked her, even though the life Myra wanted wasn't anything Matt had considered. She enjoys making her own decisions about what's important; what other people expect doesn't impress her. Opposites attract, I guess. I think she fascinated him."

Franklin looks at his notebook. "And he was what, in love with her?"

"They were friends. And he tried. He even talked about taking a creative writing course."

"Speaking of writing..." Kevin walks over to a bookcase. "Are these yours or his?"

Henry shrugs. "I read more than he does; non-work-related stuff, I mean."

Kevin peers at a book. "Lovecraft?"

Henry manages a weak smile. "That's H. P. Lovecraft, Detective—the author. I'm a member of the Lovecraft Historical Society. You've heard of *The Call of Cthulhu*?"

"Who?"

"I like sci-fi and horror stuff. Sterling wrote science fantasy poetry, but I thought it was boring and pompous."

"Oh." Kevin fingers another book. "So, horror stories next to *Taking Confucian Ethics Seriously: Contemporary Theories and Applications*?"

"That's a gift from my grandfather. He's a traditionalist."

Franklin reins things in. "So how can we reach Myra?"

"I don't know where the commune is, but I can give you her cell phone number."

"Any idea what's happened to her previous boyfriend?"

"I don't know anything about him, but I think she said his name was Toby something."

"Do you have a number for Matt's parents? We haven't found his phone."

"I can get you that." Henry heads for another room and returns with a computer printout.

"Do you think Myra would be likely to answer if we tried calling today?"

Henry hesitates. "I have no idea. She hasn't been around much. Matt said she was preoccupied."

"With what?"

"Her play, I guess. It's about some people in Carmel. She was going to play a poet named..." He stops for a moment. ".... named Nora May French. Myra was doing a lot of research about the characters. I've heard that actors like to immerse themselves in a role, and I think Myra was trying to become Nora May."

Franklin frowns. "How did Matt feel about that?"

"He spent a lot of time with her at the commune, so I guess he was OK with it. It just sounded like she was really into it."

"Swept up in her writing?"

Henry shrugs. "I suppose so. Almost more like being possessed by it."

A dead software engineer with a girlfriend off in her own world. It's only been eight hours, and this investigation is already getting complicated. "Thank you for your help. One other thing: Matt had a note from Myra in his backpack."

"A note?"

"Something about Jack London."

"Oh yeah. Jack London is also in the play, and Myra thought Matt might find that interesting." He turns to Franklin. "A person who might know more is the writing instructor Matt contacted. She's written a book about the people in Carmel."

"Do you know her name?"

"Elizabeth something. She teaches at the San Francisco Writers Collaborative."

"Thanks. We'll follow up on that. Could you provide us with a list of some of Matt's friends?"

"I can try."

Franklin stands, and Kevin takes his cue. "Again, we're sorry for your loss. We may reach out to you again as things develop. If you think of anything else, here's my card."

Henry walks with them to the parking area. "This has to be some freak accident. I can't think of anyone who would want to hurt Matt. He wasn't a guy who made enemies."

Kevin nods his head in understanding as he climbs into the crappy Ford Taurus the pool has given them. "The law says that all unexplained deaths have to be investigated. We have no reason to suspect any wrongdoing."

Franklin can see Henry still standing in the apartment parking lot as they pull out onto Dixon Street. Kevin is quiet for a minute. "Get the feeling that there's more going on here than someone falling down some stairs?"

"They sound like complicated people, but sometimes even complex people die of simple causes. We'll find out more when we get the ME's report." He glances over at Kevin. "I'll take care of calling Matt's parents. Ortega won't do it, and I've had more experience with this than you have."

"Thanks. That's got to be hard; I think it isn't a job for an amateur."

"No problem, but don't sell yourself short. You did a good job back there."

Kevin raises his eyebrows. "I don't have any illusions about my position here. One reason I got the promotion is because the department wanted a gay guy in some position other than a beat cop. I've been out since I was twelve, so I already knew how people may react to that. And guys on the force haven't been shy about suggesting which of my many skills got me here. So I tone down the gay sometimes, just to annoy them. But thanks for the vote of confidence."

If today has been you in toned-down mode, I can't wait to see what you're like unrestrained. But Franklin decides some things are better left unsaid.

FIVE

A fountain occupies the middle courtyard of the Hayward apartments, and the space by the railroad tracks has the swimming pool. But it's the tree-lined Dixon Street courtyard, the sort of green space that Matt liked, that speaks to Henry this morning. He'd awakened wondering when Matt would get back; it took a few seconds before he remembered Matt wouldn't be coming home. And then the movies in his head started playing.

It's their first day at Janus Health. They're in Dr. Atkinson's office; a man in a wheelchair is also there. They're both there "because of your outstanding potential, the best of the best." Atkinson has decided that Henry will work in his division, and Matt will be part of "a groundbreaking new venture that Dr. Walker is developing."

Henry grabs some coffee and walks to the concrete bench that's farthest from the road. It's cool in the shade. Perhaps that's something he can use to anchor him in the present.

Henry watches Matt's reaction; he's like a kid on Christmas morning whose excitement has gotten the best of him. What's Dr. Walker's project?

That was Matt all over. The world was a big playroom, and Matt was a kid running from one toy to another, trying to decide which he wanted to try next.

Atkinson looks annoyed by the question, but Dr. Walker senses an opening. Dr. Atkinson's is a "Big Data" program to identify connections in pharmacology databases, while Walker's will design new versions of drugs.

It was the first real job for both of them; looking back, Henry can remember that it also excited him in his way. The new position was going to be great. Matt was going to be a great roommate. Everything was going to work out fine. And now it was all gone because of a stupid accident. *I miss Matt. I need this time to say goodbye.*

Atkinson interrupts; there will be time later for Matt to hear the technical details. And with that, he dismisses Matt and Walker and summons his Administrative Assistant. It's only as Matt stands to leave that Henry glimpses something, a hint of surprise and envy that the CEO chose Henry for his division assistant.

He'd never doubted that Matt was smart. It was only after living with him he began questioning the depth of his understanding. Ideas flooded Matt's brain by the dozens, and each time he was sure that the latest one was better than the last half dozen. Henry watched with interest at first and then with bemused detachment as Matt outlined and began a new project, only to abandon it for the Next Big Idea.

Later, at the apartment, Matt had congratulated Henry. He had protested that his assignment might not be as glamorous as Matt assumed. As CEO, Atkinson spent most of his time on administrative issues rather than research. Matt had looked surprised; that possibility hadn't occurred to him.

Flaky creative types aren't rarities in Silicon Valley, so where are these judgmental memories of the friend he's lost coming from? We are all more than the sum of our parts; even if Matt was sometimes unreliable, he was still a good person. And besides, what difference did any of this make to Henry? He hadn't had to work alongside Matt.

"And what's Dr. Walker about?"

"Hey, it's only Day 1. I'm not sure. He spent today talking about theoretical approaches to artificial intelligence but said nothing about any functioning applications he's designed. I don't know what I'll be doing. And he's sort of weird about security. We're not supposed to share any existing or future code with other divisions, and we're all assigned private e-mail accounts."

"What are you working on, the next Manhattan Project? Most of the programs Janus has produced sound just like typical 'AI in Medicine' applications every other IT company is trying to market."

"I guess recruiting an academic like Walker was a big deal for Janus. Do you think all this 'top secret' stuff is supposed to emphasize Janus Health's position as a major player?"

Henry wonders if the detectives have found Myra yet. He's worried about her and wanted to call her himself, but he's held off after the detectives made Matt's death a police investigation. What weren't they telling me? The red-headed one had been very interested in the books in the apartment. Was it that obvious that Matt wasn't into plays and poetry? He'd told them that himself, but it was true; even Myra saw that. I worried that Myra might just be another bright idea Matt would lose interest in. And she deserves better than that.

"Dr. Atkinson seemed less than overawed by your boss this morning."

"When was that?"

"When he cut Walker off in mid-sentence and sent us on our way. I'd guess there's some tension between the two."

"Guess I didn't pick up on that."

No, he hadn't. Poor clueless Matt, lost in his own world. *Overall, I liked him, even though he could be obtuse and self-absorbed. Perhaps Grandfather has a point, and I've absorbed more Confucian concepts about relationships than I realize.*

By rights, Henry should have been the one working with Christopher Walker; he would have known how to take advantage of the opportunity. Instead, Matt just sat there oblivious, pissing it all away. *That was the problem; if anyone would have missed danger signals on Lombard Street, it was Matt Glover.*

This isn't working. The apartment is too full of Matt, but coming out here hasn't changed how I feel. Perhaps he'll hike out to Dry Creek or visit the Japanese Gardens later; right now, he needs to get control of his intrusive memories.

Henry walks back to the apartment to sit before the corner shrine in his bedroom. This morning, it takes extra time to settle himself and focus on the verses.

> *Sariputra, all things are empty.*
> *Nothing is born, nothing dies,*
> *Nothing is pure, nothing is stained,*
> *Nothing increases and nothing diminishes.*

As he finishes, the phone rings and voice mail kicks in to record a message from Sergeant Washborne. Matt's parents have arrived in San Francisco

.

SIX

Dense fog has grounded the planes at the airport and muffles the sounds of everyday life in San Bruno, and Franklin sleeps late. The Golden Gate National Cemetery, San Francisco County Jail #5, and Artichoke Joe's Casino define his neighborhood. It's not Nob Hill, and the apartment is cramped and noisy. But he doesn't care; it's affordable, and he doesn't spend much time there, anyway.

He's glad for the extra sleep; it will let him get by with just two cups of coffee on a morning when he needs to avoid caffeine over-stimulation. Matt Glover's parents are at the Airport Marriott, having spent ten hours getting from Albany to New York and then to Detroit and finally San Francisco. Sudden loss, profound grief and bone-crushing fatigue, all as prelude to a ride to the shiny new institutionally sterile Public Safety Building on Third Street that houses what was once their son. The sisters taught Franklin that God does not ask of us anything that faith will not make us able to bear. *Lord, I want to believe; help Thou my unbelief.*

What will the best time to call the hotel? It's an impossible question to answer because there is no good time, and God isn't being any help this morning. *It could be worse; the old Medical Examiner's Office in the Hall of Justice was so grim that even the experienced pathologists didn't want to go there.* Somehow, the thought doesn't help.

His grandfather had been insistent; if he was going to be a cop, the one thing he couldn't afford was to stop feeling. "Whoever fights with monsters should see to it that he does not become a monster in the process; when you gaze long into an abyss, the abyss also gazes into you." *Well, Granddad, you can be proud of me today.* And his grandfather would be, if Alzheimer's hadn't stolen his thoughts and erased his memories.

Thinking about the old man only depresses him more. *Don't go there, Franklin. You learned how to avoid these head games in Afghanistan; don't let this*

22

become a problem for you. Least of all on this morning. He gets himself a glass of water and takes a prophylactic Advil; then he dials the Marriott.

In the fog, the drive into the city feels disorienting and malign, like some German Expressionist silent movie about some voyage to the underworld. Riding in a police car is an unfamiliar experience for Mr. and Mrs. Glover. As he drives, they tell Franklin about Matt; even though it's painful, talking is less toxic than silence.

"How did it happen? He fell down some stairs? Outdoors? In public? But he was so healthy. And fit—hiking was his favorite activity. He was never happier than when he was backpacking in the Adirondacks."

"Yes, I understand, Mrs. Glover. But sometimes San Francisco can be deceptive. For a modern city, it has plenty of antiquated streets and steep hills."

"How dangerous is it here? It seems like some thug must have attacked Matt. But why? He's not careless, or a person who draws attention to himself or makes enemies."

"The neighborhood where the incident occurred is a low crime area. We have no evidence so far your son was doing anything that put him at risk."

"So far? What are you implying?"

"Nothing, Mr. Glover, other than that the investigation is still in its early stages."

"Our son was a serious, hardworking young man who understood the value of a first-class education, Sergeant. He didn't engage in risky behavior. We had our doubts about his moving here. So many of these new businesses don't seem to work out, and the world is changing so rapidly. But what else was there? Nothing upstate could compete with Silicon Valley. We didn't feel we could ask Matt to give up his dreams."

Denial, anger, bargaining; he knows the sequence by heart. It's impossible not to feel sympathy; no parent should have to bury a child. And yet… *"There's nothing for you here in Albany, but moving to San Francisco is too risky."* Few of us are good at hearing the mixed messages we give. *Do the Glovers believe Matt was as diligent and prudent and passionless as the man they're describing?* That person doesn't sound like someone who'd go drinking at the Black Magic Voodoo Lounge or date a poet living in a commune.

Who was Matt Glover, and what don't his parents know or want to know? He's reminded of a presentation he'd attended on the unreliability of eyewitnesses. The speaker argued the problem wasn't a failure to observe; it was a matter of competing interpretations. "The eye will only see what the brain already knows—the Rashomon effect".

Rashomon. Franklin feels like he's in the middle of the second reel and there are no subtitles.

They're buzzed into the Public Safety Building, and he guides the Glovers to the Medical Examiner's suite. Even on a Sunday, the office is busy. An older woman appears to lead Matt's parents into the office. *I wonder how many sets of grieving relatives it takes before even the promise of a county pension can't make the job worth it?*

Dr. Olsen, the pathologist on duty, comes into the anteroom. "Morning, Sergeant. You here about the young man from Lombard Street?"

"Yeah. His parents just flew in from New York."

Olsen shakes his head. "None of these cases is easy, but it's always harder when they're young."

"So how does a healthy guy his age kill himself by falling down some stairs?"

"He didn't."

Franklin holds his breath.

"Your man died from a cerebral hemorrhage caused by blunt force occipital trauma. That's not an injury you sustain if you fall face forward. Somebody knocked this guy down Lombard Street by smashing his skull in with a heavy object, something like a baseball bat."

"A homicide."

Dr. Olsen nods.

"Anyone told his folks?"

"No, I haven't finished my report. But I thought that the cause of death was obvious enough to warrant giving you a preliminary."

"Thanks." Franklin sits down again to wait for the Glovers.

SEVEN

MONDAY, AUGUST 22, 2016

"So who do we like for this?" Ortega swivels his chair, glaring over his coffee cup at Kevin. Franklin guesses he must be wearing his special invisibility underwear this morning because Mike doesn't even acknowledge his presence in the small conference room.

"We interviewed his roommate Saturday, we're tracking down his girlfriend, and we're developing a list of friends. So far, nobody stands out."

"Obvious enemies? Drug issues?"

"No evidence of either. The guy was a real straight arrow."

Ortega smiles. "As your friend, let me share two facts of life with you, Kevin. Number one: there are no straight arrows. Everybody has something they want to keep hidden, usually for good reason. Your job is not to believe people, it's to uncover what they don't want you to know. And number two: you don't wait for somebody to show up wearing a sign that says 'I did it'. You start with whoever you got and work on him. Most of the time, your first guess will be right. Even if it isn't, that person will end up pointing you to the real perp. OK? Now, tell me about the timeline here—three sentences."

"Matt and his roommate were at a bar after work on Friday night. Matt left first; the roommate assumed he was going to see his girlfriend. Roommate returned home around 1 AM; they found Matt dead on Lombard Street at 5:30."

"So, there you are; two guys and one girl turns into one guy and one girl. Sound like anything you've heard somewhere before?"

"Yeah, though I didn't get any jealousy vibe off the roommate."

Kevin is a quick study; he's already figured out how to challenge Ortega while seeming to agree with him.

"Which should be a red flag right there; that's what he *doesn't* want you to see. This kid on the stairs, he was tall, blond, muscular, is that right?"

"More or less."

"So what's the roommate look like?"

"Asian, a careful dresser, a literary type, geeky."

"The jock and the metrosexual. Two guys work together, live together, and then a woman shows up. Which one's she gonna choose, and how's the other guy gonna feel about it? Christ, it's the oldest story in the book."

Kevin tilts his head and says nothing. Ortega leans back again; Franklin winces as he sees the light bulb go on over Mike's head.

"Oh shit! No wonder you can't see this; I keep forgetting that you don't think like a straight guy. So just take this on faith, Kev; jealousy over another guy getting a piece of ass can turn anyone into a killer. That's why we need to haul the roommate in for questioning." Ortega pauses for a second. "You met with him what, two days ago? We'll give him a few more days, so he thinks he's in the clear and then catch him off balance and hit him hard. Meanwhile, get on the paperwork; I want all that done and filed so that we're good to go when the roommate spills his guts. And find the girlfriend, Myra, or whoever, because once one lovebird starts singing, the other one will join in the chorus to save her own skin."

He turns to Franklin. "What's your plan for the day?"

"I want to go back to the scene. Things are different when you know you're looking at a homicide. There could be something we were looking at but didn't understand."

"The eye cannot see what the mind does not grasp, eh?" Ortega glares at Kevin again.

Christ, no one could ever accuse Ortega of subtlety. Hell, no one could accuse him of having a thought that wouldn't be more at home in a Dirty Harry movie.

"Yeah, the Rashomon effect."

"Huh?"

"Nothing. Myra originally came to California with a boyfriend that she dumped before she hooked up with Matt Glover. If jealousy is the motive, I want to talk to him too."

"We know where he is?"

Franklin shakes his head. "A guy named Toby something; worked for a startup that didn't make it. We know when he and Myra moved here and when Matt met Myra. We check tech companies that went south during that window, one of them might know where their former employees are now."

"OK, let's get on it, people."

Franklin stands up. *Maybe my eagerness to leave will look like investigative zeal. Somehow, though, I doubt it.*

26

EIGHT

The Black Magic Voodoo Lounge is just a doorway with a black awning that looks like Edward Gorey designed it and a window with a neon Fleur de Lys Abita beer sign. When the Saints are playing, the bar opens at 8 AM, but today's opening time is 3 PM. No matter; Franklin isn't interested in the bar's innards. He needs to see what Matt's last night was like.

It's three blocks uphill from the Black Magic to Hyde Street; not a challenge to an athletic 20-something backpacker, but enough to remind Franklin that his Army days are in the past. As he stops to catch his breath, he notices that the north side of the street has nose-in on-street parking. *Anyone who'd had a few would likely cross the street and take the sidewalk on the south side.*

The sidewalk ends in a steep flight of stairs at Larkin Street, where a sign tells Franklin he's reached Sterling Park. Matt might have walked in the road, or he could have gone into the park. *Sterling's charisma and high spirits inspired fellow writers and artists to dub him "King of Bohemia"* a bronze plaque declares. On the opposite side of the stairs, George Sterling himself proclaims

> *Tho the dark be cold and blind,*
> *Yet her sea-fog's touch is kind,*
> *And her mightier caress*
> *Is joy and the pain thereof;*
> *And great is thy tenderness,*
> *O cool, grey city of love!*

Charisma and high spirits win out; Franklin takes the stairs.

'Great is thy tenderness.' Well, maybe, George, but I'm not sure what I'm feeling in my legs is the pain of joy. The path at the top flattens out to a gentle series of switchbacks meandering past fenced beds of succulents that look like

extras left over from *Little Shop of Horrors.* On a clear day, the view from the tennis and basketball courts at the crest of the hill would be spectacular. But today George Sterling's Cool Grey City is just that, cold and blind. What would Matt have expected to find here at night other than the Golden Gate foghorns? *How drunk would you have to be to pick this as a destination for your last night on earth?*

Sterling Park

More curving paths and stairs lead down to Hyde Street; Lombard is a block further south. As he walks, Franklin tries to envision an inebriated Matt staggering up to the park and then down Hyde to the Lombard steps, where someone is waiting for him with a baseball bat. It's possible in theory, but it feels implausible, a "Colonel Mustard in the conservatory with the lead pipe" solution to this homicide case.

There's still yellow police tape strung across parts of Lombard. Does the SFPD still consider this an active site? Or has some member of the Lombard Hill Improvement Association decided to make this a permanent tourist attraction? Auto traffic is back to normal, but a crowd of pedestrians still mobs the accident site. They're unimpressed by the tape's "Police Line Do Not Cross" injunction; the homeowners must be pissed.

Franklin joins a group walking down the first switchback and waits as people take selfies in front of 1079. If nothing else, this case proves that crime still sells. A few minutes is enough to convince him that he's unlikely to find anything new here. He is almost back at the intersection when he sees the woman.

The House on Hyde Street

She's short and elderly and wears a fussy old-fashioned dress, and she's leaning out a second-story window. Her house is the huge yellow ark that occupies the entire northwest corner of the Hyde-Lombard intersection. Hanging out a window must violate some neighborhood bylaw here, but given the house's size and prominence, Franklin guesses she's both rich and impervious.

It takes a few seconds before he realizes that she's looking straight at him. No, not just staring; she's waving at him. And as he watches, she extends an arm and starts pointing. *Southwest. There's something to the southwest that she wants me to see.*

Franklin turns, but he can't see anything that looks different from usual. Perhaps the surrounding buildings are blocking his view of whatever she's pointing at. One thing is clear; wherever the something is, it isn't in Sterling Park.

He scans the surrounding crowd. No one else appears to have noticed the woman. A squeal of steel on steel and a clanging announce the arrival of an inbound Hyde Street cable car. It stops to disgorge more tourists into the intersection. By the time it has passed, the woman in the window is gone, and the window is closed.

Franklin crosses the street. A dense growth of rhododendron obscures the lower story windows of the house. A short flight of stairs at the north end leads to an elaborate iron and glass gate flanked by potted topiary. Franklin can see the main door of the home and an enclosed side yard. He rings the bell and knocks, but there's no response.

A walk around the perimeter reveals garage doors on the south side of the building but no other entrances at street level. All the windows are closed, and the shades are drawn. The woman seems to have vanished as abruptly as she appeared, and the house feels empty.

Rich, elderly, reclusive, eccentric; it's not an unusual constellation in San Francisco. It also makes it unlikely he'll be able to interview her. That's not a significant loss. She might have a good view of the murder scene during the day, but no one could see much on a foggy night.

He can't even be sure that she was signaling him. She might have been pointing something out to someone inside the house. *Perspective, Franklin. You see this as a crime scene, but she sees a neighborhood she's looked at every day for years.*

At least there have been no headaches this morning, and this was a real person, not some shadowy figure in his peripheral vision. No one ever said anything about hallucinations being a consequence of head injury. The only guys with any doubts are the jerks in the squad room who are heavy into "us versus them" cop-think. *I mean, how far can you trust some dumb fuck who got his head almost blown off in the Sandbox? Doesn't matter what anybody says, Humpty Dumpty has to have gotten a little scrambled after that. And when it's my ass on the line, I want to make sure I can count on the guy who's got my back. Ask me, I wouldn't want to risk it with him.*

The main thing he's learned this morning is how unlikely it is that an intoxicated Matt Glover could have negotiated Russian Hill, let alone the Lombard Street stairs. *But if that didn't happen, what did?*

NINE

Christopher Walker is trying to decide which picture of the Turing statue at Bletchley Park he'll put in his PowerPoint when his secretary sticks her head in. "Dr. Atkinson wants you in the executive conference room."

"Tell him I'll be there presently."

"I'm sorry, Doctor; he says he needs you there now. He sounded quite adamant."

Monday morning, and there's already smoke and steam issuing from Mount Atkinson. *A position at Janus Health should require a degree in seismology as a prerequisite.* The observers awaiting this morning's eruption seem more subdued than usual as they cluster around the wall-mounted flat screen. Atkinson himself stands off to the side, talking with Theo Markham, Janus Health's Marketing Director.

"Police discovered the body of the victim early Saturday morning..."

"Have you seen this?" Atkinson has spotted him.

"No. Someone's been attacked?"

"It's Matt Glover. They found his body on Lombard Street. We've already contacted the police, but there's not much other information yet." He nods to Theo. "We're preparing a statement for the press."

Walker's annoyance at being interrupted has evaporated, replaced by confusion and disbelief. "Matt's hurt? I don't understand. How...?"

Atkinson shakes his head. "Dead. The police interviewed Henry Qu Saturday morning, but they still seem to have no working theory of what happened. That reminds me..."

He strides back towards the main group of employees; the news anchor has moved on to a story about a homeless encampment in the Memorial Court. "I'm sure I don't need to tell you to refer any request for comment to Public Affairs. I expect the police to go through the usual channels; you needn't worry that they will interrogate any of you. The press may be another matter. Be very cautious about anyone claiming to be a friend or relative seeking information."

Theo turns to Chris and rests a hand on his shoulder. "We're all shocked by this, and I know how painful this must be for you. Matt was a bright, successful young scientist with so much promise."

"Yes, he'd already distinguished himself and was reaping the rewards that await a man of his abilities."

"Coming from you, that's high praise, Doctor. I know he viewed you as a mentor."

"I was happy for him, and also a little concerned. He's had a series of successes, and that sometimes makes people take success for granted. I've seen too many young scientists whose careers ended up being a flash in the pan. But I had great hopes for Matt, and now all of that is gone."

"I am sorry, Doctor."

Atkinson rejoins them. "Chris, I think the best thing is not to worry about this. We'll sit down to discuss your division's needs when you get back from Chicago; we should know more about what happened by then." A clap on the shoulder and Atkinson turns away; after another sympathetic glance, Theo turns to follow him.

Back in his office, Chris Walker stares at the monitor; Alan Turing is still fiddling with the keyboard of the Enigma machine. *Matt Glover was a good worker, someone who was both smart and lucky. What had happened?* Did Matt's strong start go to his head and make him feel invincible? Matt had seemed more distracted than reckless, but still; should he have suspected something and asked more questions? *I'd hoped that my behavior could serve as a model of what could work, even if it may provide limited immediate gratification. It's still an effective way to avoid losing perspective.*

Enough. No point in going on like some sententious academic advisor; whatever had happened, it's all over now. He needs to calculate how much corporate political capital it will cost to replace Matt with someone competent. And he has to do something soon; how dysfunctional Atkinson may become if the police investigation drags on is anyone's guess.

He glances at his desktop; it's sprouted a couple of Post-It's with messages from Darryl Lockheed, the Human Mosquito, during the time he was gone. *Thank God I'm leaving town.*

His secretary is at the door again. "It's Mr. Lockheed again; he wants to know if you got his messages."

"Yes, thank you, but I'm behind schedule. I still have a lot to do before I leave. Tell him I'll call him after I get back."

32

"I've already tried that, but he's quite insistent. Is there someone else I can refer him to?"

"I'm afraid I'm the only one he thinks able to solve his problems. But I can't talk to him now."

"What research project is he interested in? I could offer him a few staff names as substitutes."

"Thank you for trying to run interference, but that's part of the problem. What he's obsessed with isn't a Janus program. Just tell him I've already left."

It's no use; he gives up on Dr. Turing and closes the PowerPoint file. Dealing with Darryl has been a two-year roller coaster ride. Every time he assumed the ride was over, Darryl has wanted him to buy another ticket. *It's long past time to leave Seven Flags.*

The first call had sounded innocent enough, just an inquiry from a new group of potential Janus clients. "Dr. Walker, I represent scientists who are creating a new pharmaceutical start-up. We're familiar with your work on Deep Learning and are eager to avail ourselves of your expertise."

"Genomics? Personalized medicine?"

"No sir; we're interested in developing designer pharmaceuticals whose actions are well defined."

"Dr. Ehrlich's magic bullet?"

"Excuse me?"

"I'm sorry, Mr. Lockheed; an obscure private joke."

"Oh. Well, our physicians are distinguished psychopharmacologists knowledgeable about current agents, but we also realize just how haphazard their development has been. The field needs a systematic analysis of the characteristics of effective agents to guide the formulation of new ones."

"I understand your thesis. Do you have data you need to analyze?"

"We've done our homework, I assure you, Doctor, and we're ready to move to the next phase."

"Good. If that's the case, then you also know about Janus Health's current projects. They include developing programs for drug design. If you wish to submit a formal proposal, I'll connect you with the Scientific Advisory Committee."

"We can describe our plan, but what we need is someone to tell us if what we're looking for is possible. If it is, then we can talk about how to do it. If it's not, then we'll need advice on how to modify the original concept."

"My contract with Janus limits the outside work I can accept."

"What if we just wanted a theoretical discussion unrelated to any commercial considerations?"

"I'm not sure that piece of sophistry would withstand legal scrutiny."

"We're not asking you to *do* anything. Think of it as a mathematical riddle; your contract can't forbid you to think. It would be like saying you're not allowed to solve crossword puzzles."

"I can't promise anything, but if you framed a question in general terms, I suppose it would do no harm to take a look and perhaps jot down a few thoughts."

"That's all we're asking, Doctor. I think you may find this fun."

No mention of deadlines, or that with Darryl, answers to questions only beget more questions. He's had enough stress for one day, and it's not even noon. He crumples the Post-Its.

TEN

"A BAC of 0.06? What's that, three beers? You walk into the Elbo Room any night of the week, you won't find any SF's Finest that under-medicated." Kevin passes the tox screen report to Franklin.

"So the theory that inebriation contributed to Matt's death just shit the bed. After hiking up and down Russian Hill, that doesn't surprise me. Anything else show up in the screen?"

"None of the usual suspects. The ME has asked for some exotics, but we won't get those results for weeks. So what was Matt doing, where was he going, and why did he get himself killed?" Kevin ticks possibilities off on his fingers. "A random mugging? Something work-related or drug-related? Another weird California cult thing?"

"Don't forget Ortega's favorite, death by jealousy."

"Oh yeah, that. Us queers keep forgetting just what sex-addled maniacs breeders are. Hey, how come you never talk about that part of your life?"

If we're going to work together, I might as well meet him where he lives. "With you? You wouldn't understand, anyway; weren't you listening yesterday?"

Kevin looks pleased. "Must've zipped right past my Clueless Queer headphones. Anyway, we canvassed the neighbors and came up with zip. The hardest to prove will be if this was a chance attack."

"Matt's wallet and cell phone are missing. He wasn't rich by San Francisco standards, and so far his bank has reported no activity from his credit cards. There's no real foot traffic on Lombard Street at that hour, and the neighborhood isn't popular with the homeless or the under-medicated. This doesn't feel like a typical mugging and robbery."

"Henry didn't know of any drug issues with Matt, and no one would look to score on Russian Hill. How likely was it that he was selling? Just as a sort of side business?"

Franklin thinks back to his time in Narcotics. "A courier to the elite? He wouldn't be the first squeaky clean professional who decided drugs could be a good way to supplement his income because no one would suspect him."

"Leaving a dead guy on display at a major tourist destination has the sort of dramatic flair major dealers use to send a message."

"I still have some contacts; if this was a drug hit, somebody on the street may be talking."

"And I can press Henry some more on the drug question during the Mike Ortega Baseless Accusation Hour. If nothing else, it'll piss Ortega off to have his uppity subordinate deviating from the script."

"Are you sure Mike isn't bugging our office?"

Kevin snickers. "Absolutely. Otherwise, I'd already have been busted and would be walking foot patrol in Hunters Point."

"We still need to check out Matt's workplace. You been able to find the girlfriend?"

"Not yet. No answer on her phone and her mailbox is full. No Facebook page or Twitter account for anyone by that name, and a Google search didn't turn up anything."

"Seems a little strange. Someone her age who wants to be on stage but she has no online presence?"

"Henry described her as pretty retro; my guess is it's part of her being hung up on people who lived a hundred years ago. And I haven't found anyone who knows about this writers commune, where it is, or who's in it."

Franklin is checking his notes. "The website for the San Francisco Writers Collaborative lists Elizabeth Mills as an instructor and the author of *San Francisco Bohemia*; sounds like a person Matt could have contacted. While you're hunting for Myra, I'll see if Ms. Mills can tell us anything."

"I'm guessing 'Bohemia' could be code for sex and booze, so are we back there again?"

"I suppose. Ortega's *True Crime* pulp fiction approach notwithstanding, we still can't exclude the jealousy angle out of hand."

"Ask me, I can see Henry cranking somebody's baser passions up a few notches."

Franklin glances up. "I thought you were partnered."

"I am now, but a good metrosexual is a terrible thing to waste. If Myra met both Matt and Henry at a bar and picked Matt, she could have had second thoughts when she figured out which roommate was more simpatico with her literary world. I know I don't think like a straight guy, but I bet I can understand Myra."

"So Myra decides she likes Henry better, and Matt goes off and commits suicide by bashing himself in the back of the head on Lombard Street?"

"Very Quentin Tarantino. But I hear you. I think Henry deciding to kill Matt because of some femme fatale is also a stretch. How about this? Myra was so distraught that she decided murder-suicide was the only solution, which is why I'm having trouble finding her."

"You're serious?"

"Me? I..."

Kevin's phone rings. He answers, scribbles a few notes, and makes a face. "A call from the Russian Hill Open Space. Somebody at the Norwegian Seaman's Church was standing on the landing when he noticed a guy sleeping on the ground across the street."

"Sort of strange place to pick for a nap."

"Since it's all fenced in, yeah."

"Did the sleeper tell the unis anything?"

"Uh, no. Doesn't sound like he's going to be doing much talking to anyone about anything."

ELEVEN

The phone at the San Francisco Writers Collaborative has gone to voice mail and Franklin is leaving a message when a real live person breaks in. Yes, Elizabeth Mills teaches a course there on Thursdays and weekends. Franklin can also enjoy her television series, which features captivating stories about San Francisco writers past and present on KQXR.

"Thank you. What about Tuesdays?"

A brief pause. "Today, Elizabeth is leading a tour of some of San Francisco's most fascinating literary locales. You can still make a reservation; I can give you *Exploring San Francisco*'s number if you'd like."

"Thanks; I think I've already got it."

"They're conveniently located on Market Street; that's where the tours start."

"Thanks."

"You're more than welcome. Have a truly rewarding day."

When Franklin dials "San Francisco's Number One Location for City Tours", Elizabeth Mills herself answers on the second ring. "The police? I hope none of the students has gotten into trouble."

"No, we're just following up some leads on a matter that doesn't involve the Writers Collaborative. I have a few questions I need to ask, though they may have nothing to do with anything."

"I'm just about to begin a tour now, and I'm starting another at ten tomorrow. Would nine AM then be too early for you?"

"Not at all. You're at Market and Third?

"Right on the corner. I look forward to meeting you, Sergeant Washborne."

Her sangfroid piques his curiosity; most people don't agree to meet cops without a barrage of questions or a display of wariness. He should see what else he can find out about Ms. Mills—but he wants to meet her in person first.

38

"When I got here, I thought it was a mannequin somebody had dumped. We couldn't find anyone to unlock the gate, so I ended up scaling the fence." The officer still sounds a little winded. "We're checking now to see if somebody's making a movie."

Kevin stands in the middle of a rectangle of bare dirt, weeds, and trash. It's surrounded by sloping concrete walls and a chain-link fence. A hundred years ago, this had been the Francisco Street Reservoir At his feet lies the body of a middle-aged man of slight build. He sports mutton chop sideburns and wears a tweed wool suit and vest, complete with a watch chain and pince-nez. He's cold and pale, and his skin and his clothes are soaking wet.

"There was no pulse when we got here. He was so wet when we rolled him over, the water just poured out of his mouth. We started pumping on his chest and some more came out, but we never got him breathing or got a pulse."

"Sounds like something a drowned guy would do. Next question: how do you drown in a reservoir that's been empty for seventy years?'" He regards the body again. "You weigh more if you've drowned. You'd need at least two guys to lug him here. You said the gate was locked?"

"Yeah. We had to radio for a bolt cutter."

"If anyone had carried him, there'd be water be pouring off of him and out of him. But all the ground around here is dry. You see any drip patterns on the ground?"

"No."

"You look?"

"We would've seen it."

Kevin scans the perimeter. "Somebody placed him here. There's no way anyone could just toss a body into this lot without a catapult, and he doesn't look like he dropped out of the sky. So how did he get here? Someone have a key to the gate?"

"If they did, they locked it again afterward,"

The other cop says, "And Francisco Street's been closed to traffic at both ends for years."

"So you could get to the gate on foot, but that means you'd have to bring the body from Hyde or Larkin in broad daylight. There's no easy way here from the Chestnut Street side." Kevin glances to the south. "And anyone near a window in those high-rises would have a good view of someone hauling a stiff up the road."

The officer shakes his head. "Makes me glad you're the detective."

"Yeah. That makes one of us."

The Russian Hill Open Space

Toby O'Neill's small but overpriced apartment on Natoma Street is littered with packing boxes, some only half-filled. Franklin's offered the one remaining chair; Toby perches on a sealed box.

"Yeah, of course I knew Myra. We went to school together back in Illinois."

"Chicago?"

"Elmhurst; same difference. After graduation, she got an entry-level advertising job in Chicago that she couldn't stand, so she moved back home."

"That must have been a little discouraging for her."

"Yeah. Her major was communications and theater, but her folks thought communications meant advertising and theater meant making commercials. They weren't what you'd call imaginative. She was dying there."

"So you both moved to the Bay area?"

"It was already 'Anywhere but here' for her, and San Francisco sounded like there'd be more opportunities for doing what she wanted. I told her that dot-coms are always risky and this might not work out for me, but what the hell—nothing to lose, right? If it didn't, we'd be no worse off than before."

Franklin looks around the room. "Looks like you're getting ready to move."

"Been through two start-ups here. Both took off fast, and when they went public, I was a rich guy, on paper. But none of it lasted, and the cost of living here has gone through the roof. I figure three strikes and you're out, and I've got a solid offer back in Chicago. At least I was smart enough not to get rid of my down parka."

"And Myra?"

"She found some people who were interested in theater and writing, though none of them ever had a steady paycheck. I was working my ass off while they all sat around in their fantasy world. It got to where Myra and I had nothing left to share."

"You know we're investigating Matt Glover's death. We understand he and Myra were friends. What can you tell us about him?"

"Mr. Grandview Technogeek? Never met him. Myra had already started getting weird, and it seemed like he just encouraged her, like it was all just a game. I suppose I should thank him for showing me just how shallow she could be—willing to dump me to become a trophy girlfriend in return for a steady meal ticket."

"Sounds like you didn't like him much."

"Like I said, I never met him, but he sounded like an arrogant piece of shit. I wouldn't kill him if that's what you're asking, but those two deserved each other. I won't be all that upset if they both got what's coming to them."

"You seem bitter."

"I just don't have time for fakes or people who sit around waiting for things to be handed to them on a platter."

"So where were you Saturday night and Sunday morning?"

"Out with friends—at a 'Last Hurrah and Fuck You San Francisco' party."

"You want to write down their names and contact info for me?"

"Sure, and I'll give you my work contact in Chicago too because I'm not hanging around for much longer. You got a problem with that?"

"If your alibi checks out, no. If not, we'll want to talk more."

"Knock yourself out. These guys can tell you where I was."

TWELVE

WEDNESDAY, AUGUST 24, 2016

"Big day ahead?"

Kevin is in early. "Just came from the Medical Examiner's. The guy in the empty reservoir drowned."

Franklin leans back in his chair. "Accidental death?"

A shake of the head. "No definite evidence of foul play at autopsy; the tox screen is pending as usual. But how do you drown when you're six blocks from the Bay?"

"Bathtub. Swimming pool." Franklin shrugs. "Puddle in an alley, if you're drunk enough."

"The guy's clothes were soaking wet, so scratch the puddle option. Myself, I prefer a Speedo to a wool suit when I go for a swim and my birthday suit in the shower. And he was wearing vintage clothes, they think Victorian. I'm checking to see if anyone's staging something or filming a costume drama in the City, but no luck so far."

"How many plays can there be where some nineteenth-century hero jumps fully clothed into a river?"

"I dunno. Didn't somebody fall through the ice in *Uncle Tom's Cabin*?"

"Little Eliza crosses the Ohio River, but it's frozen over and she doesn't fall in."

"This dude had pretty fancy facial hair; unless the play's *Uncle Tom* in drag..."

Franklin grins. "Did you think about checking the bars south of Market?"

"I always do. But another thing; the ME isn't sure where this guy is even from. The dental work doesn't look like anything you'd get in the US. And of course, there's no identification on him."

"Another case with nothing to go on. If these things come in threes, we're in for a hell of a week."

"You're scaring me. I'm already girding my loins for the Ortega onslaught tomorrow."

"Sufficient unto the day. This morning I'm going to meet the only person I've found who knew both Matt and Myra."

"Great. I'm going to keep reading *Hollywood Insider*. If I can't find anyone working on the movie I'm looking for, I hope there's one I can star in about a cop who flunks out of detective school."

"Now, now, none of that."

"Easy for you to say." Kevin turns back to his computer.

Elizabeth Mills is a petite redhead whose figure tells Franklin she spends more time climbing San Francisco's hills in service to the city's literary heritage than she does lecturing in a classroom. He has to hustle to keep up as he follows her into the office. *What must her tours be like for out-of-towners?*

"I remember Matt Glover as a pleasant young man; I believe Myra Johannsen referred him."

"So you know Myra as well?"

Elizabeth smiles. "One of my interests is the lives of early Californian authors. I wrote a book about a writers' community that began in Carmel back when that was an unsettled area. The book got polite reviews from academics, but it didn't fly off the shelves. Finding someone who'd read it and then looked me up to discuss it made an impression."

"I understand Myra is interested in one poet in particular."

"Nora May French. It's a tragic story. Her family moved to Los Angeles in the 1880s and went broke. She went back to New York, worked in a factory, and then came back to Los Angeles. She moved to San Francisco after the quake, working at low-paying jobs and trying to write poetry. Then she went to Carmel, was unlucky in love, and killed herself at 26."

Franklin's eyes widen enough for Elizabeth to notice. "Has something happened? I don't want to make assumptions about the Police Department's literary interests, but I've never had an officer stop by to discuss California poets before."

"I'm sorry; there's no easy way to tell you this. Matt Glover was killed Saturday, and we haven't been able to locate Myra."

Surprise, shock, sorrow. "Oh my God. He seemed like such a gentle man. How did it happen?"

"We still don't know all the details, which is why we're reaching out to people who knew him. I was wondering what you could tell me about him."

"I only met him a few times. He was..." She takes a few seconds. "I'm not sure how to describe it. I know a very nice woman who runs a business fostering stray cats. Some of them turn into good pets, but she had one who remained aloof. If another cat was being petted, he'd come over and sniff at it, as if he couldn't understand what was happening—he could never quite put the picture together. I had a similar feeling about Matt. Myra immersed herself in her writing and wanted to create her version of the Carmel experiment. And Matt hovered nearby, looking like he didn't get what the appeal of a writer's life could be."

An author with a gift for metaphor. "So he wasn't that interested in writing himself. Was he doing it to please Myra, or hoping you could explain her to him? I assume he didn't become a student himself."

"Neither of them did. Myra enjoyed our discussions and wanted to enroll in a course, but her finances wouldn't allow that. As someone who works three jobs, I can empathize. I never felt that Matt was on fire about writing. He was an engineer who'd had little exposure to literature, and I doubt he'd ever met anyone as passionate about poetry and theater as Myra."

"Sounds like he was in over his head."

"I think it was a whole new world for him, something like when Captain Cook's sailors landed on Easter Island." She smiles ruefully. "You found me through the Collaborative, so I'm sure you already know about our television series. Janus Health is a sponsor, and I assume that's how he heard about me. I think the television show appealed to the engineer in him."

"Is there anything you can think of that might could put Matt at risk?"

"I don't see how."

Franklin shrugs. "In my line of work, I sometimes come in contact with people who harbor strong negative feelings about 'San Francisco Bohemians'."

She laughs. "I'm not old enough to remember the Summer of Love, but I understand. A hundred years ago, people were scandalized by Nora May and George Sterling and Jack London. They all lived together and loved together, and some of them drank themselves to death. Artists of all stripes have been doing that for centuries, but only a few of them ended up getting murdered. "

"Matt's body was found close to Sterling Park. What would be the significance of that site? Any ideas?"

"Not really. Sterling's friends put a park bench on Russian Hill and called it Sterling Glade, but the city didn't build the current park and the tennis courts until 2005, so they're not 'historic'. George didn't live anywhere near the park; he couldn't have afforded to. When he was in town, he rented a room at the Bohemian Club. Myra would have known all that; she was a serious student of these writers. But Matt? No, I don't think so"

"Would Matt or Myra be interested in that location for any other reason?"

"None that I can think of. They named the tennis courts for a 1930s tennis champ who also served as a secret agent during World War II. But Matt and Myra never said anything about tennis or espionage."

"I'm curious. Why isn't the land used for condos? It must be worth a bundle."

She shakes her head. "It can't be sold. The Marble tennis courts sit on top of the Lombard Street Reservoir."

"I thought the old reservoir was next to Hyde Street."

"The abandoned one is. There were two reservoirs on Russian Hill in the 1860s. When the city upgraded the Lombard Street one around 1930, the Francisco Street Reservoir was decommissioned."

"Excuse my asking, but is there anything you don't know about San Francisco's history?"

"Plenty. I'm always learning something new. That's what happens when you lead walking tours; people ask questions about everything they see." She stops abruptly, blushing. "I'm sorry. I've lapsed into tour guide mode and told you almost nothing about Matt. My tour is about to start. Let me see what else I can dig up or remember. The forms we use at the Collaborative ask lots of questions; Myra must have filled one out. My class is on Friday, and I'll be free afterward. There's a nice cafe right across the street; do you ever eat lunch?"

"Yes, I could do that. And thank you, you've already been very helpful,"

She smiles and heads toward a group of people assembled on the sidewalk, leaving Franklin surprised at how quickly he accepted her offer.

THIRTEEN

THURSDAY, AUGUST 25, 2016

This isn't going to go well.

The three of them are sitting in the observation room, where Mike Ortega is explaining his approach to interviewing. On the other side of the one-way mirror, Henry Qu looks composed as he sits in the empty interrogation room.

"We establish who's in control from the moment we begin. We control the narrative from the time we open the door until we've got him signing a confession."

"Assuming there's going to be a confession." Kevin sounds like a hard sell.

Ortega gives Franklin his "Can you believe this kid?" look. "Kevin, Kevin, Kevin. We're already five days into this. *Somebody* murdered our guy, and most homicides are committed by somebody the vic knew. You said yourself, the kid was a loner; this isn't some Agatha Christie novel with ten suspects at a dinner party. You found anyone else you think could be the guilty party?"

Kevin shakes his head.

"Our boy Henry here had means, motive, and opportunity. Sometimes, it looks like a duck and quacks like a duck for a reason. Sit in, shut up, and watch how I do this. You're about to learn how to close a homicide case. Franklin can stay here and take notes."

The two of them head into Interrogation. "I'm Sergeant Ortega; you've already met Inspector Loeffler." Ortega takes the seat opposite Henry and drops a thick folder on the table separating them; Kevin takes a chair behind him. "So how ya doin', Henry my friend?"

"OK, though I'm confused about why I'm here. Everything I know I said to the detectives last Saturday."

46

"Yeah, and that's a problem." Ortega pats the folder. "Because we know that's not quite how things went down."

"What I reported was accurate."

Ortega nods in agreement. "You told Inspector Loeffler and Sergeant Washborne you and Matt were roommates, and you both know a woman named Myra Johannsen."

Henry nods.

"And last Friday night, you and Matt went to the Black Magic Voodoo Lounge."

"We were both there, but we didn't go together."

"And then Matt took off to go see Myra."

"I guess so. I looked around, and he wasn't there, so I assumed that's where he was going."

"And you went out after him."

"No. I stayed at the bar until almost one when I went back to the apartment."

Ortega shakes his head and holds up the folder. "Suppose I told you we got an eyewitness who saw you leave and follow Matt."

"I would tell you that person was mistaken."

"You think I'm making this up?"

"No, I said that whoever you talked to saw someone else. When I left the bar, I drove back to Hayward."

Kevin glances at the one-way and Franklin can see the thought balloon. *As a tactic, Ortega's belligerence isn't likely to work unless Henry has a phobia about cranky chihuahuas.*

Ortega tries a different tack. "You work as a computer programmer, that right?"

"I'm a software engineer. I help design programs and write some of the code."

"You've got to be a pretty logical guy to do that. I mean, computers work on logic, don't they?"

"That's an oversimplification, but yes."

"So then you understand how hard it is to prove that something *didn't* happen."

"That was Karl Popper's thesis."

Ortega is caught off guard by the reference. "Whoever. Henry, let me explain to you what we know. An eyewitness who has no reason in the world to make this up saw you take off after Matt. He <u>saw</u> you, Henry. C'mon man."

Henry's looking at Ortega as if the sergeant had spinach stuck between his teeth.

"I guess it's true, then; all us Asians look alike."

"Hey, Henry, I understand. You and Matt were roommates and coworkers, and you both liked Myra. And it makes no sense that a smart, attractive woman like her would pick a nerdy kid like Matt instead of you."

"Myra liked Matt, and I was fine with that."

"So you're saying you didn't like Myra?"

"I liked her, but it was clear from the start that she was attracted to Matt."

"News flash, Henry! Sometimes women change their minds. You know what I'm saying? You may have been a little slow on the uptake, but this Myra, she sounds like she was a free spirit who might, you know, find a good-looking Asian guy with a big egg roll more interesting than plain ole vanilla Matt."

Franklin winces. *How could anyone misread Henry this badly? And Ortega is acting like he's enjoying this. He's leaning back in his chair with his chin up like he's waiting for someone to hand him the Bigot of the Month prize.*

Mike starts in again. "You and Matt both work at Janus Health?"

"Yes."

"That's a pretty competitive business, isn't it?"

"I guess so."

"Who do you work for at Janus?"

"Dr. James Atkinson."

Ortega raises his eyebrows. "The CEO, am I right? That's impressive."

Henry does not react, so Ortega keeps going. "And you're UC Berkeley. Also very impressive. You're very good at what you do, and I'm betting you didn't get where you are by being Henry Milquetoast. You had to work twice as hard as other guys who were handed things because of their pedigree, or Daddy's money, or the color of their skin. Believe me, I know how that works. I mean, what it comes down to is you're a superstar. And when somebody gets to your level despite it all, who could blame you for wanting to stick it to the white boy."

Ortega stands up and leans over the table at Henry. "I don't think that this thing was something you planned; maybe it wasn't even something you wanted consciously. I'm even willing to bet you didn't get the messages Myra was sending. It was just a spur of the moment, impulsive reaction."

The interrogation room door opens, framing a man in an expensive-looking suit. "You can stop now, gentlemen. Arthur Granger, counsel for Dr. Qu. Dr. Atkinson did not appreciate your grandstanding this morning when you sent uniformed officers to abduct Dr. Qu from his place of employment. This interview is over. Unless you are prepared to place him under arrest right now, Dr. Qu will be leaving."

As he watches the backs of the departing attorney and engineer, Ortega looks annoyed, like a man who was just getting to the juicy parts. Kevin knows enough to stay seated, and for once, he says nothing. Ortega turns and stares at the mirror as if he could see Franklin through it.

Yes, Mike, I watched you blow this, and I heard the mindless racism pouring out of you. We don't know if Henry killed Matt, and Kevin is a bright guy who wants to solve this one. But that won't happen with you in charge. We'll do this my way.

FOURTEEN

Kevin brings two cups of coffee. "Well, that was awkward."

Ortega has just wound down his post-interrogation debriefing. "We were almost there. Fucking lawyers! And you two were no damn help!" Franklin says nothing, which only precipitates a new volley of accusations. "It should be clear to anyone who's made it past second grade that Henry Qu is Matt Glover's killer, and no fat cat corporate lawyer is going to change that. Why the hell hasn't anyone located fucking Myra when it's also obvious she's up to her tits in this too? And has anyone found time in his busy social schedule to interview the other coworkers? In a gossipy place like Janus, this little ménage à trois couldn't have remained a secret. Please, could someone direct this Sergeant to wherever the hell the Homicide Division has gone?"

Franklin toasts Kevin with the coffee, even if it is station house brew. "Which, the amateurish interrogation or the whining that followed?"

"Do I have to choose?"

"OK, then here's an easier one. What did we learn this morning?"

"Let's see. Ortega is pissed about being Latino and uses racism to attack others. Henry is a cool customer and not very suggestible. Janus Health looks out for its own. And an expensive lawyer can end the show-and-tell hour in a hurry."

"Go to the head of the class, Inspector Loeffler. And what else?

"I'm not sure. You're supposed to be a pretty good interrogator; what did you get out of this morning? It sure as hell didn't produce the Perry Mason moment Ortega was expecting."

"When you were a beat cop, did you have trouble deciding if somebody was up to something?"

"Not really. After a couple of minutes, it was pretty obvious. Sort of like when I worked security at the casino; it was easy to tell the sharks from the first-time visitors. Not like at crime scenes where it took a while to learn how to spot when something was out of place."

"That's how we start every case, with a gut feeling. Mike's first idea was that Henry killed Matt; by the time he came in this morning, he was already so sure of it he ended up ignoring every sign to the contrary. You were in the room with him; did you get a shark vibe off Henry?"

"No, he seemed pretty cool, almost detached. If we'd hooked him up to a polygraph, I'd bet he'd have passed."

"You remember going to court after making an arrest? The guys on trial all act the same. Everyone's got it wrong, they didn't do it and if they did, it isn't their fault because the rules don't apply to them. Hear any of that from Henry?"

"No, though Mike was the one doing all the talking."

"So, we haven't caught Henry doing anything or even acting like a guy who did something. We don't even have enough for Probable Cause to get a search warrant to search Henry's possessions for a weapon or blood spatter on his clothes. Though if I know Mike, he's already twisting some prosecutor's arm to find a judge to get one. And meanwhile, the guys searching Matt's belongings will probably also search Henry's stuff, just by accident."

Kevin makes a face. "If Henry isn't our killer, does that mean this whole thing was a waste of time?"

"It means that if Henry is a killer, he's a slick one."

"And now you're about to tell me what I missed that proves he's a total sociopath?"

"You give me too much credit. But think about him at his apartment last Saturday."

Kevin looks puzzled. "He seemed shocked. You think that was all an act?"

"Not what I meant. Imagine it's a Saturday when you're off work, and I drop in on you unannounced. What would you be wearing?"

"A clean pair of Fruit of the Looms, if you're lucky, and if I'd made it to the laundromat that week."

"So you wouldn't look like Henry, sitting at home with every hair in place and with answers at hand for every question we might ask."

Kevin raises his eyebrows. "The thing that was out of place was that nothing was out of place?"

Franklin shrugs. "So is Henry just an ultra-smart, very fastidious guy? Or should we be suspicious of the image he's cultivated because it's a little too good? That's also a possibility. Or maybe chronic exposure to race-baiting has taught Henry how to stay in control of himself. If that's the case, it's no wonder that Ortega's rant got him nowhere."

"But if Henry is the murder, what was his motive—discounting Ortega's 'big egg roll' theory?"

"I'd guess ambition, money, power; not some tabloid crime of passion. Henry wanted Matt's position or project or whatever because he's in a hurry to climb the ladder of the Grandview corporate hierarchy."

"OK. How do we find out whether he's just a together guy or a total psycho?"

"Nothing. We let him do all the heavy lifting."

"Please explain, Captain Enigma."

"Smart sociopaths who get away with things are exceptional, and they know it. They can get arrogant and slip up. If that's Henry, we stay in touch, ask for his help in solving the case and wait for him to get over-confident. No need to go all Ortega-melodramatic."

"So sitting back and waiting is better than going all gangbusters? And a lack of passion is better than being passionate about crime? Not what they teach at the Academy."

"I've found that dispassion can be a useful interrogation tool. A guy will be more likely to open up or slip up if he thinks you don't much care what he's saying. Show him your agenda and you're tipping your hand; sociopaths are good at reading people."

"But you should still act like you give a damn sometimes, like when you're talking with the families of vics, yeah?"

"That's different. There, I take my lead from them and try to be supportive. It's not all about us. Righteous indignation is for *Law and Order* episodes and the Mike Ortegas of the world."

"How'd you learn to think like this?"

Franklin is quiet for a moment. "By getting my ass kicked as a cop, and before that as a soldier. No matter how hard we try, every day somebody ends up in the wrong place at the wrong time. We can't change that. And that's not counting the people who with a genuine gift for putting themselves in harm's way,

"That sounds a little cold."

"I suppose. But having been in a war, I've seen how much damage zealous good guys can do. That's tempered my enthusiasm for our 'war on crime'."

"So what do we do next?"

"Ortega has put Henry out of reach for the moment, so we go on tracking down Matt's other friends and circle back to Henry later."

"Guess I'll keep hunting for the missing Myra, along with solving the Case of the Man Who Drowned on Dry Land. What about you?"

"I need to visit Janus Health, but right now I'm about to lead a Peer Support System meeting."

"Boy, some people catch all the breaks. Good luck."

FIFTEEN

"When I joined the force, I thought this was the greatest job in the world. I was going to do something, protect people, make a difference. What a crock of shit! I go out each day and risk my life, and for what. No matter how many lowlifes I take down, it doesn't seem to make any damn difference. And nobody cares! My wife has given up listening, and I've got a sixteen-year-old daughter who refuses to talk to me because I run background checks on her boyfriends. And my son thinks cops are lame, period."

Isolation, depression, anger, burnout: the Emergency Responders Exhaustion Syndrome. *OK, buddy, perfect score. You've shown me all four, and we've been talking for what, ten minutes?* Cops like to bitch about things at work, just like everybody else. But we expect to always remain in control; confront people, and encourage them, and warn and manipulate and intimidate them, if it comes to that. It's all part of the job. *When all is said and done, we're still the police, and we're in charge, and you're supposed to do what we tell you to. Why can't any of you assholes get that?*

"You know that thing they use in AA—the Serenity Prayer?"

The officer turns defensive. "What, you think this is about booze?"

"No. It's about perspective. You've heard it before; 'Accept the things I cannot change and change the things I can'."

"How the hell am I supposed to 'accept' that a mother leaves her kid with her pimp to go buy crack? Or a 16-year-old knifes another kid for a pair of Air Jordans?"

"Trust me, I've been there too; I worked Vice and Narcotics before Homicide. It doesn't mean liking what goes around us. It's about recognizing that we can't control or take responsibility for every godawful thing that happens in the world. Every one of us joins the force with the idea that we can make a difference. And at some point, the world turns around and says, 'Yeah, every one of you says that in the beginning. But no matter what, there will always be more of them than there are of you. It's the way things are'."

"So, what? You just shrug it off? 'Another dead kid? That's life.' I can't do that. I can't look away, and I can't stop feeling and getting pissed off. I know guys on the force who give up and check out or just go numb. I don't want to end up like them, but how am I supposed to live with this shit?"

Franklin is about to answer when time stops. *They're driving along when there's a sudden shout, and then a flash of light and a noise so loud he's deafened. And everything goes black.* Then he's back in a conference room in San Francisco, sitting across from a surprised brother officer.

"Sorry, I just got blown up."

"What?"

The officer sounds confused. *That makes two of us, friend.* "I mean, I got myself blown up. By an IED in Afghanistan. It ended my Army career."

"Geez, I'm sorry. You came out of it all right, though?"

Franklin's ears are still ringing. *What the hell just happened?* The officer is waiting; he needs to say something. "It got the message across that there were things in my life that I couldn't prevent and couldn't control. It wasn't easy. I wasn't very good at handling the anger and self-pity and whatever. Eventually, something gave me room enough to see how much I loved being military, and how much I hated it. Just like police work."

The officer is listening. "Because you almost got killed?"

"That, and the searches. On my first tour, we were doing routine searches for weapons caches. We'd bang on a door and order some family out of their home and make them lie on the ground while we went through their belongings. They hated us for that, and it got so I could feel their shame and helplessness in my own body. And for what? The one time we got in a firefight, we still didn't find any weapons or Taliban. Just a bunch of dead villagers, old people and children."

Why is this piece of my life back now, in living color with all the noise and dust and stink and fear? "I'm sorry. I'm not sure what I'm trying to say here; I don't know if I'm making any sense."

"No; you make a lot of sense. Sometimes life just sucks, and being forced to admit that at least does something. A lot more than the psychobabble I've been getting." *He looks perplexed, but he doesn't seem as angry; does that count as progress?* "I need some time to think about this."

Franklin sits in the small office after the officer has left. First, the headaches came back, and now the flashbacks; symptoms of PTSD? But why? This session wasn't different from others he's conducted, and the officer didn't sound suicidal or homicidal. Why would that trigger all of this?

Like the man said: *Shit happens*. Kids in Kandahar Province get killed, and an IED blows the guy next to you into oblivion, and Matt Glover leaves his friends at a bar and ends up with his brains bashed in. "It's all about perspective." *What did you tell Kevin this morning? "Be dispassionate"? Dispassionate, or just numb? How you doing with the acceptance stuff, Franklin, when you keep remembering things you know you can't accept? Not just remembering; reliving.*

So are Ortega's ideas about the case wrong because they're too understandable? They make sense at least to some reptilian part of the brain. Matt Glover was most likely murdered for no reason at all, and his death was a senseless, meaningless act that even the perpetrator can't explain. *And I don't want that. Right now, I want to track the guy down and wring an answer out of him that will make sense of it all.*

He takes his time walking back to his desk The image of the road in Afghanistan is gone, and instead, he's on Hyde Street, where a woman is leaning out a window, trying to tell him something.

SIXTEEN

FRIDAY, AUGUST 26, 2016

He almost misses the cafe, an unpretentious storefront at the convergence of Noe, Market, and 16th Streets. The Castro being the Castro, the restaurant looks out on an AIDS mural from the 1990s. Inside, it's all natural wood, with a striped awning that shelters the enclosed patio. The place feels upbeat and matches Elizabeth's mood as she zips through the door.

The AIDS Mural

"How did your tour go?"

"Pretty well for a Friday morning. This time we did Dash Hammett and the Beat poets."

"City Lights Bookstore?"

"Very good! City Lights and the Vesuvio Cafe and the alley in between that Larry Ferlinghetti got the city to name after Jack Kerouac. And a stop at the Beat Museum on Broadway."

"I see you know how to keep the folks on your tour occupied. Is there a Maltese Falcon Museum, too?"

"Might as well be. Don Herron has recreated Hammett's apartment on Post Street, and I take clients to John's Grill; there's a replica of the Falcon in a case at the top of the stairs. If it's too busy there, there's also one in the lobby of the Flood Building and one at the Hotel Union Square."

"Copies?"

"Uh-huh. The one used in the movie was auctioned off a few years ago for about four million."

"If only I'd known."

"We also visited Dash Hammett Street and Burritt Street—that's where Brigid O'Shaughnessy shot Miles Archer."

She just got here, and this already feels like lunch with Wikipedia. "You must be starving after all that."

"Famished. The fish tacos here are great, by the way."

Franklin takes her suggestion, grateful that she didn't suggest the fried chicken po'boy sandwich. She decides on *loco moco,* a hamburger on steamed rice topped with a fried egg. *I'd guess Elizabeth isn't the salad bar type.*

"I mentioned that when anyone contacts the school, we ask them to fill out a personal information form. Even though she didn't register for a course. Someone's looking up any information Myra left with us for me, though I don't know how current it is. How else can I help?"

"We're still looking at motives for Matt's… demise." He stops. "I'm sorry; perhaps this isn't an appropriate conversation. Homicide detectives are used to looking at the seamy side of things."

"Have you read the stuff Hammett and Lillian Hellman wrote? Or heard about the lives they led?"

"Point taken. Matt sounds like a well-adjusted guy leading a normal life. Most people would find that unremarkable; for a homicide detective, it's an invitation to pry into his private life."

Elizabeth smiles. "Then should I also tell you where I hid Aunt Tillie's body? Just to keep you from wasting your lunch hour wondering what I've been up to?"

"So you admit that Aunt Tillie is missing? Where were you when she disappeared?"

58

"I was visiting the grave of my fourth husband, who died after falling off a cliff on our honeymoon. But I already told the police his death was an accident. Just like the previous three."

"I can see why your writing courses are standing room only."

"I wish. As far as I knew, Matt was a straightforward man. Of course, it's also true that we don't include a checklist of vices in the Collaborative course application form. Perhaps we should; life experience is an excellent source of literary inspiration."

"Does that ever invite people to confuse creative writing courses with group therapy sessions?"

"It's something we talk about. One thing I want my students to learn is the difference between writing fiction and journaling."

"Do you think that's a distinction Myra understands?"

Her playfulness subsides. "I don't know the details of Myra's theater training, but I'd guess she's familiar with Stanislavsky's concepts. What started as a theater piece about little-known authors became something more intense. She immersed herself in their lives the way a Method actor might. I'm flattered by her interest in my book, but I found her preoccupation unnerving."

"Coming from someone who knows so much about those authors, I'd say that's significant."

"My book is a layperson's version of an academic study that documents an overlooked chapter in California culture. A few of the writers—London, Upton Sinclair, Sinclair Lewis—became well known, but most of them lived and died in relative obscurity. I think their lives were more interesting than their writing, but not in a good way."

"The lives of troubled people can make good theater, can't they?"

"George Sterling was very charming, and Nora May was a vivacious young woman, but too much of their story sounds like *As the World Turns*, or worse. Everyone remembers *The Call of the Wild* as a story about a dog's devotion. It's also about a pet that turns feral and kills Native Americans, written by an alcoholic who espoused eugenics."

"Ouch!"

She frowns. "It's easy to let where we are now color our reactions. They considered George Sterling a poet of great promise in 1910, but no one reads him today."

"So what happened? I would think that if you get a park named after you ..."

Elizabeth sighs. "I always bring a copy of my book on my walking tours. So sit back for a minute, close your eyes, and listen to this."

The Black Vulture
Aloof upon the day's immeasured dome,
He holds unshared the silence of the sky.
Far down his bleak, relentless eyes descry
The eagle's empire and the falcon's home —
Far down, the galleons of sunset roam;
His hazards on the sea of morning lie;
Serene, he hears the broken tempest sigh
Where cold sierras gleam like scattered foam.
And least of all he holds the human swarm —
Unwitting now that envious men prepare
to make their dream and its fulfillment one,
When, poised above the caldrons of the storm,
Their hearts, contemptuous of death, shall dare
His roads between the thunder and the sun.

Franklin puts his fork down. "Uncle! I'm sorry, but that's awful."

"Particularly if you remember that while he was penning this, T. S. Eliot was writing *Prufrock*. Anyway, if you want to find *La Vie Boheme* in San Francisco these days, you'll have to think about getting tickets for Puccini night at the War Memorial. What disturbs me is Myra's willingness to pursue what had proved to be a dead end in the 1920s. I imagine some part of her understands that, but I worry she may be mixed up with people who have embraced a formula for personal disaster."

"Would you include Matt in that group?"

"I suspect he didn't know what to think. She kept him off balance, perhaps because she had no set plan herself. She saw Nora May as a victim of fate rather than someone who created a lot of her own problems. That sort of self-deception can come with at a high price."

"Which is why I need to find her and her friends. But thank you; you've been a real help."

She blushes. *Pink is an excellent color for her. She also seems as surprised by my response as I am at how good I feel watching her reaction.*

She's finishing her coffee and he realizes she polished off her *loco moco* a quarter-hour ago. "I didn't notice that they mentioned dessert on the menu."

"I know I shouldn't say this to the police, but the 'Dynamo Donuts' here melt in your mouth."

Franklin signals the waiter.

SEVENTEEN

He's unpacking when the phone rings; a call from Janus Health.

"Dr. Walker, I apologize for interrupting you at your conference, but Dr. Atkinson thought he should notify you that a detective will be here Monday."

"Are they still pursuing Henry?"

"No sir. Corporate counsel is representing Dr. Qu."

"What do they want then?"

"Dr. Atkinson assumes they want to talk to the other employees. He intends to head them off at the pass. Since you were Dr. Glover's supervisor, he wanted to give you a heads up."

"I'm sorry I'll miss the opportunity to chat with them. Please keep me posted. Is there anything else?"

"Just that Mr. Lockheed called again. He'd like you to call back."

"Of course. I will call him from the podium in the middle of my address."

"Sir?"

"Please tell Mr. Lockheed I'll be in touch."

"Yes, doctor. Have a good evening."

What law of physics makes pains in the ass come in pairs? Darryl Lockheed and the San Francisco Police Department promise to be twin nuisances. The police should be a self-limiting phenomenon, but Darryl has already proven he has an extended shelf life.

It would help if Lockheed's understanding of pharmacology derived from something other than Marvel comics. Drugs are molecules that interact with the body's chemical machinery. It is an understanding of those interactions that shows how a medicine will effect that machinery's operation. But Darryl's ignorance left him looking for *Zauberkugeln*, magic bullets that always hit the target.

How could he explain to this ignoramus what he's expecting the program to do? A birthday announcement in *Nature* and a television commercial gave him an answer. 2016 marks the 100th birthday of Francis Crick, co-discoverer of the DNA double helix. It wasn't the helix itself but the way base pairs arranged themselves within it that revealed what DNA did and how it did it. The key was to grasp why the geometry had to be what it was.

There was also the TV commercial about the stinky teenager. The active ingredient in Fabreze is cyclodextrin (he'd had to look it up), a ring of glucose molecules that meant nothing to him. But he gave the computer the formula and watched the three-dimensional structure emerge. And then he saw how cyclodextrin worked; it was a tunnel that vacuumed up the offending molecules.

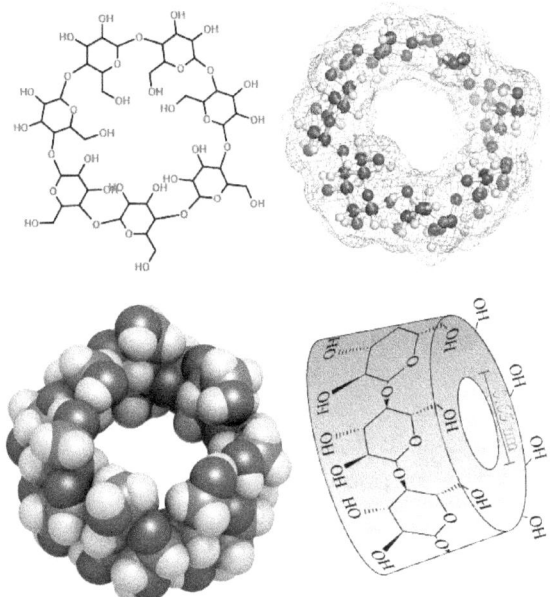

In chemistry, geometry is destiny. Conway had proven that simple rules can generate complex structures; atoms also followed simple rules to form complex molecules. The National Institute of Standards and Technology Chemistry Reference Database contained forty thousand examples taken from the real world. With those data, a program would be able to deduce the rules that govern the structure of organic compounds and set about assembling new ones.

He would use the database and computer visualization to create Darryl's new drugs. Give the program a sample molecule and let it search the database for similar molecules. Analyzing the structure of the related compounds should give clues about how their geometry made the compounds work and about possible variations. Darryl's scientists could review the results and select the ones that made the most sense.

But the elegance of his solution didn't impress Darryl. "So you're saying that what we want is possible, but you aren't telling us how to do it?"

"The question was whether we could construct a program to do this; I have shown that it is possible and outlined the approach. That was our agreement, Mr. Lockheed."

"But you haven't written the program, so how do can you be sure it will work?"

"Because I have proven it. During World War II, no one had found a solution to the Enigma code. But Alan Turing understood it would be possible because of work he had done in the 1930s. I've shown the conditions under which you can use computing to attain your goal. What do your coders think?"

"We're all pharmacology types here, Doc. We have a few computer people, but what you've sent us is over their heads."

"No reflection on them, Mr. Lockheed; I've been doing this for quite a while."

"And you're very good at it. The people who cracked the Enigma code saved a lot of lives, and saving lives is what we want to do."

"That's also my goal at Janus Health, Mr. Lockheed."

"I don't doubt that Dr. Walker, but are any of your projects as exciting as this one? We're looking for drugs whose impact will be huge, and virtual chemistry would give us a quicker, cheaper way to create them. You're a smart man; this will be an undertaking worthy of your skills."

"Now you're sounding like my wife."

"I ought to; she's the one who suggested I contact you."

In the end, it was fear of the repercussions of ignoring Grace that persuaded him. He'd create a simple mock-up as proof of concept. After that, Darryl would be on his own.

He unpacks tomorrow's keynote. He'd toyed with introducing his new idea at the meeting but decided against it. A rigorous mathematical argument in a first-tier journal would be a better choice. He'll start on it when he gets back to San Francisco.

EIGHTEEN

Kevin is already working the phones, wearing an "I can't believe this shit" expression. Franklin can feel his pain from across the room. "Another busy morning?"

"Ortega came down from the mountain with the tablets and the key to my redemption. Since I've failed to find Myra, he's chosen a simpler goal: just find her dead body and prove that Henry killed both her and Matt."

"Great! How's that working for you?"

"Piece of cake. No live Myra, no dead Myra, no friends of Myra, no relatives of Myra. It's obvious: the whole thing is an example of mass hallucination. Case closed."

"OK, you've solved that one. How's the drowning case coming?"

"You're not going to believe this."

Franklin settles into his chair and plants both feet on the floor. "I'm ready; hit me!."

"He's gone."

"Your drowned guy?"

"Yep. The tech in the ME's office discovered that him missing this morning. Dude was still on ice and they hadn't released the body. There's no record of anyone coming to ID him or claim the remains."

"How could anyone steal the body? And why?"

"No clue. Security tapes don't show any movement in the area. Just *poof*! Into thin air."

"Same way he appeared."

"Easy come, easy go. At least I can't get blamed for this one."

"I always like a positive attitude, but don't underestimate Ortega's capacity for irrational behavior."

"Gee, thanks. So what's our War Hero got going this morning?"

"I'm visiting Janus Health. I want to see if anyone besides Ortega knows about Matt's secret life and Henry playing hide the weenie with Myra."

"Great. Look for Myra's head while you're there; I bet it's sitting in a bell jar somewhere. You ever see *Donovan's Brain*?"

"No."

"Nancy Davis costars with a rubber brain in a goldfish tank. I don't remember whether she'd become Nancy Reagan by then. Myself, I see the movie as the prequel to *Ronnie Goes to Washington*."

"I'll keep that in mind during my visit."

Why would a major Silicon Valley player house its latest undertaking in a 1929 building that radiates early Great Depression chic? To call Janus Health's office choice idiosyncratic is an understatement. 450 Sutter Street is twenty-six stories of Art Deco Mayan fantasy. The front entrance is straight out of *Raiders of the Lost Ark*, and bronze glyphs surround even the parking garage entrance and the ATM.

A security guard watches Franklin survey the small lobby, all black marble and patterned bronze panels. "A dentist with terrible timing built this place. It opened in 1929, just before the market crashed."

"I notice a lot of the offices still are doctors and dentists, but Janus occupies the top three floors?"

"Yeah. Used to be *Health! Now! Informatics*, some electronic medical records business. The Grandview Corporation bought them. Renovations were a pain in the ass; we got a ton of complaints. But I guess these big tech companies don't give a damn about small private practices."

Inside the office, no trace of Hollywood Mayan décor remains. Franklin wonders if Angelina McCarthy, the head of HR, is registering some sort of protest by wearing a 70s block print kurta.

"I can tell you without violating privacy considerations that Dr. Glover was a hardworking and competent young man who was well-liked. He passed all our screenings, and his behavior and character raised no red flags. He'd worked here for over 2 years and was an up-and-coming scientist with a professional demeanor. I'm sorry I can't offer you more."

"Matt's privacy isn't an issue in a homicide investigation, Ms. McCarthy. Who could answer some questions about Dr. Glover?"

Underneath the considered professionalism, Franklin senses puzzlement and confusion. *Matthew Glover was not someone Angelina McCarthy expected to be the victim of ill luck or ill will.* "Dr. Christopher Walker is director of the division where Dr. Glover worked, but he's delivering a paper in Chicago and won't be back until Wednesday."

"Then perhaps there's someone else ..."

He stops as two men in thousand-dollar suits appear. One of them shoots out a hand. "Jim Atkinson, Janus CEO. And you are?"

"Sergeant Franklin Washborne, SFPD Homicide Division."

"It's about Matt Glover." Angelina McCarthy looks worried.

"Terrible thing." Dr. Atkinson turns to his companion. "Glover was that scientist who died this weekend."

Franklin must be wearing the right tie because Atkinson continues with the introductions. "Andre Kortov is Grandview Corporation's Vice President for Development and the visionary behind Janus Health. How close are you to finding Dr. Glover's killer?"

"We don't discuss active investigations, but we have identified a person of interest."

Atkinson purses his lips and nods. *The man isn't fussy; even that little is enough to serve as an acknowledgment of his special status.* "Good! What else?"

"I've told the Sergeant that Dr. Walker..."

Atkinson cuts Ms. McCarthy off with an impatient gesture. "I can give you anything you need."

"I confess I'm unfamiliar with what exactly Janus Health does."

Atkinson turns to Kortov. "Just what Andre and I were discussing. I have a few minutes; let me explain Janus to you."

Andre Kortov turns to the door as Atkinson gestures to Franklin to follow him. Angelina McCarthy sighs and turns back to her workstation.

450 Sutter Street

NINETEEN

"Fill-in-the-blank medical questionnaires, cut and paste medical histories, smartphone self-help tools—Janus Health's predecessor was an example of 21st-century technology being used as if this was 1975. Sophisticated data mining and analysis is going to transform medicine, and we'll be leading that revolution. In an era of super-computing, what will move us forward will be algorithms and statistical tools that will sift through information and transform it into knowledge."

Franklin's done his homework, but his skepticism must be showing. The area's second-biggest tech giant has had previous forays into healthcare, and this latest attempt is being led by one of the Bay area's loudest proponents of Better Living Through Big Data.

"You're familiar with digitalis, Sergeant?"

"The drug? I've heard of it."

"What do you know about its discovery?"

"Nothing. I'm all ears."

"An 18th-century doctor found a local herbalist who could treat dropsy. He took her concoction, decided that foxglove was the active ingredient, and then wasted a decade figuring out how to use it. A success story, but an inefficient one."

"Chinese medicine uses 50,000 different compounds, and the National Cancer Institute Natural Products Repository holds tens of thousands of specimens from all over the planet waiting to be characterized. How long will it take to uncover the next wonder drug in all of that? A well-programmed computer can sift through it and unearth connections, detect patterns, develop insights. Imagine what we can accomplish once we translate these data into treatment goals defined in the language of modern molecular biology. Humans have been concocting medical treatments for thousands of years. The only thing lacking is the data analytics that Janus Health will engineer. "

He stops to catch his breath. *Is the man a genius, a con man, or a lunatic? Probably some combination of all three.*

But Atkinson's not done. "The scope of the undertaking proves it's the work of a true visionary. Andre Kortov conceived it and got Grandview's buy-in, and he chose James Atkinson to direct it."

"Yes, and Dr. Glover?"

The man doesn't seem to hear him. "I was the one who picked the name and chose this location. Janus was the Roman god who could look both forward and backward. We're taking the past and turning it into the medicine of the next generation. This building is part of San Francisco's past, and we're taking it into the city's future."

Franklin tries to look fascinated. "You run all your operations from here?"

"Massively parallel processing; Grandview's computational facilities are widely dispersed. Hell of a job getting all that Depression-era wiring upgraded." He grins wryly. "You've had the experience of riding our elevators?"

Franklin nods. "So, Doctor—Matt Glover?"

"Yes. Dr. Glover was involved with the Molecular Synthesis Division, another of our major programming initiatives."

"That would be for designing drugs?"

"Very good, Sergeant!" *Atkinson looks like he's about to ask how the GED is coming.* "Assembling molecules is a little like playing with a Tinkertoy. Computers are good at that; it isn't difficult to build a program that takes some starter molecule and creates variations on a theme."

Franklin tries again. "And Matt?"

"A member of a team of software designers."

"So Janus plans to join the pharmaceutical industry? "

"Not directly. We're a data analysis company. Some of our business comes from pharmaceutical companies looking for drugs for specific conditions. And there are always unexpected discoveries that we may recommend to our clients. Matt helped evaluate some of these 'bonus' ideas."

"Was Matt working on anything that might put him at risk?"

"All research companies generate proprietary information which has potential commercial value, but something worth killing for? Glover was just one person working on a piece of an enormous puzzle."

Atkinson seems more interested in his Big Ideas than in the people he's hired to implement them. The Law of Diminishing Returns predicts that continuing with

70

this infomercial won't get me any closer to finding the killer. "Well, Doctor, thank you for your time and all the information you've shared. I'll also need to arrange a time to meet Dr. Walker."

Atkinson gestures expansively as he ushers Franklin into the waiting arms of Ms. McCarthy. "Of course! Angelina, will you arrange that for our visitor?"

As Janus Health's Captain of Industry departs, Ms. McCarthy concedes defeat and calls Dr. Walker's secretary.

TWENTY

The desk sergeant sticks his head in. "Franklin around?"

Kevin shakes his head. "Out on an interview."

"There's a woman who has information for him."

"I'll take it."

An attractive redhead strides over to Kevin's desk. "I'm Elizabeth Mills. Sergeant Washborne was trying to contact Myra Johannsen, so I brought the contact information she had left with the Writer's Collaborative. I'm sorry that this is all the information I have."

"Thank you. I'm Inspector Loeffler; I work with Sergeant Washborne. I'll make sure he gets this." He smiles. "Are you the *San Francisco Bohemia* lady?"

She laughs. "Yes, I am. Would you like to buy a copy of my book? It would boost my sales by about 15%."

"I'm afraid I'm not much of a reader; I'm dyslexic. But I'm also working on the Glover case."

"That's so sad. I met Matt only a few times, and I'm afraid all I did Friday was bore Sergeant Washborne with literary trivia. I guess I thought he looked professorial."

Kevin grins. "High school football star, Purple Heart war veteran, ten plus years on the force, but I don't know about any professorships."

"A Purple Heart? I hope he wasn't badly injured."

"Had an IED blow up near him. Left him unconscious with broken bones and stuff, and he was one of the lucky ones." He stops himself. "Sorry; sometimes I can get a little graphic. I just mean he's tough and, uh, multi-talented."

"Well, I'm glad that you're both working on this, and I'm sure you'll get justice for Matt. This can't be an easy job."

"It has its challenges."

"Then I shouldn't take any more of your time."

"Thank you for your help, Ms. Mills." Kevin holds up the envelope. "I'll make sure Franklin knows you stopped by."

Perhaps because he's spent his morning listening to Atkinson's visions of corporate splendor, Franklin can feel a headache bearing down on him. It's already becoming intense enough to interfere with the afternoon's paperwork. *This one doesn't feel like Advil's going to touch it; I may need to pack it in for today. I ought to google Elizabeth Mills or George Sterling and the Carmel writer's colony before my eyesight goes.*

The first site he finds is the program guide for KQED's *Literary San Francisco*. "Previous episodes have included biographies of Dashiell Hammett and Lawrence Ferlinghetti, and next up will be *The Lost Tales of Robert Louis Stevenson*." But Franklin's more interested in Elizabeth's commentary. "Friends ask why I choose to live in a world of dead writers. I've always loved a good story, and I appreciate good writing. Over time, I've become more interested in the lives of the authors themselves and the connections between their lives and the fictional worlds they created. Life in early California could be rough, dangerous, and violent. For me, it's not just about their writing but about writing under those circumstances. What made it all worth it? And I enjoy leading literary walking tours because they give a kinesthetic dimension to that history."

Life as a form of literature immersion therapy; no wonder she understands Myra. But can she help us find out what's become of Matt's missing girlfriend? The headache won't let him pursue the question further. *I'd better leave while I can still drive.*

As it is, the ride home is challenging. When he reaches San Bruno, he swallows an Imitrex and collapses on the sofa, trying to center his attention on the cat who's settled himself on Franklin's knees.

They can hear gunfire as they approach the village; an ambush. The artillery is heavy at first, and they wait until it stops before advancing. Bodies lie scattered on the ground.

A convoy of Humvees straggles down the road; the dust obscures almost everything. The vehicle ahead slows. Then there's the explosion, and he's on the ground; someone is shouting. "Shoot him! Shoot him!" Another explosion; this one is deafening.

He's jogging near Land's End, along the coastal trail, and then the path to Mile Rock Beach. Stairs and then a low hill where people are standing. On the peninsula in front of them, someone has arranged stones to outline a labyrinth. A tall, thin man in a dark jacket is traversing the maze. He turns to look up as if suddenly aware of Franklin's presence and drops the sheaf of papers he's holding. The breeze carries the sheets out over the water. Other people have also stopped to watch as the pages blow away; one holds a pair of binoculars. The man has reached the center of the labyrinth, but it's hard to see him in the fog. Franklin turns back to the path; the others have already left. He's jogging again, leaving the man in the labyrinth behind. It's time to head back.

Lands End

TWENTY-ONE

Kevin's all smiles as he pulls a chair up to Franklin's desk. "So, what did you get from your visit to Janus Health?"

"A headache and a bunch of weird dreams; not much else."

"That sounds like a good day's work. Nothing more about Matt?"

"No. The good news is that I got to meet Dr. Atkinson, the Janus CEO. The bad news is I got to meet Dr. Atkinson, the Janus CEO. I doubt he even knows who Matt Glover was and assumes the police visit local businesses because we're studying corporate infomercials."

Kevin makes a face. "Do you suppose he understands what 'homicide investigation' means?"

"I'd guess his enthusiasms crowd everything else out of his field of view. I wonder how a guy that self-absorbed gets to run a company the size of Janus Health."

"By filling the role of a figurehead while others sail the ship?" Kevin frowns. "Although he'd be vulnerable if other people also knew that. A CEO who's all bluster and isn't on top of things leaves room for lots of imaginative corporate diversions. And if some bright, idealistic underling were to stumble across things he wasn't supposed to know..."

"... then the boss or his handlers might consider said employee an encumbrance rather than an asset."

"Unless..." Kevin pauses. "Unless Atkinson's dumb like a fox. He comes across as flamboyant because he wants people to underestimate him. He started as a program designer at Grandview and climbed through the ranks; he's not a stupid man. If I wanted to lull my competition into a false sense of security, letting them conclude that I'm as shallow as a dinner plate might be a good strategy."

"You have a devious mind. I like that in a partner."

"Hey, I'm only half German. My mother's family name was Machiavelli."

"No kidding?"

"No, O'Rourke." He points to his hair. "Just in case my theory is a little too clever, should we maybe pull Janus Health's financials."

"OK. And tomorrow I get to meet Matt's actual boss. We both go?"

"Sure! I'll bring the aspirin."

"You have time?"

"Yeah. My workload's a lot lighter since the Department has decided the best way to deal with the Case of the Misplaced Drowned Man is to deny he ever existed."

"That's creative."

"Hey, we don't know who he was or where he came from. We don't know how he drowned or where he went. Unless something else turns up, there's not a lot more to do. The ME's office would like this all just to go away."

"And it did."

Kevin flashes a grin. "My second piece of good news is that I tracked down where Myra lives. It's a place near the Cow Palace. She hasn't been there for a week, but she's done this before, so no one paid any attention to her absence. I just got off the phone with the founder. I wanted to go down today, but they put me off until tomorrow. Guess they may need time to dispose of any pieces of communal living they don't want to show the SFPD."

"A reasonable concession if we're trying to get their cooperation."

"That's what I thought. And besides, there's more stuff I've still got to check out about friend Matt."

"Somebody else knows him?"

"Yeah, the Saratoga Springs Police Department."

"I thought Janus screened applicants for any criminal record."

"They did, and Matt came up clean. But one of his fellow grad students got arrested for assault back in New York. The Saratoga Springs Casino accused him of cheating, and he took it personally."

Franklin grimaces. "He's lucky the police got to him before the casino heavies did. Any connection to Matt?"

"Both grad students in computer science who had worked on some programs together. The casino claimed Matt's friend was consulting his smartphone while playing poker. The cops invited Matt to drop by to answer some questions.."

"And?"

"Matt wasn't at the casino and had a solid alibi. And the programs they'd written needed huge amounts of computing power to run; they weren't anything you could pull up and use on your iPhone. Only the assault charge stuck, which must have pissed the hell out of the casino management."

"So the boys hadn't actually been caught cheating?"

"The casino argued computers pose a major threat to the industry. After that MIT Blackjack Team stuff in the 80s and 90s, they got paranoid about math and technology types. Ask me, I bet the only reason the cops got interested was they wanted to hear more about a computer program named *STUD*."

"*STUD?* You're kidding, I hope?"

"The card game, as in 5-card stud? Our boys were trying to teach a computer to play poker."

"What was supposed to happen if the computer lost? Was Rensselaer going to foot the bill?"

"Never found out because they couldn't get *STUD* to work. But I still want to know if Matt was a gambler. Call me cynical, but I'm still having difficulty with our boy being Mr. Purity Supreme."

"Perhaps. I think you're just disappointed that *STUD* turned out to be a program about a card game."

"Only trying to find out who in upstate New York stole my online handle."

Franklin just shakes his head.

TWENTY-TWO

Franklin spends several hours studying Janus Health's business model before deciding it's a dead end. Like many start-ups, *Health! Now! Informatics* had been a money-loser throughout its existence, and Janus Health is only one piece of the byzantine corporate structure of Grandview. Making sense of it will take a team of forensic accountants and a subpoena.

He still feels hungover after last night's headache. Some of it felt like a regular dream. *I've jogged past that part of Land's End lots of times. The labyrinth--"a shrine to peace, love, and enlightenment"--has been there since 2004.* But why are these memories of the war popping up again? *The pages blowing out to sea; was that intended as a message about letting go of the past?* He doesn't put much stock in dream interpretation.

The phone rings. It's Elizabeth.

"Hi! How are things going?"

"OK. We've located the place where Myra is living and are going there tomorrow."

"Have you spoken to her? Is she all right?"

"The co-op leader or founder or whatever that she hasn't been there for a week."

A silence. "I hope nothing has happened to her."

"Why would you think something might have?"

"Many people would see the characters in her play as foolish, if not out-right delusional. Myra acted as if she had a calling; she wanted to prove that their experiment could work. Living in an intentional community sounds to me like another attempt to rewrite history."

"I understand your concern, but let me play devil's advocate. Imagine that things don't work out for her, and Myra emerges sadder but wiser and decides she'll write TV sitcoms instead."

"It's possible, but I'd like to know who her housemates are. This feels a lot like a descent into romantic fantasy and escapism."

"And in my line of work, when someone says 'intentional community', I hear 'cult'."

Elizabeth sighs. "I don't know what happened to Matt, but I see them both as lotus-eaters, two people who mistook San Francisco for a mythical Aegean island in the Land of Make-Believe."

"Which could make them sitting ducks. You seem to be very intuitive about people."

"Perhaps. Sometimes things just fall together in front of me in ways I can't ignore. Does that ever happen to you?"

"Not often enough. You're thinking of Hercule Poirot."

"Oh, have you read…."

"No, but I saw the movie."

"You're impossible!"

"You're just noticing that, Ms. Intuitive?"

"A lady never reveals all she knows. So what's new outside of work, Sergeant?"

"Recently? The only thing close was a dream about someone throwing papers into the Bay."

"Did you arrest them for littering?"

"No, though I should have. How are you on dream interpretation?"

"I tell my students to avoid it in their writing. It's been done to death."

"So, no theories?"

More laughter. "The only theory of dreams I find interesting comes from Robert Louis Stevenson. He claimed the 'little people'—he called them Brownies—produced his dreams and filled them with stories. Over time, they got good enough at it to provide him with sections of novels while he slept."

"So are there little men who will help me if I'm stumped by a case?"

"Wouldn't that be handy?"

"Only if I were planning a career change. I doubt the San Francisco Police Department would accept even a good detective story as a substitute for something that would hold up in court."

"Anyway, he didn't mean that the Brownies were real. He was trying to explain the inexplicable, why he was such a born storyteller. I dream, but my dreams don't turn into bestsellers. I'd suggest you continue to rely on your excellent deductive skills and not count on crime-solving little men."

"I took something for a migraine last night; that could account for the vivid dreams."

"I know very little about medicine, but it sounds reasonable."

"Was Stevenson a drug user?"

"Louis suffered throughout his life from lung hemorrhages. The treatments of the day included opium, ergot, and cocaine."

"No wonder he heard little men talking to him. You called him Louis, though."

"Everyone did. He and his cousin and his grandfather were all named Robert; using his middle name simplified things. Anyway, that exhausts my knowledge of dream interpretation and medicine, and I've taken too much of your time already. I hope I'm not being intrusive in asking about Myra."

"No apologies needed for being a caring person. It's not against the law, and I should know. I promise I'll keep you posted."

"Yes, Officer."

It's only after she hangs up that he realizes he hadn't intended to tell anyone about the dream. *But it doesn't matter. What does matter — a lot — is just how comfortable we are around each other and how good I feel after talking with her.*

.

TWENTY-THREE

The fog is thick enough to slow the trip to Vienna Street, which is just as well. Otherwise, they could have missed the generic four-bedroom house in the packed Outer Mission district. A playground and a park separate it from a squalid square mile of dilapidated World War II concrete barracks where even Muni drivers refuse to go after dark. The Cow Palace sits to the south, buried in the fog.

Franklin is peering into the gray monotony when Kevin breaks the silence. "Never been down here before, but after looking at Google maps last night, I'd already decided I wasn't missing out on anything."

"Yeah. If I wanted to recreate the experience of some early California writers living in Carmel-by-the-Sea, this isn't a location I'd pick."

"Playing a starving artist may sound romantic, but trying to live in San Francisco with no money sucks. I mean, what kind of poetry are you going to write when you're stuck down here?"

"We're an intentional community embodying the Fieldstone principles. Each member is responsible for his thoughts, emotions, and behaviors—for every aspect of his existence. We're convinced human beings thrive in groups; our goal is pleasurable living and responsible hedonism."

Carl Holton is tall and bearded and fills the small living room with his presence. He looks like a slimmer version of Paul Bunyan. *If there's a Mesomorphic Inspirational Speakers Bureau somewhere, Carl is a charter member.*

"Fieldstone, as in Fieldstone University?" Kevin is also responding to Carl's aura. Franklin wonders; *is it the persona or pheromones that are grabbing his attention?*

"Yes. I took courses and then conducted workshops there, though these days, I prefer to teach experientially among people living as a community. There's just so much you can accomplish with words. Are you familiar with the Fieldstone concepts?"

"A little." Kevin looks at Franklin. "The idea of 'responsible hedonism' is sort of interesting."

Franklin clears his throat. "We're trying to find Myra Johanssen; we understand she lives here."

"Yes, Myra has been a full-time member of the Inner Freedom family for four or five months. She's interested in intentional communal living and wants to model her life after what people in an earlier Monterey community enjoyed."

"And you both thought here would be a good place for that?"

Carl shrugs. "I don't know much about California history. I got the impression that the previous group was much looser and less structured than the first Fieldstone family, which has been self-sustaining since 1968. I can tell you that these things won't work unless every member is invested in communication, sensuality, and decision-making. But everybody has to start somewhere, and Myra is smart and committed."

"So she's a good fit?"

"She has potential. Like many people, she ended up here because of what she didn't like about her previous life. She grew up in Illinois, got a dead-end job she hated, and followed a boyfriend out here. Big surprise: she ends up unemployed, he ends up frustrated and resentful, and the relationship falls apart. Welcome to your life, everybody. At some point, she figures out what's important and comes to us."

"And she's happy now, yeah?" Kevin sounds less than convinced.

"As long as she is present when she's here, yes."

Classic Ploy #17: Be enigmatic. Franklin decides to play along. "Sorry?"

Carl flashes a knowing smile. "We emphasize living in the immediate present. Wandering off into your thoughts may let you daydream about happiness, but our goal is to experience genuine pleasure in the real world. When she is on, Myra is great; she enjoys being in her own skin and brings other people pleasure." He smirks. "That's something we're all still working on."

Carl seems to enjoy playing provocateur in front of narrow-minded cops. But he's never met Kevin.

"And that's something you're taking a personal interest in helping her with, yeah?"

"I try my best. But she keeps returning to fantasies about recreating that particular writers' group. Some in our family are active in the arts, but we're not an artist's commune as such. We're welcoming to anyone who sincerely wants to practice our principles. Her fixation, her obsession, started interfering with some aspects of life here. She becomes withdrawn and focused only on her poetry. I confess I've been disappointed that her writing keeps displacing us and taking possession of her life

Kevin interrupts. "Possession? Like some dead poet is taking over?"

"A fanciful description, but as a metaphor, it captures how she's living somewhere other than *here*. I suggested she take some time to delve into what she's looking for. The day after that, she disappeared."

"Did she take her things with her?"

"No. She's a grown woman, and participation here is voluntary. The work we have to do on ourselves can be intense and requires a serious commitment. Many people come here but leave in a few weeks, and even the most dedicated may need to take a break."

OK, this continuous patronization is getting to me. Franklin tries to keep his tone neutral. "Did you file a Missing Person report?"

"Why would I? If she wants to do something else, that doesn't mean she's missing. It's a big world, Sergeant."

"I assume you realize we're investigating the murder of Matt Glover. He was a friend of Myra's; was he ever here?"

"Matt? Yeah, that was weird. He visited from time to time, and he seemed curious, intrigued. But he wasn't committed to our community." He looks at Kevin. "That's not surprising. Lots of people find the idea of responsible hedonism titillating. It usually means they don't understand the concept. Myra was more engaged when Matt was around. It could have turned into something positive if they'd decided to involve themselves by living here as a couple."

"So they could also become apostles of 'responsible hedonism'?"

"I don't expect cops to understand this, but when you put people together for an extended period and let them jettison mindless Puritanism, there's a lot more sensual energy to tap into. And experiencing and sharing sensual energy—pleasure—isn't against the law. People should be able to do whatever they want, as long as everyone involved agrees."

I've heard enough of this BS. "That sounds like a nice theory, but getting people to behave rationally when they're swimming in a sea of 'sensual energy' is asking a lot. So who here might be less evolved and could have reacted with 'mindless Puritanism'?"

"People who don't want to live the principles leave on their own. Everyone here is working every day to rid themselves of personal negative energy. Matt was never a member of Inner Freedom, and nobody here had anything to do with his death."

The resistance is abrupt and intense enough to tell Franklin there's something Carl is avoiding. *Time to play chastened civil servant.* "Well, we'd appreciate it if you'll let us know when Myra shows up again. We'd like to talk to her." Franklin hands Carl his card. "Thank you for your time. We'll be in touch."

TWENTY-FOUR

It's started to rain. Kevin stares out the window as Franklin drives. "Well, he makes it sound like he's been to the mountain. Wonder how much he believes this stuff."

"What the hell is Fieldstone University?"

"All I know is they used to offer a Ph.D. in Sensuality. It took the state of California like twenty years to figure out they weren't Stanford or UCLA and that the legislation that created Fuck U needed to be repealed."

Despite the fog, Franklin takes his eyes off the road. "Please tell me you didn't choose police work because the state killed the doctoral program you were counting on."

"Of course not! I elected to work with you so I could stay pure and innocent. Besides, I'm from Reno, so I've already had plenty of training in advanced debauchery."

"But there are people around who take this bullshit seriously?"

"Fieldstone has a set of rules about 'intentional communal living' that makes sense. They might work if anyone could follow them."

"And since nobody can..."

Kevin looks serious for a change. "Take one troubled young woman, one naïve boyfriend, add in a bunch of horny 'anything goes' strangers, shake, and serve well chilled over the Lombard Street steps."

"Matt may have been a little unworldly, but he was still a healthy male 20-something. Myra may have wanted a literary enclave, but you heard Carl. She's been an 'active participant' in his community. Matt follows Myra, he doesn't want to share, and somebody gets upset. So was he some devious little shit living a double life?" Franklin shakes his head. "Inner Freedom my ass; Inner Sleaze is more like it. This polyamory stuff is a formula for jealousy and violence just waiting to ignite. It sounds like Ortega may be at least half right."

"We've got to talk to Myra. And let me see what more I can find on Fieldstone and Carl."

"We might still learn more this afternoon at Janus. I'm glad you're going to be there."

"Thanks. I never bought the 'Henry is the only plausible suspect' thing, and this morning throws more cold water on that." Kevin is silent for a few seconds. "Seriously, you think polyamorous relationships can never work? I read an article in *Scientific American*. There's something called compersion; it's supposed to be an alternative to jealousy."

"What the hell's 'compersion'?"

"It's the joy you feel when your partner encounters love from any source."

Franklin shakes his head. "*Scientific American* isn't my strong suit, and I've never heard of compersion. But I don't know anyone who'd react like that, and I can't see myself being able to feel that." He hesitates. "Are gay guys able to do that, or at least do it better than straight guys? This is a real question."

"I don't know. At least some gay guys seem to be OK with open re-lationships, even though that gets us labeled shallow and promiscuous. Which reminds me to say thank you. I mean, a lot of military guys get squicked by this whole gay thing, and plenty of gay guys have a uniform fetish. That's not my thing, and you seem to be OK with me, which is cool. If you had to be a walking sex machine and me the perpetual nympho-pansy, solving this case would be a lot more complicated."

Franklin nods his acknowledgment. *I'd already figured out that weaponized candor is your default mode, but still—where this conversation has gone is a surprise.*

Ahead of them, the Vallejo Street garage emerges from the rain.

TWENTY-FIVE

Kevin studies the directory in the lobby of 450 Sutter. "Even if you didn't have a thing about dentists, I wonder who would pick one whose office is part of the set for *Dr. Frankenstein Meets the Mummy*?"

The rain has stopped, but fog still envelops the upper floors of the building, and the black marble lobby feels claustrophobic. "The glyphs look more Aztec than Egyptian."

"OK, so it's an Aztec mummy. I'd still decide to live with my toothache."

They're invited to take a seat in a tiny waiting area on the twenty-fifth floor. "So who is this Doctor Walker?"

Franklin checks his notes. "Christopher Walker, PhD., director of Janus Health's Artificial Intelligence Virtual Pharmaceutical Task Force. Impressive educational pedigree, a bunch of academic appointments, has published a ton of papers. Sounds like he's a big deal in the Artificial Intelligence world."

"Then why would he leave academia to work at a start-up run by a blowhard like Atkinson?"

Franklin closes the notebook. "Full professor, but not department chair. Grandview has more money than God. Maybe dangling an offer of a research institute let Atkinson snag him. He gets to be his own boss, and Janus gets his expertise and the publicity value of his reputation."

"And private business is a lucrative place to do research. What's not to like?"

"You haven't met Dr. Atkinson."

A secretary leads them to Dr. Walker's small, cluttered office. *This man has to be the most colorless guy I've ever met.* Walker wears a white shirt, ivory slacks, and a pale gray tie. Clean-shaven, pale white face, almost albino hair, and nearly invisible eyebrows. *As a kid, I thought skin that white looked wrong somehow, and that feeling's just come back.*

Dr. Walker rolls his wheelchair out from behind the desk and stands to greet them. His gait is stiff and awkward, but he's not paralyzed. He's also prepared for others' reactions. "Neurosarcoidosis—an uncommon auto-immune disease. It's not fatal or necessarily progressive, but it makes walking and prolonged standing difficult. I am sorry to have caused you the inconvenience of a second trip; I was in Chicago, addressing an international AI forum."

Kevin smiles. "Anything I would have been able to understand?"

"My topic was 'Can Machines Think—Turing Re-Visioned'."

"Turing? The Enigma code?"

"The same." Walker looks pleased.

"And can they? Weren't early computers called 'thinking machines'?"

"They were. You've seen *The Imitation Game*? Turing suggested a computer could be said to think if a person couldn't tell whether answers to questions came from a machine or a human being."

"But is mimicry the same as thinking?"

"I can posit that you are smart and observant, detective, but I doubt that you're clairvoyant. How do you know I think? We deduce what we call thinking in other people through assumptions about universal human experiences. Perhaps the question should be 'Do Humans Think?' "

Is this another interrogation ploy, or is Kevin's interest genuine? A taste for metaphysics? My partner, the philosopher. "We were wondering, Doctor, what you could tell us about Matt Glover that might help our investigation."

"I don't know that I have much to offer. Matt was part of a team whose goal is to teach a computer to design drug congeners."

"Congeners?"

Walker points to two wooden squares on his desk that have been cut into pieces. "You've no doubt seen dissection puzzles like these. The larger one is Archimedes' Ostomachion, and the smaller one is a Chinese tangram. The tangram has only seven pieces, but one can construct thousands of intriguing shapes from them. It makes for an interesting exercise in geometry, imagination, and intuition. Atoms can also arrange themselves into molecules in multiple ways. All the cholesterol-lowering statin drugs, for example, have similar structures—congeners is the technical term. Some work better than others; deducing why and making more like them is the intuitive part. Computers can manipulate shapes; the challenge is to give them the equivalent of imagination and intuition. "

The Ostomachion

"And Dr. Glover?" *Is Walker being avoidant or just discursive?*

"Some people have a knack for solving geometric puzzles; Dr. Glover was someone who could translate them into computer code."

"So he was a valuable resource."

Walker looks pensive. "Over the months since we hired Matt, he and I worked together on a drug synthesis program and were making progress. It was a good start for someone new to this work. Recently, though, he was distracted and less engaged."

"Can you give us any idea why?"

"I suspected it might be a manifestation of his attaining success too early. I would expect that as detectives, you've encountered cases where a belief in one's exceptionalism has led to poor judgment."

"Is there a particular incident you could share with us, Doctor?"

"No, it was just an impression." He pauses for a moment. "I make it a policy not to involve myself in employees' lives. But I couldn't avoid hearing about Matt's involvement with a woman who was—I don't know—what used to be called a hippie. I wondered if she might distract Matt from his work."

Kevin makes a choking sound that he attempts to disguise as a cough. Franklin has a hard time imagining this intensely cerebral man noticing social dynamics. "How about Matt's coworkers or friends? Are there other aspects of his life that might have been bothering him?"

"No. As I said, I try to keep out of people's private lives. The only extracurricular reference that ever arose was in the context of artificial intelligence and game theory." He pauses, waiting expectantly. When no response comes, he adds, as if for clarification, "Specifically, imperfect information games."

Does everything in life remind Dr. Walker of some interesting theoretical question? Franklin tries to sound apologetic. "I'm sorry, Doctor; can you give me an example?"

Walker looks puzzled. "In a perfect information game, each player can see all the details of the state of play; tic-tac-toe or chess would be examples. Many card games are imperfect information games because a player can't see all the cards."

"Like blackjack, for example?" *Kevin's interest is beginning to make sense.*

"Yes. Poker was the example Matt used."

Bingo! "But what would poker have to do with pharmacology?"

Walker ponders the question. "Nothing, I think. In a paper I wrote on virtual pharmacology, I pointed out that our lack of knowledge about biological molecular structures is a major technical limitation. But Matt insisted that a modification of classic game theory could somehow compensate."

"Did Matt like to gamble?"

"I'm not sure. He had shown me work on a prototype program he contributed to in grad school. They wanted the computer to play poker." Walker looks as if even the memory of the conversation is painful. "Regrettably, the program was called *STUD*."

TWENTY-SIX

"I dismissed the whole thing as a stunt. Junior engineers often display an affinity for creating flashy applications that make eye-catching poster presentations or marketable game ware rather than concentrating on fundamental principles. The seductions of glamorous applications are an occupational hazard in computer science. To his credit, Matt's later work showed original ideas and interesting insights that made me revise my initial assessment."

Franklin assumes his "mature fellow professional" demeanor. "I can understand how that exploit might have made Dr. Glover look frivolous."

"It's said that Sir Isaac Newton laughed only once in his life. The Newtons of this world distinguish themselves by their capacity to focus on the important while avoiding whimsical projects or trivial distractions."

Franklin glances at Kevin. *We're learning a lot about Walker but not much new about Matt.* "Wouldn't creating this poker program pretty much require someone to be an experienced poker player?"

"No. There are plenty of 'How To' books around—ones for all sorts of games and players at all levels. If Matt used a compendium of examples of successful strategies an expert player might use, he could transform those into algorithms to include in the program."

"Another question: did Matt's work require a knowledge of chemistry?"

"Again, no. The rules governing chemical syntheses are well established; one could use the same approach to provide the computer with them. Matt had no pharmacology background, but he did not need one."

"Can you think of anything in Matt's work that would give someone a motive to harm him?"

"No. Nothing he was doing would be of use to anyone outside his group. His work was part of a very complicated undertaking." He turns to scan the bookcase near his desk. "Do either of you gentleman have time to read?"

Kevin smiles back. "No, sir. I don't even have time to watch *Law and Order* reruns."

"At Yale, I studied enough molecular biology to see that the discipline bordered on the chaotic—endless catalogs of variations on every chemical theme imaginable. And I later found this opinion validated in an unlikely source."

"And which was that?"

"Annie Dillard." He pauses, looking for any sign of recognition. "*A Tinker at Pilgrim Creek*?" Another pause before he pulls a book from a shelf and puts it on the desk.

"In the book, Dillard argues that not only has the Creator made things we know about; He seems intent on making everything and anything imaginable. It's not the intricacy of the world that amazes her, but the endless variety of forms she sees everywhere. As she puts it, 'anything goes' appears to be a fundamental guiding principle of the universe."

Walker gazes at them with a triumphant smile. "So I looked to computer science, logic, and mathematics, to impose order on what she calls 'the extravagance of nature'. After reading her work, I became persuaded that whatever pharmaceuticals we're looking for may already exist. We need only to construct a program to discover where it's hiding."

Franklin nods his understanding. "Dr. Atkinson's 'Big Idea'. Matt was working on it?"

Walker puts the book back and shakes his head. "Pharmaceutical companies are conservative. They prefer 'me-too drugs', variants rather than anything too novel. But they pay the bills."

"So Matt's was a second-tier undertaking?"

"It's a useful project well suited to his knowledge and experience." He turns to Franklin. "You've met Dr. Atkinson, Sergeant Washborne; I'm sure he's shared his vision for Janus Health with you. But a project of such complexity will take time to implement. We need interim revenue-producing programs while we're designing true deep learning systems."

"Slowly now, Doctor; deep learning?"

"Programs that mimic the way the human brain works. The design of artificial neural networks has been a principal interest of mine."

"Which is why you give lectures entitled 'Can Machines Think'?"

This time, Walker almost laughs. "Bravo, gentlemen! Your astuteness makes you welcome visitors indeed. I'm only sorry I can't be any help with your investigation. Matt was a fine engineer working on a non-controversial program. His worst failing was a temporary romantic distraction. If that were a crime, we'd all spend time in jail."

There's a knock at the door, and an elegantly dressed woman steps into the office.

"Gentlemen, my wife, Grace. Dear, these detectives are investigating Matt Glover's death."

"Such a terrible thing. I heard about it on the news. But I didn't mean to interrupt."

"You're not interrupting, Mrs. Walker; we were just leaving. Your husband has already been very generous with his time."

Grace Walker beams her approval. "It's a failing of his, I'm afraid. I take advantage of it all the time." She turns to her husband. "There's a meeting of the S21CBR board tonight. Can I tell them you'll have a presentation? Something short—it may be better if it isn't anything too complicated."

"Not tonight, please. I have nothing prepared, and I wouldn't want to short-change your board members."

"Of course. I'll tell them you'll be at their next meeting—it's in four weeks." She turns back to Franklin. "My husband has a distinguished academic background, and he treats every invitation to speak as if he was defending his thesis. The Society for 21st Century Biomedical Research is just the sort of group that needs to learn from him. They'd love to make him a regular consultant."

"So you've said. And I'll make space in my schedule for their next meeting, I promise."

They file into the outer office. "Nice to have met you, detectives, and I hope you find the person who committed this terrible crime soon." Mrs. Walker smiles and takes her husband's arm to guide him back into his office. With a grimace, Franklin starts toward the antique elevators.

TWENTY-SEVEN

He wishes he'd brought a rosary to clutch as the elevator shudders its way back to the lobby.

"Somehow, I get the feeling they're not interested in letting the worker bees talk to us." Kevin stands by a door in the lobby that looks like it should lead to the Sapa Inca's tomb instead of a parking garage. "So where would we go if we wanted to meet them?"

"Wherever they hang out. Did Walker's office look plush to you?"

"Not hardly. Even low-end casinos in Reno can do better than that."

"Janus may be a prestigious place, but being housed in this relic has to limit staff perks. Where would their employees take a break?"

"There are two Starbucks and a McDonald's across the street that looked crowded. There are plenty of bars around here, but Janus doesn't feel like a mid-afternoon-martini type of place."

"You've got a good eye for these things."

"Hey, I used to be in the hospitality industry. Maybe everybody's so dedicated that they don't take breaks? Walker seems oblivious to anything other than work. Think we'd get any clues if we drove around a bit?"

They start back to the car. Unlike the revamped offices on the upper floors, the parking options for 450 Sutter reflect the building's 1920s origins. "Jeez, they must have built this garage with Studebakers and Model A Fords in mind."

"And Nob Hill must complicate the traffic flow. The main Sutter Street entrance is on the first level, but where we're parked, the Bush Street exit is three levels up."

By the time they reach the car, the rain has started again, and the narrow alley outside is wet and slick. Ambling down it is a tall, thin figure with longish hair wearing a short black velvet jacket. *It's not likely this guy is a Janus employee or a dentist.* It takes Franklin a few seconds to realize where he's seen the man before and to head down Pfleuger Place after him.

The man turns onto Bush Street and walks toward Stockton. Franklin is moving fast, but Velvet Jacket is still pulling ahead. By the time Franklin reaches the intersection, he's gone. A tattoo parlor and a laundromat occupy the northwest side; a Windham hotel is across the street. On the south side, stairs lead down to the Stockton tunnel. Franklin scans the entire area, but the man has disappeared. There are too many buildings to check and it's raining harder. Franklin turns back toward the garage.

Kevin stands at the exit, studying his drenched partner. "Where'd you go?"

"Thought I saw someone I was interested in, but I lost him."

"Someone from Janus?"

"No, someone I recognized from the crime scene. But I could have been wrong."

"Oh." Kevin's face is non-committal.

I'm glad the curiosity you gave free rein in Dr. Walker's office is in check. It's a stretch to describe a dream about Land's End as part of the crime scene. And explaining why he was chasing someone he saw in the dream is more than he wants to tackle right now.

"Hey, you're pretty wet." Kevin cocks his head toward the parked cars. "Let's head back. I'll drive."

The Garage

TWENTY-EIGHT

THURSDAY, SEPTEMBER 1, 2016

"I take it that the interview with those detectives went well?" James Atkinson takes a wooden puzzle from Chris Walker's desk and runs his thumb over the cut surfaces.

"For the life of me, I can't imagine what they expected to find."

"They're grasping at straws. I suspect they haven't any idea who killed Dr. Glover; it was probably just a senseless mugging by some homeless guy. The public would be better served if the police addressed that problem rather than running around interrupting our work."

"People don't get killed for writing code. Matt was off his game in the past few months. I still worry his extracurricular interests somehow gave rise to what happened. I'm just glad I don't know any of the details."

Atkinson suppresses a laugh and puts the puzzle back on the desk. "Chris, I admire you as a scientist, but sometimes I swear you sound downright Victorian about people's personal lives."

"He had so much going for him, and then —. If your homeless conjecture is right, it was a random event, nothing that he could have prevented. What bothers me is the possibility that it might not have been random. What is it about these junior engineers that makes them so blind? Part of our training is supposed to be about learning to foresee consequences."

"Chris, all I'm saying is that in any field where people work hard under pressure, sometimes they need to blow off steam. You knew Matt well; he never struck me as someone who would make a fool of himself."

"Success can make fools of us if we let it. I've seen too many people decide they will always succeed at anything they try, no matter how reckless their decisions turn out to be. That's why I found Matt's interest in that poker program disturbing."

"I didn't; if you got it, flaunt it. A program that can play poker would be a reason to hire him. Nothing succeeds like success, Chris. Your belief in seriousness and modesty can also be a formula for being left in the dust, underestimated and ignored. 'Just keep your head down and the world will beat a path to your door' is unrealistic."

"And the alternative? After he was killed, I went through Matt's files and found items that weren't connected to his assigned projects. Some files were encoded and password protected; what was that about? Yes, I thought I knew Matt, but now I wonder."

A shrug. "Well, what's done is done. I'm sorry this happened, but it has nothing to do with Janus, a fact I expect the police now understand. In the meantime, we still have projects with deadlines. I feel Henry Qu should take over Matt's assignments."

"Is that going to work? Henry has his own work. Is it realistic to expect he can do both, get up to speed on my projects while working with you?"

"I know it's not ideal, and I assure you, we're trying to recruit someone for your very important work. Given the sophistication of your field, I'm sure you understand why that could take time. Software engineers capable of appreciating and understanding the subtlety and complexity of your thought are uncommon. Given our immediate needs, Henry is available; he's bright and a quick learner. He'll do for the present; there's no need to catastrophize."

Atkinson shifts in his chair and looks around, but there's nothing left to fiddle with on the desk. "I also appreciate that this may not be the best time to remind you of our other needs, but we have still to address this un-resolved issue of product impact assessments. We're a young company with a lot of balls in the air. What we need is a 'real world' assessment of every Janus Health product. Not just the usual measures, citations in journals and such. The reactions of other scientists don't interest me; they're a chorus of carping idiots picking things apart for secondary gain. What we have to foresee is how much each product will change the medical world. And how much it's likely to enhance the reputation and profitability of Janus Health."

"Right now, what we're producing is task-oriented software designed for individual clients. If the client is happy, what more do we need?"

"We're never going to dominate this field by wasting our time on other people's trivialities. That was *Health! Now! Informatics* problem. They jumped through everybody else's hoops and ended up with a line of pedestrian products. If somebody offers us a minor challenge, we need to counter with a proposal that's a lot bigger, something that will put them and us out in front. We don't shrink our vision down to their perspective; we open their eyes to the broader view we enjoy. Going forward, Janus Health will need an ongoing assessment of each project from its inception through its development and successful completion. I believe Matt Glover was already considering this."

"I was not aware of that."

Atkinson waves a hand. "You have far bigger issues to deal with. I sent a memo to junior staff, telling them that this should be one of their ongoing activities. The way to get this done is to insist that everyone be part of it. But Henry will be by later so you can help him get started."

He stands up with the air of a man who's about to state an unarguable truth. "Andre Kortov could have had anyone he wanted for Janus, and he chose you and me. Have you ever wondered how or why he reached that decision? By performing a similar sort of impact assessment. He studied all the candidates and found the two men who could change the world. And that's us, Chris. I've always appreciated all you do for the Institute and the long hours you've been putting in. I know, as you do, that you're a man who's going to make a difference in people's lives. So work with Henry, because we're going to accomplish great things together."

TWENTY-NINE

"I don't know what it is about fecundity that so appalls." Christopher Walker puts the book back on the shelf. It's a safe bet that James Atkinson has never read Annie Dillard, but he'd probably agree with her; life is astonishingly cheap. Is Matt Glover dead? Well, it goes with the territory, a regrettable consequence of blowing off steam. The good news is that Janus is in the clear, and Atkinson's found another warm body to replace Matt without missing a beat.

Everyone sees Atkinson as a "big data for profit" entrepreneur known for exaggerated claims and oversimplifications. It's difficult forging an iden-tity as a serious AI researcher while working for such a shameless self-promoter. But this is the company Grace championed as an alternative to life at a university. A place where he wasn't just tolerated because political correctness required that a man in a wheelchair be appointed to a named chair.

And even Janus may not be enough for her. "These 21CBR board members know just the people you need to meet. They're very creative men who want to use computers to design pharmaceuticals."

"... Which is what I'm doing at Janus, Grace."

"They're bright, ambitious, disaffected scientists who would benefit from the advice of an experienced senior specialist. You can't say that about Janus. Why must you so undervalue yourself? Your work has so many fans."

"Fans? I am a scientist, Grace, not a rock star."

"No, that's where you're wrong. You ARE a rock star. Why not loosen up just a little and enjoy it? You make it sound as if I'd been hawking your CV on a street corner."

"Because I am not a performer! What do you want me to do, open an act in Las Vegas? 'Dr. Walker and his Performing Computers'?"

"Sometimes you're impossible. I almost wonder which you fear more, failure or success. Just come speak to my board. Please?"

Speak to my board. He knows the speaker she wants, the confident young man she married, or the powerful academic she expected him to become. And if Darryl Lockheed represents the membership of her board? They must all be people with no interest in the complexities of theory. They don't want advice; they want someone to hand them the results they want to hear on a platter.

The prototype program he sketched for Lockheed was very basic. It played with the structures of two molecules over four or five iterations to generate plausible new variants. It wasn't much, but it got Darryl's attention.

"Dr. Walker! It works!"

On the phone, he'd tried to keep the annoyance out of his voice. "Yes, Mr. Lockheed, it works. Mathematics is a rewarding area of study; you should look into it some day."

"So that means our idea will work!"

"Within the constraints imposed by the theory, your problem remains a calculable one, yes."

"Can we structure this so that it could handle other molecules?"

"The algorithm's function is independent of the input data." The conversation is growing more tedious by the minute. For a group intending to build a business based on digital simulations, these people understand less about computers than the average seventh-grader.

"How many sets of revisions can it make?"

"The program will continue until repeated trials yielded no better results."

"So the computer keeps going until it gets things right?"

"I suppose that would be one way to put it." *Perhaps I can fake an accident, tell Lockheed I've just fallen out an upper-story window.* "It's artificial intelligence, Mr. Lockheed; computers can learn."

There is a long pause while Darryl Lockheed absorbs this.

"We've got to get one of those!"

"I'm afraid you won't be able to pick one up at Best Buy. We're talking about sophisticated software concepts."

"Perhaps not Best Buy, but I know who has what we need."

"Please, Mr. Lockheed. I have already provided you with far more than we had discussed."

"Look, Doctor, so far the human genome mapping has produced little that's useful. Personalized medicine is going to depend on new individualized drugs if you will. Our supporters want us to get ahead of the curve."

"Then they should get ready to provide the facilities you'll need."

"They are ready. Or rather, they were until we saw there was no need to reinvent the wheel. You're the expert in this field, and you're already working at Janus. How much revenue would a single new drug generate if it were the equivalent of the next Viagra?"

"Computer-assisted drug design should lower costs and decrease gross revenues."

"Even so, there will be rewards. That's what Grandview must assume as well. From where I sit, you're the man who knows how to do this. You can be the progenitor of a truly scientific pharmacology. And you already have resources at your disposal. Yet you want to argue that we should find someone of your stature elsewhere instead and build a program in parallel to what you're creating."

"I'm sorry, but I see no point in continuing this conversation. I've proven that the approach can work; that's all I proposed to demonstrate."

"No, you've only shown that you can design a couple of simple compounds."

"The principles of machine learning networks are more universal than you seem to understand. Start with the database of chemical structures of your choice and use it as a template. Let the programs run and fine-tune them and see for yourself what the results are."

"And that's what we want you to do. Just name your price."

"I do not work for your company, Mr. Lockheed, and I have no intention of doing so."

"My apologies, Doctor. It's just that we believe that no one else can replace you. I'm asking you to consider our position. We're working against a deadline. The win-win solution would be for you to implement some expanded software where you are. Grandview Corporation is one of the world's computing powerhouses. You are a senior scientist there, and it's unlikely they would refuse your request. Upload the data we will supply and let the program create a few examples of novel compounds. If your theory is correct, the results will convince everyone and guarantee you a place in the pantheon instead of being consigned to a footnote in the history of computing."

"If your company wants Janus Health to create and run your program, then submit your proposal."

"I just did, Doctor. I just did."

THIRTY

"So who do you want to hear about first, Fieldstone or our buddy Carl?" Kevin has his notebook open and a half-dozen printed sheets spread out in front of him.

"Background first, then the specifics. Sandwich?" Franklin holds out a paper bag.

"Thanks, I'm good. A guy named Marion Campbell founded the Fieldstone Commune back in the 1960s. Depending on who you read, Cabello was a brilliant psychologist, an expert on human potential, a paranoid schizophrenic, or just your basic sociopath. Anyway, he started what he called 'an experiment in pleasurable group living'."

"Where the hell do you get this stuff?"

"The Internet. Fieldstone has a website. There's also a book about them; it's called *Mindf**king.*"

Franklin almost chokes on his lunch. "I applaud your investigative zeal, but maybe just the highlights?"

"Good idea; I hate it when coffee squirts out your nose. Fieldstone's history is a mixed bag. They've had like fifty years of communal living, and their ideas about what makes it work sound like Psych 101. But they also claim that the world is perfect as it is, which sounds... I dunno, Taoist maybe? Except I've never heard of Taoists charging a thousand bucks for a personal investigation of my perfection. Carl is right about their responsible hedonism ideas, but some of their projects stretch the concept of 'responsible' a bit."

Franklin forgets his sandwich. "Getting laid, I understand, but how do you get rational people to buy the rest of this stuff?"

"That's the problem; the reasonable stuff kept getting drowned out by Cabello's *agent provocateur* act. Carl talks about hedonism, but how you get a bunch of hedonists to live together without letting selfishness and alpha male power games tear things apart is always TBA."

"No big surprise there." Franklin picks up his sandwich again. "So what about Carl?"

"A couple of run-ins with San Francisco's Finest; bad checks, some minor drug charges. Nothing big, but not the guy I'd pick for my life coach."

"OK, so sex, jealousy, something drug-related; which one do you like?"

"Me, I'd bet it's drugs. Where I come from, jealousy is overrated. You ever heard of the Palm Springs White Party?"

"A white supremacy group?"

"No, it's a circuit party, a rave. Thirty thousand gay men at a three-day music bash where everybody wears white. Or at least the guys who bother with clothes at all."

"I can't wait to see where you're going with this."

"Just that if polyamory is going to drive guys to jealousy and mayhem, I'd expect that a bunch of my music-loving brethren would never to make it out of Palm Springs alive. But there's no violent crime at the thing, despite all the mixing and matching. It's the drugs that fuck people up, so to speak. So you can take the jealousy angle, and I'll do the drugs."

"OK. I'm not sure which bothers me more, though: the idea that jealousy is a mental illness limited to straight guys or the reason you know so much about what goes on at this White Party thing."

"Like I said, I learn a lot on the Internet."

Kevin's gone back to his desk, and on an impulse, Franklin puts in a call to Alfred Lansing, a shrink at Langley Porter. Lansing provides forensic psych evaluations to the Department and has impressed Franklin with the variety of human behaviors he knows about. To his surprise, Lansing himself answers the phone.

"Ever heard of Fieldstone University, Al?"

"Both them and some others of their ilk."

"There are others?"

"There's a course that teaches orgasmic meditation and a book that made the New York Times Best Seller list by promoting a regimen that combines weight loss and incredible sex. And a couple in Walnut Creek offers courses on Extended Massive Orgasms."

"Orgasming must be quite a cottage industry. Myself, I can't remember needing a course to get the hang of it."

"Sex sells, Sergeant, but I'd guess you already know that."

"We're working a case where someone has been living in what they call a Fieldstone-inspired commune. Do such groups ever turn into cults?"

"In theory, there's nothing intrinsically pathological in the concept of communal living, and psychological rigidity or a puritanical suspicion of pleasure aren't signs of mental health. At times, Fieldstone has promoted some semi-reasonable interpersonal relationship rules. The question would be why a well-adjusted man or woman would choose to live in that environment. I'm not saying that there aren't reasons. What I'd want to know is whether the person is moving toward something affirmative or avoiding something aversive. A closed group with rigid doctrines and a forceful leader could have the potential to become cult-like."

"One of our persons of interest is a young woman who feels frustrated in her attempt to pursue a literary career."

"Do you know any writers who haven't felt frustrated at times? I've never met one."

"She also seems obsessed with a dead writer, so much so that some of her friends describe her as seeming almost possessed."

"I make a point of avoiding the Armchair Psychology Club. One person's obsession is another person's intense interest. If I claim my friend is possessed, you may decide I have a taste for romantic hyperbole or that my friend suffers from an autism spectrum disorder. The differential could also include delusional states and schizoaffective or dissociative disorders."

"We haven't interviewed her yet; in fact, we don't know where she is."

"Sounds like you have your work cut out for you, Sergeant."

"Well, I'm glad I don't have to be looking for a Manson-style cult."

"Nothing you've told me would point to such, no."

"And I can also cross ghostly possession off the list of potential motives for murder?"

"I don't believe in ghosts, but from a scientific standpoint, their existence can't be proved or disproved. There's a neurologist at Boston University named McNamara who's written a book on spirit possession and exorcism. It's quite a scholarly work, written from a cognitive neuroscience perspective."

"Always a pleasure, Doctor. You're very good at reminding me the world is a complicated place."

"Yes it is, isn't it?"

THIRTY-ONE

"PTSD is a mental health problem that some people develop after experiencing or witnessing a life-threatening event, like combat. It's normal to have upsetting memories, feel on edge, or have trouble sleeping after this type of event. If symptoms last more than a few months, it may be PTSD. People who have PTSD also have other mental health problems like depression, anxiety, alcohol or drug abuse."

"When PTSD isn't treated, it seldom gets better, and it may even get worse. It's common to think that your symptoms will just go away. But this is very unlikely, especially if you've had symptoms for longer than a year. Even if you feel you can handle your symptoms now, they may get worse."

No mention of hallucinations, but he knew that already. Franklin puts the VA booklet back in his desk. *So why didn't you tell Al about what's been going on with you when you were talking with him? Other than you didn't want to hear his answer.*

He's still staring at the phone when Kevin comes back. "I just got a call from somebody who has stuff about Carl she says we need to hear."

"Who's that?"

"She's a commune member. Seems that not everyone there sees Carl as the Mentor-in-Chief of South San Francisco."

"When do you plan on talking with her?"

"Right now. She called from Cafe Trieste and is making herself at home in our interview room."

Maggie Chadwick is in her early 40s, has graying hair cut short, and wears bib overalls. She stands and holds out a hand as they enter. She reminds Franklin of some of the nuns at Junipero Serra High. *I bet Ms. Chadwick owns only sensible shoes.*

Kevin plays Master of Ceremonies. "Ms. Chadwick, this is Sergeant Washborne. You said on the phone you had something to tell us."

105

"Yes. I saw you at the house yesterday and heard Carl giving you his usual line of bullshit. When I found out why you were there, I decided someone needed to set the record straight."

"So what are the non-bullshit parts?"

"You may not understand this, but some of us at Inner Freedom are committed to true communal living. Carl Holton isn't one of those people."

"He isn't?"

"No. He's a selfish sleaze who enjoys manipulating people to feed his ego. Inner Freedom means just that: freeing ourselves from the self-imposed constraints that limit our happiness. Carl talks about freeing oneself from outmoded thinking, but he uses the commune to dominate women and humiliate men while telling them they shouldn't feel what they're feeling. He doesn't support self-empowerment; he's all about finding needy people and making them even more dependent."

Franklin nods. "And that isn't what responsible hedonism means. Inspector Loeffler has been updating me on polyamory and ... What was the term?"

"Compersion. It's ..."

"Thank you, Inspector; I'm familiar with the concept." Ms. Chadwick studies them both for a moment. "I see communal living as a milieu in which we can develop deeper interpersonal relationships that can be a source of genuine pleasure. Too many people—men especially—treat sex as the principal source of pleasure. Responsible hedonism isn't about trying to fuck everything in sight just to see how many notches you can cut in your belt."

"And this misplaced emphasis on sex is what you find objectionable in Carl? *And in a lot of the other males who hang out at your place?*

"The videos were the last straw."

"Videos? Why am I not surprised?"

Ms. Chadwick frowns. "We're not opposed to recording lovemaking. If you've freed yourself from all the 'sex is bad' indoctrination you've absorbed, they can be another way to enhance enjoyment in a relationship. But it has to be by common agreement. We have what we call an automatic veto rule. We refrain from doing something if even one participant isn't cool with it. And Carl's been recording people without checking how they feel about it."

"I can see how that would make people angry."

"It violates the core principles that make the community work. Videos can be affirmations, but not the way he's getting them."

Kevin puts on a puzzled-but-thoughtful face. "I've read that Marion Cabello could be intentionally provocative to get people to break out of their old beliefs. Some people also claimed that he encouraged drug use for the same reason."

"A lot of that's just spiteful gossip. In the early days, Marion was still figuring out what could work, and that included drugs—it was the 1960s, after all. Early on, I'm told our community had some heavy drug users, but they're long gone."

"So these days, nobody at Inner Freedom is into pharmaceutical enhancements?"

"Like what? Viagra?" She laughs. "For the record, I neither confirm nor deny any allegations about drug use anyone has made, officers. By our principles, if it enhances pleasure and doesn't violate the automatic veto rule, we won't oppose any behavior out of hand."

Kevin looks chastened. "I didn't mean to imply anything, Ms. Chadwick. But a general principle in law enforcement says that people who ignore rules in one setting are also prone to ignore them under other circumstances. We're Homicide, not Vice, but drugs and violent death have a way of going together."

"No offense taken. Your general principle would apply to Carl. I can't give you any specifics, but I suspect that he's provided 'party favors' of dubious provenance to the family."

Kevin shakes his head. "I don't get it. If this guy's such a creep, why do you put up with him?"

"There are a variety of historical and legal reasons. But a group of us are trying to draw the community away from his perversion of the principles. That's one reason I was happy that Myra was joining us. I was trying to help her bring Matt to the light. If you should find evidence of criminal wrong-doing on Carl's part, few of us would be unhappy to see him go."

"Wow, you do sound like a genuine family."

THIRTY-TWO

Franklin holds his breath, waiting to see if Maggie Chadwick is going to deck Kevin. When she doesn't, he cuts in. "So Myra is in tune with your principles?"

"Yes, a very sweet person who's committed to the concept of living in community. She enjoyed connecting with the other members."

"And Matt?"

"Matt was her anchor. When she first arrived, she developed crushes and over-invested in uncomplicated pleasurable experiences. I suspect she hadn't had all that many of them. She didn't realize they're the rule rather than the exception for us. That subsided after she met Matt."

"Did her behavior make anyone unhappy?"

"No one except Carl. Myra's become quite skillful at maintaining positive connections with everyone. We all realize there's a learning curve for life at Inner Freedom."

"I'm afraid I can already guess the answer, but how did she make Carl unhappy?" Kevin looks and sounds serious for a change.

"Carl needed Myra to be needy and pliable, another woman for him to dominate. When she proved she could remain her own person, she bruised his ego. He was furious with her."

"It sounds like you took Myra under your wing."

"I knew she was sincere, and there is a synergy. Her writing builds community, and the community helps sustain her writing."

"And Matt was going to join your family?"

"I wanted him to. At first, Matt felt possessive about Myra. He got all 'either-or' when he found out that she was living with us. I worked with her and with him to explain our true objectives."

"How did that go?"

"He started spending more time at Inner Truth, joining in with whatever was going on if Myra was part of it. I expected he might become a positive counterbalance to Carl's influence."

"How did Carl feel about that?"

"Frustrated. Carl likes to fuck with people. I could tell that Myra's obvious intellect and artistic gifts affronted him; it's why he tried to humiliate and dominate her. And Matt was smart and sensitive, which meant naïve and weak to Carl—you've met him. But he underestimated both Matt and Myra."

She stops to gauge the effect of her words. "I don't see Carl as someone who would resort to murder. Like a lot of bullies, he's all bluster, and he knows he's already lost the battle for Inner Truth. I expect that one of these days he'll just leave and form another group he can dominate without as much resistance."

"Well, thank you for providing so much background. Is there's anything else?"

She shakes her head and stands. Then she pauses. "I don't know if this means anything, but there was one time months ago when Carl was talking with Matt and a visitor I didn't recognize. Carl wandered off, but Matt and the other man kept talking."

"Did you find out who that was?"

"Someone told me he had been a member of Inner Truth back in the freewheeling early days."

"Did they know his name?"

"Yes. Let me see, it was… It was Enright. Andy Enright. I can't tell you how much involvement Carl Holton may have with drugs, but someone from that era showing up made me wonder."

"Thank you. I promise we'll follow that up."

"We believe we're perfect, as is the world because there's a self-righting mechanism always at work. Perhaps you're intended to be part of that."

Kevin smiles. "Thank you. People have called me a lot of things, but being part of the world's self-righting mechanism is the nicest one to date. Have a safe drive back."

Franklin leans back in his chair. "Someone who believes in group polyamory but not in Carl Holton."

"Doesn't seem like Carl's charisma has swept her off her feet, does it?" Kevin looks at Franklin. "What's the likelihood she's just trying to use us to topple Carl from his top dog position at the commune?"

"It's possible. What struck me was how she made it sound like Matt was there a lot, even if he wasn't a card-carrying member of the club. If that's the case, was he as much of a straight arrow as Henry thinks?" Franklin grins. "You ready to rethink your 'it was about drugs' theory?"

Kevin shakes his head. "Maggie as much as told us Carl's dealing. Do you suppose your old friends in Narcotics could give us a list of the top Ecstasy sources in South San Francisco?"

"Or GHB and Rohypnol."

"You figure Carl for date rape?"

"Why not? I mean, what the hell does 'consensual' even mean if you're swimming in a stew pot full of people extolling the virtues of fucking your brains out?"

What the fuck, Franklin; this is not the time to go all judgmental. Kevin looks up. "I hope you don't think that when I was talking about the White Party..."

Dammit! What part of that puppy-dog eagerness to please haven't you been seeing? Kevin knows how to flaunt his gayness, but he's also looking for someone who can look past that and see him as something more than a libido on legs.

"No. I'm sorry; I was thinking about some people who live in the Outer Mission who aren't what they claim to be. Someone, and perhaps more than one someone, has been lying through their teeth, and it's pissing me off."

Kevin relaxes."You know what they say on TV. Murder cases are easy because there are only three motives: money, sex, and revenge. If it's about money, then it's also likely about drugs, and I'm right. If it's sex, then you win. Revenge, it could be either. Let's go find out. I'm going to run a search for this Andy Enright for starters. If he dates back to the early days of the commune and Carl is still chatting him up, he'd be my bet for our missing drug connection."

"And you're still leaving me to work the sex angle?"

"Serves you right, straight guy."

THIRTY-THREE

The first thing Franklin notices when the phone awakens him is that he doesn't remember having any dreams.

"Hey, it's Kevin. They've found Myra."

Fog blankets the Bay, but the crest of Nob Hill is clear. Lights are coming on in the hotel rooms and condos, and the Fountain of the Turtles and the facade of Grace Cathedral remain floodlit, but the small green rectangle of Huntington Park is dark. Franklin walks to the bench where Myra sits. She looks like she'd stopped here to absorb some of the early morning calm.

"Rigor has set in; body temp says she's been dead about five hours. No obvious signs of trauma."

"Did she have anything with her?"

"Just what she's wearing. Her ID was in her coat pocket."

"Anyone around see anything?"

"We're still looking. There isn't a lot of foot traffic up here at night."

"Ophelia." Kevin is backlit by the patrol car headlights, and his face is difficult to see.

"Who?"

"Ophelia. It's a painting by Millais. Myra looks a lot like the model he used."

"In the play, Ophelia commits suicide, doesn't she?"

"She's in love with Hamlet and goes insane and drowns in a brook after her father's murder."

A play with another young woman doomed by love and tragedy. *Art imitating life imitating art—this is getting way too confusing.*

The officers who found Myra have little to add. "A car discovered her on routine patrol. They only come by here once or twice a night. No one at the

Huntington noticed anything. The Hopkins and the Fairmont have their own security, but they're too far away."

Franklin turns back to look for Kevin, but his partner is walking toward the cathedral. *Where is he going? The church is closed at this hour.* Franklin follows the path past the fountain where four youths reach for the tails of the turtles in the basin above them. By the time he's crossing Taylor Street, Kevin has climbed the stairs and has walked to the roof of the cathedral garage. Franklin follows. Kevin is traversing the labyrinth laid out in multi-colored granite just to the north of the main entrance.

"A labyrinth is not a maze, because a labyrinth has only one path. But the journey inward and the journey back are still different." He hadn't thought of Father Morales in years. What had the old man told his students? "To enter a labyrinth is to travel inward, to shed mundane distractions and find your true self. That is the path of Purgation. When you return, even though you follow the same route, some of the sharp boundaries in your life have dissolved. That is the way to Union. And in between, at the center of the labyrinth, is Illumination, the place of clarity."

For now we see through a glass, darkly; but then face to face: now I know in part; but then shall I know even as also I am known. Perhaps. Perhaps if the first step wasn't always the hardest...

Franklin remains standing at the labyrinth's entrance, watching Kevin circle inward.

The Cathedral Maze

THIRTY-FOUR

Like most people who work at Janus Health, Chris Walker knows there are two Jim Atkinsons, the grandiose demanding one and the genial cajoling one. *Yesterday afternoon I had a visit from the admonishing Ghost of Christmas Yet to Come. This morning, the jovial Christmas Present has appeared, and he's brought a gift.*

Atkinson himself is in front of his desk, Henry Qu in tow. "I've been telling Henry how important the Deep Learning programs you're developing for Janus Health are, and how labor-intensive. I've decided he'll be part of your team on a full-time basis, even though it will be a temporary inconvenience to my division. I'm sure he'll make an excellent addition."

So this is the spoonful of sugar to sweeten yesterday's medicinal surprise. At least there's a full-time replacement for Matt now; no need to tell Atkinson his latest pet project has already taken its place on the back burner. "I don't doubt that you're right, Jim."

Atkinson almost manages to mask his surprise at the first-name familiarity. He turns to Henry. "Losing Matt was a tragedy, and no one here thinks for a minute that you could have anything to do with it. The best thing is to let this go and move on. The police will lose interest soon enough." A nod to no one in particular and Atkinson is gone.

"Welcome to your new position, Henry; everybody knows you're not a murderer, except the police. But that's enough to make you damaged goods in my book, so you're Chris Walker's problem now." How am I supposed to undo this? "I understand this must all be distressing for you; Matt was a good friend and a colleague. None of us needed this distraction. Dr. Atkinson is right: we are scientists, and we should continue to devote our energies to our work. That's what Matt would want, and it's a fitting way to honor his memory."

Henry takes a deep breath, like someone who's coming up for air. "Thank you, sir. I already know a little about what Matt was working on because we were roommates. He didn't talk about anything confidential..."

"Henry! Relax! My name isn't Atkinson!"

Henry manages a weak grin. "Yes, Dr. Walker...you are Dr. Walker, aren't you?"

"Good; it sounds like you're recovering already. Matt kept an electronic notebook, and his code is well-annotated. But I admit I've been pushing to have you here full time, less because of the ongoing work than for a new program."

"That sounds intriguing."

"You've been working on Dr. Atkinson's Whole World Therapeutics Program, cataloging and evaluating pharmacologies. Uncovering, digitizing and analyzing that data will be a long-term project to which we'll all contribute. Then there's the Congener Program, which was Matt's principal focus. Both projects take what we know and build on that. The Origami Program will be forward-looking, an exercise in extended visualization."

"The Origami Program, sir? Does that have to do with folding things?"

"Exactly so, Dr. Qu. Specifically, the folding of proteins, their tertiary structure. Architects may believe that form follows function, but for proteins, the opposite is true."

"Function will follow form." Henry holds up his hand as if cupping some invisible molecule. "And if a computer can visualize the shape of the molecule, or better yet, all the configurations it could assume under different conditions..."

"... then we gain insights into how things work at the molecular level. Instead of thinking of molecules as static objects, we need to visualize them as dynamic structures. I see you've studied some molecular biology, Dr. Qu."

"More general principles than specifics. But I guess this would be like giving a biochemist three-dimensional models and inviting him to play with them."

"Yes, though we're getting ahead of ourselves. Let's set you up with a workstation and access to Matt's files. Familiarize yourself with his existing body of work. Once you're settled in with Congener, then we can talk more about Origami."

THIRTY-FIVE

The commune on Vienna Street is almost empty. Neither of the two members who let Franklin and Kevin in asks any questions as they lead the detectives to the bedroom Myra shared and point out her belongings.

"They look like they've been crying, and nobody asked to see a search warrant. I thought these people didn't like authority figures."

"The TV was on in the living room; it looked like ABC7 News. So they must have heard about Myra." Franklin scans the room. "Even allowing for the constraints imposed by communal living in a smallish house, Myra's space here is spartan. I don't recall Carl saying anything about people here having to renounce earthly possessions."

"Yeah. Offhand, I'd guess life here isn't the same as in a convent." Kevin is still standing in the doorway. "It felt like her housemates didn't want to intrude on her space."

"I'm sure in a house this small there must be rules we don't know about. Let's get pictures of everything and see what we've got."

The photographing doesn't take long; then they begin with her clothing. What there is has a retro look. "Vintage—economic necessity or preference?" Kevin wonders aloud. "I'm no authority, but I'd guess this isn't your standard line of St. Vinnie de Paul couture. I'd bet you'd have to hit some-place like Relic Vintage."

"Would make sense if you liked the style and were writing a play with a protagonist who dressed like this. Everyday wear plus costuming and dressing in role; a smart plan if you're on a tight budget."

There is no laptop or tablet or cell phone. The bulk of Myra's other possessions is books and notebooks. Kevin holds up "*The Poetic Sensibility; The Poems of Nora May French*, and *San Francisco Bohemia.*"

Franklin opens a notebook. "Here's something about Nora May." Taped to the page is a reproduction of an obituary from the San Francisco Call.

November 15, 1907.
Nora May French, Writer, Ends Life With Poison.
Friend Has Telepathic Vision of the Poet's Death Scene
While dying at Carmel in the midnight hour Thursday morning, Miss French sent a telepathic message to an intimate friend in San Francisco. This friend, whose veracity cannot be questioned, saw the act in a dream. It is firmly believed by the one who dreamed of the act of suicide that the vision came at the moment when Nora French, moved by some impulse which is not understood by her friends, ended a life that gave great promise.

Nora May French was a poet of rare talent. Her output was small, but everything that she had written was invested with haunting beauty.

"Suicide and telepathic dreams—all the makngs of a period theater piece."

Kevin has picked up another notebook. "These are some of Myra's poems. She wrote them out in longhand. Seems like she was pretty hard on herself when it came to her writing." He flips through the pages. "Four different versions of the same poem, one to a page. And a bunch of others that are just fragments or have half the lines crossed out."

Franklin picks through scattered piles of sheets. "This may be the play, or at least pieces of it. There are individual scenes and sections of dialogue, but nothing is in any sort of order. I don't see any outline or plot summary. Scenes are started at random and are left unfinished or are revised multiple times. Lots of blank pages too, just like the poetry." He pulls a few pages at random. "This part's got three characters: Nora May, George Sterling, and someone named Henry Lafler. At least this confirms what Henry and Elizabeth told us. But It's hard to find much that Myra completed or ever considered finished."

"So, like what? You fall in love, but your love remains unrequited, you go through life unfulfilled, and then you die without ever finishing anything? I'm sorry, but reading this stuff is a real downer."

"No disagreement from me. In this scene, a character in the play is reading a story aloud where another character says, 'Someone has to die so that the rest of us should value life more'. A play about unhappy people who spend their time reading stories about unhappy people—feels like I'm stuck between a pair of infinitely reflecting mirrors."

"Great, a funhouse for depressives. That's a Virginia Woolf quote from *The Hours*. Some friends made me watch it because there's a gay character in it. The guy has AIDS and commits suicide just before he's going to receive

117

some literary prize." Kevin shakes his head. "Must be something wrong with me, because if I was doing things right I would be a lot more miserable."

Franklin chooses a bound notebook. "This looks like a diary or journal. The first entry was on June 6. Seen any others like this? There should be some earlier volumes?"

"Haven't found any yet."

Myra had covered the journal's pages with densely written entries; whatever else she left unfinished, she had been diligent in her journaling. Near the end of the entries is a poem—Myra's? Nora May's?—entitled *At the End*:

> *Trembling and spent I ran and fell,*
> *And ran again, a sorrow made me fleet.*
> *For very fear its shape I could not tell—*
> *The briars tore my feet.*
> *In broken flight across the cruel land,*
> *So weary was I that I only smiled*
> *When, swift and strong, a tender, mighty hand*
> *Upraised me like a child.*
> *"It was not you I feared," rejoiced, I cried,*
> *(His touch had healed my hurts, no more they bled,)*
> *"Life radiant, God has sent you to my side."*
> *"Nay, I am Death!" he said.*

She'd also glued reproductions of two photographs to the last pages. One is a vintage soft-focus studio portrait; the other is a snapshot of the same woman sitting on a rock. She has an attractive oval face with striking eyes and a mass of blonde curls. Under the second picture, Myra had written a quotation from someone: "We had the lifeboat out, but we were only hitting her on the head with our oars."

Franklin closes the diary. "This looks like our best bet to find out what was going on with Myra and Matt. Let's bag this stuff."

Kevin nods. "Even though she didn't leave a note, Myra comes across as pretty depressed and fixated on death. I'm betting the ME decides it was suicide."

Myra's belongings fit in three plastic bags. They walk back into the main room, which is empty. "Do we just go?"

"Leave our cards and come back later. It wouldn't be a bad idea to give everyone a little grieving time, especially in a close-knit community like this."

Kevin hefts the bags; they don't weigh much. "It's not a cop thing to say, but I could use a little time myself."

THIRTY-SIX

Chris Walker lifts himself from the wheelchair into the more comfortable office chair behind his desk and takes a deep breath. *O Fortuna, you are as changeable as the moon.* This morning, the news had a piece on an upcoming Hindu holiday. *Monday marks the birthday of Ganesha, the elephant-headed god who is the Patron of Scholars, the Lord of Beginnings, and the Remover of Obstacles.* Perhaps that explains Atkinson's decision to give him Henry full-time, a short miracle that should qualify as proof of divine intervention.

The Remover-in-Chief has been very busy of late. After all the fanfare, the police interviews have amounted to nothing. The response to his presentation in Chicago has been more positive than he had hoped. And before that, there was the Miracle Deluxe that started the sequence by providing a chance to appease Darryl Lockheed.

And to restore some semblance of marital tranquility. "Grace, he's like the camel with its nose in the tent; he moves in and takes over, inch by inch. You call it consulting, but Darryl wants me to work for him on Atkinson's dime."

"Are you surprised? Of course they'll try to get all they can at the lowest cost; they're businessmen, after all. Tell me: will this program you're contemplating be an important one? Does it have the potential to be a great one? A revolutionary one? "

"Yes, yes, and possibly—if I can get it done."

"Then why not at least try? After years of academic wheel-spinning, you've had a breakthrough, so why won't you use it to get what you deserve: public acknowledgment and meaningful financial reward? You are a brilliant man, Christopher, but you feel that to acknowledge that would be vulgar. If I had a brain like yours, I would want to take advantage of it. You've been patient and tolerant for years, almost inhumanly so. You have every right to be furious about the academic politics and at shallow

120

bureaucrats who think that a man in a wheelchair has to live in the shadows."

"You keep giving mixed messages, Grace; you want me to be decorous and assertive and scholarly and charismatic."

"I would like you to be less puritanical with yourself. Work with Darryl. Take your place in the spotlight for a while. If Atkinson complains, show him your ideas. The man can smell money a mile away. After that, you can always retire back to the obscurity of some emeritus academic position."

It's been a recurring motif in their marriage. The beauty and precision of mathematical concepts have always fascinated him; to be distracted by the external trappings of success feels like a lack of commitment. His wife is different; position, social status, and money enough to sustain the Good Life matter to her. As she put it, "I didn't realize I was marrying St. Christopher of Assisi."

And I wasn't planning on marrying Lady Macbeth.

And then Ganesha had intervened at a Corporate Senior Staff meeting, in the guise of Andre Kortov. Andre had pulled him aside afterward. "You're always quiet at these meetings, Chris. I like to check in from time to time. How are things going?"

"Just fine, Andre; I believe we're soon going to see major transformations of AI as we know it."

"As the person who recruited you, I can't say I'm surprised to hear that. Of course, I also selected Jim. Do you know why I chose both of you?"

"Because we are both well-qualified individuals, I would assume."

Kortov waves a hand. "Of course you are. But in a business as competitive as ours, Janus Health needed high visibility from the outset, and Jim Atkinson guaranteed we would always have that. It also needed brilliant scientists, including at least one we could count on to remain stable despite the firestorms we expected Jim might ignite. I believed you could do a better job in that role than anyone else." He frowns. "One issue has always concerned me, though. We very much value your academic credentials, but Jim can be so results-oriented sometimes that he sounds downright anti-intellectual. We're a both-and company, not an either-or one. So are you getting enough time to pursue other intellectual interests here?"

"The work I'm doing is satisfying, yes."

"But is it enough? Blue-sky thinking has been responsible for some of the most creative work I've encountered. Are you getting to do some of that?"

"I hadn't thought about it."

Kortov stands and rocks back and forth on his heels. "There's a story Abe Lincoln told about always putting two pumpkins in a sack. That way, their weight balanced each other out. I'm not that folksy, but I hired you both, and I want to keep you both happy. If balancing your workload with resources for 'what if' projects will do that, I'll see that you get it. I don't pretend to understand what you do, but I want to make sure you have all the resources you need to do it. I've read that Einstein became something of a recluse at Princeton, absorbed in his theories. But no one complained, because when all was said and done, he was still Einstein."

"The comparison is an exaggeration, but I appreciate your understanding and your solicitude."

Andre's candor about just how calculating he had been in his hiring choices caught Chris off guard. The question wasn't about good guys and bad guys; in this business, it was which SOB would prove the least toxic at the moment. Perhaps Grace was right, and the only rational choice was to play the hand he held to his best advantage. And now he was being offered resources and permission—a virtual mandate—to pursue whatever projects he chose. Which meant whatever Grace and Darryl wanted.

Not everything possible in theory can be translated into reality; there was a reason he had been wary about promising Darryl anything concrete. But if he succeeded, then Dr. Christopher Walker, whom no one saw as flashy or sexy or able to leap tall buildings, would become Super Scientist, creator of the smartest, showiest, and most outrageously successful deep learning program around. Grace would be happy. Darryl would be happy. And he might even find how pleasurable it could be to build machines that would thumb their virtual noses at his critics.

So what does one do to celebrate Ganesha's birthday? Light some incense? He must remember to ask his Indian coworkers.

THIRTY-SEVEN

With Henry engrossed in his review of what had been Matt's files. Chris Walker can turn back to his notes on Origami. The first step should be straightforward but tedious. The amino acid sequences and tertiary structures of thousands of proteins are already known, but they'll have to be translated into a form the program can recognize. That's work an assistant can do. Then he'll need to create a program that can use the data to deduce the rules governing protein folding. After that, the program will have to test those rules on novel amino acid sequences.

The firepower requirements will be daunting. Once again, he's thankful that Kortov has provided him access to the extended network of computers he'll need. And Origami will still be an easier undertaking than Darryl's program had been.

His simple proof-of-concept model program had prompted Darryl to up the ante. "Hey doc, our scientists want to know if we could use this as a universal synthesis machine. You said the program could work with any drug we plugged into it; what about giving it two drugs and asking it to create a new one, one that combines the properties of both?"

Developing multifunctional agents would complicate the program exponentially. How drugs work in the brain was still an unknown for many agents, and their effects on other tissues could be variable and unpredictable. Darryl knew so few details about the physical chemistry of the agents he wanted to create that guessing any new drug's properties was less an imperfect information problem than a crapshoot. Agreeing to tackle Darryl's project had turned out to be a bigger gamble than he had expected.

And that was the revelation. *He had to create code that could learn how to gamble and win.* He would write a deep learning program that contained data on the known physiologic functions of drugs. The first step in designing a new variant would be to make an educated guess—in effect, a bet—and then test it against the table of known physiologic responses. The first attempts

123

would likely be wrong, but the program could learn from its errors, modify its bets and continue trying *ad infinitum*.

He retrieved the jejune-named program files and game theory applications that comprised Matt's poker software. It still looked like an incoherent mess; Matt just hadn't understood the nuances of game theory or artificial intelligence. Still, occasional sections of sophisticated code were scattered among the jumble of poorly written and rewritten sections.

A few days' study revealed where Matt had gone wrong and what modifications he needed to make. *Nothing like studying other people's mistakes to show you what not to do.* The review had even allowed him to uncover a few functional pieces of code he could incorporate into his work. Lockheed was continuing to make a nuisance of himself, and anything that might reduce his workload would help. *Any port in a storm; the sooner I can deliver a working version, the better.*

That completed program felt as if too much of it was held together with duct tape, but sending it off to Darryl had produced weeks of blissful silence. Until the most recent phone blitz.

He glares at the latest Post-It sitting on his desk; he's run out of credible excuses. Time to see if the Lord of New Beginnings is still listening. He takes a deep breath and asks his secretary to dial Darryl.

"It's amazing, Dr. Walker! We ran two test cases, more complex compounds than your 'baby steps' examples, and the program delivered. It took several days to find the first solution, but when it tackled the second one, it found an answer in half the time."

"Perhaps a coincidence, but the program should learn from each problem it solves, just like humans. That's why it's called artificial intelligence."

"So this program can use the results to create more sophisticated drugs as we go on?"

"That would be one way of putting it."

"And could the computer take prototype drugs and use them to make second-generation agents?"

"I suppose. Deep learning programs have sometimes performed at levels of generalization and abstraction that we had not expected. We write the code but can't always tell how the programs derive solutions."

"That doesn't matter. We're designing drugs that haven't existed before, and now we can see ourselves being able to synthesize small amounts in our lab."

"I'm glad to hear that. The program relies on the ChemSynthesis database to make your new molecules; it sounds like that part works."

"When we reach the point of clinical trials, we'll have to address large-scale production issues, but our chemical engineers are used to dealing with those problems. Right now, making testable amounts of product will be a big breakthrough."

Two test cases and you're already talking about clinical trials? "Excellent! It doesn't sound as if you need anything else from me."

"Thank you, no. Your program has turned out to be a tremendous resource; we'll be exploring its potential for some time to come. The reason for this call is to give you this update and to let you know that we're creating the Christopher J. Walker Research Grant. You'll be receiving information on how to access it."

"A grant?"

"For you to use as you see fit. We expect to supplement it and continue to renew it."

"I don't recall that we ..."

"This was a decision of our philanthropic affiliate."

"I feel honored. This comes as a complete surprise."

"I understand. I'm pleased but not surprised at all. Our assessment of your skills has proven more than accurate. The grant reflects our satisfaction in having helped inspire such a successful application."

"I admit it presented a few challenges; the devil is always in the details."

"You're too modest, Doctor; it's an unqualified success. I hope you'll get some personal time to relax now.

He glances at his Origami notes. "I'm just happy to get back to my day job."

"I understand how much extra work this project has made for you. Can we offer you anything to make up for it? The corporation has a very nice sloop; perhaps a weekend on the water?"

A start-up that owns a yacht? Someone has deep pockets. "Thank you, but I'm not much of a sailor."

"Just wanted to offer. I find sailing addicting. But I shouldn't keep you longer. Again, Doctor, our sincere thanks."

No glitches and no demands for additions or alterations? This has to be a result of divine intervention. He hasn't looked at the program since he sent it off, and it sounds like he won't need to any time soon.

He's completed his 'blue sky' undertaking. No one at Janus has even noticed its existence. Perhaps he'll make a presentation about it at some point; Andre will appreciate the update. Even a very general description of the results should be enough to vindicate his advocacy of Deep Learning programs. And Grace will be pleased.

ILLUMINATION

THIRTY-EIGHT

SATURDAY, SEPTEMBER 3, 2016

Contrary to what television producers believe, the Law of Everything in Triplicate dominates a cop's life, even on a Saturday. Franklin is deep in paperwork when Kevin sticks his head in. "Got a hit on Andy Enright. Maggie Chadwick's instincts were right; he had a couple of arrests for possession six or seven years back."

"With intent to distribute?"

"Tried, but they couldn't make it stick. He had a pretty good stash of acid, more than what most people would need to maintain an alternative version of reality for themselves."

"Do we have an address?"

"Not a current one. I wonder if Henry or any of Matt's neighbors have seen him around. I'm waiting for a call back."

"Henry seemed pretty certain that Matt wasn't a user or a dealer."

"But did whoever killed Matt realize that? Matt wouldn't be the first victim of Death By Association. You know how paranoid people from the World of Pharmaceutically Enhanced Reality can get."

"Why would Matt hang out with a tripper? Some moth and flame thing?"

"I don't know. But I believe that if something sounds too good to be true, there's a reason. I still don't buy this Saint Matt story."

"Then keep digging. I so want this to be something other than a random killing." Franklin's phone rings. He listens for a minute and then holds up a finger to Kevin. "It's Inner Truth; Carl just got attacked and beaten up."

"At the commune?"

"Yes. Seems it was another member."

Kevin's already pulling on his jacket. "I just knew Maggie Chadwick had a mean left hook."

The Inner Truth Commune

It's a full house at the commune. A muscular, dark-haired man with a bruised face is sitting on a couch, rubbing his knuckles. Franklin looks around. "Where's Carl?

"At the Urgent Care Center in Daly City. We had someone drive him there; he looked like he might need stitches and an x-ray or something." Franklin doesn't recognize the speaker, a wide-eyed young woman who acts like she'd rather be somewhere else right now. He wonders if she's one of Carl's latest recruits.

"Has anyone reported the assault?"

"No, we called you. I didn't know where this was going, and our experiences with the local police haven't been that positive." Maggie Chadwick and another woman—her partner?—have taken control as the voices of the community elders. "You already know about us, and I was pleasantly surprised by your lack of judgmentalness. 'Judgmentalness'—is that a word?"

"No idea. I try to limit myself to police work, like investigating a possible assault." Franklin turns to the man on the couch. "What's your name? You know anything about what happened here?"

"My name is Carter Albemarle, and I got in a fight."

130

"You shouldn't say anything else until you get a lawyer." It's the newbie again. *She's been here long enough to have decided whom she wants to protect.*

Franklin holds up a hand. "Let's slow down, folks. We haven't Mirandized Carter because we haven't established that anyone has committed a crime. We also haven't heard Mr. Holton's side of events, and he isn't here to talk to us. That he's at an UrgiCare could be circumstantial evidence of assault, but Carter's face suggests that this could also have been self-defense."

As he had hoped, stepping it back a notch gives Carter the space he needs. "And I'll tell you why I got into that fight."

"Because Carl's an asshole?" Kevin tries to look innocent.

"Damn right. That fucker was videotaping people! And you know why?"

"Something other than the obvious reason?"

"Bastard's created a blog, and he wants to turn us into an Internet version of a reality show. Can you believe that—a fucking reality show!"

They both look at Maggie. "I told you I knew about the videos, but I had heard nothing about this other."

Carter is rubbing his cheek. "I only found out for sure a while ago. Pay-per-view online porn, and then he was going to take viewers' requests and use them to plan parties here, while he's telling us he's going to lead us to some responsible hedonism Wonderland. So I'm supposed to do what? File a complaint with the police? 'Hi, I live in that group sex place you'd like to see go away, and I want to report someone who's into some sketchy stuff. Can you come right over?' I wanted the sonofabitch to know that I was on to him, and I wasn't going to let him turn this into an even bigger pile of crap, and I think he got the message, OK?"

Maggie's heard enough. "Between our recent loss and this incident, I think the community has a lot to discuss. I gather Carter is not under arrest?"

"Not at the moment. We'll want to talk with Carl before we make any final determination."

"I understand. At the moment, I think we've had enough distractions. Perhaps we should take some time to ask ourselves what each needs to re-establish equanimity, in our own lives, and our life as a group together. Life is perfect, just as it is. We've seen this proven time after time—if we can bring ourselves to stop clinging to automatic judgments. Life is giving us another opportunity to let go of old baggage."

She looks at Carter, who gets up slowly and limps towards the small yard at the back of the house. Other members pair off and leave the main room. "Impressive," Kevin says *sotto voce.*

Maggie turns to them. "Carl may still be at the UrgiCenter. His injuries didn't appear to be severe, but Dignity Health can be slow."

The front door opens, and a somewhat battered Carl shuffles into the room. He has a black eye and stitches in a laceration on his right cheek. The way he holds himself suggests that he's cracked a rib or three.

"Well, good morning, Carl! Glad to see that the reports of your death are greatly exaggerated, just like Mark Twain."

I have to hand it to Kevin: he has a gift for putting people off balance.

Carl's grimace is a mix of pain, anger, and fear. "Somebody call you?"

"Out of concern for your well-being. So what happened here?" Franklin glances at Maggie, who takes this as her cue to withdraw to some area where she'll still be able to hear everything.

THIRTY-NINE

"We had a disagreement, is all. It happens. Like I told you, changing old mental habits can be hard work."

Kevin snickers. "Painful too, it looks like. Do old habits include going around videoing people without their knowledge?"

"I don't know what you're talking about."

"What Kevin means is we heard a story about people feeling that someone was invading their privacy. We're not here about any of that now. We just want to make sure that you're going to be safe. Of course, we'd also be interested if you've recalled anything else that could help our other investigation."

Carl lowers himself gingerly into a chair. "Yeah, well, I'll be all right. Carter's a hothead, and he doesn't get that family is all about sharing. You can't share if you keep drawing lines in the sand."

Kevin switches gears. "I can see how that could be a problem for some people, particularly beginners. Anybody else having problems like Carter?"

"Everybody struggles a little, but most people see the benefits pretty quickly if they're willing to try new things."

"I'm thinking in particular about Matt." Carl looks up, but Franklin can't read his expression. "You said he wasn't a committed member of your family, but it sounds like he hung around a lot because of Myra. Were there any misunderstandings?"

"No. I mean, he was around but he wasn't here, if you know what I'm saying. It was like Myra letting her little brother tag along. He was the kid that people tolerated; nobody got worked up over him."

"So if he got wind of someone being filmed…?"

"Don't know if he knew about the videos or not. We didn't hide any of our activities from him, but he was pretty clueless."

Kevin smiles. "You know, Carl, I'm wondering if we're not barking up the wrong tree here. It's like your lifestyle is the shiny object that grabs everybody's attention. Me, I think that what gets guys Matt's age killed are things like drugs. Am I way off base?"

"We don't allow illicit drugs here."

"We're not suggesting that you do, Carl. We're just asking if you suspected Matt might have been using."

"Don't know for sure, but I don't think so." He smirks. "He was real closed-minded about a lot of things."

"What do you mean?"

"After Myra told me what he did for work, I started asking him about that computer stuff Janus is always talking about in their ads. You know, 'Using the wisdom of the past, blah blah blah'."

"And you were asking if...?"

"If what his boss said in a TED Talk about searching the world's pharmaceutical resources" —he makes finger quotes—"was true."

"You're thinking about branching out?"

"Aphrodisiacs, man; why not? This guy I know got me information about them from a couple of Indian dudes."

"You're serious?" Franklin suppresses the urge to tell Kevin his mouth is hanging open.

"Those guys were. I read it in *Pharmacognosy Review*."

"Pharmacognosy yet, you old intellectual! So you asked Matt?"

Carl ignores Kevin's sarcasm. "Like, could he do a computer search for some stuff? I even offered to get him a copy of the article."

"What did he say?"

"He said that he couldn't work on that because he was busy redesigning penicillin or some crap like that. So I asked Pharma Bro if a computer could design an aphrodisiac, and he gave me all these excuses about how he'd get fired and a bunch of other BS." Carl's face darkens as if he can see Matt across the room even now. "What a loser. A total fucking loser, always sure how things were supposed to be. Added nothing to the community and sucked the life out of Myra."

Another thought occurs to him. "And the guy had no imagination. If I was Janus, I'd make it a top priority. I mean, how much money could an aphrodisiac earn you?"

"You've got a point there, Carl. But I thought aphrodisiacs didn't work that well."

"So what? Janus claims they're digging stuff up from the past, but they don't promise it will work. Ever hear of the placebo effect? 'I can get it up if

I think I can'. And what if they worked? Don't tell me there aren't plenty of guys who'd like to be randy teenagers again."

Franklin grits his teeth. "The biggest sex organ is the one between the ears, huh? It sounds like you have a good head for business."

Carl attempts a self-satisfied smile that is cut short by pain. "Yeah, I do. Did you know there are people out there selling kits that let you grow magic mushrooms?"

"You just said you don't tolerate drugs here, Carl."

"Hey man, mushrooms are food, that's all."

Kevin looks disappointed. "OK, so Matt wasn't into drugs. Who here is?"

"I told you, none of that shit goes on here."

"So I'm supposed to believe that here in Hedonism Central, no one ever wants to get high? Do I look that naïve, Carl?"

"I'm telling you how we live. We used to have a few members who liked to trip, but they left because they were more interested in acid than in the people they were with."

"When was that?"

"I don't remember; years ago."

"Know what happened to any of them? Ever run into them from time to time?"

"Guy came by a couple of months ago, just to stick his head in and say 'Hi'. And before you ask: no, he'd didn't come to sell anything. Just a social visit."

"What's his name, and where is he now?"

"Andy Enright. And I don't know where he lives now or what he's into."

Franklin pumps the brakes. "Again, Carl, we're Homicide, not Drugs or Vice, OK? I appreciate that you've told us what you know. You going to be OK?"

"Yeah. The other members of the family are helping Carter think about his role here. He won't do this again."

"This fits the definition of assault and battery. If you wanted to press charges to recoup some of your medical expenses?"

"Seeking retribution is a lousy way to build community, Sergeant. I'm fine as I am."

"Your choice, Carl. Guess I'm just not used to dealing with magnanimous people."

"That's the sort of life experience that we're trying to help people develop here."

"And we wish you success. But you should take it easy for a few days, OK?"

FORTY

I wonder if there are Brownies who would do paperwork while I'm asleep? The thought prompts Franklin to put the report he's working on down and check his voice mail.

"I heard about Myra on the news this morning. I'm devastated. Can you call me?" Elizabeth answers on the third ring. "Oh, thank you! I don't know what to say. Do you know if it was suicide?"

"There was no evidence of foul play, but there was no note. We're still waiting on toxicology. I'm sorry that I didn't call; it's still an open investigation of an unexplained death."

"I wouldn't want you to violate any protocols. I was also wondering how you're doing. You never got to meet Myra in person, but you know enough about her to have established a connection. I think an investigator would have to."

Except that cops can't afford feelings on the job. We have to be in control—of the situation, of the suspect, of ourselves. It was the basic rule drilled into him at the Academy and before that, in basic training. Sherman was right; war is hell. *But you won't find its torments described in Dante. It's the gradual loss of your ability to feel things, to feel anything, that marks the stages of your descent. At least Elizabeth thinks I haven't reached the last circle. Yet.*

"Thank you. Homicide detectives sometimes get a little numb after being exposed to death often enough. All you want is a suspect to confess and get locked up. A death that isn't a homicide leaves you with no crime to solve. And no place to hide from the senselessness."

"I'm sorry if I seemed flippant during our meetings. My only exposure to murder has been through literature. Sam Spade or Philip Marlowe can afford to be hard-boiled because they're fictional. I guess fiction is one way of managing the troublesome parts of reality."

This isn't the conversation I'd expected. Hell, it isn't a conversation I could even imagine myself having. What's going to come out of my mouth next? "I didn't find you flippant at all. What have you been doing to take care of yourself?"

"Funny you should ask. I've buried myself in my work. But that's not quite true; it's more like work has buried me."

"Walking tours seven days a week?"

She laughs. "No, it's the television program."

"NBC has hired you to host the Today show?"

"No, thank you! At least my show doesn't require a move to Rockefeller Center."

"Glad that you'll be sticking around. Whatever it is, you make it sound exciting. When do I get to hear more about it?"

"'Sound exciting'? Only after a couple of glasses of Pinot Noir."

"Well then, what are you doing tonight?"

"I have a tour this afternoon—no, don't laugh—but nothing after that."

"Where does your tour end?"

"Near Post and Grant. But won't that be a little early for dinner?"

"On a Saturday night when we don't already have reservations some-where? Our choices will probably be 4:30 or 9:00."

"I can't do 4:30, and I don't think I could last until 9:00. There's a nice little French restaurant around there, and it has a good bar right next door to it."

"Which will take care of the Pinot. Give me their names; I'll get to work on it."

"Thank you very much. That sounds lovely."

Only after he hangs up does he realize how much he wants this, and how much of the tongue-tied adolescent he still has in him.

The call has left him unfocused, but if it shows, Kevin doesn't comment on it.

"I knew Carl was a sleaze, but I'd hoped he was at least a little smarter than that. 'New from Janus Health: Designer Aphrodisiacs!' The guy is a con man who's as gullible as his marks."

"Yeah. No wonder people like Maggie think he's a waste of time."

"To say nothing about being unimaginative. Pay-per-view online sex shows? That's so fifteen years ago. I guess Mr. Hedonism figured that making you a porn star without your knowledge is a great way to enhance interpersonal relationship skills."

"Yeah, he's a repulsive character, but once again, how would that explain why someone murdered Matt Glover?"

Kevin drums his fingers on the desktop. "Carl is a voyeur and a manipulator, but do you think he's a wimp?"

"He looks pretty solid. He's scared of Maggie Chadwick, but all that proves is he doesn't have a death wish."

"Carter is about three inches shorter and twenty pounds lighter than Carl, but there's no question who got the worse end of the deal. So what provoked all that frenzy?"

"You don't think the betrayal those non-consensual videos represent is enough?"

Kevin looks serious. "As a sex-positive guy, if a video of me screwing ended up online, I wouldn't fret because people found out I'm a sexual being. I know who I am and that I'll never get rid of the bigotry in the world, so what the hell? I might as well enjoy doing what I like because they're going to hate me whether or not I'm getting laid. The one thing I would be concerned about is my job. It's easy to guess what Matt Glover's reaction would be under similar circumstances, and Carl understood that. I wouldn't put it past him to try a little blackmail. And if Matt called his bluff, or just laughed at him..."

"...Carl might decide to show Matt who's boss. So on whose behalf was Carter exacting revenge this morning?"

"A person who would find Carl's actions hurtful. Someone Carter had powerful feelings about and whose emotional state mattered to him."

Franklin frowns. "Myra. Matt and Carter were both mad at Carl because of Myra. Were both of them also in love with Myra? This is making my head hurt."

"You said you wanted a sexual jealousy theory, and I'm offering you one, in spades. 'The shocking truth about what happens when a ménage à trois turns into the Eternal Triangle! Film at 11, courtesy of Carl Holton'."

"Tell me, does everyone in Reno talk like you?"

"Hang around casinos long enough, you start sounding like a con artist. What can I say?"

"Anyway, on the positive side, now we have two more guys Ortega can try to bully confessions out of. At least I'm right about motive."

Kevin grins. "I can afford to be magnanimous because this morning also boosted the drug angle."

"You mean Andy Enright?"

"You heard Carl confirmed Maggie's identification. Andy is a known druggie who's still around and visited the commune recently. And—fanfare please—when I called Henry yesterday, he told me Matt had gone hiking with someone named Andy."

"Hiking?"

"Point Reyes. That's how I got a phone number for Doper Dan. Turns out Matt kept a hiking diary that included a list of contacts."

"Didn't Ortega have them execute a search warrant on the apartment while he was interrogating Henry?"

"Yep. But a North Face backpack sitting in a closet with a notebook full of maps and trail descriptions didn't pique anyone's interest. Calling the number got me Andy's voicemail: I'm waiting to see if Verizon can attach an address to it."

"Dropping acid at Point Reyes—sounds like a 60s thing."

"Gotta love the classics. At least we've got more leads than we had last week."

"Progress of a sort. And how are you doing?"

Kevin looks almost surprised. "OK. Pretty good."

"How about taking a little time for yourself this weekend?"

"Gary and I are going to *Beach Blanket Babylon* tonight."

"Good. Say hello for me."

"Will do."

It's the first time Franklin's heard Kevin mention his partner by name.

FORTY-ONE

Against all odds, Cafe Claude has a cancellation with a table available at 7 PM; Franklin leaves Elizabeth a voice mail. It's not worth trying to drive to San Bruno and back, and it's too early to go meet her. He should have asked what the tour route was and surprised her by joining it in progress. But it's been a hectic Saturday.

He looks at the unfinished reports on his desk; they'll keep. This would be a good time to read Myra's journal. Franklin heads to the property room.

The first pages of the journal are a mix of warm thoughts about Matt and confident statements about Myra's literary aspirations. But the tone darkens as doubts about the possibility of realizing her plans and about her abilities crowd the pages. *"I realize that I'm becoming infatuated with the idea of a writer's commune. Carl's family is the closest thing I've found, but it's not what I had hoped. Was this a mistake, or was this also part of Nora May's experience, to be surrounded by people who underestimated how difficult it would be to build a cooperative entity? This too could be a gift from her; it will make the play Nora's authentic story."*

"The other commune members are self-absorbed, and it's difficult to relate to the women here. They're too dogmatic,"—was Myra thinking of Maggie Chadwick?—*" or naïve, insecure, always too eager to please the men. They look to others to fill the void in their lives—that sounds a little like Phyllis too."*

Entry after entry reflects a growing kinship with Nora May, whom she calls Phyllis. *"I know she had been strong and healthy when she started, before everything wore her down. I wonder if Jack London was as big a self-congratulatory jerk as Carl is. How much rage did she feel? I can sense Phyllis' spirit in the Genthe portrait at the Bancroft Library, but I can't feel her at her Lombard Street address, or anywhere else in the city. Is this a direct 'understanding' from her, that she'd never felt at home anywhere? The thought depresses me."*

"Matt is such an attractive man, intelligent without being arrogant, funny, innocent in a charming, even sexy sort of way." Nothing in the entries suggests

141

these feelings changed, but they seem to have lost their salience, and all mention of Matt eventually ceases. So do references to almost everything else in the external world. By the last pages, the journal is a record of Myra communing with her vision of Phyllis, only to realize why Phyllis decided there was no way out left.

His sense of foreboding increases as he reads. The entries remind Franklin of being called to a nasty accident. You see the evidence of what's happened before you get there; you don't want to look at it up close, but you can't look away. It's clear why Myra's friends thought her personality was being subsumed by Nora May's. And sometime early yesterday morning, Myra and Nora May both went away.

The entries end abruptly; blank pages follow, along with the two photographs. But there's been a change. These pictures are not the ones he saw yesterday. In place of the soft-focus portrait of the young blonde woman, one photo shows a dark-haired woman wearing a dark blouse and jacket and a knotted neckerchief. And instead of a girl sitting on a rock, the second picture is of this other woman in a formal gown, leaning against a table, her left index finger against her cheek. Yesterday's photos were early twentieth-century, but the ones in the diary now are vintage nineteenth-century.

He pages through the rest of the journal, but there are no other pictures. The two new images are solidly mounted and don't appear to overlie yesterday's photos. Franklin sets the diary aside and Googles "Nora May French". A quick search is enough to convince him that yesterday he was looking at Nora May. The woman whose photos are in the diary this afternoon is someone else.

He examines the journal carefully. There's no doubt that this is the same volume he placed in the evidence bag yesterday. He photographs the new pictures with his phone. Then he closes the diary and carries it back to the evidence room. The officer on duty confirms that no one has done anything with the journal since he checked it in yesterday. There have been no apparent breaks in the chain of custody.

He returns to his desk. It's almost five; Elizabeth will be waiting.

FORTY-TWO

The bar is at the end of an alley decorated with a giant carp swimming along the brick walls and antique signs advertise tea, gin, cigarettes, and beer. Elizabeth is wearing a tailored blue silk dress, a patterned silk shawl, and pearl stud earrings—a definite upgrade from her usual walking tour uniform.

"Very striking; I like it. Was it a high society literary group tour?"

"I suppose this would be a good choice for a *Thin Man* tour; Nick and Nora were pretty ritzy. But this is going to be my new SFPD look. Hope you like it."

"A fashion plate like me? You bet."

A waitress with a subtle brogue takes their order. People at tables are celebrating, and the Irish cheer helps wash away the despair he felt reading Myra's diary.

Elizabeth senses it, too. "In the *Divine Comedy*, Francesca da Rimini tells Dante that the greatest sorrow is recalling past happiness when surrounded by misery. But this is the reverse. Right now, being surrounded by all these celebrations while I'm mourning Myra is challenging."

"I don't know if it helps any, but when we found her, Myra was sitting across from Grace Cathedral. She looked at peace."

"Thank you for that. My disquiet is due more to my knowledge of Nora May's story than anything about Myra herself. It felt like a premonition."

"I'm still having difficulty wrapping my head around Myra's infatuation with these writers."

"Nora May was in her 20s and had published just one poem when she found herself rubbing elbows with the likes of Jack London and George Sterling. Heady stuff to be part of that crowd, and discouraging at the same time. Jack was rolling in money and planning a trip around the world on his yacht, and she was working as a telephone operator and getting nowhere."

Franklin remembers the journal entries. "Who was Phyllis?"

143

Elizabeth looks startled. "That's what her Carmel friends called Nora May. You knew that?"

"I didn't; Myra did." He takes a sip of his drink. "Do you believe that under the right circumstances, the spirits of some people persist—live on—in places?"

"The spirits of people and of peoples. Do you remember the King Tut exhibit at the De Young six or seven years ago?"

"Uh-huh. Traffic in Golden Gate Park was a mess."

"Spoken like an officer and a gentleman. It upset some people that Tut's death mask wasn't part of it, but the simpler artifacts were the ones that spoke to me. There was a chair made for a child. I realized I was looking at something someone's son sat on 3,000 years ago, and I could almost feel the boy's presence."

"Do you think you're a... what's it called? A sensitive?"

"I'd guess we all have these feelings. Look at people's responses to Stonehenge. What makes so many people feel it's a special place? I think human lives leave traces on the places where they've lived. Some of those locations seem to hold life imprints more strongly. San Francisco may be one of them, and I think other people can sense that too. That's how I earn my living. Perhaps individuals like Myra are so empathic that their lives resonate with those who have come before. Human needs and experiences are pretty universal. It doesn't seem odd to me if we encounter the same ones over and over, generation after generation."

"I read some of Myra's journal this afternoon, and I got that same sense of foreboding you mentioned. It was like watching someone sinking in quicksand."

"Myra's writing skills were exceptional, and I expected she could have crafted a powerful play. But I had trouble sorting out what in Myra's life was a consequence of a well-developed sense of empathy and what was an expression of her depressive tendencies. I'm still not sure how such a promising young woman ended up there."

"I saw people trapped by hopelessness in Afghanistan. But their assessment of their lives was accurate because their situation *was* hopeless."

Concern spreads across Elizabeth's face. "I'm sorry. That must have been difficult."

He can feel the heat radiating from the vehicle and smell burning fuel. Someone near him is yelling. "Shoot him, damn it! Shoot him!"

And then he's back, sitting at an outdoor table in Mark Lane. *This isn't where I want the evening to go. Nora May, if you've followed me here, it's time for you to leave.*

"That was in a different world, not one I made or that I live in now. So here and now in San Francisco, what's Elizabeth been up to? On the phone you made it sound like you were running away to join the circus."

If Elizabeth had noticed any change in him, she's hiding it well. "Pretty close. But can we save that for dinner? It's complicated."

"And it's also time." He waves down a server and pays the tab.

The Carp

Elizabeth's walking in the carp's wake as it swims toward Bush Street. Franklin makes it to the fish's tail when he sees a too familiar figure. Just under six feet and thin almost to emaciation, he's still wearing the same improbable outfit, a short black jacket and white linen trousers. It's only a few yards to Bush Street, yet the man is gone by the time he reaches the sidewalk. He turns to catch up with Elizabeth.

"I hadn't realized that these side alleys had so much art on their walls."

"Oh yes. In Claude Alley, there aren't any fish, but there is a flower garden. And also an attractive woman with a provocative expression who watches you."

"Tell her I'm spoken for this evening."

"I certainly intend to."

FORTY-THREE

"So, your television program—biographies of writers who have some connection with the city?"

Elizabeth studies the plate of charcuterie and eyes the Jambon de Bayonne before deciding on a taste of Pork Rillette instead. "Yes. I'm trying to make literature interesting while telling a bit of San Francisco's history. It also helps promote the walking tours."

"Your website mentioned something about stories that had gotten lost?"

She smiles, pleased that he's visited the site. "I should check to see if you liked me on Facebook. The episode we've been planning is *The Lost Tales of Robert Louis Stevenson*. Though that's misleading; most of them weren't lost. He just never finished them."

"What's Stevenson's connection with San Francisco? I thought he was Scottish and ended up somewhere in the South Seas."

She nods. "He was born in Edinburgh and died in Samoa."

"And on the way, he stopped off at Treasure Island for the World's Fair?"

She makes a face. "As I was going to say, he died in Samoa, but he lived in San Francisco in 1880 and married an Oakland girl. She was ten years older than he was and already married when they met."

"So he comes to San Francisco and falls in love in Oakland?"

"He'd met Fanny in France in 1876 when she was studying painting. It was love at first sight, at least for him. When she moved back to California, he followed her, but he got sick and almost starved to death in Monterey."

"Sounds like he was lucky to survive the courtship."

"Fanny was the more practical one. Back then, he wasn't famous; in fact, he was broke. She dithered for a while before getting a divorce. In the meantime, she stayed in Oakland while he rented a room on Bush Street."

"You mean right here?"

"Yes, near the Stockton tunnel, though it wasn't there in 1880. There's a bronze plaque near the site of his boarding house; we were filming there this afternoon. Where we're sitting now is pretty close to where he used to eat dinner."

"Did you find any lost stories while you were there?"

"'Fraid not. The house is long gone; a laundromat and a tattoo parlor are there now. Not the sort of places I'd expect to find lost manuscripts." She takes a bite of pâté. "Mmm, a little black truffle. Anyway, the reactions we're getting about the upcoming episode surprised me, especially since my producer's idea hadn't wowed me at first."

"His idea being?"

"To make the show more popular. *Literary San Francisco* gets positive reviews, but our ratings aren't that great. My producer argued that my approach is too highbrow; he proposed renaming the series *Once Upon a Book*. I vetoed that, but I agreed we should pick a popular author for an episode. He suggested Stevenson; even people who've never opened a book have heard of *Treasure Island* and *Dr. Jekyll and Mr. Hyde*. I made the mistake of mentioning that Stevenson had lots of ideas for stories that he started and then put aside. That's when the staff came up with the *Lost Tales* concept."

"That makes sense. People get intrigued by a story that breaks off just when it's getting interesting. Are you going to invite them to come up with endings themselves?"

"It's worse than that. Someone suggested that we add a treasure hunt and try to track down an actual missing story."

"A treasure hunt, like in *Treasure Island;* I get it. But how likely is it you could find one?"

"No idea. A man named Swearingen published a list of stories Stevenson mentioned in his letters; there were over 350 of them. We don't know how many he ever started or how far he got. Fanny saved his papers, but her children auctioned many of them off when she died in 1914. Aside from disliking the 'reality TV' approach, I was afraid we might give forgers an invitation to create 'lost' documents. Stevenson memorabilia still command good money at auctions."

"Thinking like a cop! I like it!"

"So did corporate counsel. I agreed to advertise the segment on the station's website and app, though the writers made everything sound more mysterious than it is. What I wanted to talk about were the ideas behind the unfinished stories and the whole creative process."

"I understand now why you've been busy."

"Oh, that's just the beginning. I may need some salad and a little Petrale Sole to get through the whole saga."

"And I bet a little more wine will help."

FORTY-FOUR

"So the marketing department made the ads, and the *Lost Stories* concept must have struck a chord. We got more responses than usual from viewers. Some wanted to know where Stevenson got his ideas or why he abandoned a story, the sort of interest I was hoping for."

"So far so good, except that you had to admit that your producer wasn't wrong."

"He's educable, at least a little. We also got a lot of pet theories, like Dr. Jekyll had been a French serial murdered or a dentist in Boston who got addicted to chloroform. I sent all of them polite responses and applauded their erudition. It was a man in Santa Barbara who got everyone excited, though."

"And are you going to tell me why?"

She sticks her tongue out at him. "It's because Mr. Arthur Jackson's great uncle Brad knew Isobel Osbourne Field."

"Who?"

"She was Stevenson's stepdaughter, and Mr. Jackson claims that Belle once showed his Uncle Arthur an actual Stevenson manuscript."

"Bingo! But is he credible?"

"Credible enough to make my producer call him and schedule an on-camera interview. Belle's job was to take Stevenson's dictation in Samoa; there's even a recording of her talking about the day he died. She owned homes near Toro Canyon and what's now the Polo Club in Santa Barbara, so Mr. Jackson's claim is at least plausible."

"So when's the interview?"

"We recorded it earlier this week."

"You do have an author's gift for suspense, don't you? It's a good thing we're still on the entrée."

"One reason I suggested a French restaurant; this is a four-course story. Want the abbreviated version?"

"Just the facts, ma'am."

"Aren't you going to warn me of my right to remain silent?"

"Too late. You can't stop now."

"Well, this is my story, and I'm sticking to it. Arthur Jackson is a 72-year-old financial analyst from Los Angeles. He moved to Santa Barbara in 1970 to take a job with Raytheon and worked there until he retired six years ago. His Aunt Dottie was active in the city's artistic and literary circles, and she was the one who became friends with Ned and Belle Field."

"Belle was a literary fixture because she was Stevenson's stepdaughter?"

"Yes. She'd also been painting ever since she and Fanny studied in France. Dottie's family had money; Belle inherited Stevenson money and then became a millionaire in her 60s when they discovered oil on one of Ned's properties. Like attracts like, I guess."

"I'm confused. Where does Uncle Brad enter the picture?"

"Sorry. Somewhere around 1925-1935, just before Ned Field died. Uncle Brad would have been in his early 30s, and Belle was in her late 60s or early 70s. Mr. Jackson says that Belle took a liking to his uncle; she had a thing for younger men. Her husband Ned had been her mother's companion. He was only three years older than Belle's son."

"Her *companion*?" Franklin shakes his head. "This family..."

"I know. Not stuff you'll find in *A Child's Garden of Verses*. But if we wanted to spice up the show..."

"On public TV? Shame on you! So what happened between Belle and Uncle Brad?"

"Shame on you too! According to the very proper Mr. Jackson, Brad provided a chaste but attentive audience for Belle's stories about her colorful life. Having tea with Oscar Wilde when he visited San Francisco, hobnobbing with the King of Hawaii, sailing all over the world. I would love to have been there to sit in on those conversations."

"At least this way, your show will keep its 'G' rating."

"Anyway, on one of his visits, Belle was reminiscing about how sick Stevenson was in San Francisco and how much better he looked when she visited the newlyweds at Silverado in 1880. Brad asked how Stevenson felt about doctors, and Belle laughed. Her mother was unhappy with the doctors; Fanny claimed she kept Louis alive despite them. Louis never criticized doctors, but the doctor in *The Body Snatcher* is a murderer, and Dr. Jekyll leads a secret life. And there was also Dr. Montfort." Elizabeth puts down her fork, glowing with excitement.

"OK, so who is Dr. Montfort?"

"That's just it; there is no Robert Louis Stevenson story about a Dr. Montfort. Belle told Uncle Brad that Louis heard about Montfort from a sailor in San Francisco. Her stepfather began a story about him but never completed it. She still had the manuscript somewhere—it was only a couple of pages—along with a letter telling about his meeting with the sailor. He toyed with *Dr. Montfort's Prescription* during their stay in Silverado but set it aside once he and Fanny started planning their return to Scotland."

"So the man you interviewed this week had an uncle who knew about a 'lost tale'?"

"His uncle saw it and heard it. Belle was as good as her word. She produced a sheaf of pages and read what there was of the story aloud. She had been her stepfather's amanuensis and had no trouble reading his handwriting. She also had a commanding stage presence. I guess her performance made a powerful impression on Brad."

"And you got this all on camera?"

"Pretty much, yes. Mr. Jackson heard about the story in the 1970s, but he seems quite sharp and comes across as genuine, even if he doesn't share Belle's theatrical flair."

"So do I get to hear the story?"

"Just as soon as the tarte Tatin arrives."

FORTY-FIVE

"Just one bite first!"

Franklin waits for her blissful smile to subside. "So it's 1880, and?"

"In San Francisco, Stevenson kept to a schedule: write in the morning, eat at Donnadieu's at noon, explore the city in the afternoon. Sometime early in that year, he met a sailor in Portsmouth Square who told him about Dr. Charles Montfort, a European-educated physician who'd set up practice in San Francisco. Montfort had observed that there were places where everyone seemed to live to an advanced age. Infectious diseases were the most common cause of death back then, and he wondered if something in the area could be protecting people."

"After several years of visiting exotic locales and collecting samples of what he hoped might be his universal cure-all, he settled here and started testing various concoctions. Most failed, but one combination seemed promising, and some of his patients recovered. But there was a problem; the patients who recovered all went mad later. And that's the story in a nutshell."

"It's an interesting anecdote, even if it doesn't sound very plausible."

"There's no evidence Stevenson thought otherwise. I'd guess he envisioned writing a cautionary tale about the dangers of tampering with the natural order, but he never took it past those preliminary sketches. I suppose you could see it as a sort of precursor to *Jekyll*; at least that's how my producer wants to pitch it. 'The incredible story of the San Francisco physician who was the inspiration for the most famous horror story of all time!'"

"I take it you would prefer a more understated approach."

"It's a tale I can imagine someone telling in a waterfront bar anywhere in the world. Dramatizing an apocryphal story won't make it real. For the program, I'll need evidence that an actual manuscript once existed."

"How likely is it you can prove that?"

"As you would say, the chain of custody hasn't remained intact. After Samoa, Fanny and Belle lived in San Francisco and then in Montecito. They brought a lot of Louis's miscellaneous papers with them. Some were donated or auctioned off in the following years; Belle kept the rest after Fanny died."

"So she might have them in the 1920s and '30s?"

"Oh yes. She outlived her son and her second husband and died in 1953. Have you ever been to the Stevenson Museum in St. Helena?"

"No, I didn't know there was one."

"There is, and I've been there. After Belle died, her nurse inherited what remained of Louis' papers and donated them to the museum."

"So Belle had kept some items until the very end, sixty years after Louis' death."

"Yes. For a man who died at 44, Stevenson remained a presence in his family's life even into the mid-twentieth century."

"That's a theme to explore right there. Can you convince your producer to ease up on the treasure hunt idea?"

"I think I know how. Stevenson liked ghost stories, but he wasn't Jules Verne or H. G. Wells. He didn't write science fiction, and I doubt a story about making people almost immortal would have interested him. When Fanny married him, he'd just survived a serious hemorrhage and wasn't expected to last a year. It's no wonder a story about living free of the threat of disease might capture his imagination. But whatever his personal views, he was still living in a Victorian world."

"And this is important because?"

"Name an infectious disease that was common in the 19th century and could cause insanity."

"Uh-huh. And a discussion of syphilis is nothing either the author or your producer would touch. So what do you do with Mr. Jackson's story?"

"Oh, he's still the perfect spokesman for *Literary San Francisco* and the living literary past of the city. You could feel the excitement that Robert Louis Stevenson can still generate, even at third hand, while he was talking."

"Which is sort of where we began, isn't it? People living on because of the way their lives and accomplishments can influence later generations."

"It happens all the time in my classes and on my tours."

"You'll have to add a stop at the site of Dr. Montfort's office to your tours."

"Oh, stop! I'm going to search the minutes of the San Francisco Medical Society to look for some mention of Dr. Montfort. If I can't uncover anything, we may have to change the theme to what a convincing storyteller Stevenson could be."

"Him, or a drunken sailor. It sounds like you're preparing for any eventuality."

"My life hasn't been dull in recent weeks. I'm just happy it's been exciting in a good way."

Franklin raises his eyebrows. "I'll drink to that."

"What will you have? A Rusty Nail? Drambuie and scotch would be an appropriate toast for a Scottish author."

Franklin catches the waitress's eye for the menu and scans it. "There's one here called 'Our Last Word'. That might be appropriate."

"Last Word? Never! Perhaps I should order a 'Blessing in Disguise': sparkling wine with berries and amaretto and gin."

"I may have to carry you to your car."

"Oh, that's right; the police are watching, aren't they? Perhaps just a cup of French Roast instead, then."

Even without an after-dinner drink, Franklin is feeling mellow. *And I don't want this to end.* "So, did Stevenson ever come back to San Francisco?"

"Only once. He came to New York on a boat full of zoo animals in 1887 and spent the winter at a sanitarium in the Adirondacks. Then he came to San Francisco in June and set sail for the South Seas. He never returned and died of a stroke in Samoa."

"Wasn't he young to die of a stroke?"

"Yes—even back then. Who knows what the diagnosis would be today. He was chronically ill; people who met him always commented on how thin he was."

Franklin is suddenly alert. "And Fanny and Belle ended up back here?"

"Yes. After Louis died, Fanny and her children moved back to San Francisco; Montecito came later."

"These people didn't like to stay in any one place very long, did they?"

"No, but they could afford to come and go as they pleased. Fanny must have felt vindicated. First she married a philanderer who dragged her off to a mining camp in Nevada, and then she divorced him to marry a penniless Scotsman. But she ended up the wealthy widow of a world-famous author, living in a mansion on Russian Hill."

Don't tell me. "Is the house still around?"

"Yes, it survived the quake. We walked past it on the tour today."

"And it's a pale yellow, three stories, at the intersection of Hyde and Lombard."

"So you know it?"

"It's near the murder scene we're investigating. Who lives there now?"

"Someone with the University of Phoenix bought it, but he died a couple of years ago. I don't know whether anyone lives there now full time."

"I saw a woman there the morning they found Matt's body."

"What did she look like?"

"At least late middle age, short, full head of short curls, wearing a white blouse with a scarf, and a fussy old-fashioned jacket, all frilly cuffs and elaborate brocade."

Elizabeth smiles. "Do you always pay so much attention to what older women wear?"

"It's how I make my living, ma'am. She stood at an open window for several minutes, so I got a good look at her." He hesitates. "I thought she was trying to flag me down, but when I went to the front door, no one answered."

Elizabeth's sudden silence takes him by surprise. "Did what I just said ring some bells?"

"The woman you're describing sounds a little like one of the previous owners."

"Could she have come back to visit the house?"

"I suppose it's possible, except she's been dead a hundred years. The person you saw fits the general description of Fanny Stevenson."

The Woman in the Window

FORTY-SIX

"Is it possible that this was some sort of stunt?"

"It sounds like something my producer might like. But most people don't know the house's history, and the present owners keep a low profile. I don't know of anyone using the house for anything other than a residence."

"Perhaps it was part of a cleaning crew or a realtor."

"Do you believe that?"

"No."

"I didn't see the person you saw, but that's the way Fanny dressed at the time she lived in San Francisco. And I doubt that any realtor showing a house with a Russian Hill price tag would dress as eccentrically as she did."

"So you are suggesting that Fanny Stevenson is still living on Hyde Street, one hundred years later?"

"It wouldn't be the first time someone saw a ghost there. Fanny believed in spirits. She held seances at Hyde Street, trying to contact Louis. And she sold the place in 1908 because of malevolent deities. She left San Francisco and moved into a haunted estate in Montecito instead."

"She sounds a little odd."

"Odd, but high class; her Montecito home's ghost was a dead countess. The man who bought the Russian Hill property in the 1980s also claimed the place was haunted. I don't know who or what you saw, but you're not alone, and not all the people who've seen ghosts there were as dotty as Fanny Stevenson. "

"Or me." He looks around; the restaurant is almost empty. "I'd guess that if we sit here much longer, they'll bring us a breakfast menu. But this has been an interesting evening."

"An endless lecture on clan Stevenson from a person who is crazy enough to believe in ghosts. That sounds like a pretty unusual meal, even to me. What did they slip in our food, I wonder?"

"I didn't hear any lectures tonight. A glimpse into the lives of some real Bohemians, accompanied by excellent wine and French food, and excellent company. Those are all things I haven't had in my life very often."

The tip is on the table, they've reclaimed their coats, and he's trying to walk slowly. It isn't working, and the parking garage is just a block away. He walks Elizabeth up the two levels to her car. "Well, it's a long drive back to San Bruno."

"... and your dog is waiting for you."

"Just two cats. I'm gone too many hours a day for a dog."

"Whereas the cats spend the day asleep and don't even notice when you're not there."

"Probably."

"Lucky for us that there's a store in the Mission that's open late and has a pretty sophisticated liquor selection."

"Why the Mission?"

"Because that's where I live, and it's a lot closer than San Bruno. You can follow me while I get the Drambuie to go with the scotch I have at the apartment. We can have a nightcap to toast dead Scotsmen everywhere. Along with deceased wives who like to hang around San Francisco just for old times' sake."

"That won't make the drive to the East Bay any easier."

"Which is an even better reason not to make it." She unlocks her door. "I'll wait here while you get your car."

He closes her door for her and watches her start the engine, turn on her lights, and sit with the engine idling. Then he finds his keys and heads toward his car.

FORTY-SEVEN

SUNDAY, SEPTEMBER 4, 2016

On a clear day, the view from the base of the KNTV tower at the Radio Road-Ridge Trail intersection is spectacular, but the two cyclists out for an early ride don't reach the summit this morning. They're about a half-mile from the Guadalupe Canyon Parkway when they spot the orange Camaro. It's off the road, sitting among the trees at an angle that suggests sudden rapid deceleration. An airbag has pinioned the driver, but he's still breathing. By the time the EMTs take him to Seton Medical Center and the police are finished asking their questions, the riders have abandoned the idea of bicycling to the tower. Instead, they pedal back to Brisbane, where they're still in time for Sunday brunch at the 7 Mile House Grill.

Elizabeth makes strong coffee. Franklin is standing in the center of her living room, drinking his third cup. *From now on, no more Drambuie at bedtime.*

Elizabeth's computer sits on a small desk in the corner, surrounded by piles of books stacked on the floor. Papers and books also cover what may once have been a coffee table. He decides he'll try the loveseat; it has only three books and what looks like an old-fashioned photo album. *I wonder if Elizabeth drinks her morning coffee standing up or sitting on the floor?*

He opens the album gingerly; it looks like it's an heirloom. The first pages contain yellowing black and white photos of landscapes. Spidery handwriting identifies locations: *Zaca Lake, Toro Canyon.*

"That's Mr. Jackson's." Elizabeth finishes toweling her hair and gives it a toss. "It had been Uncle Brad's. Those pictures are of properties the Fields owned."

"And Uncle Brad gave this to Mr. Jackson?"

"Yes. Nephew Arthur was genuinely interested in his uncle's friends and stories, which wasn't true of Brad and Dottie's children. The kids thought that Belle Field was a tiresome old woman and their parents were behaving like sycophantic fools."

"That's harsh."

"Not the first pair of well-heeled entitled brats to bite the hand. Eventually, they moved to New York City, more or less to get away from boring Santa Barbara. Mr. Jackson ended up with the miscellany that Brad's kids didn't think was worth claiming."

"Like this album."

"And odds and ends of furniture, books, some paintings, the sort of stuff you'd find at an estate sale." She moves books to the floor to sit beside him and takes the album from him. "Here's the one I want to show you."

Toward the back of the album is a snapshot of three people in wicker chairs on a veranda. "That's Uncle Ned and Aunt Dottie; the woman in the middle is Belle."

Even in the fading photograph, the round-faced woman with short hair, dark brows, and large dark eyes is a commanding, even imperious, presence. "She has the air of a determined survivor, someone who lived through a lot and came out the other side intact."

Franklin studies the photo. "There's a painting on an easel in the background. It's just visible there, on the right."

"Yes. That's what's interesting. Mr. Jackson says that's the one Belle gave to Brad, or rather to Dottie. Look at this."

On the next page is a close-up of the painting, an island scene done in watercolor. Scrawled in the lower margin is a handwritten note. *I know your wife loves art, so this painting is for her, along with something for you.*

"Isn't that cool? It shows that at least the part about Uncle Brad knowing Stevenson's stepdaughter is true. That could be enough of a surprise discovery for the show right there."

"Where is the painting now?"

"Mr. Jackson still has it. He brought it down from his attic to show us when he heard we were coming. I took a picture." She hunts around among the papers for her purse and pulls out her phone. On the screen, a gray-haired man is holding a framed painting. He has the air of a boy who's just won a blue ribbon at a 4-H fair.

Franklin takes the phone from her and studies the photo.

Elizabeth frowns. "You agree that it's the same painting?"

"Yes, it appears to be the same. That's the first point that I think is interesting. This is an actual painting by Belle Field. She gave to Uncle Brad, who later left it to Arthur Jackson."

She looks at him with a shrewd smile. "If that's the first point, then there must be a second."

FORTY-EIGHT

"The second point is that someone photographed the painting and added a note to the photo indicating it was a gift for Brad's wife. A logical assumption would be that the writer most likely was Belle herself."

"We haven't had a chance to contact a handwriting analyst yet, but the content would suggest that Belle wrote it."

"Let us stipulate for the moment that she did. I would guess that the photo served as a notice of her intent to give Dottie this painting."

"That's what it says, yes."

"In the inscribed photo, the painting is not framed."

"Yes, it's still on an easel. But I suppose if you're giving a painting as a gift, you'd want to frame it first." She's squinting at him, trying to guess where he's going.

"The frame is interesting; it's a good deal larger than the painting itself."

"Yes, the frame and the matting are pretty elaborate."

Franklin takes the phone and enlarges the image. He holds the phone at arm's length. "To the point where they threaten to overwhelm the artwork itself. That's not something I would expect an artist to do."

"You think perhaps Dottie had it framed?"

"In the nineteenth century, elaborate frames like this were common, but by the 1930s?"

"They were out of style by then, especially for works under glass like a watercolor."

"So why would Dottie have done that? It makes no sense."

"Not for someone with her sophisticated taste in art."

He smiles. "Unless someone had a specific need for the frame to be that large."

"Which would be?"

"I don't know for sure. But listen to Belle's syntax. Does 'this painting is for her, along with something for you' sound a little odd? What was the *something*?"

She looks up. "The thing she'd shown to Uncle Brad. The *Montfort* manuscript. A painting for Dottie and a special something for Brad."

"I'd guess that the photo with her note accompanied her gifts: the watercolor and the Montfort story. At some point, someone framed or reframed Belle's watercolor to make a space where the second gift could be concealed."

"A frame large enough to hold both!"

"How many mysteries stories have you read where an important clue gets hidden in the back of a picture frame? I hate it when life imitates art."

Elizabeth smiles. "Louis was the member of the family who had a gift for original plots. I guess Belle's Brownies only provided ideas for pictures."

"Or maybe the frame was Brad's idea."

"Could he have been the one who hid the manuscript?"

"It's conceivable. Brad's kids may have felt his stories about Belle were tedious, but he suspected they would be happy enough to get their hands on an original handwritten Robert Louis Stevenson manuscript. They hadn't treated either Belle or him with respect, so he left Belle's gifts to his favorite nephew instead."

"But why didn't he tell Mr. Jackson about it?"

"He might have intended it as a test to see if Arthur's friendship and affection were genuine and not based on any expectation of material gain. If Arthur accepted the painting as the intended gift, he passed. If his response was to ask about Stevenson's papers, he failed. The painting is worth something, but not as much as the manuscript."

Elizabeth gives Franklin a look. "'Always trying to find the ulterior motives behind things. I suppose that must be a necessary mindset for a homicide detective."

He shrugs. "Brad's test may have worked a little too well. He left it to his nephew to guess what he'd done, but Arthur never picked up on Belle's hint."

"An ironic plot twist! Do you think this could be true, or are we both just hopeless romantics making up fanciful stories? I'd hate to make the program about our *folie à deux*."

"At least it's a testable theory, as we say in the trade."

She stands up. "Even though it's Sunday, I'm going to call my producer and tell him we've got to visit Mr. Jackson again tomorrow. But I'll try to sound enigmatic. I've raised so many objections to this project that my enthusiasm might tip him off that I'm up to something."

"Perhaps we should think about breakfast first?"

"Yes, please! I'm starving! Jim's Restaurant or crepes at the Little Heaven Deli?"

"Just plain Jim's, and then you can call your producer."

"And how would you like to spend the rest of the day?"

"I'm sure something will come up."

Elizabeth is still on the phone when Franklin's cell rings. He's tempted to let it go to voicemail until he sees it's Kevin.

"Sorry to be a pest on a Sunday, but I wanted to give you a heads up. Early this morning Carter Albemarle disrupted Sergeant Ortega's usually sunny disposition and equanimity."

"I thought we were going to be questioning Carter pretty soon. What's up?"

"Carter's in the ICU at SF General. Seems he got drunk last night, went for a drive on Guadalupe Canyon Parkway, missed a turn, and smashed into a tree."

"He going to be all right?"

"He's still unconscious. Far as I can tell, they think he should be OK, but it may take a couple of days."

"So a temporary delay."

"Sounds like it, but Ortega's having difficulty seeing the glass as half-full. He wants this case closed yesterday."

"Hey, what if he just shows up at the hospital and flashes his badge, and Carter wakes up and confesses all?"

"I'll suggest it to him. If Carter doesn't respond, he can always arrest the doctors on an accessories charge."

"It's worth a try. Keep me posted."

He looks back at Elizabeth, who is now holding her phone a foot away from her ear. He can hear her producer from across the room. "No, Glen, we won't need a camera crew. I just have a few more questions I thought of for Mr. Jackson. No. No; I'm sure."

Perhaps there are worse bosses than Mike Ortega in the world, after all.

FORTY-NINE

After some searching, Henry has found what appears to be the master index of his former roommates' projects. He's relieved to see how organized Matt had been. Still, some entries are puzzling.

MENU

Congener Program
- ChemSynthesis database
- Macrolide Scaffolds examples
- NCI Natural Products Repository
- PDSP Ki database

Impact Assessment
- RoFF
- Criteria

Protein Programs
- AtomNet Neural Network
- CSF Chimera
- FrgBag

--MORE--

There are two versions of the Congeners program, the code intended to design new drugs. Pick a molecule, drop it into the computer's version of a Waring blender, chop it into pieces, and then rearrange and replace some parts to make new compounds. This had been Matt's baby. He had a working model up and running and ideas for an expanded version aimed at potential future clients.

The collection Matt called "Protein Programs" contains projects in the planning stages, and their functions aren't obvious. *The concept of a protein data bank I get, but what the hell is a FrgBag?* And after hearing Dr. Walker describe the technical challenges of the Origami program, why was Matt even thinking about attempting anything in that area. *I wonder if Dr. Walker even knows about any of this?*

The other two categories are also problematic. For starters, the "Other Programs" folder contains locked files that are inaccessible without passwords. Locked files within protected folders; what did Matt have that needed such security?

Roff stands for Recognition of Familiar Faces—but what does facial recognition software have to do with pharmacology? The most Henry can piece together is that Matt was toying with the idea that receptor recognition of drugs somehow resembled the way we recognize friends. As a metaphor, it's a fanciful idea; as a programming concept, it verges on the incoherent.

So what had happened to the man I met a few years ago, the guy who could create substantial pharmacology applications until he wandered off into non-assigned projects, bizarre speculations, and secret files? Perhaps the detectives are right, and there's another side to Matt I never saw.

Or maybe working at Janus Health had pushed Matt over the edge. The Janus institutional persona was schizophrenic enough, with a manic CEO who was indiscriminately passionate about everything and a chief scientist who seemed almost devoid of emotion. It was always Dr. Glover and Dr. Qu, never Matt and Henry, all formality and self-control and a life undisturbed by enthusiasms or passion. Matt had wondered aloud how Walker did it. "I'm not sure how long I could last in his world." *Perhaps the answer was "not long enough".*

But Matt is gone, and Matt's projects are now his. There are immediate concerns he needs to address. He'll study the congeners first; he can get up to speed on those programs quickly. Dr. Walker will tell him when he wants Henry for Origami, but there's no need to be as scattered about it as Matt had been. RoFF is unlikely to go anywhere, and his 'protein programs' are not a priority. And whatever is in the locked files will remain out of reach unless someone discovers the passwords. *Let sleeping dogs lie.*

That leaves a few remaining files that aren't password-protected. Many of those cover aspects of game theory. There's also a collection of modifications and variations for a program called *STUD*. That rings a bell. *What was the story Matt had told him about some stupid scheme a classmate had cooked up? Something to do with playing poker with computers. But why was Matt continuing to work on that program now?*

FIFTY

Kevin sits glaring at his phone. Matt's LUDs show that he'd made multiple calls to this number, often on weekends. But Kevin's calls go to voicemail and are not returned. Reverse phone lookup produced no results, and Andy Enright has left no social media trail. That's unusual, but it's not enough to compel a carrier to provide him with what he wants. *This is crap.*

Kevin punches redial, and this time someone answers.

"Hello, I'm trying to reach Andy Enright."

"This is Andy."

"I'm Inspector Kevin Loeffler with the San Francisco Police Department. We're investigating the death of Matthew Glover. I understand you knew him?"

"Yes, I read about Matt's death in the Chronicle and am remembering him in my prayers."

"I would appreciate anything you could tell me about Matt, even if it doesn't seem important. When can we talk?"

A momentary pause. "Would 9 PM tonight be too late for you, Inspector?"

"No, that would be fine. Where can we meet?"

"I'm in San Mateo; I'll be at 100 Ellsworth Avenue."

"100 Ellsworth in San Mateo at 9 tonight; I'll be there."

Franklin is standing by his desk as Andy Enright hangs up. "He's ready for us."

Sergeant Ortega sits with his chair tilted back against the wall and raises both arms in mock supplication as Franklin and Kevin sit down. "So tell me, people, where are we in this investigation?"

We could get this over in a hurry if he'd just lean back a little more. "I checked this morning. The doctors expect Carter will be able to answer questions in a day or two. He's still good for this as the third partner in the jealousy triangle."

"A better suspect than Henry Qu," Kevin points out.

Ortega makes a face. "Damn Janus lawyer already sent me a letter. Since you guys managed not to get anything useful on him, I'm up shit creek on that one. So what do we do when your next pet suspect craps out tomorrow?"

Kevin clears his throat. "I'm meeting tonight with a friend of Matt's who has a long drug history. They spent time together on weekends. This looks like another senseless drug-related killing."

"Any evidence that Matt was dealing?"

"None yet. But my guy is into psychedelics, so I wouldn't assume that rational thought governs his actions at all times."

"What's his name? Let's go pick him up."

"Grounds?"

"Possession with intent to distribute, for starters."

"We don't have evidence of either, Mike."

"And what's the likelihood that will change if you show up at his door unannounced? Pretty much 100%, I'd say."

"Arrest them, and the evidence will appear. You expect a judge to buy that?"

"Who the hell are you working for anyway, Washborne, the SFPD, or the ACLU? We're supposed to be in the business of busting bad guys despite the lawyers' best efforts to fuck things up. And you two have done a piss-poor job of doing that. Now one of you two is going to produce an arrest, and soon, or there's going to be hell to pay."

Kevin looks at Franklin. "I think that's our cue to leave."

FIFTY-ONE

"So where has our friend Andy been hanging out?"

"San Mateo. I just got off the phone with him. We're meeting tonight."

"You want some backup?"

"I didn't get a bad vibe off him."

"Famous last words. They'll look good on your gravestone."

"Don't take my word for it. He didn't ring any alarm bells for Maggie Chadwick or Henry either."

Franklin considers this, and Kevin takes advantage of the pause. "Speaking of drugs, I'm still puzzled by Carter's accident. Was he on anything?"

"Nothing except booze, according to his tox screen."

"A Saturday night traditionalist. Makes you wonder what sort of sorrows he wanted to drown."

"We'll have to hear it from the horse's mouth. Like a lot of Inner Truth's members, Carter just drifted in; I wonder how well anyone there knows him. Ortega's right; there's an awful lot we don't know, despite the interviews."

"Hey! Recite some affirmations or something. I don't agree that we've been the idiots Mike thinks we are." Kevin tries to look affronted.

"I made a mistake in assuming there were reasonable people in Carl's family. If this was a bunch of gangbangers, I wouldn't have wasted five seconds listening to them. They're well-heeled and college-educated, but this responsible hedonism stuff sounds like self-serving BS to me. Hogs at the trough."

Franklin's surprised by his own vehemence, and Kevin looks taken aback.

"So your theory is that it's not about jealousy, but just plain selfishness? 'I'll take what I want; you get in my way and I'll kill you'?"

"Yeah, though that may be a distinction without a difference."

170

"I dunno; jealousy feels like it's a special type of greed." Kevin hesitates. "I know I sounded like a smartass when I said jealousy was a het thing. But for me, the whole 'You belong only to me' thing hasn't come up. I guess it could be because I've never expected anything more than one-nighters and quickies, anyway. Since I met Gary, I'm noticing little tugs of possessiveness. I can't see myself killing anyone over a guy, but it got me thinking. What if I've been doing some sort of 'If you don't stick around long you can't get rejected' thing?"

I haven't seen you this serious before. You're funny and sarcastic and flamboyant—pretty much what I expect a gay guy to be like. And I've been content to leave it at that, without bothering to ask why my new partner is always in performance mode. It's a lot easier just to sit around passing judgment on commune members and responsible hedonism and guys who know too much about the White Party.

Franklin takes a deep breath. "Listen. Sometimes listening to myself makes me wonder who that judgmental asshole who's sounding off is, so let me try again. I have nothing against pleasure or sex or personal freedom; I just don't see a lot of freedom at Inner Truth. It's all about bullying and manipulation and at least one arrogant bastard taking advantage of women who aren't sure what they want. A lot of deception and self-deception goes on there, and that makes them all potential suspects in my book."

"I still hope I'm right because solving a drug-related case should be a lot simpler than diving into that morass."

"Which Andy Enright used to call home in the 'freewheeling days'. So please think about some backup?"

"Andy seemed pretty skittish; I think low-key will work best. You go home and take a night off."

"OK, I admit I'm being a pain in the ass. But you know for yourself; every interaction is unpredictable. Henry and Maggie are nice people, but how well do they know Andy? And even if they did, what would that tell you about how he'll act when confronted?"

"OK, now you sound like Ortega. I haven't forgotten what it's like to be on patrol and get called to a domestic dispute that goes south. But those are disasters looking for a place to happen; this is just an initial sit-down."

"... With a druggie who you suspect may be a murderer."

"This guy's no drug kingpin; he's just another stoner. If he killed Matt, it was because he was hallucinating, and it was an accident."

"You don't know that."

"No, I don't. What I know is that a lot of police work is routine stuff and not all about the Adventures of Junior G-Man Kevin. I don't buy that crap from the guy on *Police One*: 'Everyone is sizing us up, so remain humble and compassionate and have a plan to kill everyone you meet'. And when I hear guys at the cop bars talk about all the assholes out there, I'm pretty sure that would include most of my friends. And I'm damn sure they wouldn't join me at the bars I like. So yeah, I'll use my good judgment, but don't ask me to join the Thin Blue Line Paranoia Brigade."

Franklin leans back. "I'm not questioning your judgment. Just stay safe."

"Thanks. I appreciate you saying that. I won't do anything stupid, I promise. Now go home and get psyched for tomorrow. I'm hoping we'll have suspects to interview and even some red meat to throw to our lead investigator."

"You sound downright optimistic."

"Like I said, I think we've done a good job. One of these two is our culprit, or else this was just a stupid random thing that's not gonna ever get solved. Either way, the end's in sight."

He's almost at the door when he turns to Franklin again. "Besides, this one's still way simpler than the Case of the Disappearing Drowned Man."

FIFTY-TWO

He takes Kevin's advice and heads home early. The cats are reproachful but accept a can of Fancy Feast Savory Salmon Paté as a peace offering. A shower, a change of clothes, a quick check of e-mails that can wait, and he's on his way back to the Mission.

If it's possible, Elizabeth's apartment is even more awash with papers. Before he can ask, she hands him a drink. "So how did things go with the investigation today?"

"Oh, fine. Carter's still in a coma, Kevin's gone off to meet a drug-addled homicide suspect, and Ortega's threatening to get us both busted back to foot patrol. Just another day at the office."

"Is it just me, or has everyone around you gone crazy?"

"No idea. Sometimes things just get into people."

It takes about three seconds for her to dig out a pillow to throw at him. "You're terrible, although you may have a point. Today was full of little surprises along with one biggie in *l'affaire Montfort*."

"Did you and your producer see Mr. Jackson today?"

"Yes, and that's not all. After I called Glen yesterday, he called Mr. Jackson and told him your theory. Then he raced down to Santa Barbara, but Mr. Jackson had already cut into the backing on the picture."

"Walt a minute. You said you wouldn't tell Glen our theory."

"I wasn't going to, but he beat it out of me with a rubber hose."

"Always a favorite interrogation technique. So, Mr. Jackson opened the frame, and?"

She smiles triumphantly. "There were papers tucked in behind the painting. They looked old, so he didn't want to handle them. He also had the good sense to keep Glen at arm's length; for a senior citizen, Arthur can be surprisingly forceful."

"So he found something, but we're not sure what?"

"But not for lack of trying. This morning an army of KQXR staffers descended on Santa Barbara. Glen brought a camera crew and wanted to film a re-enactment of the discovery. He also wanted me to drag you down there as 'the detective who cracked the case'. I had to remind him you're a detective in real life, not just someone who plays one on TV."

"Thank God for small favors."

"I don't know who pulled what strings, but someone also got hold of a curator who knew about handling historic documents. I guess it may be because we're an NPR affiliate. With his help, we extracted the pages intact and got them photographed. Mr. Jackson wants to contact the UCSB Humanities and Fine Arts Library and ask them to evaluate them. That was my day."

"Sounds strenuous. How are you holding up?"

"I'm tired. I don't know whether I'm happy or disappointed by all this. It threatens to change the entire tenor of my show. Besides, what will I do for an encore?"

"I understand your dilemma. But why do I think you're not telling me everything?"

A giggle. "I have to keep reminding myself just what a good interrogator you are. When we got back to Mariposa Street, I asked for copies of the pictures they'd taken. I needed to decide how I was going to fit them into the program. Glen is still trying to track down a handwriting expert, but the Stevenson Museum in St. Helena isn't open on Mondays, and they're the people who have actual samples of Stevenson's handwriting. Otherwise, we'll need somebody at Yale or the Morgan Library in New York."

"So, absent a local expert, what did Clever Betsy do next?"

That earns him another pillow aimed at his head before she walks over the computer and holds up a thumb drive. "These are the copies of what was behind the painting. I've played with the contrast because the ink has faded. Have a look and then compare them with what's on this website. There are multiple sheets, and you can enlarge the images."

Franklin peers at the two windows open on the desktop. Each displays pages written in a regular hand. He studies them for several minutes.

"I'm no expert, but I don't see a big difference between the two samples. That doesn't mean a good forger couldn't have created Mr. Jackson's finds. I take it that someone has authenticated one of these as an example of Stevenson's handwriting?"

"The one on the left is the manuscript copy of *Jekyll and Hyde* Stevenson sent to his publisher. For reasons known only to itself, the Morgan Library has published it online. I thought they look alike. Besides, why would Belle Field give someone a forged manuscript? She had so many originals that she gave away random pages as Christmas presents."

"Have you read this?"

"Yes. The handwriting isn't difficult, and I practiced with the Morgan *Jekyll*. What we're looking at is a story about a doctor who invents a new treatment. It's the same story Mr. Jackson recalls hearing, with a few extra details. In the sketch, Montfort discovers the secret ingredient for his universal antidote at Woodward's Gardens. The story breaks off just as the doctor decides to try it on a patient."

"Woodward's Gardens?"

"A combination amusement park, garden, and zoo in the Mission District during the late 1800s. Woodward was a friend of Virgil Williams, the director of the San Francisco School of Design where Fanny and Belle studied."

"Talk about a small world."

"Louis included local details in his first draft. I feel good about having this in the program; it's a genuine piece of San Francisco history."

"So the *Lost Tales* episode will feature an actual lost tale. Sounds like a win to me. Congratulations."

"Thank you. But I have to tell you: I'm more excited about the other papers."

"A second lost tale?"

"Not exactly."

"So, are you going to tell me, or do I have to get my rubber hose?"

FIFTY-THREE

"The second document is a letter Stevenson started but never finished or sent."

"It must have something pretty interesting in it to make you like it more than the new story."

"I think it shows where Stevenson got the idea for a character in a story he did complete."

"Don't a lot of writers create characters based on people they know?"

"Yes, and it's a marvelous way to lose friends. The rule is you pick the salient characteristics, not the person; it's something we practice in my writing classes. Long John Silver had the physical characteristics of a friend of Stevenson's, but his villainous personality was pure invention."

"Stevenson had a one-legged friend?"

"Treated by Dr. Lister himself."

"So the inventor of Listerine went around treating pirates?"

"Will you stop! Henley wasn't a pirate; he was the author of *Invictus*— you know,

I am the master of my fate:
I am the captain of my soul."

"I never knew you were such a Stevenson expert."

"I'm not. He's always been part of the *Literary SF* tours, but I've had to brush up on Stevenson factoids for the program. We like to pose 'Did you know?' questions in between segments."

He gets up from the computer and walks back to the littered coffee table. "For the last couple of years, I've spent my life looking for people who kill other people. Before that, I was chasing kidnappers and drug dealers. I'd almost forgotten there's a world of normal people out there who read poetry. A lot of the people I deal with have never read a book cover to cover. And I don't mean just criminals. I can hear Mike Ortega now. *'Haven't seen*

176

you at any cop bars, Frank; whaddya been doin' when your shift's up?' 'Been discussing Victorian inspirational poetry by a guy with one leg, Mike'."

"I'm sorry. I've gotten so wrapped up in this episode that Fanny and Louis almost seem more alive than the people I'm working with at KQXR."

"That's because you leading a normal life. Just this afternoon, I had to remind Kevin that the guy he's interviewing tonight could turn homicidal. I need more contact with your world if I'm going to avoid drowning in police-think. So tell me about—who was it?"

"The man mentioned in the letter was a sailor named Liam Cromartie. He told Louis the Montfort story, and I think Louis used him as the model for Gordon Darnaway, a madman who shows up in *The Merry Men*."

"A story about Robin Hood has a madman in it?"

"No. The 'Merry Men' are rocks. Darnaway can hear the voices of drunken men in the sound of the breaking waves. He's a superstitious religious fanatic who's also prone to hallucinations."

"Wait, this is the world of normal people?"

"Liam Cromartie was just an average uneducated man who believed that foreigners were heathens in league with the Devil."

"I take back what I just said about wanting more contact with your world."

"Or Mr. Stevenson's, which was full of people like the ones you arrest and work with and we know...and like us. In some ways, you and he think alike. He'd agree with your advice to Kevin."

"You're confusing me. Again."

"You just said you live in a world where everyone may be a criminal. You're convinced I live in some innocent world full of creative literary types, both living and dead. The authors I like are engaging, but most of them had few illusions about people. Remember Long John Silver? He's the friendly guy who's also planning to lead a mutiny, steal a treasure, and murder everyone on board the ship. And this is a story Stevenson wrote for children."

"And after that, he writes a story about a madman—another kiddie's tale?"

"No, he intended it for adults. Nobody reads it, though, because the crazy character talks in an incomprehensible Scots dialect."

"Just like Cromartie?"

"I think so. That may be why he ended up telling Montfort's story to Louis. Nobody else would have been able to understand half of what he was saying."

"Then I'd suggest you omit the story of Cromartie and the drunken rocks unless your show's audience includes a bunch of people from the local Robbie Burns Club."

"Roger that. Now can we get something to eat? I'm hungry again."

FIFTY-FOUR

100 Ellsworth Avenue turns out to be the San Mateo Masonic Hall. Kevin arrives early and parks across the street. Just after nine, seven or eight people walk down the double set of front steps. One of them stops and sits on the side of the upper flight.

The San Mateo Masonic Hall

Franklin has nothing to worry about; Andy Enright is five foot five and perhaps one hundred thirty pounds. His close-cropped hair is pale blond or prematurely gray, and his features are almost elfin. He sits with his palms on his knees, eyes closed.

179

"Good evening, Mr. Enright. I'm Inspector Kevin Loeffler from the San Francisco Police Department. As I mentioned this morning, we're investigating the death of Matthew Glover."

A pair of blue eyes examine Kevin with mild curiosity. "Good evening, Inspector." He gestures to the step beside him. "I'm afraid this is the best I can offer as a seat unless you'd prefer the lawn. But I imagine you'll want to talk here, under the light."

Kevin sits on the stairs next to Andy and stretches his legs. Aside from an occasional passing car, the street is empty. "There was a function here tonight?"

"The regular Monday meeting of the San Mateo Zen Community. We're part of the Pacific Zen Institute. We also hold events at the Santa Rosa Creek Zen Center, in case you're interested. It's Rinzai Zen." A pause. "As opposed to Soto Zen, the practice at the San Francisco Zen Center."

"Thank you for the clarification. You're a Buddhist, Mr. Enright?"

"A practitioner. Still a beginner on the path."

"Was Matt Glover a practitioner?"

"No, at least not yet. I sensed an awareness of the natural world in him that might have provided a path to the Dharma."

"What was your connection with Matt?"

"I met him at the Inner Truth commune. I had been a member years ago, and I drop by sometimes to look at my past with my present eyes. There is a mindset among the members I still recognize in myself and seeing that can be a useful exercise in mindfulness. Matt drew my attention because he seemed..." He pauses, searching for words. "... In a liminal space, one foot here and one foot still in his previous life."

He makes a wry face. "My path at the commune had been quite different. I dived in headfirst and spent several years trying to convince myself I could swim underwater without ever needing to come up for air."

"And you suspected he might do the same?"

A smile. "Buddhist practice hasn't made me clairvoyant. We view not knowing as a natural state of affairs. I just went over to him and asked him where he was."

"And what was his answer?"

Another smile. "It's not a question whose answer we can express in words. It took me a while to make clear what I was asking. Our conversation confirmed that Matt was in transition. His assumptions about the world and life were springing leaks, but he seemed uncertain whether the commune's answers would be any more satisfactory. That can be disorienting, but also liberating."

"Forgive me for being frank, Mr. Enright, but in my line of work, people who enjoy the confusion of others sometimes turn out to be predators."

"Yes, that would be your world, Inspector. Have you read the *Dhammapada*?"

"I'm afraid not."

"'All that we are arises with our thoughts; with our thoughts, we create the world.' That's not a literal translation, but I find it a comprehensible one. In my life, losing the labels and not knowing who you are can be useful. When someone asked the Buddha who he was, he answered, 'I am awake'."

Way too much acid for too many years, dude. Do you even remember why I'm here? "May I ask what you and Matt talked about?"

"He said he enjoyed hiking, and I could feel the earth energy in him, so I asked if he had ever been to Point Reyes, which can be a koan in itself."

"Point Reyes is your koan?"

"No, my current koan is 'Stop the fighting on the other side of the river'."

"Oh. That's interesting. I'm sorry I have to ask, but Carl Holton said that you had been into drugs. We know you've had a couple of drug arrests."

A slight nod. "At one time, I thought I could find what I was looking for through acid, and then through commune life. Those were unskillful means that I put aside once I set my foot on this path. But then, they say the practice is always the last house on the block."

"So you no longer use or sell drugs?"

"Not in years."

"Was Matt into drugs?"

"No, not at all. Unless you consider his addiction to computers."

"No sir, I was speaking of illicit substances of abuse."

"As was I, Inspector." He closes his eyes. "We went hiking at Point Reyes. Andy's body was there, but not his full awareness. So we tried a little mindfulness practice. I took him to the tunnel of cypress trees at the Point and asked him to close his eyes. 'In a moment, I'll ask you to open your eyes and just see. No conditions, no interpretations; just be the seeing itself.' That's a path to awakening, bringing the present moment to life and living in it, seeing things for what they are. 'You are a computer scientist; you use computers to solve problems. But your life is not a problem to be solved'."

"How did Matt respond to all of this?"

"He seemed puzzled but receptive, or at least curious, an interesting reaction from someone I had expected to be entrenched in Engineer's Mind."

"Did he talk about anything that was bothering him?"

"No, though knowing the commune, I could imagine the interactions and conflicts he might have encountered."

"We're looking for concrete motivations for homicide: jealousy, betrayal—things like that."

"Those do arise and increase suffering in the world, but there have been no deaths at the commune. Matt seemed to be aware of the basic unsatisfactoriness of transient events—the First Noble Truth. My impression was that any interpersonal challenges the commune had created for him were less unsettling than whatever made him question his concept of himself as a scientist."

"What do you mean?"

Andy shrugs. "From the little he said, I felt it might involve an issue that violated some core value, or something over which he had no control. But he never went into any detail."

"So you think you may have caught him at a time of change in his life?"

"Perhaps so, though awakening is always only a half breath away. I do not know what karmic debts he might have accumulated."

There's a brief silence before Kevin stands. "Thank you for taking the time to speak with me, Mr. Enright."

"I am known as Hokashi now. Have an awakened evening, Inspector."

Kevin walks back to the car, contemplating the demise of his drug theory. *I wonder what the Masons would make of an acid-head Buddhist sitting on their steps.* Andy Enright may have pickled his brain and exchanged one escapist activity for another, but he had no obvious reason to kill Matt Glover.

Fort Point

FIFTY-FIVE

Elizabeth has drifted off to sleep, still pressed against him. Franklin lies awake, listening to the light rain pattering on the roof of the building's entry. It's a soothing sound, and he's content just to lie there. Somewhere in the distance, dripping rain is echoing in an enclosed space.

The Golden Gate Bridge arches over the west end of Fort Point, rain cascading from its undergirding. The pavers of the central parade ground are wet and treacherous. In the intervals between blasts of the foghorn, he can hear someone shouting. The man seems to be somewhere in the brick casemates above him near the east spiral staircase. Who would be in the fort at this hour?

He crosses the parade ground, but the door to the staircase is locked. Whoever the screamer is, he's on the upper level now; incomprehensible words echo off the brick walls. He climbs the open stairs by the officer's quarters and peers into the darkness and the repetition of brick arches. Somewhere someone has struck a light.

Searing heat and dense smoke radiate from the burning Humvee. His ears are still ringing and he's having trouble hearing. Someone grabs his shoulder, pointing to the Humvee. "Shoot him! Shoot him, Goddammit! Don't let him burn!"

He can see an infantryman trapped in the burning wreckage trying to raise his arm. But Franklin's frozen in place; he can't feel the weapon in his hands. Then someone nearby is shouldering an M4. He hears a volley of shots, and the man in the burning Humvee stops moving.

No, he's sitting on the edge of the bed in an apartment on 20th Street in the Mission District of San Francisco, awake and drenched in sweat. The attack in Kandahar is fading, and the shouting man at Fort Point is also gone.

Franklin waits for his pulse to slow before attempting to stand. There's a familiar flickering at the corners of his visual field; luckily, the current bottle

184

of Advil Migraine is almost full. He fumbles for his pants and heads for the kitchen, where he washes two down with a glass of water.

He can see the glow of his cell phone on the computer table, though he doesn't remember leaving it there. The picture gallery is open to the photos he took of Myra's journal. As he walks back to the cluttered love seat, the phone illuminates the books on the coffee table. The top one is *Robert Louis Stevenson: A Life.* The dust jacket shows a group of people on a veranda.

In Samoa

The men in front appear to be Polynesian. Behind them, a man with a parrot on his shoulder leans against a post. Next to him is an elderly woman wearing a Victorian widow's cap. But it's the two figures in the center of the second row that catch his attention. A thin man with long hair and a drooping mustache sits with his arms crossed. Beside him, a short woman with dark hair and a steely gaze sits with her hand pressed against her right cheek.

The biography contains more pictures, including a painting of the same man pacing and tugging at his mustache. The caption reads *Robert Louis Stevenson by John Singer Sargent, Bournemouth, 1885.*

It takes Franklin only a few seconds to leaf through the remaining photographs. He finds two of Fanny Stevenson that match the ones on his phone. Below a third is a portion of a letter:

She runs the show… handsome waxen face like Napoleon's, insane black eyes, boy's hands, tiny bare feet, a cigarette…. Hellish energy…. Is always either loathed or slavishly adored. The natives think her uncanny and the devils serve her. Dreams dreams, and sees visions.

The photograph is labeled *Mrs. Robert Louis Stevenson, from a photograph by Hollinger, London.* Gazing calmly out at him is the woman he saw in the window on Hyde Street.

As he sits holding his discoveries, Elizabeth comes to sit beside him. "Are you having trouble sleeping?"

"Just a dream. I was walking around in the rain at Fort Point; then I woke up with a headache. The Advil seems to be kicking in."

She looks at the book in his lap. "I'm sorry I don't have any other reading material. My life has been pretty monothematic these past few weeks."

"After hearing so much about them, it's nice to see what your friends looked like." He puts the book down. "Do you have any pictures of Nora May?"

"Yes, she's in my book. I can get it. Do you want coffee?"

"That would be great. Caffeine is good for migraines."

Among the pages of *San Francisco Bohemia,* he finds the familiar images.

"She was quite attractive." Elizabeth is looking over his shoulder.

"We found copies of these photos in Myra's journal."

"The formal portrait is by Arnold Genthe. He was quite a well-known photographer in San Francisco."

"We had inventoried the journal as property. When I looked at it again on Saturday, things had changed. These were the pictures I found instead." He shows Elizabeth his phone.

She stares at him. "But why would someone put Fanny's portraits in Myra's journal?"

"And who. No one else checked the journal out between the time I logged it in and when I read it on Saturday. And the evidence room is secure."

She goes to the kitchen and brings back two cups of coffee. "Sherlock Holmes was the world's greatest detective, and Conan Doyle was an ardent believer in spiritualism. That's the only connection I know of between crime-solving and contact with the Great Beyond. So you're breaking new ground here. First, you see Fanny on Hyde Street after Matt's murder. "

"If that was Fanny, I didn't just see her. She saw me—and waved."

"Everyone said she had an eye for good-looking young men. And when you open Myra's journal, she pops up again, displacing poor Nora May. I'd say it's pretty obvious she has a thing for you.

"I'm not that young."

"You're younger than her. She was born in 1840."

"You're telling me I saw a dead woman flagging me down after we found Matt's body, and then she put pictures of herself in a journal after Myra's death? An erotic haunting? I can't believe that we're sitting here at 1 AM having this conversation."

FIFTY-SIX

Elizabeth smiles sweetly. "Your romantic life is your affair, and I'm not trying to tell you how to run it. Though I have some ideas of my own on the subject."

"OK, Ms. Sherlock, what connection would there be between a murder, a suicide, and Fanny Stevenson? Was she connected with the Carmel Bohemians?"

"No. After years in Europe and Samoa, Fanny didn't have many literary associations here. The only American writer she knew in California was Frank Norris."

"This is ridiculous. The woman I saw in that house couldn't have been Fanny Stevenson. Maybe no one was there. What if this is all some late effect of head injury?"

"That thought occurred to me. But all you have is headaches; your cognitive skills are unimpaired. And a head injury wouldn't explain how those photos got switched. I don't understand what's going on, but I doubt you're hallucinating."

"Because hallucinations are your area of expertise?"

"Well, I did once lead a seminar on Oliver Sacks' book on hallucinations. *Literary San Francisco* stuff again; Dr. Sacks is a well-known author who interned in town here at Mt. Zion Hospital."

"Of course he did. Why didn't I think of that?"

"And why should there be any plan behind these appearances? Fanny never stayed put for long. Who knows; she may still enjoy roaming the world to make appearances at random."

"As does her husband. I saw someone who looked very much like this"—he points to the book cover—"at the parking garage at 450 Sutter, and I saw him again Saturday night on Bush Street. Do dead couples always haunt in pairs?"

"Ghosts often appear in locations where they once lived, so Hyde Street and Bush Street would make sense. Of course, you'd have to accept that there are ghosts traipsing around the city."

"Have you met anyone else who has experiences like this? I still think it's more likely that I'm going nuts."

"And I don't. I admit I haven't *seen* these people, but I have *felt* their presence. My original plan, long before the whole 'missing stories' thing, was to create an episode about Louis and Fanny's multi-continent courtship. I wanted to use some of his love poems until I read them. They sounded more Victorian dutiful than passionate, so I chucked the idea."

"I was leading a tour on Bush Street a few weeks later. We passed the tattoo parlor, and I mentioned Stevenson had lived nearby. The tour came alive with questions; people could almost see Fanny rushing to her sick lover. I knew then and there that a Stevenson program would work, insipid poetry be damned."

"Because of the aura of a building that isn't even there? So you believe all this New Age woo-woo? "

"All I know is how people responded and what they felt." She pauses and sips her coffee. "I've read police procedurals where someone solves the case when he realizes what he's been missing. Does that happen in real life?"

"It's a sort of sixth sense about something being out of place that you acquire if you're lucky. If you don't, you may not last long."

"So humor me. You've described a bunch of occurrences that feel 'out of place'. What would your Inner Detective's response be?"

Franklin considers the question for a moment. "I'd develop a theory that would explain the anomalies. An obvious one: this must be some sort of scam. The question is who's running it, and how is he using these 'ghosts' to rip somebody off?"

"Would leaving a dead body in front of Fanny's house affect property values?"

"The people living on Lombard Street think so. I'm told condos there go for three or four million."

"The current asking price for Fanny's house is fifteen million."

He raises his eyebrows. "'Return to Treasure Island' anyone?"

"Someone at the network once asked me for a list of locations where authors featured in the episodes had lived." She flashes him a wry smile. "You know, just in case any realtors wanted to become sponsors."

"So the Stevensons are trying to cash in on the current real estate market?"

"Stop! I'm trying to take you seriously! You said to follow the money, and in San Francisco, it's in real estate. Any other theories?"

"Someone's gaslighting me, trying to convince me I'm going crazy."

"Is there anyone on the force that you suspect might try to do that?"

"No; cops aren't that subtle."

"OK, what else?"

"Nothing, except that this could be somebody's stupid prank that they're going to post on YouTube or their Facebook page. Your turn now: if this were a novel you were writing..."

Elizabeth closes her eyes. "The typical ghost story involves malevolent spirits or the shades of people who still have unfinished business. The Stevensons don't fit that description; they seem quite benign. A story about ghosts just cruising the city would be boring, so in my novel, Louis and Fanny would be trying to get your attention. The next question is 'Why?'"

FIFTY-SEVEN

"Damn, you're good! I can see the headline now. 'A Voice from Beyond the Grave Helps SFPD Solve Crimes!'."

Elizabeth has returned with coffee refills and peers over the rim of her cup at him. "In literary circles, when we speak of an author's message, we're referring to a theme that recurs in his works."

"So Stevenson had a theme? Did it also involve Fanny? Please don't tell me she's the one who wrote the novels."

She laughs. "They tried writing one book together; it wasn't a success. But she read and critiqued everything he wrote."

"Which is why they're still joined at the hip now?"

"They were inseparable in life. And she certainly influenced his output; his writing changed after he married her."

"Porn instead of soppy Victorian love lyrics?"

"Don't make me hit you again. Before 1880, Louis was a feckless young writer cranking out stylish lightweight travel essays. After he got married, he changed course. His stories are full of danger and treachery—*The Body Snatcher, The Merry Men, Treasure Island*. And he continued in that vein thereafter."

"A peculiar response to marital bliss. 'Life is good, so let me tell you about murderous pirates and crazy uncles and doctors who concoct potions to turn themselves into monsters'."

"You're thinking of the Hollywood version, but *Jekyll and Hyde* is a good example of Fanny's editing. We can all recall things we've been tempted to do when no one is watching. In Jekyll's case, he decides to use Hyde as his disguise to avoid getting caught. But Fanny found that storyline too pedestrian and made Louis rewrite it."

"What did he change?"

191

"In the revised version, Jekyll is obsessed with propriety. He wants to excise all his wayward impulses, split them off and stuff them into an alternative persona."

"So his behavior will be beyond reproach."

"No such luck. Stevenson was a Calvinist. All men are sinners, so it's never possible to be completely good, no matter how hard you try."

"Given the people I deal with, I'd say that's a reasonable first assumption."

"Does that include you and me?"

He remembers the dream—no, the flashback—that awakened him. "You never can tell."

She raises an eyebrow. "Stevenson is clear that Jekyll isn't a bad person. He's overly fastidious and too concerned with other people's opinions—your average upper-class Victorian. For Louis, Jekyll's minor failings are significant only because they're evidence of everyone's capacity for wrongdoing."

"Sounds a little like Broken Windows Theory."

"I don't know what that is. Have you ever heard of a 1950s sci-fi movie called *Forbidden Planet?*"

"Nope; I'm a *Star Trek* guy, but only the original episodes, please."

"In the movie, a scientist becomes annoyed when some astronauts land on his planet and start hitting on his daughter. Later, an invisible alien attacks the astronauts. The creature turns out to be a projection of the scientist's unacknowledged rage. The script calls it a 'monster from the Id'."

"Very Freudian. You also teach sci-fi?"

"I teach writing; I don't choose genres for my students. Henry Jekyll's worst failing is a desire to cut loose a little. But he decides that's too unseemly to acknowledge or tolerate. Stevenson argues that we can never eliminate those impulses, and people who insist on denying them may be potential tinderboxes. His stories feature reasonable people who are also capable of dishonesty, cruelty, vengefulness, or murder under the wrong circumstances. If he had a message about human existence, that would be the one I'd look for."

He takes a deep breath. "So, who's going to pop up next? Scrooge and his three ghosts?"

"Wrong famous British author, dear. I realize I see everything through the lens of what friends call my literary ivory tower. I'm surprised that my enthusiasm doesn't seem to bother you."

"It's because I take you seriously—all of you. But I'm still not sure why dead people are helping me solve a case."

"Not because you need them; you're a fine detective in your own right."

"And one who's may wake up any minute and realize this is all just some weird dream."

"Sorry, you're not allowed that out."

"Why not?"

"How many times have I told my students that 'And then I woke up and realized it was all a dream' is a terrible plot device?"

"Yes, teacher. I'll try to remember that."

FIFTY-EIGHT

Dr. Walker looks up from the monitor and nods his approval. "Very good, Dr. Qu. You appear to have grasped the essentials of our approach to the Congener Program. I'm confident you'll be able to continue to expand the program even though you are new to this."

"Thank you, sir. I'm fortunate to be building on the foundation you and Matt laid down. I hope my contributions won't prove a disappointment."

"Always the faithful friend and roommate; loyalty is a commendable virtue, Dr. Qu. As it happens, I agree with you. Dr. Glover did fine work." He watches for any reaction, but Henry's face remains a study in composure. *If he knows what was going on with Matt before he died, Henry Qu isn't about to share that information.*

"So I should continue developing the Expanded Congener Program? Most of the changes should be simple; increasing the program's capacity to access additional data sources and addressing a couple of issues around prioritizing."

"An opportunity to enhance the program's utility by an order of magnitude with a modest investment of effort. Dr. Atkinson always welcomes programs with the potential to attract a larger pool of clients."

"Yes, sir; I'm on it. I guess it makes sense to build a robust version of the expanded program and have it up and running before I tackle anything else."

Walker pauses for a few seconds before leaning forward almost conspiratorially in his chair. "Are you familiar with AtomNet?"

"No sir, I'm not."

He pushes a journal across the desk. "It's a convolutional neural network intended to predict the bioactivity of small molecules. The Congener program can design new structures, but that's of little use if we can't predict what they could accomplish as therapy."

Henry thumbs through the paper. "I can see I still have a lot to learn."

194

"One sign of a good AI researcher, Dr. Qu, is that the more he learns, the more he realizes how little he knows. Humility isn't a virtue in our field; it's a necessity. Your work on Congener will be a good start; then your task will be to make it design drugs that are both new and useful."

"That sounds daunting. Thank you for your faith in me."

"The result will be useful in itself and a necessary step for constructing the Receptor Program."

"Sir?"

"Computer modeling of drug-receptor interactions, Dr. Qu; what I suspect may be the most important step forward in pharmacology research in our lifetimes. Receptors are the structures to which pharmaceuticals bind. The Receptor program will be an exercise in reverse engineering. Drug development usually starts with an observation about a biological event. Fleming noticed the Penicillium mold halted the growth of bacteria. It took years to identify and produce the active agent in quantity and decades to establish a mechanism of action. What if we chose a receptor we want to target and then engineered a drug to fit it? Rather than trying a ring full of keys in a lock, let's study the lock's innards to deduce the shape of the key that will fit it."

"That sounds very ambitious, sir. I wouldn't know where to begin."

"The answer is Go."

"Excuse me, sir?"

"Go, Dr. Qu; the game created by your forebears."

"I am familiar with the game, but I'm still not sure I understand."

"Do you recall the stir when Big Blue won a chess competition? What made computer analysis of chess possible is the fact that the game has a limited number of pieces, each with a circumscribed set of permitted moves. Go has simpler rules, but the number of possible plays is immense. That's what makes it a challenging game, even for experts. To understand how to teach a computer to play Go, we need to understand how humans become adept at Go."

"Your smile suggests you have an answer, but I'm not qualified to venture a guess. As a Go player, I'm a total beginner."

"Not an answer, Dr. Qu; a procedural approach. People learn to play Go by playing Go, game after game. To teach the computer Go, we program in some basic rules, some recommendations on strategies, and examples of winning games. But the critical step is to have the computer play against itself repeatedly. Over thousands of games, the program will evolve its own style of play. Experience leads to knowledge and then to intuition, both in humans and in Deep Learning programs." He leans back and folds his hands. "And I would argue that an analogous approach is a key to problems of protein fine structure. The only difference is that the two players are now the drug and the receptor."

Stop; you hadn't intended to say this much. Henry needs to concentrate on the Congener Program, nothing else.

But Henry already has a question. "In chess and Go, the pieces are all visible, but is the same true of receptor molecules?" He hesitates. "Isn't this a version of an imperfect information game?"

"It could be. But I see Dr. Glover shared some of his ideas with you. I assume you're familiar with his poker fixation?"

"Yes, sir. I guess back in school, some of his classmates liked high-risk 'go for broke' gambling."

"That explains a good deal. There are valid mathematical techniques for dealing with imperfect information games, but I don't believe many gamblers use them. They prefer to put their faith in 'luck' and superstitions rather than the laws of probability. They also count on their ability to detect non-verbal cues from other players."

"A tell."

"Excuse me?"

"In poker, it's called a tell; some involuntary behavior that reveals what a player is attempting to hide."

"Ah! The phenomenon is common enough to have a name. And these tells—is their information content always obvious? Do players ever bluff by displaying a false tell? I'd guess the expression 'poker face' exists for a reason. No, Dr. Qu, there are too many untested assumptions in Dr. Glover's ideas. I'm afraid that relying on superstitions and luck won't help us much."

He stops and glances at his watch. "I'm sorry; I've been rambling. What I intended to say was that you're on the right track. We'll be taking baby steps for starters; crawl before you walk, and walk before you run. But I hope this gives you some idea of the scale of our future projects."

"Yes, sir. I'll remember that; walk before I run."

FIFTY-NINE

Franklin is on his third cup of coffee when Kevin drags himself to his desk.

"Late night?"

"Early morning. Some drunk was shouting at the top of his lungs around 2:30. Couldn't make out what he was saying; it almost sounded like a foreign language. I was about to call the cops until I woke up enough to remember that I am the cops. Grabbed a flashlight, but I couldn't see anyone in the courtyard or tell where the sound was coming from. Whoever it was finally quit." He yawns. "Strangest thing was that nobody else's lights were on, even though he was loud enough to wake up everybody in the complex."

"I think I know the guy. A sailor named Liam Cromartie."

"Friend of yours?"

"Never met him. He's been dead about a hundred years."

"Cool! How does that work?"

"It's a long story. It might be better to let Elizabeth explain it over lunch sometime."

Kevin grins. "Damn! You're finally doing this?

"Doing what?"

Kevin makes a face. "You and Elizabeth, I mean. Do you know how many times during this case I wanted to say, 'Dude! Whatever it is, I'll handle it; she's waiting for you!' "

Franklin stares at him. "Was it that obvious?"

"To everybody in the squad. Except you, I guess. But this Liam guy; does he have anything to do with our case? I'm assuming he's been yelling at you, too. Why else would he be pestering both of us? And what would a drunken sailor, dead or otherwise, want with Matt Glover?"

"Good question. But right now I'm interested in another drunk. The hospital called; Carter Albemarle is awake."

"Great! Paper, scissors, rock; loser has to call Ortega and tell him."

197

"Hate to disappoint you, but he's the one who told me; he's already on his way to the Trauma Unit."

"And he didn't invite you to come along? I get that I'm the reason Captain America hasn't already cracked the case, being a pervert and all. But you're supposed to still be in his good graces."

"Shows what you know. Let's both go over to the General. It'll annoy the hell out of him."

San Francisco General Hospital

"Good afternoon, Dr. Walker. This is Fred Willoughby. I'm taking Darryl's calls while he enjoys a little well-earned time off."

Now what? "How can I help you, Mr. Willoughby? I received a message from Darryl saying he had something important to discuss."

"It's more about how we can help *you*, Doctor. Our team has been reviewing the results that your program has been producing. We're *very* impressed. I'm told Darryl has already mentioned the research grant we established in your name."

"He referred to it, yes."

"We felt it an appropriate gesture of thanks. Since then, we've gained a greater appreciation of the program's productivity, and it seemed only reasonable to adjust the size of the grant. We're seeing results that are more sophisticated than those produced by our rather tentative first steps. Perhaps we've been too timid in our expectations. That's why we're making the grant incremental and contributions proportional to the results. I don't understand how you created this, or what you may have done to it since, but the results are gratifying."

"I've made no recent changes."

"Still, it seems to us its operation has improved."

"That would be expected with this form of Artificial Intelligence. The program can enhance its performance by learning as it goes."

"Quite remarkable! We had no idea."

"Deep Learning is an emerging technology, Mr. Willoughby, and none of us yet knows what the full potential of such programs could be."

"So it's possible it's still not maxed out even now?"

"I don't think there's any way to predict that, but it's conceivable. I appreciate your keeping me abreast of things, and of course your generosity as well."

"You've earned it, Doctor. And may I also say how sorry we all were to hear about your associate."

"My associate?"

"Yes, Dr. Glover. Have the police apprehended anyone?"

"Not to my knowledge, no."

"Well, let us pray for closure. Again, our thanks and congratulations, Doctor. Take care."

He should be elated by the news. *But how did Willoughby know Matt had been working for me? Could this be Grace's doing?* The grant might be a spontaneous gesture, but if there's money involved, Grace likely had a hand in it. *In any case, the call was just a pro forma expression of generic corporate sympathy.*

For all of his effusiveness, Darryl's flattery has always sounded empty. He and this Willoughby are clueless. They have no idea what the program does or can do. *Oh, we're so amazed by your work; we'd assumed you were just a lot of hot air. Like Atkinson, your CEO—and like us.*

Idiots. He'll check in on the program at some point, but there's no rush. At least Darryl is out of his hair for the moment.

SIXTY

They've moved Carter out of the ICU, and Ortega is already at his bedside. As expected, he doesn't look pleased to see them. "I've already read him his rights."

Kevin smiles approvingly. "Always a good icebreaker." Carter winces as he grins; Ortega looks even more pissed.

Franklin shoots Kevin a glance. They'd already discussed their strategy on the drive to the hospital. "We're assigned to the case, so he can't throw us out."

"That may not keep him from trying." Kevin closes his eyes. "I'm not sure I'm ready for another dose of the Ortega Interrogation Hour."

"Our role is to lend Carter enough support so that he can get his story out before Mike blows it. So please just chill, OK? I'd like to see Carter get an opportunity before Ortega trashes the interview by plugging one of us."

Ortega has developed a case of selective deafness this morning. He ignores Kevin and turns to Carter. "You've got a lot of questions to answer, my friend; you're in a shitload of trouble."

The cervical collar he's wearing muffles Carter's soft drawl. "Is that so? Because I wrecked my car after spending an evening with Jack Daniels? I heard you were the homicide squad, not the traffic detail." *We're just getting started, and this already sounds like an installment of Smokey and the Bandit.*

"Yes, Sergeant Washborne and Inspector Loeffler and I are from Homicide, and we're investigating the murder of Matt Glover. And that's where you come in. You can make this easy on yourself and tell us how it went down, and we'll let the prosecutor know you've been cooperative. It may help with the sentencing recommendation. Or we can do this the hard way: you can be a pain in the ass, and I'll sit here and ask the questions and get the answers my way."

"No, I don't think so. You're not going to be asking questions; you're going to sit there with your mouth shut and listen."

200

Despite himself, Ortega's mouth opens, and Franklin can hear his teeth click when it snaps shut again. *This isn't what Mike intended, especially with us here.*

Before Ortega can counter the challenge, Carter is talking again. "How well did you know Matt?"

"I never met him."

"Figures. Anyway, it didn't take me long to get that Matt's friends had always been people pretty much just like him. A nice guy from a conventional community, decent, well-behaved, brought up to always be polite—just like that Albemarle kid."

Franklin sits forward, elbows on his knees and chin on clasped hands. *Show some interest; keep him talking.*

"Always dated nice girls who lived in that same world with the same rules, everybody looking for a future that was going to be comfortable and secure. And so fucking bland that it makes you want to puke, or scream, or just cut loose. And do something that would at least let you know you're alive."

"So it's no surprise Matt assumed Myra was like all the other women he'd met, except I suppose he was used to more family-oriented ones. She's a writer and poet, and he has no fucking idea what that even means. She ends up in Carl's 'family' because she's hung up on some idea about writers' communes, though the one in her play sounds like it was a real clusterfuck. And Matt follows Myra to Inner Truth, even though he has nothing in common with the people there, except being the proud owner of a dick. She's the flame, and he's one dumb moth."

Ortega makes a face, looking bored. "What the hell does that mean?"

Kevin interrupts. "What he means is, 'How ya gonna keep 'em down on the farm?' Our boy Matt turns out to have been more amenable to Carl's ideas about responsible hedonism than anyone, including himself, had expected."

Ortega glares at Kevin again but stays quiet. *He's already figured out that it's three against one.*

Carter nods. "Carl's a total sleaze, but he's good at reading people and figuring out how to manipulate them. It didn't take him long to guess what buttons he could push with Matt. Bastard thought it would be funny to make sure Mr. Computer got some real-life experiences, just to see if he could fuck with Matt's head."

Here it comes. "So what did he do?"

"Twice a month, the commune has social evenings, a chance for everybody to get together and show where they're at in communal living. Carl made a point of inviting Matt. He said our boy should be ready 'to take it to the next level'. He was afraid Matt might not come, so he was super nice to Myra for a few days before."

"And you know this how?" Ortega sounds like he's about to lose it again.

"Because Carl told me himself. And unlike some of the selfish bastards around the commune, I gave a damn about Myra as a person. Of course, you never met her either, did you? I guess that's one advantage of being a homicide detective. You get to look at cases and theories without having to get involved with real live human beings."

Franklin tenses and glances at Kevin. *Please don't make us have to tackle Ortega because he's attacking a man who just got out of ICU.*

"Myra used to alternate between being a free spirit and being very needy. She wanted a community that could give her the emotional space she needed, and affection and support. Carl didn't get that. He likes to dress up fucking your brains out by calling it hedonism. The idea that for Myra, physical pleasure might be an add-on rather than the main event didn't compute."

"I liked Myra a lot, and I had a clearer idea of Myra's needs than even Matt had. Not that he wasn't a decent guy, but he was pretty conventional in his ideas before he got into the commune thing."

Ortega looks up. "So you're admitting that you liked Matt's girl. You thought she'd be better off with you than with him."

"What did I tell you about keeping your mouth shut? You want to learn something about Matt, then you listen to me instead of that 'Fun with Dick and Jane' tape you got running in your head."

Franklin is settling back in his chair. Despite his soft drawl, Carter is a commanding storyteller, and Ortega's body language says he knows he may not be able to control the flow.

"I could tell that Myra needed both Matt and me. Matt saw women as sexual partners who you treated politely. I dunno; I guess he liked computers better than people. Anyway, emotional intimacy wasn't his strong suit. I wanted Matt to see things from Myra's point of view. And Carl knew how I felt, so he made a point of telling me that Matt and Myra were both coming to Hospitality Night. He said I could help ease Matt into seeing how it could work for the three of us. He knew Myra liked us both, and he figured our boy might have some interest in me. And even if he didn't, it would still be fun to watch what Matt did when I came on to him."

"And you bought all that?" Ortega snorts derisively.

"Knowing Carl, I figured he was just bullshitting, like always. But I got a vibe off Matt when he was around the commune. He acted like a kid in a candy shop where all the bins are unlocked. It was obvious even to him just what kind of hospitality would be available that night; you'd have to be brain dead not to figure it out. But he still showed up."

Carter isn't big, but he's muscular and Southern charming. He's an alpha male in his way, the sort of guy Matt knew he was not. What did anyone think would happen when Matt found Carter and a bunch of women interested in him? Take one healthy male and one party loaded with sexual opportunities; his libido will provide all the means and motive any jury could want. That's our theory, Your Honor; case closed.

SIXTY-ONE

"So then what happened?"

"Myra and Matt came in together, but Matt still looked like he wanted to play observer. No surprise there; that's why I got picked to serve as his guide and fluffer. So I tried to give him permission to be himself, loving or playful or aggressive or whatever he was feeling at the moment. What I didn't know was that Carl had also helped things along."

"And how did he do that?"

"He'd dosed the refreshments with a shitload of Ecstasy."

"I supposed you understand that's an illegal drug, and drugging unsuspecting people is also a crime. If it had anything to do with Matt's death, then Carl or whoever can be charged with reckless endangerment. And I'll make sure you're named as an accessory."

"Sorry to disappoint you, Sergeant, but Matt left the party alive, and all your evidence has long since been flushed. In case you haven't already heard, we're all about responsible hedonism. If you're too damn arrogant and rigid to bother finding out what that means, that's on you."

"Keep going, cracker. Since you're OK with all this, I'm sure you're going to enjoy telling us all the slutty details."

Franklin intervenes. "I think I can listen without passing judgment. We're trying to find Matt's killer, and I'd appreciate anything you think might help us."

"Matt and the ladies were having a good time, so I went over to Myra and just held her for a while. She seemed like she'd been pretty down."

"And what did Matt do while you were feeling her up?"

Got to hand it to you, Mike; you never let go of your chosen approach, no matter how wrongheaded it is.

"Nice mouth you got on you, Sergeant. At first, he didn't even notice. I guess he was pretty well buzzed by then. When I came back and he saw Myra wasn't with me, it was like he was feeling guilty that he was enjoying himself without her. I told him that was the sort of mental programming we were trying to learn to overcome. Myra was free to engage or not, and so was he, as long as everything was consensual."

"Even if everybody was stoned? I've never heard so much bullshit in my life."

"You get off on this, Sergeant? You dig phone sex too, huh? Then you're gonna love this next part. The ladies and I invited Matt to a foursome, and he went for it. Just like that, boys and girls together. We had a real good time playing mix and match."

Ortega's disgust is palpable, but Franklin sits listening intently.

"People started splitting off as the party wore down. Matt was pretty out of it, so I helped him to bed."

"Alone or with Myra?"

Franklin can see the thought balloon over Kevin's head. *What the hell, Ortega; does he need to draw pictures?*

"Alone—I didn't see where Myra had gotten to. So it was just four of us, more or less, for what was left of the night. I was in the shower when Matt came to in the morning. He'd looked for Myra and couldn't find her, and then he realized how late it was and headed off to work. She must have shown up during the day because she was there when he came back that evening."

Kevin makes a sympathetic face. "How did that go?"

"I think he wanted to confront me. I just told him how much I admired him and how much I liked him. I understood Myra and was sure she wasn't angry with any of us. After all, she'd been a member here a lot longer than he had. But I didn't need to tell him that, because Myra showed up and told him herself. She wanted Matt's affection and his support for her literary efforts; those were more important than anything about who might sleep with who."

"And Matt?"

"Confused as hell. I think he wanted to blame me or tell me to go to hell or pop me one. He couldn't imagine Myra could be happy with either of us after what happened. The concept of poly-partnership as a way to meet multiple human needs wasn't part of his world."

"No shit!" Ortega is on his feet. "I ought to bust you right now!"

"You want to hear the rest or not?"

Ortega hesitates and then sits back down.

SIXTY-TWO

"Myra kissed Matt. She said she just needed some time to sort things out."

Kevin nods. "Sounds like she wanted time to process, not that she was bummed out. We know she'd been depressed; how was she after this?"

"A little more upbeat. Matt was worried she would disapprove of his participation in what was a regular commune activity. Myra expected he'd reject the family's acceptance of all forms of sexual pleasure and turn his back on her too."

"And why the fuck wouldn't he?" Ortega's Inner Cop is back. "You think this guy was going to risk his job by getting mixed up with a bunch of sickos like you? You just admitted that you lured him there under false pretenses and drugged him so you could use him for sex. That's called rape, asshole. You know what I think? I think you're a predator who gets off on seducing and humiliating people, and two people are dead because of you."

Is Ortega still expecting threats and righteous indignation to cow Carter?

"Have you heard anything I just told y'all? Myra lived in our group because she wanted to, and she also wanted Matt to be part of it. She was happy that he had come. She knew what happens at our get-togethers, and she wanted Matt to join in. Listen to me, troglodyte! Nobody's interested in your tired old tropes about the evils of free love. What do you think, we sit around wearing togas and peeling grapes? Hospitality Nights are about experiential learning."

Ortega snorts. "With the ladies?"

"Yes, with the ladies. And with the men. And with me. I think finding out much he enjoyed himself with us surprised Matt. Real-life experience was telling him that his opinions were bullshit, and it was time to wake up. It was like he had found a part of himself he hadn't known about."

"So he was bi."

Carter's expression makes it clear what he thinks of Ortega's formulations. "It's called ambivalence, Sergeant. Matt wasn't used to having anyone, female or male, enjoy him physically. It's possible to enjoy someone who's enjoying your physical being with no praise, no blame, and no shame. You don't understand any of this, but responsible hedonism includes feelings of warmth and genuine affection towards *all* partners, including yourself."

"And you want me to buy that? What you were feeling when you were shagging Matt that night was 'warmth and affection'? You make me want to puke."

"No, asshole. It wasn't generic warmth and affection I felt for Matt. I LOVED him."

His forcefulness takes Ortega by surprise. Carter turns to Franklin, whose face remains non-committal; Kevin flashes a look of understanding.

And that's why I would never have harmed him."

"Because of some perverted one-night stand?"

"It wasn't one night, or one week, for that matter." He shakes his head. "But you couldn't imagine that. You wouldn't recognize love if it came up and bit your scrawny ass—not that anyone would ever want to."

It's time to defuse things. "We never got to interview Myra, so we don't know her side of the story. I would imagine that in a small community like Inner Truth, someone else could confirm what you've told us. The sort of commitment you're describing would be hard for you to hide or for anyone to miss."

"I had no reason to conceal it. So ask anyone you want."

"Thanks, we'll do that."

Ortega glares at them both as if he can't believe what he's hearing. He hadn't lost control of the interrogation because he never had control of it. "We're not done here."

He stands and turns towards the door. Franklin and Kevin are already on the way out.

SIXTY-THREE

WEDNESDAY, SEPTEMBER 7, 2016

James Atkinson puts down the *Chronicle* and peers over his reading glasses at his Director of Marketing.

"I've scanned the Obituaries twice, and the only names I recognize are Phyllis Schlafly and Hugh O'Brian. Since Janus Health has no involvement with either the ERA or the old *Wyatt Earp* TV show, I assume I must be missing something."

"On the right, towards the bottom. Johannsen, Myra."

"Not a name I recognize. Did she work here?"

"She was Matt Glover's girlfriend. They're reporting she committed suicide."

"I'm sorry to hear that. Do we know anything more?"

"No. A few employees heard Matt mention her once or twice but never met her or saw them together. No one else knows anything about her."

"And the police? They don't see her death as connected with Matt Glover's murder? Not that they're making any headway with his case."

"I've seen nothing that says her death was anything other than a suicide. And as for Matt, it's the usual; they don't comment on active investigations."

"Which means they still have nothing solid. At least they've given up on Dr. Qu. You've done an excellent job with this, Theo; Matt's death is already yesterday's news. Chris Walker was fretting that there might be more to come. It looks like his fears were groundless."

"I hope so, though I got a call from someone at the *Examiner* asking if we had any comment."

"Any comment about what?"

"That was my reaction, too. Someone had told her that Matt knew Myra, but that's all she had. Sounds like she wanted to play investigative reporter."

"One with nothing to investigate."

"Yes; these are two separate and unrelated events."

"Then I don't think there's anything to worry about. But we need to monitor this—and Chris Walker."

"I'm not sure I understand."

He pushes the newspaper aside. "Chris is an intelligent man, but sometimes I think he should have stayed in his Ivory Tower. He has no street smarts and can worry himself to death over anything. I'm not confident about what would happen if an aggressive reporter got to him, and I don't want anyone to reignite the story. Send a memo to all staff and tell them to go through channels if anyone from the press contacts them."

"We could, although we reminded everyone during the grief counseling sessions." She pauses for a moment. "Another approach might be to put our name in the news with something that would change the topic."

"You've been putting out a steady stream of press releases."

"Yes, and they're seen as just that, press releases. All our competitors do the same. I was thinking about something non-technical, perhaps a little warm and fuzzy."

Atkinson shakes his head. "You marketing gurus. What will it be this time, the Janus Health Teddy Bear?"

"No. Do you remember that Public Television show we're sponsoring?"

"Yes; dry as dust, and ratings that barely register."

"Even a broken clock is right twice a day. They claim they've come up with something interesting, though they're being very hush-hush about it. If public reaction matches their expectations, this might be an opportunity to associate our name with something interesting that's focused on San Francisco's past rather than on current events."

"You've got my attention. What's this show about, and how do we use it?"

SIXTY-FOUR

"We're both members of Inner Truth, though we don't live at the house. Rachel's a CPA, and I'm a sculptor; the realities of earning a living make stuffing everybody under one roof 24/7 impractical." Jeremy and Rachel are a married couple who've been Fieldstone community members for six years.

Kevin flashes his best boyish smile. "I'm a little confused here. I thought that communal group living meant just that."

"Being part of an extended close-knit family doesn't require us to spend all our time sitting in each other's laps. The concept of group living has evolved since the 1960s when rents were cheap and nobody had a job."

Rachel nods in agreement. "We have friends who lived together in a house on a lake in Oregon when they were in their 20s. Now they all have JDs and MBAs and are judges and investment consultants. They only use the place on weekends in the summer when they take their grandkids swimming. We're trying to find a happy medium."

"And you're able to maintain close ties, even though you live on the outside?"

"We think it helps. It's good to be reminded how few of the people we know in the larger community have genuine pleasure in their lives."

It's time to play focuser-in-chief again. "I assume you know that Inspector Loeffler and I are investigating the death of Matt Glover. Yesterday we spoke with Carter Albemarle. He thought you could tell us a little about Matt."

"Sweet guy. I can't imagine what happened."

Rachel nods, "And he loved Myra. I still can't believe they're both gone."

"Carter told us he also liked Myra a lot."

"Oh yes, and Matt too. They were a good threesome."

"So they were all involved with each other?"

Even though he tries to make it sound neutral, Franklin sees the couple stiffen. "Yes, detective. Believe it or not, we see sex as a normal part of everyday life. We call that reality, not immorality."

Jeremy smiles as his wife speaks. "You've met Carter. You must have picked up on the aura of Southern charm and physicality he exudes. Quite a few people at Inner Truth, ourselves included, found that very attractive."

Franklin suppresses an urge to nudge Kevin, whose expression suggests he had no trouble at all noticing Carter's physicality. "Matt became a part of life there, even though he wasn't a full-fledged member of Inner Truth?"

Rachel turns to Jeremy. "Excuse me, dear, did you remember to bring our membership cards? I think the detectives would like to see our papers."

Jeremy frowns at her. "Please excuse my wife, detectives; she has a quirky sense of humor. Matt was with Myra; that was enough to make him a part of our family. The rules, such as they are, are about acting responsibly. There are no other requirements, especially since the goal is individual freedom for each of us."

Rachel smiles. "Matt was smitten with Carter. It's a common and harmless occurrence among new members and evens itself out over time. And Carter didn't wish any ill to either Matt or Myra."

"What about Henry, Matt's roommate? Did he ever visit Inner Truth?"

"No, not that we know of."

Kevin makes a puzzled face. "This sounds very loving and harmonious. So why was Carter was so angry with Carl?"

Their expressions change. "I assume you've already heard part of the answer from other members. Carl sees himself as the founder and leader of Inner Truth, and we're all aware of the effort it took to get the community started. But he's had difficulty letting go, even though we've been a going concern for years. And he can be abrupt, even high-handed when he's trying to direct the community. You don't help people free themselves of concepts that have outlived their usefulness by ordering them around."

"We'd also noticed that Myra seemed fragile. She was prone to mood swings, up one day and down the next. She joined Inner Truth after she'd broken up with her previous boyfriend, and I guess she'd been hospitalized for a while after that relationship fell apart. It had gotten bad enough that a doctor had prescribed medication. That's what set Carl off."

"He doesn't approve of medications?"

Jeremy grimaces. "Sometimes it can feel like we're living with Tom Cruise's evil twin. Carl will get going on his anti-psych med rant, and there's no stopping him. I suspect it may be because of what happened when he

211

first started talking about his ideas. His parents' response was to ship him off to some shrink. He can get pretty obnoxious, and that pissed Carter off big time."

"How did Myra react to Carl's tirade?"

"She withdrew into herself even more. She agreed with him a little because she didn't like the idea that she needed drugs. Money was also an issue. She didn't have any health insurance, which was one reason she got off them. But then the mood swings got worse. She must have felt she had no choice except to go back on medication, a new one this time."

Franklin looks up. "A new medication? She found some way to pay for it, then? Or was Matt helping?"

"He'd always been willing to; he even talked about getting Myra added to his health plan. But Myra was her own woman and didn't feel she needed anyone to rescue her. Then she got this invitation to join some drug company study and started getting pills for free."

"I wonder how the company got her name?"

"We assumed it must have been from the clinic that had written her previous prescriptions. I mean, they had to be aware of her financial problems."

Jeremy sighs. "Of course, that set Carl off all over again about how all doctors are in the pocket of Big Pharma. 'That's why they're always forcing drugs on you. They're all just glorified drug pushers, and on and on. And that got Carter going. You know the rest of the story."

"So the conflict here was between Carter and Carl. Matt and Carter and Myra were all OK with each other." Franklin makes it a statement rather than a question.

"Yes; that's why none of this makes any sense. Matt was expanding his horizons; there was no reason for anyone to want to kill him. Myra had two people in her life who cared for her. I don't understand why she wasn't happy."

"She was still depressed, despite taking the pills?" Kevin sounds concerned. *He's still mourning his Ophelia.*

"Yes. It was a new drug, and I guess nobody could tell how well it might work. It didn't seem to do anything for her."

"Do you know the name of the drug or the company?"

"No. I thought she had talked to Matt about it. Anyway, she filled out paperwork, and a few weeks later pills just started coming in the mail."

"There wouldn't be any of them left at the commune?"

"We'd have no way of knowing since we don't live there."

Franklin suppresses a sigh. "Well, thank you for your cooperation. If you remember anything else..."

SIXTY-FIVE

"So, it's been what, two and a half weeks, and we've got nada." Ortega is sitting with his eyes shut, his usual belligerence tempered by case fatigue.

"Or at least not a lot. Those Inner Truth folks confirmed Carter's claims about his relationship with Matt. Listening to its members, this commune may be the only place in California where a list of motives for murder doesn't include sexual jealousy."

"You believe that shit?"

"I didn't when we started." Franklin taps his notebook with his pen. "But we've spent a lot of time with them, and they sound like they're pretty good at self-policing. They get rid of potential troublemakers before conflicts can tear the place apart."

Kevin's looking at his notes. "And I have a couple of people who can vouch for Carter. He was at the commune at the time Matt was killed."

"And they're sure about that?"

"Yeah. They were both in bed with him all night long."

Franklin pretends not to notice the satisfaction that flashes across Kevin's face as Ortega opens his eyes and hisses. "Fucking perverts! And this Carl guy?"

Franklin closes his eyes. "Everyone agrees Carl is an asshole. They just ignore him and don't take him seriously. He'd done a lot of talking about drug connections, but the signal-to-noise ratio seems to be an issue with him."

"So that story about Carl working out some business deal with Matt?"

"Again, the likelihood of finding anything substantive is small."

"You find out anything at Janus?" Ortega's expression says that he doesn't expect much either from Janus or from Franklin.

"A few people knew Matt was dating Myra, but nobody knew of any dark secrets. No one at Janus heard anything about Matt dealing or saw changes in his behavior to suggest he was using."

"What about his boss who said he was what—'distracted by a hippy girlfriend'?"

"More likely the hippy boyfriend, I'd bet." Kevin turns to Franklin. "Anyone at Janus know about Carter?"

Franklin shakes his head.

"And the ME's positive his death wasn't an accident or suicide?"

"Nope. Homicide; he's positive."

Ortega turns to Kevin. "What about that druggie guy?"

"Clean. Seems he's turned his life over to the Buddha and spends his time listening to the sound of one hand clapping."

"Jesus! I know California is the land of fruits and nuts, but did you guys have to go find every damn one of them? You ever consider that your bullshitter could be lying?"

"He has the vocabulary down, and he does a good enough imitation of serenity. If he's faking it, it's not obvious why he'd concoct such an elaborate story to hide what's a pretty routine crime."

"My guess? He's just fried his brain. Should we bring him in for a sit-down?"

"Only if you're in the mood for an hour of enigmatic pronouncements that sound like *Kung Fu* reruns on steroids."

"OK. We've already wasted too much time on this one and are getting nowhere. It's time to think about cutting our losses. Write up your report about this guy, and I'll show it to the prosecutor and tell him that Buddha Junior is our most likely suspect, but he's a couple of French fries short of a Happy Meal, and chances of a successful prosecution are low. Then we can close the case and move on."

"But he's not an actual suspect."

"You got something wrong with your ears, Loeffler? What I said was that he's our *most likely* suspect. You got anyone better?"

"No, but..."

"One, there's no proof he *didn't* do it. Two, he's got a record. And three, no prosecutor who wants to keep his job is gonna put him on the stand. No harm, no foul. Just write it up." Ortega stands up; the meeting's over.

Franklin shrugs and stands, but Kevin stays seated as Ortega leaves.

"What's on your mind?"

"Two things. First, I liked the way you handled the Carter thing. Ortega was trashing the interview, and you yanked it back from the brink."

Franklin smiles. "It's an acquired skill; some days it's harder to pull off than others. What's the second thing?"

"I'm not sure. It's just that I've never heard of someone suddenly getting free prescriptions in the mail."

"You see ads on TV all the time. New stuff for halitosis or the heartbreak of psoriasis or whatever."

"Yeah. 'Ask your doctor if Whatchamacallit is right for you'. And starving grad students get recruited to play guinea pig in drug trials at universities all the time. But a poet in a commune getting new drugs for free just when she's running out of pills and money? That sounds like too much of a coincidence to me."

"Maybe." Franklin shrugs. "I'm not sure what I think, except that Matt and Myra weren't what people assumed. But it may not matter. You heard Mike; we're about to get shut down. Unless you find a smoking gun to wave under his nose, it's going to be the Gospel According to Ortega from now on."

450 Sutter Street

217

SIXTY-SIX

Please join us this afternoon in the Large Conference Room for an exciting event with Dr. James Atkinson, CEO, and Ms. Theo Markham, director of marketing. We'll be introducing the latest chapter in Janus Health's ongoing support of San Francisco's proud history and legacy. Here's your chance to meet Elizabeth Mills, author and host of Literary San Francisco, *the critically acclaimed Public Television program supported by Janus Health. Light refreshments will be served.*

Special events and team-building exercises are common events at Janus. Chris Walker can recognize the obligatory ones, and a meeting to promote a TV show doesn't fall in that category. So why is Atkinson's assistant calling to confirm? "Dr. Atkinson considers you one of our pre-eminent scientists and feels that your presence will add to the meeting." *A summons delivered via a secretary; what's this about?* Negotiating a crowded room in the wheelchair will be a challenge, but knowing the way these things drag on, he doesn't have a choice. *And I'm damned if I'm going to allow myself to be ferried around by security.*

He's barely in the door when Atkinson is upon him. "Good that you could make it, Chris. I'm sure you'll agree that what Theo's come up with promises to be very useful."

"I'm pleased to hear that. How so?"

"By lighting a backfire. Matt Glover's death's put our name in the news, and not in a way we wanted. This should help change the direction of the public narrative. I'd like you to be part of it, to associate your division with something other than this stuff about Matt and what's-her-name."

Seeing Walker's puzzlement, he searches for the name. "Myra, Matt's girlfriend. She also died recently."

"You can't believe that anyone at Janus had anything to do with that?"

"Of course not. But the police haven't solved Matt's case. If they do, we'll be in the news again. And if they don't, the press will still talk about it; unsolved murders make good news stories. That Sergeant—Washborne or something—keeps showing up. We don't need any of this; we should bury it for everyone's sake." A nod, a smile, and Atkinson's moved on before he can make any response.

Where is he going with this? Why is Atkinson so concerned if he's convinced that Matt's death has nothing to do with Janus? *What's he holding back?*

And here he comes again with a young woman in tow. "Chris, this is Elizabeth Mills, the host of *Literary San Francisco.*"

He manages a smile. "A pleasure. Dr. Atkinson tells me you're preparing something special, Ms. Mills."

"We hope so, Doctor, but we're all sworn to secrecy about the details. I hate to be a tease, but I promise that our next episode will be worth watching."

"Congratulations to you and your team, then. I'm just surprised that Dr. Atkinson is suggesting I could contribute anything to your excellent program." *Did that sound as clumsy as I think it did?*

Atkinson interrupts. "Given our support for the program, it could be useful if your surprise included something to remind the viewers of Janus Health's mission."

Elizabeth laughs. "You're putting me in an awkward position. Our featured author wrote a famous story about a doctor, but if I wanted someone to endorse the benefits of medical research, I wouldn't pick Dr. Jekyll."

"Ms. Mills, I have to agree with you; you are a terrible tease."

Elizabeth looks at the scientist in the wheelchair and relents. "I know; it's not fair to leave you hanging, especially after I've already given away a piece of the puzzle. But you must promise not to tell anyone. We've discovered a forgotten Stevenson story based on real life. It's about a doctor whose discoveries land him in trouble. The story's only a fragment, but it appears to be genuine. There, that's already more than I intended to say."

Atkinson is beaming his appreciation as he leads Elizabeth back into the growing crowd of employees. The presentation is about to start.

Chris Walker wheels himself toward the door. *A doctor whose secret discovery lands him in trouble.* And James Atkinson has decided that this program should feature Chris Walker rather than any other Janus scientist. The message is obvious; the "discovery" is the blue-sky project that is about to "land him in trouble". *And I can already guess what form the trouble will take.*

219

Even though it has Kortov's blessing, the new program is still something that could be seen by his CEO as preferential treatment, even a potential usurpation of power. *"One God in heaven, one Atkinson on earth"*; it's a foundational concept at Janus Health.

Kortov had expected him to generate papers full of theory rather than anything practical. And Darryl's decision to include a financial reward complicates matters. But it's a "research grant"; perhaps Janus will ignore the legal questions if he signs the money over, especially if doing so puts him in the top tier of revenue generators.

No, this is just another example of Atkinson's jealousy and skepticism about anything he doesn't understand. A television appearance that likens me to Dr. Jekyll would be excessive, even for him. But it's too late; my program is running, it's a success, and it's making money. Sorry if I hurt your feelings, Jim.

Atkinson most likely learned about the project from Kortov himself and is just venting his outrage in this bizarre fashion. It's unlikely he knows any of the actual details of the project. *Though what's the chance he might try to sabotage it, just to make me look like a fool?* No, not possible, if for no other reason than that it's beyond him technically.

He'll check the software again to be on the safe side, though he can't imagine how anyone could get past the firewall. He heads for his office.

SIXTY-SEVEN

A preliminary inspection of the program code and its protections is reassuring. There's no evidence anyone has penetrated the defenses or hacked into the program. There are no error messages; everything seems to be humming along. He smiles to himself. *Perhaps my next presentation should be "Computers <u>Can</u> Think: Artificial Intelligence in the Post-Turing Era".*

What surprises him is the variety of molecules the program has designed. It's generated dozens of structures, complete with outlines of protocols for their synthesis. Darryl's group has been busy providing examples of drugs they'd like the program to emulate, change or combine, and it appears to be doing just that.

The complexity of the compounds has grown, while the time to provide solutions has improved. *True "deep learning" behavior, occurring in real-time!* The program also has expanded its repertoire of potential templates by modifying the originals. Newer compounds are being built from earlier ones, in effect creating a second generation of pharmacologic progeny.

He needs a minute to think about what he's seeing. *Darryl's company isn't directing this process; the program is acting on its own. It's simulating the behavior of a successful pharmacology R & D team and the usual progression of drug development—except that humans couldn't collect data, analyze it and test hypotheses with this speed and efficiency.* It's no wonder Darryl has been so enthusiastic and Willoughby so generous with grant money.

He should feel triumphant about creating this. It's a considerable vindication, both of him and of the promise of artificial intelligence. *But that's not how I feel.*

In part, it's the conflict inherent in his position. The program falls between two stools. He developed it on Janus Health's dime, but it's solving problems for Darryl. Both organizations could have grounds for claiming it, and its success could invite a series of protracted intellectual property suits. There's no explanation he could offer Kortov or Atkinson for his actions, other than he hadn't expected the damn thing to work. Or worse, that he had but didn't give a damn about the consequences.

Some unsettling changes have also appeared. There's now a system for assigning a "score" to each compound. This must be the mechanism Willoughby is using to determine his 'incremental grants', or perhaps some version of Atkinson's product impact assessment. *Who inserted this? Matt or one of Darryl's coders? The program itself?*

And why would any start-up pharmaceutical company want to create so many drugs? He doesn't know enough chemistry to recognize the identity or function of the compounds, but there are already more potential products than Darryl could hope to develop, given his company's entry-level status. *Even allowing for what I know AI can accomplish, things are happening that I can't explain. Who can I ask to find out what's going on? Who can I trust?*

A few moments' reflection puts things in perspective. The actions of a program that's the product of rational thought must have rational explanations. The logical thing to do is to consider the facts instead of wasting time on suspicions or suppositions. *Emotion will only prove a distraction; I need to deal with realities.*

The data he does not understand are the chemistry of the compounds the software is designing. There's no reason to assume the code isn't working. Excluding a "garbage in, garbage out" situation, the output should represent the best possible configuration of a desired new drug. He needs to find out what an authority in pharmacology thinks about the potential utility of these new compounds.

He still knows people in academic circles who could help him. It should only take a few phone calls.

SIXTY-EIGHT

THURSDAY, SEPTEMBER 8, 2016

Kevin has to run for the elevator. The man in the car is so engrossed in his reading that he hasn't held the doors. Even after Kevin is inside, his fellow passenger continues to thumb through pages, oblivious to Kevin's presence, until the elevator comes to an abrupt halt between floors.

The emergency lights are dim enough to make the man stop reading. As Kevin reaches for the alarm button, his companion thrusts the booklet at Kevin. He grabs it reflexively just as the car jerks into motion again. When the doors open on the third floor, he finds himself alone.

He scans the corridor, but his companion is nowhere in sight. The booklet's title is familiar: *Computer Poker and Imperfect Information: Papers from the 2014 AAAI Workshop*. There's also a penciled note scribbled on the cover: Monte Carlo counterfactual regret minimization. *This was in the backpack next to Matt's body on Lombard Street.* But the backpack and its contents are in the Property Room, logged in as evidence.

Kevin is leafing through the pages as he walks when he spots the single loose sheet. The heading catches his attention; the leaflet is an invitation-from a company called Feldborg Pharmaceuticals.

While he waits for a reply from the associate professor of pharmacology a friend contacted on his behalf, Chris Walker is downloading examples of the compounds the program has designed. There are also physical chemistry data and synthesis guidelines, but these might as well be in Sanskrit. The question he has is simple: given parent compounds whose medical utility is known, what does his consultant think of their computer-generated pharmacologic offspring?

The e-mail that arrives as he's finishing satisfies him on several levels. The professor thinks it's an interesting question. In theory, predicting the effects of the derived compounds should be straightforward. There are already programs under development to do just this. It's easier to identify agents that won't work, and predicting the full spectrum of a new drug's effects can be complicated. If Walker wants to send him a few examples, he'll challenge his students to figure out what the drugs do. It shouldn't take long to have a preliminary answer.

It's as much as he could have hoped for. It will be a relief to find out what's going on.

Unless. His conversations with Darryl have always been about the program; he knows very little about Darryl's company. Willoughby's said they're planning to synthesize product, but he has no proof of that. What if the pharmacologist decides that none of the new drugs will work? Then what would they do?

Or what if they don't care? For all I know, this could all be some elaborate scam, a Ponzi scheme. Coax gullible investors to sink money into a new pharma company that's planning to disappear once it's fleeced enough unsuspecting souls. He knows he's prone to become absorbed in scientific questions while ignoring the less elevated aspects of real life. That he hadn't foreseen this possibility wouldn't protect him from angry investors. *They'll see me as a willing participant and co-conspirator.*

The idea is absurd. *Too much coffee this morning, Christopher.* Such a flight of paranoid fantasy is groundless. Grace knows these people, and she's never shared what she calls his otherworldliness. "You're my balloon, and I'm your anchor; that's why we make a good pair." Besides, the Society for 21st Century Biomedical Research had already vetted Darryl. It's time to return to the world of rational thought.

He's done what he can to learn about the program's output. There's nothing in this morning's e-mail to suggest that the answer will take much time. He'll find out what else Grace knows about Darryl. It's a conversation to have over lunch, a little personal time together.

And Ms. Mills seemed friendly; it's unlikely she's involved in any Janus cabal, even if one existed. He'll arrange a visit to KQXR to show his enthusiasm and interest in their creative process. The attention may be welcome enough to make them willing to share things they couldn't reveal in a public meeting.

He checks his calendar. Lunch with Grace tomorrow and a visit to the *Literary San Francisco* set before the weekend. With any luck, he'll also hear from his consultant soon. *There; I feel better already.*

SIXTY-NINE

"Expecting to have extra time for some light reading now that Ortega has solved the case for us?" Kevin drops the brochure on Franklin's desk and picks up a book. "*Hallucinations?* Isn't Ollie Sacks the guy who wrote about Parkinson's disease? They made it into a movie with Robin Williams."

"Never saw it."

"And *Treasure Island*. I never read it, but I saw the Disney version when I was a kid."

"That's Elizabeth's; she's using it for her show. And I'd hope that this *Treasure Island* isn't like any movie you've ever seen."

Kevin pages through the book; images of disheveled, grim, scarred men stare back at him. Even Jim Hawkins looks a bit shifty-eyed. He points to a picture of a toothless blindfolded man clutching a staff. "You're right. I'm glad I never read this as a kid. I'd have had nightmares for weeks."

"That's her point. She likes this edition's illustrations because Stevenson set his 'boys' adventures' stories in a gritty world Hollywood would never recognize." Franklin notices the booklet. "What's that?"

"Computer poker; something I remember seeing in Matt's backpack."

"What made you pull it now?"

"I didn't. Someone handed it to me in the elevator, just before he disappeared. I haven't checked the backpack yet, but I'm willing to bet something is missing."

"So how did your friend get hold of this?"

"No idea, just like I didn't see how he slipped past me."

Franklin frowns sympathetically. "If you'd like to borrow it, I'm done with the hallucinations book."

"I may have to. But first, look at what I found tucked among the pages."

The infomercial for Feldborg Pharmaceuticals is a single sheet printed on both sides. "Your Gateway to 21st Century Personalized Mental Health." A brief bio of the company's Danish founder follows the enthusiastic sales pitch; a mission statement and summary of current Stage 3 clinical trials fill the second side. There's a website address at the bottom of the page.

Kevin taps the sheet. "I bet we've just found the source of Myra's free antidepressants. Feldborg could be one of Janus Health's clients."

"That would make sense. Matt knew about Myra's depression, her financial problems, and her stubbornness. If he found a company looking for study volunteers, that could have been a way to get her some help. Especially since her problems had been severe enough to get her hospitalized once already."

Kevin is on his phone. "Hello? Yes, this is Inspector Kevin Loeffler with the San Francisco Homicide Division. I need to speak with whoever is in charge of industry outreach." Ten seconds later, He's speaking to the Vice President for Public Relations.

Franklin enters the website into his computer. It takes only seconds for the playful *"Oops! There's nothing there!"* message to appear. Perhaps they deactivated the link once the trial had completed enrollment, but Google should still find all internet references to the company.

There aren't any.

He goes to https://clinicaltrials.gov/ and types in *Depression, Anxiety | United States.* The site returns a long list of entries, but none include Feldborg Pharmaceuticals.

"Yes, I realize that client information is confidential. But may I remind you that this is a homicide investigation? We wouldn't be asking for this information if it weren't necessary. We can subpoena your records if you prefer. Yes, I understand that, and you're welcome to consult your corporate counsel. But in the meantime, I need to talk to someone, please. Now."

For an easy-going, irreverent guy, you've learned how to do Inspector Hardnose real well.

"Yes. Yes, I understand. Yes. It isn't. They aren't. You're sure? Yes, sir. Thank you."

"I take it that was a negative."

"From Atkinson himself. Janus Health has had no dealings with Feldborg Pharmaceuticals, he's never heard of them himself, and Matt Glover would not have had authorization to contact any pharmaceutical company, Janus client or otherwise. So could this have been a cold call? Somebody that Janus had no interest in, but who Matt saw as a viable solution to Myra's dilemma?"

"It's possible. But where has Feldborg gone? No 'net references, no record of approved clinical trials." Franklin leans back in his chair.

"Speaking of disappearances, about your friend in the elevator—what did he look like?"

"I didn't get to see much; it all took about twenty seconds total."

"Just under six feet, real thin, like 130 pounds, dark eyes, drooping mustache, and a soul patch..."

Kevin stares at him. "You know him?"

"I saw him at the garage on Sutter Street and on Bush Street the other night. He makes a habit of rapid entrances and exits."

"So who is he?"

"I don't know, and I'm not sure what his connection with our investigation is, though Elizabeth has her own ideas."

"Should I even ask?"

"She thinks he's a ghost. I don't know what I think."

"OK, I'm cool with that. I don't know if ghosts exist, but if they do, I don't expect they give a shit about what I believe. And if my alternatives are 'Ghosts exist' or 'You both are crazy', I'll pick door #1, Vanna, because you're one of the sanest people I know."

"Whoever or whatever he is, I'm guessing our friend wants us to look at the poker thing, or Myra and Feldborg Pharmaceuticals."

"Why not ask him?"

"Good luck with that; he never sticks around for questions. But if neither Atkinson nor the Feds have ever heard of Feldborg; who else do we ask?"

Kevin ticks off names with his fingers. "Henry, Andy Enright, maybe Dr. Walker."

"Sounds about right. Henry says he hadn't seen much of Matt lately, but they still worked for the same company. And Matt still had stuff at the apartment. What if Matt said something to Henry that didn't register at the time?"

"You suppose Henry could be concealing something? Or he's just being discreet, as in 'Friends don't let friends talk about their girlfriend's mental illness'?"

"Couldn't hurt to have another conversation with him. We could also take another run at Walker. He comes across as pretty aloof, but who knows? He'd heard about the poker program and the 'hippy girlfriend'; we haven't asked him about Feldborg."

"Andy Enright is in his own world, but even he figured out something was bugging Matt. I can call him."

"And I'll call Henry. How about this afternoon, if I can set it up? Somewhere besides here or Janus?"

"Sounds like a plan. Like you said, Ortega won't keep this investigation alive much longer."

SEVENTY

"You're at home? I thought you'd be teaching or conducting a tour."

"I wish." Elizabeth sighs. "We're doing the bulk of the filming for the *Lost Tales* episode tomorrow and there are still details I'm researching, so I'm working from home at the moment."

"You mean there are still things you don't know about the Stevensons?"

"It's not that. I've been trying to track down the elusive Dr. Montfort without much success. What are you up to?"

"Kevin and I are meeting Henry Qu for lunch; something new has materialized. I may need your help."

"I'd be happy to, though I'm not sure what I can offer."

"A man who looked a lot like Louis handed Kevin our latest clue in an elevator this morning. I haven't told him the full story, and it all sounds crazy enough that I could use your help now that Kevin's in the loop."

"Louis has attached himself to this case with a vengeance. I still don't understand why, and I can't figure out the 'how'. Where are you meeting?"

"Henry suggested City Chopsticks. It's on Bush at Taylor. We're aiming for 1:00."

"I can be there about 2:00 or a little after."

"Thanks. I owe you."

"No, not really. I'll see you there."

Elizabeth sitting in on a potential interrogation is against protocol, but what the hell. It can't be any worse than having a pair of ghosts involved.

Kevin is back, radiating distress.
"What?"

"When I call Andy's phone, I always have to leave a voicemail. This time, a woman answered. She said she was a friend. Andy's dead."

Franklin gives him a few seconds. "What happened?"

"She said they're calling it an overdose. Heroin."

"I'm sorry. Are you buying that?"

"No. I'm pretty sure he was clean, and besides, his drugs of choice were always hallucinogens."

"What does his friend think?"

"She sounds like she's in shock. She didn't know he was using, and these were people who were around him a lot. They're busy arranging whatever the Buddhist rituals are to guide people to their next rebirth. She said something about avoiding hungry ghosts."

"Did you tell her this case doesn't need any more ghosts?"

"No kidding. And any more dead people, either. You noticed how the bodies are piling up?"

"Yeah. But we're not sure what Andy might have known. What if our killer was worried about how much Matt had told him and decided he didn't want to take any chances?"

"And Andy's death plays right into Ortega's scenario. The guy OD'd; that proves he's a druggy, which makes it obvious that he was the murderer. Now that he's dead, we're done." Kevin pauses. "Whoever the killer is, it sounds like he's started playing hardball. Only I don't see what the endgame is."

"We're missing something. Is he tracking us or able to anticipate our moves somehow?"

"You think he knows us by sight? When I went to San Mateo, Andy wanted to sit outside to talk. I didn't notice anyone else around, but in retrospect ..."

"I doubt anything you did made any difference. Whoever we're dealing with seems to know a lot about Matt and his friends. Someone had targeted Andy long before you met him."

"So talking to Henry today won't put him at any greater risk than he's already facing? This is getting worse by the minute." Kevin looks worried.

"If the murderer has been following the case, he may know that Henry was our original suspect. We're meeting to see if he knows anything about Feldborg or the flyer and that computer poker conference. But we could just as well be interviewing him because we have further questions."

"We make it look quasi-interrogational so that if the killer is watching, he'll misinterpret our reasons, courtesy of Fearless Crime-Stopper Ortega? Nice to know that even a douche like Mike can be helpful."

"Another interrogation sounds more plausible than a meeting because we're following a lead from someone who keeps disappearing."

"Pretty devious strategy, if you ask me. I just hope we can make it through the Hot and Sour Soup and Moo Shu Pork without someone else turning up dead."

City Chopsticks

SEVENTY-ONE

Henry is already sitting at the back of the restaurant. "Good afternoon, detectives. You said you've found something new?"

Franklin waits until they're seated with their notebooks out before he slides the AAAI program towards Henry. "Not something new; something we didn't understand when we first found it. This was in Matt's backpack."

Henry glances at the booklet. "Yeah, Matt was into game theory and artificial intelligence. He was especially interested in games of chance.." He runs his hand over the cover of the program. "Now that I'm working with Dr. Walker, I've been reading Matt's notes. He argued that computer programs needed to deal with real-life situations, and real life can be chancy. "

"Was Matt a gambler?" Franklin sees Henry stiffen at Kevin's question.

"No, he was a software engineer, detective. AAAI stands for the Association for the Advancement of Artificial Intelligence. It's in Palo Alto, not Las Vegas."

"I guess it's time to put our cards on the table, so to speak. First off, I meant no offense. In our work, gambling and money problems can be reasons people end up dead. We're not making much headway with Matt's case. We'd hoped to interview Myra but never reached her. So is there anything more you can tell us?"

"About Myra? No. I saw very little of her, and I've never been to her commune. Matt didn't talk about the place; he only went there because that's where she was."

Franklin glances at Kevin. *Henry sounds like there was a lot he didn't know. Just how many other secrets was Matt keeping?*

"So my other question: why poker? We know Matt had worked on a program that attracted the attention of law enforcement in the past. Was that just a coincidence?"

"I can fill you in on all that. But if your cards are 'on the table', tell me: am I still a suspect?"

Franklin considers the question. "We have no evidence you killed Matt. We've also found nothing that completely excludes you as a suspect."

"Which puts me in the same category as several million other people on the planet. How's that an improvement over a couple of weeks ago?"

Kevin winces. "Hey, about that jealousy stuff..."

"I'm an ambitious guy with a normal sex drive, but that doesn't make me a killer. I get that you aren't Sergeant Ortega, but cops seem to depend a lot on suspicions, hunches, and rules of thumb. In my world, that's considered non-rational behavior. So I'll answer your questions if we can talk like rational adults; any more cop-think bullshit, and we can end this right now."

Franklin's expression doesn't change. "Fair enough. What we're interested in are facts. Absent anything new showing up, you're right; you're no more a suspect than a lot of other people. Fair enough?"

Henry nods. "OK. I don't know what was in any police reports you got from New York, but I can tell you that Matt's interest in computer poker wasn't about gambling. It was about saving face. He'd come to view his ideas about the role of chance as the thing that defined him as an engineer, and he was intent on proving his theory."

"I understand that the stuff from upstate New York may be ancient history." Kevin flips a page in his notebook. "So what, computer poker somehow became a sort of life mission? I still don't get the connection between poker and pharmacology."

Henry smiles. "Which do you want to hear about first, pharmacology or poker?"

"Poker. I'm from Reno, and I know about cards. But medical stuff? Not so much."

"You already know about STUD, the poker program. Matt said the thing started as a lark, sort of a grad student project with attitude. A bunch of guys worked on it. The problems started when Matt figured out that the parts he wrote wouldn't cut it."

"I thought somebody got arrested for it."

"That was Anderson. Matt said the guy was brilliant, a way better coder than he was, but he was a total asshole. That's what saved Matt."

"Because Matt's programming skills weren't good enough to let him design a program that could win at poker?"

"Pretty much, yeah. The general approach to games in Artificial Intelligence is straightforward. You supply the computer with a ton of examples of winning moves or hands that experts have used. The program uses those to rank its strategy options during play. A well-constructed program won't win every hand or game, but it should win more often than the average player. But back then, Matt didn't understand enough about ANNs to pull it off."

"And an ANN is?" Kevin is writing in his notebook.

"Sorry. An Artificial Neural Network. It's a statistical tool that simulates biological neural networks to model nonlinear relationships, using adaptive weights between…"

Franklin holds up a hand. "Perhaps you could give us the fourth-grader's version, Doctor."

"The second-graders version." Kevin glances at Franklin. "You tried talking to any fourth-graders lately? They're scary."

Henry tries again. "It's software that works like the human brain. In theory, it makes fast, intuitive approximations of solutions and will reconsider its decisions when new information becomes available."

"Intuitive computers. Kevin's right; this stuff *is* scary."

"One problem with Matt's code was that it wasn't interactive, at least at first. It played poker by following a set of training rules, but it didn't refine its strategy based on the state of play. Anderson's program used the results of each hand to update its game plan."

"Like a guy in a poker game who notices how his opponents are playing that night?"

"You got it."

"So Anderson was the better programmer. What made him an asshole?"

"He put a piece of code he named Vindictiv into his program. It responded to any player who was winning by using dirty tricks to bankrupt its opponent, even if the computer also lost money. Anderson's theory was that you couldn't enjoy high stakes poker unless you were winning while other guys were losing their shirts."

"He could make the program do that?"

"Sure. It would start playing badly for a few hands while upping the ante—your basic 'desperate loser' behavior. When the pot got big enough, the program would revert to 'expert player' mode again."

"Nice. Where's this guy now?"

"Mexico, last time Matt knew. The point is, Matt, being Matt, all he remembered was that Anderson's program was better than his. Anderson may have been a bastard, but Matt still wanted to study his code, learn about ANNs, and do him one better. That's why he was at the AAAI."

Kevin closes his notebook. "And you're sure Matt wasn't doing anything that could piss off someone at, say, the Palace Casino?"

"Matt might have been a little obsessive, but he wasn't stupid. Anderson wanted to challenge a bunch of professional gamblers. The program would beat them, win a pile of money, and generate lots of publicity."

"You're right; that sounds stupid."

"And unrealistic. Setting up a poker tournament takes a lot of money, something Anderson didn't have. He hadn't tested the program enough to get all the bugs out. And even if everything had worked, humiliating professional gamblers in public wouldn't have ended well. After the cops charged Anderson with assault, grand larceny, and conspiracy to defraud, Matt finally recognized what the guy was, but he still couldn't let it go."

Kevin grimaces. "Still sounds like they got off easy. It would have been worse if Anderson's scheme had succeeded."

"So Matt wanted to master computer applications of game theory and somehow use them in a pharmacology program?" Franklin hesitates. "Please keep the explanation at the second-grade level."

Henry puts his tablet in the middle of the table. Kevin helps by moving the remaining Moo Shu and pancakes onto his plate and pushing the empty platter aside.

"OK; time for a quick show and tell."

SEVENTY-TWO

Henry taps the screen. "Here are two members of the penicillin family. What do you notice?"

"The right-hand parts are the same, but the left-hand sides are different."

"Good, yes. Matt's first project was in drug design. The computer would change the left-hand side to produce new flavors of penicillin."

"And then?"

"Offer them to a pharma bro to test and see if they have therapeutic potential. No guarantees they would, of course."

"Because real life is complicated?"

"Molecular biology can be. Look at these." Henry taps the screen again.

"They look similar, except for the thing in the middle. Fe is what, iron?"

"Very good again, Sergeant! And Mg is magnesium. But the one on the left is hemoglobin, and the one on the right is chlorophyll. Similar structures, very different functions."

"I gather you know a lot about chemistry as well as computers."

"Just enough to get in trouble. But this is straightforward stuff, all about 2-D models. Here's amoxicillin in 3-D."

He taps the screen again, and the molecule comes alive.

Kevin watches, transfixed. "It's like *World of Warcraft* with chemistry avatars."

Henry smiles. "Do I need to pause while you explain *WoW* to Sergeant Washborne?"

Franklin waves a hand. "I have a general idea, though what you've got there looks more like a clumsy belly dancer than a warrior."

"The point is that molecules are dynamic structures. If you want to know how they work, you have to know how they move."

"So Janus has a program that cooks up new versions of penicillin, and the next step is to create wiggly models of them?"

"Not quite. Dr. Walker wants to create a program to display protein configurations next. He's calling it Origami because proteins like to fold themselves into all sorts of shapes. Look at these."

Kevin examines the four stick and ball figures on the screen. "They look like parts of a Tinkertoy."

"They represent polypeptides, strings of amino acids. The linear one at the top is how textbooks display the formulas. The others show how polypeptides arrange themselves in the real world. Different configurations lead to different chemical interactions. The assumption is that knowing a protein's shape can tell us how it works. Origami's going to be part of a bigger program that can model drug-receptor interactions."

"But what does Origami have to do with poker?"

"It looks like Matt had been toying with ideas for building a program that worked directly with bigger structures, even though that's crazy. We couldn't model them using conventional methods. It would require statistical analysis and some way to compensate for all the unknowns."

"What was his plan?"

Henry makes a face. "He wanted to recycle parts of his poker program. Dr. Walker doesn't agree that it could have worked, but by that time Matt was pretty fixated on the idea."

Kevin looks up. "So Matt was what, crazy?"

"Not completely. The Human Genome project planned to map each strand of DNA linearly, but Craig Venter decided to chop the strands into random pieces, analyze each one, and then somehow reassemble the whole molecule. People thought he was crazy too, but it worked."

Franklin taps the table with his fingers. "So the connection between pharmacology and poker existed only in Matt's mind, and he was either brilliant or nuts. Why would that give someone a reason to kill him?"

Henry shakes his head. "It wouldn't, especially if he was crazy. I guess he hoped his idea would convince Dr. Walker he was brilliant."

"Was he in trouble with his boss?"

"It wasn't anything personal. Dr. Walker is a perfectionist. Instead of looking at how far we've come, he always sees what we still haven't accomplished."

"A challenging work environment, but not an uncommon one. Would anyone have felt threatened by Matt's efforts?"

"No one I can think of. We're all under pressure, but we expect work to be challenging. After all, we're a pretty competitive bunch, working for a leading authority on AI."

Kevin puts his hands behind his head. "Are we sure Walker feels all that secure at the top? Some of Matt's ideas sound pretty creative. Walker wouldn't be the first boss with impossible standards who felt threatened by some bright underling promising to eclipse the Master."

Franklin shakes his head. "How likely was it that Matt posed an actual challenge to Walker's position?"

"Zero." Henry almost blushes. "I know I couldn't produce anything that would pose a threat."

"And even if Matt could, Walker couldn't have killed him. He isn't up to it physically, and I can't see him arranging a murder for hire."

Kevin closes his notebook. "And he'd have no motive if he believed Matt's ideas wouldn't work."

Henry persists. "If we succeed in creating the receptor program, it will be a huge leap forward relative to existing medical AI applications. It would move Janus Health to the front of the line and cement Walker's place in the field. Matt wasn't a gambler, but in this case, the prize had to be incredibly tempting."

"So he wanted to skip a couple of steps, impress everyone, and marry the boss's daughter?"

"The way Anderson had dissed him still pissed him off; he wanted to prove he was a damn good software engineer. I had no clue until I got into his files."

"As part of your new assignment?"

"Yeah. I don't think Dr. Walker knew about his obsession either. I mean, I found a ton of variations on *STUD*. Matt had them arranged by date and gave them individual serial numbers. He even assembled trial data sets. From the header, I'd guess he'd been working on this for a while."

"How could you tell that from a file header?"

"The numbering. The most recent data set was number 3.1.1.2. There were earlier ones too, in a folder with data samples and results."

"Sounds like it was a major undertaking."

"Yeah. He'd even assigned it a project name."

"Which was?"

"Feldborg."

SEVENTY-THREE

Ten seconds elapse before Kevin says, "I'll get it" to no one in particular, and heads for the door.

Henry looks startled. "What did I say?"

"We think 'Feldborg' could refer to Feldborg Pharmaceuticals. Have you ever heard of them or heard anyone at Janus mention them?"

"No."

"Neither has anyone else, including Dr. Atkinson. What you've told us makes Matt the only person who had. Did he ever talk about a drug trial?"

"No."

"It would have been about antidepressants for Myra."

"No. I mean, it was pretty clear to anyone who knew her that Myra was depressed, but Matt never talked about it. He pretty much kept all of that private. He said he was a computer guy, not a psychologist.."

Kevin is back with the copy of the Feldborg flyer. "We found this stuck in the AAAI program."

They wait as Henry reads the flyer—twice.

"So Matt had this and knew Feldborg was recruiting people for clinical trials. Folks at the commune said Myra was getting free drugs in the mail. If she had joined a clinical trial, was it because Matt shared this information with her?" Franklin taps the flyer. "You've found files with the same name on Matt's computer; that seems like an odd coincidence to me."

Henry looks puzzled. "I don't understand what any of this means. I assumed Feldborg was a code name for a project, like the names Apple gives new versions of their operating systems."

"Do engineers at Janus get to create new projects?"

"No way; not at our level. There's a scientific development committee that sets the agenda for R & D. We don't get to freelance."

"Is there any reason Matt would use data from an outside source? Maybe someone who wasn't a Janus client?"

"No. We use NIH databases that are public domain, but everything else is proprietary. And uploading somebody else's data without approval? That'd be almost impossible."

"Could anyone at Janus do that?"

"It would have to be someone at a senior level; Dr. Atkinson, Dr. Walker, a few others."

Kevin points at the flyer. "How about this? Janus Health has pharmaceutical companies as clients, right?"

"Sure, and we're always interested in getting more. Contract work pays the rent while we're waiting for Dr. Atkinson's Big Idea project to come online."

"The way they describe themselves makes Feldborg sound like a good fit for Janus. Could Matt have seen them as a potential client?

"Yes, but he would have referred them to the Office of Program Development."

"Would Matt do that himself, or would it be his department head?"

"Anyone can make a referral, but corporate etiquette dictates we pass it up the administrative chain."

Kevin persists. "Suppose he wanted to get in Dr. Walker's good graces. He does his homework, discovers the client's needs, suggests a solution, and hands the whole thing to the boss wrapped up with a bow. Might be worth a few points."

"I suppose. I mean, sure, Matt was a little naïve, but he could see how recommending a potential client wouldn't be a bad idea."

"He wouldn't have to create a complete program; just a sketch with some data that looked like Feldborg's. If he was enthusiastic about the company, that could also explain why he decided it would be OK to put them in touch with Myra."

Henry looks doubtful. "I don't know. That's an awful lot of assumptions."

"And whether or not I'm right, the other big problem is that this doesn't get us any closer to finding the guy who killed Matt."

"What doesn't?" Elizabeth slips into an empty chair; a waiter brings a menu.

SEVENTY-FOUR

"Dr. Qu, this is Elizabeth Mills. I've asked her to join us." *Christ, I sound like a teenager introducing my prom date to my parents.*

Henry is already on his feet. "It's a pleasure to meet you, Ms. Mills. Matt mentioned you were a friend of Myra's. Are you also helping with the case?"

"Only from a distance."

Kevin steps in to fill the silence. "We were talking about computers that cheat at cards before you arrived."

"That's wonderful!" Elizabeth turns to Henry. "How do you teach a computer to cheat?"

"Not cheating, exactly; just being devious. And you would do it by designing software that mimics the way humans think—if we could understand how humans think."

"Which is why we can't tell you what the computer equivalent of a cardsharp is, or how to make one," Kevin adds helpfully. "Except that it's easier if you're a sociopath grad student who's spent time in jail."

"I see. I've always wondered what the police talk about at lunch. So how are you doing, Henry?"

"I'm all right, thanks."

It looks like the question made him uncomfortable. Franklin sits back, waiting for Henry's inner engineer to kick in. It doesn't take long.

"Strictly speaking, no one taught the computer to cheat. The program simply models the behavior of people who enjoy taking big risks and using aggressive bluffs while playing for high stakes. From a statistical standpoint, the code would be non-optimal because it doesn't maximize the probability of winning over the long haul, which is what traditional game theorists would consider the best outcome."

Kevin objects. "But doesn't doing that sort of defeat the whole point of using a computer? Anybody can bluff; the computer's advantage is its capacity to pick the best option for each hand. So who would design a program that might choose a sub-optimal strategy, even short-term?"

Elizabeth puts her menu aside. "Perhaps someone whose greed or grandiosity or competitiveness overrode his training in science and probability. I suppose anyone who gambles has to suspend disbelief, at least temporarily. I know I do when I ignore the odds and buy a Powerball ticket. The person who designed this sounds like he allowed aggressiveness or anger to overwhelm the reasoning parts of his brain and change his programming priorities. I always associate computers with mathematics and logic. But you're saying it's possible to create a program that's as irrational as a real live person?"

Franklin shoots her a bemused look. "Did I mention that as an author, Elizabeth specializes in creating believable characters?"

"Very believable. From what Matt said, that's a fair description of the program's chief architect."

"But not Matt himself?"

"No, not at all. Matt was nothing like that."

"I ran into players like that when I worked in the casino." Kevin's face darkens. "Some guys weren't playing just to win; they weren't happy unless they demolished and humiliated their opponents. But what was an easygoing guy like Matt doing anywhere near something like that?"

Henry shakes his head. "I'm sure the version of *STUD* Matt kept was his, not Anderson's."

"*STUD*? Do I even want to ask?"

"It's a long story." Franklin takes a deep breath. "Henry, could you tell whose *STUD* was whose? And would it make a difference?" Elizabeth looks beseechingly at Kevin, who just shakes his head.

"I can't be sure. Most of what's in Matt's files are just chunks of code without a lot of explanation. But it wouldn't have made any sense to use Anderson's original code. What use is an irrational gambling program if your goal is to design new pharmaceuticals."

Franklin's expression hardens. "The problem with the gamblers Kevin knew wasn't that they were irrational. It's that they were malevolent by intent. What would be the pharmacological equivalent of that?"

Kevin is right behind him. "A program designed to make malign drugs, ones that made you feel worse rather than better or sicker rather than healthier."

Franklin stares at the Feldborg invitation again. "In which case, you might not want Matt around long-term. You'd probably want him out of the way once you'd gotten hold of his code and before he got wind of what you were up to."

All the playfulness in Elizabeth's demeanor has disappeared. "You're talking about chemical or biological weapons software. That's genuinely evil!"

"I'm not sure programs can be evil. A program can be amoral because mathematical functions are outside of the realm of morals. Computers will follow whatever instructions they're given." Henry sounds distressed. "That's the problem any time we ask a machine to do something. What happens if we aren't sure what we want, or we don't define the goal narrowly enough, or we want more than one thing?"

Franklin interrupts. "Elizabeth wasn't here when you told us about programs that make informed guesses and fill in the gaps when necessary. What would happen if I trained an AI program using examples of substances whose common denominator was that they're all toxic to humans? If the computer kept designing more and more of them, how long would it take before it extrapolated a general rule about the types of drugs I wanted?"

"I don't know. I can't even tell you if something like that could happen. The problem is, I also can't tell you it couldn't."

SEVENTY-FIVE

Elizabeth looks at Henry. "So if Franklin did that, your deep learning program can't be called evil just because it's following his instructions and can guess the user's intentions. But what about the human element? Is it OK for an immoral person to use an amoral machine to release a plague upon the world?"

"Of course not. But how can we prevent that? If the program identifies a characteristic present in all the results, it will look for other formulations that also share that property. It can learn from its mistakes and will become progressively more efficient at what it does. You can't operationalize morality. The alternative would be to deprive the world of all the good this technology can provide."

Kevin frowns. "I hate to interrupt this seminar on ethics with a pragmatic question, but even if a program is malignant, its output will still be useless unless you have a lab to manufacture the stuff. Janus can't do that, so someone must be feeding chemical formulas to an illicit lab code-named Feldborg somewhere."

Franklin realizes he's been holding his breath. "And after that, the manufacturer could test the product by distributing it for free to unsuspecting victims enrolled in some imaginary clinical trial."

"While everyone else at Janus Health who isn't part of this scheme deals with the legitimate pharmaceutical companies and has never heard of Feldborg." Kevin's dismay is palpable. "To support a plan this ruthless, you'd have to be ruthless yourself, a person who's willing to risk everything and hang with sociopaths."

"And whatever his failings, that wasn't Matt Glover." Henry looks pointedly at Franklin.

There's a lot you didn't know about your former roommate, but this time I think you're right. "No. It would have to be some person or persons with power

246

and resources enough to organize the entire scheme, from initial planning and implementation through to collection of the blood money."

"If a plan like that existed, it would have to be a team effort." Henry frowns. "I can't believe there are many people at Janus depraved enough to go along with it."

Kevin adds, "And disciplined enough to keep it secret."

"You're talking about people I've worked with for three years. You've met some of them yourselves. Did any of them strike you as capable of doing this?"

"Between working in a casino and as a cop, I'm almost beyond being surprised by what humans are capable of. What's hard to imagine is Dr. Walker being able to handle the pragmatics of anything this callous. What about Atkinson?" Kevin looks at Franklin. "He's ensconced himself at the top of that weird building like the Inca at the top of his pyramid, and he talks about his Big Idea as if it's the Eighth Wonder of the World. His grandiose ideas must cost a bundle. I could see him finding an opportunity for a lucrative sideline attractive."

"I agree he's grandiose, but he's also the guy with the most to lose if this ever got out."

Henry smiles. "I think you're giving him too much credit. Deep Learning isn't an area where Dr. Atkinson is knowledgeable. I worked for him for a couple of years; he doesn't have the time or expertise or staff to create the code you're envisioning. Dr. Walker might know how to do it, but he'd want to spend a couple of years dithering over the best theoretical approach first. And the rest of the details would be beyond him; he's almost oblivious to money."

Franklin frowns. "We haven't proven that such a program even exists, let alone that it could work. We have no formulas for drugs or samples of drugs or proof that said drugs might be as dangerous as we suspect. Myra's death was ruled a suicide, and her parents took her back to Illinois for burial, so it's unlikely that we could get tissue samples to test."

"Test for what? An unknown drug we're guessing might resemble an antidepressant? I can already imagine what Dr. Olsen's response would be." Kevin looks disgusted. "What we're talking about is a pretty fantastic theory that sounds like the plot of a two-and-a-half-star movie. When someone makes it, I hope they persuade Daniel Craig to play Franklin Washborne. A computer that's a virtual chemical warfare factory sounds like something a James Bond villain would have."

"I'm flattered, but I'd remind everyone we're still working against a deadline. Henry's friend Sergeant Ortega has another suspect to blame for Matt's death and is planning to close the case soon."

Henry raises an eyebrow. "Who's the lucky candidate now?"

"Someone who's already dead; Mike wants to make sure no one will contradict him this time." *We'll break the news about Andy later; this is not the time.*

"It's depressing to imagine anyone could so misuse this technology, but if they had, there would have to be signs of their work somewhere in the system." Henry pauses. "Matt gave each version of *STUD* a unique embedded ID number. That might make any 'borrowed' fragments traceable on the Janus network. It's a place to start, even if the full program is well hidden."

"Whatever you have in mind, be careful. Anyone capable of planning this is ruthless and very dangerous."

Elizabeth reaches over and touches Henry's arm. "Not just dangerous. He's pure evil."

There's no one left in the restaurant other than customers coming for takeout, and the waiters are staring at them. Kevin stands up. "Looks like it's time to adjourn."

Elizabeth's phone rings; she wrinkles her nose as she listens to the message. "I've got to run back to the studio. Not for too long, I hope. Will I see you at home this evening?"

Franklin smiles. "It's a deal. I don't need to go to Vallejo Street; perhaps I'll surprise you and make dinner for us."

"You're a prince. Why don't you pick up some wine, too; I'm going to want a drink tonight. Maybe two or three."

SEVENTY-SIX

To be on the safe side, he buys three bottles of wine. Elizabeth hasn't arrived home when Franklin gets back to the apartment, so he sets out the ingre-dients and hunts around for a pot big enough for the pasta. He hesitates only a moment before he opens the first bottle and pours a glass as he looks up a recipe for Pasta Puttanesca on Epicurious. *After all, red wine needs to breathe.*

He's chopped the garlic and opened the can of San Marzano tomatoes and the jar of Kalamata olives when Elizabeth arrives.

Pasta Puttanesca

"So what's on the menu?"

"Pasta Puttanesca. I wanted something that I could throw together in a hurry once you got here. And having started in Vice, I feel a kinship with working girls."

"Oh. Are they the ones who showed you how to make this, or is this your creation?"

"It's mine, by way of *Epicurious*. It's still on the computer if you're curious."

"You mean if I'm epicurious?"

"After the afternoon I put you through, you can still make puns as bad as that? God, I love you!" He pauses. "I didn't see any of this stuff coming. I even forgot about filling Henry in on what's been happening with the Stevensons, which was the reason I asked you to come along to begin with."

Elizabeth shrugs. "Part of the territory. If I wanted to avoid life's realities, I shouldn't hang out with homicide detectives. Maybe my next book will be a police procedural."

"Why not? You're a quick study. Meanwhile, I want to ply you with strong drink."

"Yes, please!"

An hour and a half later, the dishwasher is making sloshing noises, and they're sitting on the couch with the remains of the second bottle of wine. Elizabeth yawns.

"Long day, huh?"

She sticks her tongue out at him. "That's putting it mildly. Makes me appreciate the quiet morning I had here. As soon as I got back to the studio, the writers announced we needed a teaser promising that there are actual results from our 'Lost Tale' search. Remember *Return to the Titanic*? Telly Savalas opens a safe from the wreck that he already knew was empty. We don't want to look like a reality show that promises a lot and doesn't deliver."

"They have a point."

"I suppose, but it still sounds like overkill. We've shown snippets of the interview with Mr. Jackson and talked about Belle. How much more do we need? And if I agree, what's next? Someone jumping out of a pirate's chest with some yellowed papers? I want to bring the focus back to the history of Stevenson in San Francisco. I just wish uncovering information about Dr. Montfort wasn't so difficult. A lot of stuff went missing after the 1906 fire, and what's left is in archives or museums."

"Stevenson never met Dr. Montfort, but what about Liam Cromartie? Any proof that he existed, or is that more fiction?"

"All we have is that one letter that he never even sent. It mentions a sailor who told Louis a story, but it can be hard to tell when author Stevenson is in storytelling mode. I don't have other evidence that Liam Cromartie existed."

"Sounds like your show's going to be a cliffhanger."

"Our producer thinks so. The staff is still under strict orders not to reveal anything before we air. That's not just to build suspense; we're still not sure what we'll end up with."

"And this was your afternoon, *after* the lunch meeting we had?"

"Yes, but the mini-dramas at the studio felt like a welcome diversion." She walks over to the computer. "Which site did you say you were on?"

"Epicurious."

"Uh, no, you're on Planetebook.com." She beckons him to a screen full of text.

"With every day, and from both sides of my intelligence, the moral and the intellectual, I thus drew steadily nearer to that truth, by whose partial discovery I have been doomed to such a dreadful shipwreck: that man is not truly one, but truly two."

which fades to:

"I do not suppose that, when a drunkard reasons with himself upon his vice, he is once out of five hundred times affected by the dangers that he runs through his brutish, physical insensibility; neither had I, long as I had considered my position, made enough allowance for the complete moral insensibility and insensate readiness to evil, which were the leading characters of Edward Hyde. Yet it was by these that I was punished. My devil had been long caged, he came out roaring."

"I had voluntarily stripped myself of all those balancing instincts by which even the worst of us continues to walk with some degree of steadiness among temptations; and in my case, to be tempted, however slightly, was to fall. Instantly the spirit of hell awoke in me and raged."

"Is that who I think it is?"

She studies the screen. "It's the last chapter of *Strange Case of Dr. Jekyll and Mr. Hyde*. I didn't open this website, and I guess you didn't either."

"So after sharing an elevator with Kevin this morning, now someone is pulling up favorite selections from his writings. Louis is having a busy day."

"Why do you suppose he's offering this literary accompaniment to our Italian meal?"

"I could try to guess, but I'd prefer my local Stevenson expert to offer her thoughts."

"It's a good question, but a home-cooked meal and that second bottle of wine are making it hard to remember what my answer was going to be. Suppose I close my eyes and concentrate hard..."

"Go ahead; close your eyes. You can skip the rest."

UNION

SEVENTY-SEVEN

FRIDAY, SEPTEMBER 9, 2016

They're at City Chopsticks. Elizabeth is sitting next to Henry, peering at his tablet. The waiters bring plate after plate of food; they're running out of space on the table.

"Who ordered all this?"

Elizabeth glances up at him "I did; I know how hungry you are. Try the Hot and Sour Cabbage."

Henry nods in agreement and holds up the tablet. "Would you like to see my new computer poker program?"

He hands the tablet to Franklin, but the screen keeps going blank.

"Here, let me." Henry taps the screen and hands the tablet back. A young Asian woman is standing next to a mound of poker chips and is speaking in Chinese.

"Seaweed Egg Flower Soup for two?" Dr. Walker is their waiter; he carries a large bowl to the table. Another waiter hurries over to remove empty plates.

Franklin opens his eyes. His head aches, and he can still taste last night's Cabernet. The predawn glow is visible through the window. The clock says 5:55 AM; he wonders if there's any significance to the number.

He makes it to the bedroom door just as his phone rings. He hurries to grab it before it wakes Elizabeth.

"I'm sorry to be calling so early. I wasn't able to sleep and decided I might as well start my search."

"No, that's fine, Henry. How long have you been up?"

"I got to Janus around 2:30."

Just the thought of staring at a computer screen for hours makes his head feel even worse. "You have access to the building at that hour?"

"It's not uncommon for people to be working all hours around here. It's a sign you're a dedicated employee."

"Sounds as bad as a white-shoe law firm. Since you're calling, I'm guessing you've found something."

"Something a little strange. I found pieces of STUD code incorporated into other programs, but they're in another of Matt's workspaces."

"So Matt was the one building the program?"

"Building *a* program. There's one that looks like it's a sample intended for Dr. Walker, as we expected. But there are also fragments with edited STUD code that don't look like Matt's at all. I've seen enough of his work to recognize his coding style, and this is very different."

"So someone else was using STUD as well. How would Matt have known that?"

"A collaboration, or else he could have found someone using his code and tracked their work. These are all programs to design drugs, variations on software we've all been working on. It looks more sophisticated, but it could be another stray trial version."

"Or the something we're worried about."

"It's possible. I haven't found a full version of anything, so I can't tell."

"And a favorite obsession: can you tell if what you're looking at is Matt's code or Anderson's?"

"I doubt original versions of either exist anymore. Matt used Anderson's program as a template. He wanted to keep the good parts and dump the rest. But he kept tinkering and revising until things were almost unrecognizable."

"If someone didn't want Matt knowing about whatever this other program was that he'd uncovered..."

"Poor bastard. And knowing him, he wouldn't have understood he was in danger."

Elizabeth comes out of the bedroom and heads to the kitchen; he can hear her filling the coffeemaker. "OK. You've already accomplished more than I hoped for. Is there any way you can get away from there today?"

"I suppose. Dr. Walker has some outside appointments and will be gone from noon on. What do you want me to do?"

"Disappear. We still don't know everything that's going on, other than that people are getting killed. After this morning, it would be good for you to stay out of sight for a while."

"I'll head home."

"No, not back to your apartment. Call me when you're ready to leave; you can stay at my place. You're not allergic to cats, are you?"

"No, but do you think that's necessary?"

"I can't be sure, but I remember what a martial arts instructor once told me. Know what the first rule of self-defense is?"

"No."

"Don't be there."

"Got it. I'll call you when I'm ready to leave."

SEVENTY-EIGHT

"Who was that?"

"Henry. He's found evidence of another program, but no smoking guns yet."

She takes a long swig of coffee. "What did you put in that pasta? I was out like a light."

"Somehow I doubt it was the pasta."

She wrinkles her nose. "I suspect you're right. Did I dream it, or was the computer being weird last night?"

"It wasn't a dream. Epicurious seems to also include literary excerpts between courses."

"*Jekyll and Hyde*, right?" She shoves papers aside until she finds the book she wants on the floor under the table. "Here it is; *Henry Jekyll's Full Statement of the Case.*"

"There were two paragraphs. The first was something about being two people, not one."

"Yes, that's a pretty famous passage from the beginning of the chapter. Here's the rest of it."

"And indeed the worst of my faults was a certain impatient gaiety of disposition, such as has made the happiness of many, but such as I found it hard to reconcile with my imperious desire to carry my head high, and wear a more than commonly grave countenance before the public. Hence it came about that I concealed my pleasures; and that when I reached years of reflection, and began to look round me and take stock of my progress and position in the world, I stood already committed to a profound duplicity of life. Many a man would have even blazoned such irregularities as I was guilty of; but from the high views that I had set before me, I regarded and hid them with an almost morbid sense of shame. It was thus rather the exacting nature of my aspirations than any particular degradation in my faults, that made me what I was and, with even a deeper trench than in the majority of men,

severed in me those provinces of good and ill which divide and compound man's dual nature."

"And that's why Jekyll started experimenting?"

"Uh-huh."

"I had learned to dwell with pleasure, as a beloved day-dream, on the thought of the separation of these elements. If each, I told myself, could but be housed in separate identities, life would be relieved of all that was unbearable."

Franklin holds up his hand. "May I see that, please?" She hands him the book, and he sits rereading the passage for several minutes. "And what was the other part last night?"

"The one where Jekyll realizes that he's no longer in control?"

"Yes, I remember." Franklin leans back and empties his cup. "I'm getting more coffee; want some?"

"Thank you, yes."

He comes back to the couch. "I think I know who killed Matt."

"Who?"

"Mr. Hyde."

"Oh? How did he manage that?"

"These days, he conceals himself in a computer, because our modern Dr. Jekyll doesn't use chemicals to partition himself or stuff his unwanted impulses into an alternative flesh and blood manifestation. He houses them in a virtual self, a separate, super-intelligent electronic alter ego."

She stares at him. "You're serious. You think that's what someone did?"

"Let me tell you what I know. Having met the guy, I'd say that Chris Walker is an uptight, very cerebral man who'd never dream of telling an off-color joke or scratching himself in public. Both Henry and Matt say he's brilliant and undervalued. His wife patronizes him, and his boss ignores him. He's the quintessential long-suffering researcher who lives for the intellectual pleasures of science. He's signed over his share of fame and glory and financial reward to Atkinson, who flaunts them and parades around in them at Walker's expense. What's the chance that some part of him is just dying to get out and shout, 'Look at me now, you pompous bastards! See what I can do when I put my mind to it!'."

"High, I'd guess."

"Even if he can't bring himself to say that out loud, could he design a program so spectacular, so showy and glitzy that anyone who saw it couldn't miss the message?"

"There are lots of not-so-glamorous people who try to live through their creations; some of them succeed."

"Which is fine, unless your amoral creation has a mind of its own and falls into the wrong hands."

SEVENTY-NINE

"Whose hands would be the wrong ones?"

"I suspect Atkinson is telling the truth, and Feldborg Pharmaceuticals has nothing to do with Janus Health. They're an outside entity, people with their own agenda, who've somehow gained access to Walker's fatally intuitive software. Henry believes there's a program out there that's incorporated parts of *STUD*. What if it includes Anderson's hyper-competitive, 'win at all costs and destroy the opposition' Super Overachiever code? Imagine that plugged into an intuitive black box, Henry's non-moral instrument. Or a program that picked up on Walker's conflicted feelings and has learned to mirror them?"

"And Matt found someone using *STUD* and tried to check it out."

"And got himself killed for his efforts."

"So, what are you going to do? How do you find these people?"

"I told Henry to get the hell out of there. I'm having him stay at my apartment until I can get him deposed. It's all circumstantial evidence, but if we get the right judge, I can get a search warrant."

She looks at him. "And you're sure about this?" It comes out more as a statement than a question.

"Yes. This is where Louis and Fanny have been trying to tell me. They've been on me since the day Ortega assigned me this case. Fanny changed the photos in the diary when she decided I was getting distracted by Nora May's story. Louis showed up when I went to Janus, and he handed Kevin the Feldborg flyer we'd missed. And when I still didn't connect the dots, he decided to beat us over the head with *Jekyll and Hyde* excerpts last night. It all makes sense—except that I don't believe in ghosts."

"Please don't ask for any more proof; we've had a pretty big dose of this dead literary couple already. That we've been a little slow on the uptake shouldn't matter; by all reports, they were very good at being direct when they wanted to be. What do you need me to do today?"

"Follow your schedule as usual—'Move along, folks; nothing at all to see here'—while I'm stashing Henry. Getting his testimony down on paper in a legally binding form is my first priority. I wish I could have one more go at Atkinson or Walker as well."

"You might get that chance this afternoon. We'll be filming parts of the episode later today, and we expect both of them to stop by the studio. My co-workers have noticed how often I seem to be in your company; I'm afraid our cover has been blown. But we can use that to our advantage. Everyone sees this episode as a feather in my cap. No one will find it strange that I've asked you to stop by to witness the filming of my finest hour. After all, you are the one who figured out Uncle Brad's little joke."

He sits looking at her with his mouth half-open. "And here I thought you were such an innocent young thing when I met you."

"Feminine wiles. Didn't those girls you met in Vice teach you anything besides how to cook pasta?"

Even though he expects his University pharmacology consultant won't have anything for him yet, Chris Walker has a few minutes before meeting Grace for brunch at the Cliff House. He asks his secretary to call and leave a reminder; to his surprise, he's put through to the professor himself.

"Dr. Walker! I was planning to call you a little later today. I've got good news and bad news for you; which would you like first?"

"Let's start with the good news."

"The compounds your program designed turn out to be easy to categorize. One appears to be a variation of an SSRI, an antidepressant. The other resembles an antibiotic in the fluoroquinolone family, and the third is a cousin of thalidomide."

"I see. At least I'm relieved to hear that I haven't asked for something complicated. And the bad news?"

"They won't work. At least, that's our initial impression. The side chain the program has changed in the antibiotic might render it ineffective as an antimicrobial."

"So biologically it would be inactive?"

"Well, it wouldn't do much to kill germs. The base structure is close enough that it still might do *something*, though what is hard to say."

"And the antidepressant?"

"Looks like it should target serotonin receptors, but it wouldn't block reuptake, which is what SSRIs do. It might even speed up reuptake. So tell whoever is working on this thing that if this is what his program can do, it's not ready for prime time yet."

"No, I guess not."

"I should have something more for you towards the end of the week. Have a good weekend."

He tries to digest this. The program works; it can rearrange assemblies of atoms derived from parent compounds. A close relative of an existing drug should have some biological activity, but these formulations lack the sought-after efficacy. *So why are Darryl Lockheed and Fred Willoughby so happy with a program that produces duds?*

The Cliff House

EIGHTY

He's wheeled to a table by large windows that look out on the Pacific. It's a cloudless day. The fog has burned off, and there's enough breeze to drive a continuous line of breakers against the Seal Rocks. The horizon is a neat line of blue against blue.

"What a delightful idea. I never think of coming here; it's so touristy, and the menu is staid. But on a day like this, everything is perfect. I could just curl up here like a cat on a windowsill."

Grace is so relaxed that he hesitates to mention the pharmacologist's findings. But she puts her menu down and places her hand on his. "Just once, dear, wouldn't you like to put work aside and enjoy your surroundings? We haven't had many days this clear all summer, and we're having a nice meal together. What is there to be concerned about?"

"The program, and my consulting work. I don't understand the output, and the program seems able to transform itself in unexpected ways. That could be a characteristic of its design, but it's disconcerting. And I don't know these people who commissioned it."

"You distress yourself over trivialities. You're such a perfectionist. These people are S21CBR members who've formed a new company, respected businessmen who left top-line organizations to strike out on their own. They wanted you as their consultant to help build a program for them. It's that simple." She smiles playfully at him. "You are a smart man, but you don't have a medical background. It's no surprise if you're finding yourself a little out of your element."

"Perhaps you're right. The program seems to run well enough on its own."

"Isn't that the whole point of Artificial Intelligence? I can remember you telling me about a program that played chess better than a Grand Master."

"Kasparov accused IBM of cheating."

265

"But your machine isn't cheating. You've created something wonderful. I can feel it. Why refuse to accept yourself as the genius that you are?"

"Please, Grace! I scarcely think... Even if I were as brilliant as you claim, I can't see myself strutting around *flaunting* it."

"But you must understand you're gifted; why not at least acknowledge that much? I suppose expecting you to enjoy yourself would be asking too much. For the life of me, I'll never understand where this puritanical suspicion of pleasure comes from. You're working with businessmen here; in their world, diffidence is not a trait that's prized."

He's losing an argument that he never wanted to start. "I think it's that Matt Glover was killed. Murdered. That still bothers me."

"I realize you were very fond of that boy, and I'm as sorry as you are that he's dead. But there was nothing you could have done to prevent it."

"But what if someone thinks...?"

"... Thinks Janus had something to do with it? Don't be absurd! The papers said he died after a night of drinking. They found his body on Russian Hill; he had fallen down some stairs. A tragic misjudgment, but I wonder if you aren't letting your sorrow about the death of your assistant cloud your judgment."

"I'd feel better if I could discuss my questions with other experts, but I don't feel that I can."

"What would stop you, other than that so few 'experts' are your equal?"

"Dr. Atkinson ..."

"Oh, please! You're not serious, are you? I know what even you think of his so-called scientific prowess; there are lots of other people, talented scientists, who feel the same way. He may be the CEO, but you are the Janus Health Institute. What would they do if you left? They'd fall apart and end up selling medical records software again. I suspect that access to this program of yours will prove more important than a lot of things in your field. Just imagine what will happen when people recognize that and accept it as a business reality. Some collateral damage is inevitable in business ventures, and if that includes Atkinson and Company, we both know that there's only one person whom they'll hold responsible."

I wish I could feel some of the conviction that informs your world. But I don't, and I can't explain why.

Their food arrives with a bottle of champagne. Grace raises her glass. "I've had quite a few conversations with Mr. Lockheed, and I've become fond of him, the same way you felt about Matt Glover. When Darryl told me that this Feldborg company needed something special, I knew at once that you were the man who could create it for them, and you did. You'll just have to accept that even though you didn't choose to be a genius, you were born one. Perhaps at some point, you'll be able to reconcile yourself to that fact."

I have created a monstrosity that has a mind of its own. I have lost all control, and I can't rid myself of the feeling that something is bearing down on me.

"Thank you. I guess sometimes I lose sight of the forest for the trees."

"I know. I've always expected you to succeed, but it can still feel overwhelming and a little disorienting when you come face to face with what you've accomplished."

She turns to flag down a waiter for coffee. "What do you have on your schedule for this afternoon?"

"I'm going to KQXR. They're taping a TV show this afternoon that Janus is sponsoring."

"Are you featured in it?"

He winces. "I'm not sure. I hope not."

She sighs again. "When an opportunity presents itself,"

He smiles wanly and turns back to his Eggs San Francisco. A riddle one of his Asian students once told him comes to mind.

Every day, a dog chases a car.
What happens on the day
that he catches it?

Sailing

EIGHTY-ONE

The breeze has picked up by the time they leave the Cliff House. The radio is on, but Walker has been ignoring the KQXR News reporter until a powerful gust buffets the car and interrupts his thoughts.

"Can you turn that up, please?"

The Coast Guard reports they've found a swamped dinghy drifting in the Bay. No one was aboard, and a search and rescue operation is underway. The identity of the boat's owner has not been released. Winds are expected to increase throughout the afternoon, with gusts up to 35 miles per hour. Boaters are advised to use caution and stay tuned for further weather updates.

He settles back in his seat and tries to quell his rising sense of foreboding.

"The rest of your morning go OK?"

Henry nods. "No problems, though yesterday's conversation is getting to me. I kept thinking someone was behind me all morning, no matter where I went."

Franklin glances at him. "That's why we're driving down to San Bruno. Give me your house keys. This evening, I'll grab some clothes from your closet, and Kevin will drive your car down. Our priority now is to get you out of Dodge."

His phone rings; it's Elizabeth. "Promise not to tell if I take this call while driving?"

Henry raises three fingers. "Scout's honor."

"Hey, I was just about to call you. I assume you'll be leaving for the station soon. What time do you want me to stop by?"

She sounds a little out of breath. "I'm running a little late, so there's no rush. It's been an eventful morning."

"Again? Even more eventful than when I left?"

"Yes. This *Lost Tales* episode is the gift that keeps on giving."

"Let me guess. Stevenson isn't dead and is holed up in a hotel with Elvis and Jimmy Hoffa in Vegas."

"Nothing that cheerful. I found Dr. Montfort's death notice in the *Transactions of the Medical Society of the State of California during the Years of 1880 and 1882.*"

"My favorite light reading. So now you have proof that there was a Dr. Monfort. Any evidence that Liam Cromartie was also a real person?"

"That too. The entire story was in the *San Francisco Call.*"

"And?"

"Liam Cromartie murdered Charles Montfort in August 1880. The *Call* said that Cromartie had been a patient of Montfort's. The killing puzzled the authorities, who believed that the doctor had saved Cromartie's life. At his trial, Cromartie justified his actions by citing 'God's laws' and Montfort's 'trafficking with devils from heathen lands and in the sea'. "

"I wonder if Cromartie had discovered the side effects of Dr. Montfort's prescription firsthand."

"Which would mean that part of the story was true as well. At the trial, the judge declared Cromartie insane, which provoked another outburst. According to the *Call* article, Cromartie claimed he knew right from wrong, and it was sinners like Montfort, whose pride caused them to challenge the Divine Will, who were deluded."

"Amen, Sister! Let's hear it for that Old Time Religion!"

"The judge remained unpersuaded, and Cromartie ended up confined to the Insane Asylum of California at Stockton for the rest of his life."

"Well, that will lend some punch to the end of your story."

"I'll say! The staff dug up photos of the old Stockton Asylum; it looks like it belongs in an Addams Family cartoon. Cromartie left a rambling manifesto before he died. He expressed no regret for his actions and swore he would 'wreak vengeance on anyone who dares to repeat such godless acts, for years at sea have shown me the face of the Devil and his works'."

"Have you shown any of this to your producer? It's lurid enough to appeal to his trashy sense of showmanship."

"Yes, it is. And here I was trying to tone down the tabloid aspects. It confirms Mr. Jackson's story, but I'm still afraid Louis will get lost in all this other."

"Had he heard about the murder?"

"It's not likely. He was back in New York by August, getting ready to sail to Scotland with Fanny."

"No wonder he never finished the story. If he knew how things ended ..."

"Though he didn't know it, Mr. Jackson was nearer the mark than he knew when he compared Belle's fragment with *Jekyll*. Montfort failed to foresee the full effects of his medical treatment and died as a result, just like the fictional Dr. Jekyll. Though I think Jekyll's story is the more artful one. Death by splitting your personality in two is a very original exit strategy."

"How did Montfort die?"

"Another gothic element in this whole thing. Cromartie drowned him in the Francisco Street Reservoir."

Franklin feels the blood drain from his face. "Where are you now?"

"At the Public Library. I'm leaving for KQXR in a few minutes."

"I'm on my way. Wait for me, and please don't go into the studio until I get there!"

"What? Why?"

"Please, just do this. I'm heading there right now."

He hangs up. "Sorry, Henry, but there's been a change of plans. You ever wanted to be on TV?"

He hands his phone to Henry as he turns the car around. "Here, can you get Kevin for me?"

The Stockton Asylum

271

EIGHTY-TWO

Dr. Atkinson is holding court with the KQXR's staff when Chris Walker wheels himself into the studio. Ms. Mills isn't there, and there's no one else to run interference and blunt the impact of Atkinson in performance mode.

"A truly wonderful discovery, a genuine Robert Louis Stevenson missing story, a piece of the past brought to light again! The perfect analogy for Janus Health's Big Data project, where we're uncovering new connections and therapeutic applications from the wealth of all the world's great healing traditions! Past and present: that's why we named the company after the Roman god." He beams. "So when do we get to see these remarkable documents?"

"They're over a hundred years old and very fragile," the assistant producer begins apologetically. Noticing Atkinson's expression, he adds, "But we have some excellent copies that you can see."

"And not just me! We want everyone to see them. This is television, and seeing is believing. I realize that you're a National Public Television affiliate, and we're happy to adhere to the model of an understated sponsorship statement that's a feature of your programming. But I think it could be educational if we used this opportunity for a few pictures for our files. No one would have any objections to that."

"It might depend. If you intend to use them for marketing..."

"No, no! I was considering a photo for our lobby, with a plaque commemorating this remarkable occasion and the productive relationship we enjoy together."

"So, a picture of you and the manuscript pages?" The assistant sounds unconvinced.

Atkinson is scanning the room and spots Chris Walker. "Not me, no. I'd like you to meet Dr. Christopher Walker, one of our most distinguished senior scientists. I can say with confidence that there is no one who better embodies the principles the Janus Health Insitute stands for. He met Ms.

272

Mills when we announced this event to our staff the other day. I'd like a picture of the two of them with this incredible discovery; the scientist and the literary sleuth with a piece of genuine San Francisco history of the first water. It will make a powerful statement. Or perhaps sixty seconds of video with comments from them both?"

The assistant producer looks dazed by the onslaught. "That sounds like a brilliant idea, sir; let me just run this by ..." His words trail off as he looks around. "I don't see Ms. Mills here yet; she called earlier and said she'd be a little late." He turns to a staffer. "Maddy, perhaps you could find a space where we could start setting up for Dr. Walker? When Elizabeth arrives, we'll have her pop in for a moment before we start filming. That way we won't be imposing on the doctor by taking up any more of his valuable time."

"Excellent! Here, let's give Dr. Walker the documents. They can set up the shoot while I walk with you. I have some other ideas I'd like to discuss with you or your superior." The assistant turns to escort Dr. Atkinson. A smiling young woman invites Chris Walker to follow her to a small side room, a cameraman in tow.

A sense of relief tempers his consternation at being swept up in one more of Atkinson's grandiose self-promotional events. So the whole improbable story about lost documents is true, nothing more than a bit of Victorian melodrama that its author had abandoned, perhaps with good reason. *As usual, I was giving Atkinson too much credit.* There's no hidden plot; it's just been another of Jim's ham-fisted attempts at a photo-op.

Ms. Mills will be here at any minute and will no doubt confirm that things are what they seem. This is just a story about a famous long-dead writer. Grace has been right all along; I allowed myself to be swept away by emotion, something I've always tried to avoid.

The photographer has set up the camera and is positioning lights. Someone applies a light coating of makeup to his face and adjusts his glasses to eliminate reflections. Maddy brings in a sheaf of papers and has him practice holding them and glancing down as if reading. Another minute and his handlers seem satisfied, but there's still no sign of Ms. Mills. Maddy looks at her watch. "Please excuse us for a moment, Doctor, while we go find Elizabeth." She and the cameraman head for the central studio.

He sits feeling his anxiety drain away until he decides it's another form of indulging his emotions. *Where is Ms. Mills? Sitting here, I feel like an exhibit at Madame Tussaud's.* He shuffles through the pages he's been holding. The writing is an old-fashioned cursive script, written with a pen that sputtered, but it's still legible. The top sheet appears to be a letter.

January 26, 1880,
My Dear Colvin,

Thank you for your letter and promise of books. I have been very much out of health and spirits, down with pleurisy again. I have taken a holiday from writing, having no style for command at the moment.

But it is not for want of material. Yesterday, in Portsmouth Square, I happened on a fellow Scot, an aging seaman named Cromartie.

Liam Cromartie

EIGHTY-THREE

Franklin heads for Mariposa Street and the KQXR studios with lights flashing and the siren echoing off the buildings. He wants to bring Kevin up to date, but driving and organizing his thoughts at the same time is proving difficult. Henry remains expressionless but has braced himself against the dash, just in case.

"So the instrument of Feldborg's malfeasance could be a version of *STUD* running inside Janus?" Kevin's on speakerphone; it sounds like he's also using his siren en route to KQXR.

"That's our belief. Henry's here with me."

"Oh. Hi again, Henry; long time, no see. Is there a chance that whoever was Feldborg's stooge got the wrong version of *STUD*, the one designed by the sociopath?"

"Hard to prove, and I'm not sure if it would matter."

"Bummer! What does Robert Louis Stevenson think? Was it somebody who couldn't figure out consequences, like Dr. Jekyll when he teamed up with Mr. Hyde?"

"Louis doesn't seem inclined to talk to me directly."

"It wouldn't be the first time somebody got mixed up in some nasty shit while telling himself it's not his fault. Just sayin'. Stevenson would have made a good cop. Anyway, what's going down at the TV studio?"

"Elizabeth is there; this morning she found out what happened to Dr. Montfort."

"Wait—so there was a Dr. Montfort?"

"Yeah, she found an old newspaper story about him."

"So what happened to the dude?"

"Liam Cromartie drowned him in the Francisco Street Reservoir."

"Holy shit!"

What the hell? It's only been how many days, and now Kevin takes the existence of ghosts for granted?

276

They drive the rest of the way in silence.

An ambulance and several police cars are lined up outside KQXR. They flash their badges and are allowed inside the yellow police tape. An officer recognizes Franklin.

"Can you have someone stay with Dr. Qu? I've got to find Elizabeth Mills."

"She's over there, Sergeant. We felt she'd be safer in the car."

Elizabeth is standing by a squad car, talking with a female officer.

"After you called, I drove over but didn't go in the studio. Then all hell broke loose. People came running out of the building, and police cars started showing up, and the ambulance. I was worried you might be in there."

"But I wasn't." He gives her a long hug. "Stay here while we find out what happened."

They push their way into the main studio. Officers are interviewing employees in a cordoned-off area. Franklin scans the group and nudges Kevin. Jim Atkinson sits staring at the floor, holding a cup of water with both hands. He looks deflated, like a balloon that's leaking air, and his usual air of command has deserted him.

The officer in charge looks surprised to see them. "Homicide here already? That was quick."

"So what happened?"

"The decedent was in the room over there. They were setting up for a photo shoot, and the photographer and assistant left to find someone. Nobody saw anyone go in or out of there, but then they heard a lot of screaming and came running. That's where they found him."

In the side studio, a camera on a tripod lies in one corner, and someone has knocked over a light panel. Chris Walker's wheelchair is on its side, and the doctor is on the floor, lying on his back on the floor. His head is twisted at an impossible angle; his eyes and mouth are still open. Even in death, his face retains a look of incomprehension.

His clothes are soaked as if he'd been dropped in the Bay. The officer beside them shakes his head. "What I don't get is how he got so wet."

On the wall above Chris Walker's body, someone has scrawled a message in chalk.

THUS IS THE DEVIL'S WORK BROUGHT LOW AND THE TRUE FACE OF DIVINE JUSTICE REVEALED.

Kevin stoops to examine the body and looks up at Franklin. "I'll call in and tell the desk Sergeant I'm already here. You want to check on Elizabeth and then find somebody to take Henry to your place?"

EIGHTY-FOUR

Atkinson spots Franklin as he's crossing the main studio and flags him down, ignoring the two officers questioning him. "What's going on here, Sergeant? They won't let me see Chris, and no one will tell me anything!"

"Someone has attacked Dr. Walker, Doctor; we're still gathering evidence. That's all I can offer you at this point."

"Is he ..." Atkinson's face is a mask of disbelief.

"I'm afraid so."

Atkinson starts to deflate again; an officer moves to get a chair under him. "This can't be happening. It's not possible. Kortov said as much when he put us together." He catches Franklin's confusion. "Andre Kortov. You met him at Janus; your first visit."

"The Grandview Vice President?"

"Yes. He said they'd spent months doing background checks and studying our track records before he chose Chris and me to run Janus. 'Virtual psychological profiling', he called it. He said it would guarantee there'd be no conflicts, no possibility of failure. Nothing like this was supposed to happen."

"Did Mr. Kortov set up Janus Health?"

"I make the day-to-day decisions, but the pre-planning, the nuts and bolts stuff, the infrastructure that supports Janus Health, that was all Andre."

"And that included the computer network?"

"Yes, of course. We told him what we needed in terms of firepower and let him run interference with the Grandview brass to get us what we wanted. He made sure it stayed up and running. Grandview had tried to get into healthcare before; Kortov promised to make it work this time. He said he could make it profitable in a hurry if they gave him free rein."

Pay no attention to the man behind the curtain. Andre Kortov was the man who used psychological profiling to pick the scientists and who set up the hardware. Franklin thinks of the poster he once saw for *My Fair Lady*. Rex Harrison is manipulating Julie Andrews like a marionette. Above him, George Bernard Shaw looks down from Heaven, holding the strings attached to Rex Harrison.

"Thank you, Dr. Atkinson. The officers will take your statement. After that, you're free to go to your home, but please don't leave town. I'm afraid the Janus offices are now a crime scene; you shouldn't go there without checking with us first."

"Crime scene? It's a business and a damn important one! Whatever happened to Chris Walker happened here, not there."

"And when two members of the same damn important business die under suspicious circumstances, we need to look at what they had in common." He turns to the officers. "Please give Dr. Atkinson a lift home after he's done here."

Kevin is back in the central studio. "OK, it's ours. I didn't have any trouble convincing them that this should be part of the Matt Glover case, now that it's turning into the Janus Health case."

"You done here for the moment?"

"Yeah, the crime scene guy's photographing everything now. I didn't find anything other than what we saw when we got here."

Franklin glances back at the small studio. "If Walker was our man, somebody else who's involved with Feldborg got pissed off at him."

"One more disposable member of the Janus team."

"There's been a change in plans; we need to get back to 450 Sutter Street. Grab a couple of officers, and let's take Henry with us. We need to see if he can still get into the program he found this morning. I'll fill you in on the way there."

"What about Elizabeth?"

"She's still outside with an officer. I think she should stay there."

"No, she's right over here."

Kevin's right. Elizabeth is standing with an officer and several studio people. They're all talking with a seated older man. She looks up as they walk over.

Franklin frowns. "I'm not sure it's safe for you to be here."

"Even though I'm surrounded by police? This is Glen, my producer, and this is Mr. Jackson. I couldn't leave him alone in the middle of all this."

"We'll take good care of everyone here, Sergeant, no worry." The officer has her notebook out and radiates an aura of control.

"I'm sure you will. We'll leave you to your work; Inspector Loeffler and I will check back later. Right now, we're needed somewhere else." Elizabeth shoots him a quizzical look. "I'll bring you up to date soon."

"I'm sure I'll be fine. I have good people looking after me, and I doubt Mr. Cromartie has any interest in me, anyway."

You are cordially invited to a

LOVE AMONG THE RUINS LUNCHEON

Saturday, October 15, 2016 at 11:00 AM

Chow
215 Church Street
San Francisco, CA 94114

EIGHTY-FIVE

Elizabeth puts her menu down and examines the invitation again. "I didn't realize you were such a graphic artist, Kevin."

Henry holds his up. "The couple in the picture, that's Elizabeth and Franklin?"

Kevin grins. "At least in spirit, though Burne-Jones's lovers are a little too heroin chic to be a good match for them. With the two of us in the doghouse, two of you unemployed, and some Silicon Valley rock stars in hot water, the 'ruins' part seemed to fit. I felt a decompression lunch was in order, and Chow's Smiling Noodles always work as comfort food, at least for me

Chow

"Are you two in real trouble?"

"Not exactly. It's more like guys in the Department don't trust cops — excuse me, 'fellow officers' — who've been mixed up with stuff as weird as the shit we've been through. We were already in bad odor because we hadn't solved Matt's murder. When four more people turned up dead and the FBI got involved, guys were like, 'Are you two clueless, or dirty, or both?' "

Gary turns to his partner. "Wait, there were five murders?"

"Looks like it." Kevin glances around, but the diners at the other tables are absorbed in private conversations. "Everyone agreed that Matt Glover was murdered. Andy Enright died of an overdose, Darryl Lockheed drowned, Myra took her own life, and Dr. Walker died of natural causes, according to the record."

"Natural causes?"

"Yeah. Just like when I throw someone off the top of a building and he has a heart attack on the way down. I didn't kill him; he died of natural causes before he hit the ground."

Franklin looks bemused. "Cases of people drowning on dry land seem to be a specialty of yours. I hope you don't make it a habit."

"What did Ian Fleming say? 'Once is happenstance, twice is coincidence, and three times is enemy action'."

"Huh? I still don't understand; you've lost me."

"Sorry; a private joke."

Franklin clears his throat. "These people all died with some outside help. Darryl was an experienced sailor, and the weather wasn't anything unusual on the day he drowned. After the Coast Guard recovered his body, the FBI ran some extra toxicology tests. They're not saying what they found, but more than just saltwater was involved."

"Andy's friends found a syringe near his body and assumed it was heroin. Heroin kills you by stopping your breathing. It happens fast; I've seen addicts who died with the needle still in their arm. But Andy died screaming and writhing in pain; his cries were loud enough to bring his friends to his side."

Kevin grimaces. "Not exactly the sort of exit I associate with Zen. I wonder if that was what his friends meant when they talked about protecting Andy from hungry ghosts."

"Everyone knew Myra was depressed and on medication. What they haven't uncovered is exactly what Feldborg Pharmaceuticals sent her and what it did to her. It may take a while before we know all the details."

"And the 'we' in this case won't include Franklin or me." Kevin smiles. "No big surprise there. As soon as Ortega smelled TV coverage coming, he grilled us and hustled off to regurgitate what we'd told him to the Feds verbatim. Once the FBI got involved, we were off the case—and so was he. With a gag order thrown in for good measure."

"And Mr. Subtlety here"—Franklin gestures towards Kevin—"reminded Mike he owed us for not submitting that, report that had him identifying Andy Enright as the killer."

No one says anything for a moment. Then Elizabeth turns to Henry. "And how are you doing?"

He shrugs. "The first week was rough until the Feds decided I didn't have the program, and I wasn't smart enough to be the brains behind the operation. By then, Grandview had announced it was suspending operations at Janus 'while the current investigation is ongoing'. The business press is already predicting Janus's demise, and we're all sending out copies of our CVs. I've updated my resume, but an affiliation with Janus isn't the draw it once was."

Elizabeth smiles ruefully. "And KQXR seems to have lost interest in *Literary San Francisco* for the moment. My producer's planning to move to LA as soon as the FBI will let him."

"But your teaching, and the tours?"

"They've survived; in fact, they're more popular than ever. But my students and the tourists are more interested in recent events than in learning to write well or hearing about local history."

"I can imagine. What happened to the Stevenson manuscript?"

"The originals are still with the conservators; they were never at the studio. The FBI wants them because the copies have somehow disappeared; it's all still in the hands of lawyers. Poor Mr. Jackson! They grilled him, even though Glen and I told them he was an innocent bystander. I bet he wishes he'd never heard of me or my program."

Kevin pulls a sympathetic face. "It's not your fault; the FBI treats everybody that way. Of course, they'd be paranoid about Arthur Jackson; Raytheon is a major defense contractor. But linking Robert Louis Stevenson to DoD contracts is a stretch, even for them."

"I imagine Arthur may feel better once the documents have been authenticated and he finds out how much they're worth. But he's made the national news and may have to face Uncle Brad's kids in court."

Gary looks at Henry and Elizabeth. "I'm sorry. I didn't realize how much this had screwed up everybody's lives. Kevin's spared me the ugly details."

"We're not supposed to be talking about this anyway. Homeland Security is also involved, but very quietly."

Gary's eyes widen. "It's that big?"

Kevin snickers again. "Yeah, and that's another reason I don't feel reassured. Remember the last scene in *Raiders of the Lost Ark*? 'We have top men working on it right now.' Fade to the giant warehouse."

"But who do you think is responsible for killing these people?"

EIGHTY-SIX

A waiter arrives with their food. Franklin stares at the pizza Elizabeth has ordered. "What is that?"

"Spicy pork, tomatillo, and cilantro. It's fantastic." Elizabeth narrows her eyes. "Let me guess. You're a plain pepperoni guy, right? So boring."

"We interrupt this episode of *Law and Order* to bring you news from the Food Network."

Gary grabs a napkin and threatens Kevin with it. "Talk quick, Franklin, before I have to gag him."

"Thank you. Just keep an eye on him and let up if he starts turning blue."

"Children! Mind your manners at table!" Elizabeth tries to look stern. "And Gary, you'd better move your hand if you don't want to get stabbed with a forkful of Smiling Noodles."

Franklin puts a slice of pizza on his plate. "A few days before his death, Dr. Walker asked a colleague to look at some computer output he assumed was the result of a coding error. The consultant said that the results resembled existing drugs but would be ineffective or toxic. If Chris Walker knew what the program was really designing, he wouldn't need a consultant. He created a deep learning program for drug synthesis, but somebody else was telling it what to make. This had been the plan from the beginning, though it was kept hidden from everyone."

"Whose plan was it?"

"Andre Kortov, Grandview's Vice President for Development. He oversaw the creation of Janus Health and had the means and opportunity to develop and implement this plan."

"Has he admitted anything?"

"He disappeared the day Walker died. He knew the game was up and had already planned his escape."

"But how did he mastermind everything?"

"Henry would call it social engineering; we'd call it psychological warfare."

"You've lost me. Again."

"Grandview Corp wanted to get into healthcare and had decided that medical information services had too small a profit margin. Kortov had heard Dr. Walker lecture on AI applications in medicine, and he sold Grandview on the idea that this could be the Next Big Thing. Once they put Kortov in charge, he started assembling a network of clients looking for new drugs, both legitimate pharmaceuticals and chemical warfare agents."

"An updated MKUltra program to serve a niche market?"

"Gary, you surprise me."

Elizabeth interrupts. "Will someone please help the English major? What's MKUltra?"

"It was a 50s covert CIA project where they fed unsuspecting people LSD and tried to put poison in Fidel Castro's underwear."

Franklin takes a bite of pizza. "MKUltra ran mind control experiments as part of its effort to combat Communist brainwashing techniques. It was a clandestine program that included chemical warfare and non-consensual human testing. Kortov was different; he hid his operation in plain sight. For starters, he recruited a brilliant academic and made him subordinate to his polar opposite in order to create an environment intensely frustrating to Walker."

"Which is why Kortov picked Atkinson as CEO?"

"One reason, yes. Mrs. Walker also contributed to his plan, perhaps unwittingly. She knew her husband was unhappy at Janus, so when an eager young entrepreneur came looking for an AI consultant, it was a virtual certainty she'd connect him with her husband."

Kevin almost aspirates a noodle. "One meeting with her was enough. Spent a week afterward trying to remember where Sister Brigid put Pride on the list of the Seven Deadly Sins."

Elizabeth smiles at Kevin. "You should take up writing. You have a gift for metaphor. But does this mean that Darryl was also in on the scheme?"

"I don't think so. Because Darryl knew very little about medicine or computers, it would have been easy to keep him in the dark. If he believed Feldborg was a legitimate start-up, it would have made his pitch to Dr. Walker sound sincere. I doubt he appreciated the true intentions of the Feldborg partners."

"And once he was no longer needed, he ended up in the bay. All very neat."

"Neat, and ruthless. But that's part of the business model when you're selling dirty tricks and chemical warfare."

"And Matt was killed because he discovered the actual function of the program?"

"Because he had an idea and was stubborn enough to hold on to it and pursue it." Henry looks reflective. "He kept working on his code and sharing the revisions with Dr. Walker. He also tracked them, which is how he discovered pieces of the hidden program and its data."

Franklin picks up the thread again. "He also assumed Feldborg was a legitimate client and printed out the flyer for Myra. That may have attracted Kortov's attention. Not knowing how much Matt had figured out, they disposed of him and keep Myra as a guinea pig. When Andy Enright became Matt's hiking buddy and sometime confidant, he also became collateral damage."

Gary looks shocked. "That's an awful lot of killing. Didn't Kortov realize he'd get caught?"

"I suspect he'd already made escape plans for every eventuality. In the beginning, he didn't know if his scheme would even work. If Walker couldn't create the program, the Feldborg clients would be unhappy, and Kortov might need to disappear in a hurry. If it did work, he'd let it create new drugs and chemicals and bail if things got too dicey. He didn't intend to hang around long in either case."

"Take the money and run?"

"Pretty much. But he underestimated Matt Glover's abilities and couldn't predict how grating a boss Jim Atkinson would be. Frustration plus self-doubt and fear of failure drove Walker to use some of Matt's ideas, which is what made the scheme detectable."

"With Henry's help." Kevin hesitates. "Which is why we had to get you out of there as soon as you found evidence that supported our theory,. Atkinson was oblivious, but Feldborg had been watching you because you had been Matt's roommate. Once you took his place, you were in their sights."

Henry takes a deep breath. "I suspected something like that. Thank you."

"And Dr. Walker? Did Kortov have him killed too?" Gary looks almost as distressed as Henry.

"It was no coincidence that someone killed him after he started investigating the program's output. He knew it would try to design anything someone asked it to. What would happen if he found that the output included things like MKUltra-style hallucinogenics, poisons related to dioxin or ricin, and 'Myra agents'—ineffective look-alike medicines, or ones that exacerbated diseases or had terrible side effects? The amount of malign creativity involved was breathtaking, and if he got even a whiff of that, Walker would have to go. But who killed him, or how, we still don't know for sure."

EIGHTY-SEVEN

"Poor Myra!" Elizabeth looks so stricken that Franklin puts his arm around her. "A life someone ended as casually as if they were tossing out yesterday's newspaper. And for what?"

"No reason other than curiosity about whether their new product worked. And of course, she was a friend of Matt's." Kevin's face is a mask. "I wonder if anyone knows how many of San Francisco's homeless have died of unknown causes in the last year? All in the name of science."

"But what sort of people would pursue such a monstrous idea?"

"You mean, other than the people who brought you impending nuclear annihilation and MKUltra? People like those who worked for the DoD and the CIA?"

"You can't be serious!"

Franklin shakes his head. "In the 1950s, some people felt the Russians wanted to enslave everyone and that Manchurian Candidate-style brainwashing was a real thing. I suspect that philosophically this was much more limited. Kortov came up with a scheme he could market to a select clientele for a short time and make a lot of money. I doubt he understood how powerful Walker's program would turn out to be. Once he did, he didn't want it shared with anyone, so he had to eliminate Chris Walker, grab the software, and disappear."

"But how did it get so extreme? Wasn't there some point along the way where someone could step back and ask, 'What are we doing'?"

"It all went so smoothly and made designing chemical warfare agents mundane, almost routine, that no one even noticed. Just like boiling the frog. My grandfather told me that when we start down a path, there'll always be a point where we're no longer in control, and we won't even realize it."

Henry fumbles for his tablet. "One day early on, Matt came home with an ebook Dr. Walker gave him."

"About a creek somewhere?"

"Yes, *A Tinker at Pilgrim Creek*. You're familiar with it?"

"Walker mentioned it at our first meeting. Something about how nature has already created everything we could want or imagine."

"That section? Interesting." Henry turns his tablet on.

Kevin looks exasperated. "Don't go getting all enigmatic on us, Henry. And please, no more chemistry."

"No. But if we're getting all literary and Elizabeth's here, I want to get this right. Here: Dillard says that right and wrong are human concepts that don't exist in the natural world. She sees human beings as moral creatures in an amoral universe that's 'a robot programmed to kill'. I guess Dr. Walker must have missed that part."

Elizabeth folds her napkin. "I wonder if Annie Dillard would say that Chris Walker's program mirrored the way the biological world operates a little too accurately. That its very success was also its major failing."

Kevin makes a face. "Sort of gives a whole new meaning to the concept of virtual reality. Being a cop is hard enough as it is. I don't need somebody building a Darwinian supercomputer that's all electronic brain without the electronic equivalent of a heart."

"Alan Turing argued that to exhibit intelligent behavior, a computer would have to function in a way that is indistinguishable from a human. Does that mean we need irrational programs because caring human beings aren't like Mr. Spock?" Henry looks at his empty glass. "Perhaps I should look at this as a new career opportunity. 'Henry Qu and Associates—Mildly Irrational Software Made To Order'."

"Do you think Turing would call what you're been creating 'intelligence', artificial or otherwise?"

"I don't know. But I suspect that the father of computer science was a hell of a lot more of a humanist than some of his heirs have turned out to be."

292

EIGHTY-EIGHT

By the time they finally get back to the apartment, the rain is coming down in buckets.

"Your weird pizza was pretty good, and I liked the stuff by local artists they had on the walls. The Castro isn't usually a place I think of for a fine dining experience."

"I suspect Kevin's more subtle, or more devious than he appears."

"Devious, perhaps; subtle I'm less sure about."

"Lunch was a nice gesture, and I doubt the invitation's reference to love was accidental. He's a romantic at heart."

"This is the first time I've seen him bring Gary to an event."

"He feels comfortable enough around you to do that."

"When he can. Even in San Francisco, cop events are aggressively hetero."

"So give yourself credit for being less judgmental than the average police officer."

He shrugs and fingers the invitation sitting on her bookshelf. "Matt, Myra, Darryl, Andy, Walker, *Literary San Francisco*, Janus Health; talk about ruins."

"It's still hard for me to take it all in. Is that what your job feels like — Official Inspector of Ruins?"

"It did when I was serving in Afghanistan."

Concern washes over her face. "I hope you don't include yourself on your list of ruins. Aside from headaches, you've recovered from your injuries."

"The physical ones. I came home having nightmares, and I wanted to avoid people. I'd guess that's why my engagement disintegrated."

"PTSD?"

"That was one label; another doc called it 'acute moral injury'. The military runs on the concept of accountability, but war is always unpredictable.

293

People get killed even when we do everything right. Feeling helpless was the worst part."

"The best soldiers in the world encounter situations they can't control."

"I understand that intellectually, but it doesn't help much. When I was in Kandahar, the first explosion missed me, but the second one blew me across the road and trapped one of my men in his Humvee. He was on fire; he was being burned in front of me. My corpsman was telling me to shoot and put him out of his misery. I stood there listening to his screams, and I couldn't pull the trigger."

She waits for the horror of the memory to subside. "But at some point, were you able to forgive yourself, or your commander, or the Pentagon? You'd have to because no one could survive long in that space otherwise."

"I didn't think it would ever let me go. It's loosened its hold a little, and I'm not sure how I feel about that. It's almost like a betrayal to stop hurting so much."

He has to move some newspapers to fit the invitation back on the shelf. "Um, I'm curious; do you ever throw anything away once it's been committed to print?" He holds up a clipping. *Esa-Pekka Salonen Gives Stravinsky's Oedipus Rex A Forceful Performance In Berkeley.* It's dated October 10.

"That was a concert I went to. It was very good."

"You're into Stravinsky and Greek tragedy?"

"I went because a friend is a member of the San Francisco Conservatory Chorus. They were part of the performance. But doesn't Sophocles count as literature?"

He puts the paper down. "The only Greek myth I remember was the one about Cadmus sowing dragon's teeth."

"Cadmus? He was Oedipus' great-great-grandfather."

"I've never asked, but do you have a photographic memory?"

"Pretty much for literature, but not for anything else. So why Cadmus? It's an obscure enough story."

"A book I had as a kid; I thought the pictures were cool. I was too young to see that everything the guy touched blew up in his face. Sort of like what my grandfather predicted would happen when I enrolled in the Police Academy."

"He told you that?"

"He believed police work was incompatible with his commitment to social justice. That and the 'Power corrupts' thing."

"Do you agree with him?"

"Not really. If anything, being part black has made me a little less judgmental about the people I end up arresting."

"I may be naïve, but in my world, that sounds like a positive." She takes his hand. "Cadmus was a man following the commands of gods whose plans he didn't understand. He couldn't win for losing. I've never been sure whether the message was that humans just can't keep from fucking up or that shit happens."

He laughs despite himself. "Do you talk like this with your students? In Afghanistan, I thought both things were often true."

"And yet you kept going, despite all that happened, and being a cop also hasn't corrupted you. I think your grandfather was overly pessimistic."

He's serious again. "He grew up in a different world than I did."

"I can imagine ... no, I can't. But you must see yourself as a decent person at heart."

"I try."

"I read something in *Smithsonian* where some psychologist showed that power strengthened ethical tendencies in people with a strong moral sense. Your grandfather had nothing to worry about; he raised you right."

"So my job hasn't corrupted me? I guess that's reassuring, even if I'm not as good a detective as a dead Scotsman." Suddenly, he starts to laugh. "I guess we can find allies in strange places. I have you, and a bunch of ghosts, and Kevin."

"Kevin is an ally, and he's also your friend."

"We were in a briefing once, and Ortega was giving Kevin grief about being a casino punk. And Kevin says, 'You know, Mike, Carl Jung said that we don't become enlightened by imagining figures of light but by making the darkness conscious.' It shut Ortega up for at least ten seconds. I have no idea where Kevin comes up with this shit."

"Do you think we should start hanging out in casinos more?"

"Dunno. Kevin claims it's because the only books at home when he was a kid were two volumes of an old *World Book Encyclopedia*. He reread them so many times that he ended up memorizing whole sections of them. But I like the casino idea; they usually serve great drinks."

EIGHTY-NINE

She stretches lazily. "I'm not sure what to do with myself now that the case is over."

"I know. Finding the people behind Feldborg is the FBI's job. They're already treating this as a terrorist plot and aren't releasing any information. Our job was to solve murders, but it's going to be next to impossible to prove what happened to Matt and Myra."

"What about Dr. Walker?"

Franklin shrugs. "The Feds have taken that over, too. When they questioned you, did you tell them about Liam Cromartie?"

"No. All they asked was if the Stevenson papers could be authentic and Dr. Walker's death might be a robbery gone wrong"

"The photographer insists they left the papers with Walker. If his assailant didn't know they were copies, seeing the attack as a robbery isn't unreasonable. Did they ask about the writing on the wall?"

"They asked if I knew what it meant. I didn't *lie*; I said I couldn't say for sure. After all, what else could I tell them? 'The ghost of a lunatic Mr. Stevenson used as a model for a character in a story and who thought Dr. Walker reminded him of someone he'd murdered a hundred years before might have written it.' Is that perjury, officer?"

"I expect the DA's office would decline to prosecute because of mental illness or defect. Or because we're about to wake up and find this was all a dream."

"Sorry, but I already told you, as a plot device, that's a cop-out."

"What about ghosts? Aren't they a clichéd plot device?"

"Louis and Fanny were originals, not clichés, and they're very real to me. Sometimes I can get more connected to characters in stories than to the people around me. Look at our dinner at Cafe Claude. I had you all to myself, and I spent the meal prattling on about the Stevensons."

"I was the one who started it, and what you told me turned out to be key to figuring the case out."

"You're so sweet. I admit I've always had doubts about the significance of what I do, just like Myra and Nora May. Then you showed up and made me feel like I'm something more than a minor writer and a tour guide and a source of literary trivia. I hadn't felt like that in a while. I could learn to like it."

"Well, I had a good time at dinner. The conversation was a lot better than talking about police work. And you must admit it ended well."

"At least you didn't say it ended with a bang."

"Listen to you! I'm shocked a second time."

"I know; I'm supposed to find Sherlock attractive because of his mind. The Stevenson bio is right in front of you; perhaps you should read about how Louis and Fanny carried on in France."

"So that's what they see in us? The universal language of love, or at least of horniness?"

"Louis had two speeds: randy teenager and excited nine-year-old. He was always enthusiastic about something, and he loved being the center of attention. Fanny often got lost in the glare of his fame and personality. I'd bet that lust was part of the glue that held them together."

"If things could be as simple as that, why wasn't Myra happy? There must be enough lust at Inner Truth to glue everybody in San Francisco together."

"Because she wasn't child-like, and Louis wasn't prone to depression? I don't know. He was sick all his life, but when someone asked how he did it, his answer was simple. 'Life is not a matter of holding good cards but of playing a poor hand well'. I can't imagine Nora May or Myra ever saying that. He just kept writing, and Fanny stayed with him through everything. The sickness and obscurity, and the fame and wealth, and life as gypsies in exotic locations. That's the message Fanny wanted to give me: just surviving together can sometimes be achievement enough. Perhaps my next book should be about her or them."

"Is that another of Louis' messages too? Besides the Walker/Jekyll one?"

"He stuffed an awful lot of ideas into the essays he wrote. Nobody reads them anymore."

"Except you."

"They're good teaching examples for students who want to hone their prose skills."

"So he's telling me to hang loose and stay randy? I can live with that."

297

She giggles but stops abruptly. "You just reminded me of something. Could you stand it if I brought out one more book?"

"I'm getting used to it."

She rummages in a bookcase and comes back to snuggle against him. "This is from *A Christmas Sermon*."

"But it's not even Halloween yet!"

"Shhh! Listen."

If we do not genially judge our own deficiencies, is it not to be feared we shall be even stern to the trespasses of others? It is probable that nearly all who think of conduct at all, think of it too much; it is certain we all think too much of sin. We are not damned for doing wrong, but for not doing right.

He looks at her. "Can I have a copy of that? Maybe Louis has a point. I spend too much time pursuing wrong-doers, including myself. After this case, perhaps I should look at some other line of work."

"What did you have in mind?"

"Psychic investigator. What do you think?"

"Somehow, I don't think you're serious. But while you're deciding, I'll make a copy of this for you. You can carry it around with you and let it sink in."

"I'll keep it in my wallet."

"Put it in your shirt pocket. That way, it's over your heart. Works way better than sticking it next to your butt."

"So that's what I've been doing wrong."

"Now you know. And don't forget Fanny's message."

"Which is?"

"That together we can survive almost anything, and in the end, that's what counts."

"Yes. ma'am. Anything else?"

"Just that the pizza wasn't all that substantial."

"Would you be interested in getting something to eat?"

"Ooh! Another date night! This time we'll talk about us, I promise. There's an interesting Ethiopian restaurant right across the street." She's already heading to the closet for her coat.

He pats the book of essays for luck and hurries to catch her.

Mr. Stevenson

ACKNOWLEDGEMENTS

I owe a large debt of gratitude to Jake Tommerup, Michael Bootz and Maria Graham for reading early drafts of the novel. You provided unflagging support of this project and also saved me from my inability to write, type, spell or stitch words together coherently.

The poems *The Black Vulture* and *At the End* were written by George Sterling and Nora May French, respectively, and are in the public domain, as are the quoted sections from Stevenson's *Strange Case of Dr. Jekyll and Mr. Hyde.*

Kevin's invitation to lunch at Chow (page 282) includes a reproduction of *Love Among the Ruins* (Edward Burne-Jones, 1894). The picture of Robert Louis Stevenson (page 299) is a modification of the 1893 portrait by Henry Walter Barnett. The woman in the window (page 157) is Fanny Stevenson in old age (photographer unknown), and the joint portrait of the Stevensons (page 127) is from a photograph taken during a visit with King Kalākaua in Hawaii. The picture of the fictitious Liam Cromartie (page 275) is based on a photograph of Tom Day, a crew member of the *Janet Nicoll*. Like the photographs of The Stockton Asylum and the Stevensons in Samoa (page 185), all of these are in the public domain.

The picture of San Francisco General Hospital is from a photograph by Jim Heaphy (public domain). The image of the San Mateo Masonic Hall is a modified version of a photograph taken by Eugene Zelenko and is used with permission under the terms of the GNU Free Documentation License (https://commons.wikimedia.org/wiki/Commons:GNU_Free_Documentation_License,_version_1.2.) Pasta Puttanesca and the man in the wheelchair are modifications of images licensed from https://www.123rf.com/.

All other illustrations are from photographs taken by the author in San Francisco and processed with Affinity Photo, Exposure X6 and Topaz Labs Simplify software.

Any resemblance of Charles Montfort, Liam Cromartie and the present day characters in *The Montfort Prescription* to actual persons, living or dead, is entirely coincidental. The lives of Robert Louis and Fanny Stevenson, Belle Field, Nora May French and George Sterling have been presented as accurately as the historical record allows. The bibliography below also lists sources that helped me understand their histories and also the story of the Carmel Writers Group, the workings of police departments, the geography of San Francisco, Post-Traumatic Stress Disorder, and the world of Artificial Intelligence. Additional information can also be found at www.themontfortprescription.com,

BIBLIOGRAPHY

Amidon, Amy. "Guest Perspective: Moral Injury and Moral Repair." *Center for Deployment Psychology*, USU CDP, 3 Jan. 2016, deploymentpsych.org/blog/guest-perspective-moral-injury-and-moral-repair.

Andersen, Ted. "Former S.F. Mansion of Author Robert Louis Stevenson's Widow Lists for $13.8 Million ." *Bizjournals.com*, 17 June 2019, www.bizjournals.com/sanfrancisco/news/2019/06/17/former-s-f-mansion-of-author-robert-louis.html.

"Basic Academy." *San Francisco Police Department*, 10 Apr. 2019, www.sanfranciscopolice.org/your-sfpd/careers/sworn-job-openings/basic-academy.

"Bid to Trace Lost Robert Louis Stevenson Manuscripts." *BBC News*, BBC, 9 July 2010, www.bbc.com/news/10569471.

Bowers, Maggie Ann. *Magic(Al) Realism*. Routledge, 2010.

Calder, Jenni. *Robert Louis Stevenson: a Life Study*. Oxford University Press, 1980.

Caldwell, Elsie Noble., and Isobel Osbourne Field. *Last Witness for Robert Louis Stevenson*. University of Oklahoma Press, 1960.

Callaway, Ewen. "'It Will Change Everything': DeepMind's AI Makes Gigantic Leap in Solving Protein Structures." *Nature News*, Nature Publishing Group, 30 Nov. 2020, www.nature.com/articles/d41586-020-03348-4.

Callow, Philip. *Louis: a Life of Robert Louis Stevenson*. Ivan R. Dee, 2001.

Crank, John P. *Understanding Police Culture*. 2nd ed., Anderson, 2004.

DeFord, Miriam Allen. *They Were San Franciscans*. Caxton Printers, 1947.

Dryden, Linda. "Life: Robert Louis Stevenson's Life." *Robert Louis Stevenson Website*, 13 Nov. 2009, robert-louis-stevenson.org/life/.

Eadicicco, Lisa. "How This Poker-Playing Computer Beat the Best Human Players." *Time*, Time, 1 Feb. 2017, time.com/4656011/artificial-intelligence-ai-poker-tournament-libratus-cmu/.

Eigner, Edwin M. *Robert Louis Stevenson and Romantic Tradition*. Princeton Univ. Pr., 1966.

Field, Isobel, and Peter Browning. *This Life I've Loved: an Autobiography*. Great West Books, 2005.

Fitzpatrick, Elayne Wareing. *A Quixotic Companionship: Fanny and Robert Louis Stevenson*. Old Monteray Preservation Society, 1997.

French, Nora May, et al. *The Outer Gate: the Collected Poems of Nora May French*. Hippocampus Press, 2009.

Furnas, Joseph Chamberlain. *Voyage to Windward: the Life of Robert Louis Stevenson*. Faber and Faber, 1952.

Gilmartin, Kevin M. *Emotional Survival for Law Enforcement: a Guide for Officers and Their Families*. E-S Press, 2002.

Grossman, Dave. *On Killing: the Psychological Cost of Learning to Kill in War and Society*. Revised ed., Little, Brown and Co., 2009.

Hammond, John Richard., and Robert Louis. Stevenson. *A Robert Louis Stevenson Companion*. Macmillan, 1984.

Harman, Claire. *Myself and the Other Fellow a Life of Robert Louis Stevenson*. HarperCollins, 2005.

Ho, Vivian. "Amid Push for S.F. Police Reform, Union Escalates Counterattack." *SFChronicle.com*, San Francisco Chronicle, 24 Mar. 2016, www.sfchronicle.com/crime/article/Amid-push-for-S-F-police-reform-union-escalates-7004239.php.

Hodges, Margaret. "When Robert Louis Stevenson Was One Of Us." *AMERICAN HERITAGE*, Dec. 1988, www.americanheritage.com/when-robert-louis-stevenson-was-one-us.

Horan, Nancy. *Under the Wide and Starry Sky: a Novel*. Ballantine Books, 2014.

Issler, Anne Roller. *Happier for His Presence: San Francisco and Robert Louis Stevenson*. Stanford University Press, 1949.

Katz, Jack. *Seductions of Crime: Moral and Sensual Attractions in Doing Evil*. Basic Books, 1992.

Kiely, Robert. *Robert Louis Stevenson and the Fiction of Adventure*. Harvard University Press, 1964.

Kirschman, Ellen. *I Love a Cop: What Police Families Need to Know*. The Guilford Press, 2018.

Kotta, Sabna, et al. "Exploring Scientifically Proven Herbal Aphrodisiacs." *Pharmacognosy Reviews*, Medknow Publications & Media Pvt Ltd, Jan. 2013, www.ncbi.nlm.nih.gov/pmc/articles/PMC3731873/.

Kraft, Robert N. *Violent Accounts: Understanding the Psychology of Perpetrators Through South Africa's Truth and Reconciliation Commission*. NYU Press, 2014.

Lapierre, Alexandra. *Fanny Stevenson: Muse, Adventuress and Romantic Enigma*. Fourth Estate, 1996.

Litz, Brett T, et al. "Moral Injury and Moral Repair in War Veterans: A Preliminary Model and Intervention Strategy." *Clinical Psychology Review*, vol. 29, pp. 695–706.

Livesey, Margot. "The Double Life of Robert Louis Stevenson." *The Atlantic*, Atlantic Media Company, 1 Nov. 1994, www.theatlantic.com/magazine/archive/1994/11/the-double-life-of-robert-louis-stevenson/306474/.

Lofland, Lee. *Police Procedure & Investigation: a Guide for Writer's*. F+W Publications, Inc., 2007.

Mackay, Margaret Mackprang. *The Violent Friend; the Story of Mrs. Robert Louis Stevenson*. Doubleday, 1968.

Maguen, Shira, and Brett Litz. "Moral Injury in the Context of War." *National Center for PTSD*, U.S Department of Veterans Affairs, 23 Dec. 2011, www.ptsd.va.gov/professional/treat/cooccurring/moral_injury.asp.

Marr, Bernard. "What Are Artificial Neural Networks - A Simple Explanation For Absolutely Anyone." *Forbes*, Forbes Magazine, 24 Sept. 2018, www.forbes.com/sites/bernardmarr/2018/09/24/what-are-artificial-neural-networks-a-simple-explanation-for-absolutely-anyone/#63fd11b61245.

Mazzocchi, Fulvio. "Could Big Data Be the End of Theory in Science? A Few Remarks on the Epistemology of Data-Driven Science." *EMBO Reports*, John Wiley and Sons Inc., 10 Sept. 2015, www.ncbi.nlm.nih.gov/pmc/articles/PMC4766450/.

McLynn, Frank. *Robert Louis Stevenson: a Biography*. Random House, 1994.

MacNair, Rachel. *Perpetration-Induced Traumatic Stress: the Psychological Consequences of Killing*. Authors Choice Press, 2005.

McNamara, Patrick. *Spirit Possession and Exorcism: History, Psychology, and Neurobiology*. Praeger, 2011.

Meagher, Robert E., and Douglas A. Pryer. *War and Moral Injury: A Reader*. Cascade Books, 2018.

Metz, Cade. "Making New Drugs With a Dose of Artificial Intelligence." *Zi-Medical.com*, 22 Apr. 2019, www.zi-medical.com/l/making-new-drugs-with-a-dose-of-artificial-intelligence/.

Nickerson, Roy. *Robert Louis Stevenson in California: a Remarkable Courtship*. Chronicle Books, 1982.

NIST Office of Data and Informatics. "NIST Chemistry Webbook, SRD 69." *NIST Chemistry WebBook*, National Institute of Standards and Technology, https://webbook.nist.gov/chemistry/.

"Nora May French, Writer Ends Life With Poison." *San Francisco Call 15 November 1907*, California Digital Newspaper Collection, 4 Aug. 2015, cdnc.ucr.edu/?a=d&d=SFC19071115.2.6&e=-------en--20--1--txt-txIN--------1.

Osbourne, Katharine D. *Robert Louis Stevenson in California*. Literary Licensing, LLC., 2014.

Plantinga, Adam. *400 Things Cops Know: Street-Smart Lessons from a Veteran Patrolman*. Quill Driver Books, 2014.

Plantinga, Adam. *Police Craft: What Cops Know about Crime, Community and Violence*. Quill Driver Books, an Imprint of Linden Publishing, 2018.

Poletti, Therese. *Art Deco San Francisco: the Architecture of Timothy Pflueger*. Princeton Architectural Press, 2008.

Press, Gil. "The Brute Force Of IBM Deep Blue And Google Deep-Mind." *Forbes*, Forbes Magazine, 8 Feb. 2018, www.forbes.com/sites/gilpress/2018/02/07/the-brute-force-of-deep-blue-and-deep-learning/#6acae11749e3.

Pykett, Lyn. *Reading Fin De Siècle Fictions*. Routledge, 2016.

Redmon, Michael. "Isobel Field." *The Santa Barbara Independent*, 6 Mar. 2012, www.independent.com/2012/03/06/isobel-field/.

Sacks, Oliver W. *Hallucinations*. Vintage Books, 2013.

Sanchez, Nellie Van de Grift. *The Life of Mrs. Robert Louis Stevenson*. James Stevenson Publisher, 2001.

Senese, Louis C. *Anatomy of Interrogation Themes: the Reid Technique of Interviewing and Interrogation*. John E. Reid and Associates, 2012.

Shea, Christopher. "Why Power Corrupts." *Smithsonian.com*, Smithsonian Institution, 1 Oct. 2012, www.smithsonianmag.com/science-nature/why-power-corrupts-37165345/.

Smith, Matt. "Once a Joke, SFPD Is Actually Solving Murders These Days" *SF Weekly*, 4 Nov. 2009, www.sfweekly.com/news/once-a-joke-sfpd-is-actually-solving-murders-these-days/.

Sterling, George, and S. T. Joshi. *The Thirst of Satan: Poems of Fantasy and Terror*. Hippocampus Press, 2003.

Stevenson, Robert Louis. ""A Chapter on Dreams"." *Selected Essays of Robert Louis Stevenson*. Lit2Go Edition. 1892. Web. <https://etc.usf.edu/lit2go/110/selected-essays-of-robert-louis-stevenson/5111/a-chapter-on-dreams/>. September 21, 2018.

Stevenson, Robert Louis. ""A Christmas Sermon"." *Selected Essays of Robert Louis Stevenson*. Lit2Go Edition. 1900. Web. <https://etc.usf.edu/lit2go/110/selected-essays-of-robert-louis-stevenson/5112/a-christmas-sermon/>. September 21, 2018.

Stevenson, Robert Louis. "Strange Case of Dr. Jekyll and Mr. Hyde Autograph Manuscript." *The Morgan Library & Museum*, 3 Apr. 2019, www.themorgan.org/collection/robert-louis-stevenson/dr-jekyll-and-mr-hyde.

Stevenson, Robert Louis. "The Merry Men." *Free Classic E-Books*, 27 Dec. 2018, www.freeclassicebooks.com/Robert%20Louis%20Stevenson/The%20Merry%20Men.pdf.

Stevenson, Robert Louis. "The Strange Case of Dr Jekyll and Mr Hyde." *Planet EBook*, 2018, www.planetebook.com/the-strange-case-of-dr-jekyll-and-mr-hyde/.

Stevenson, Robert Louis. *Treasure Island*. Palazzo Editions Ltd, 2006. Illustrated by Robert Ingpen

Stevenson, Robert Louis, et al. *The Letters of Robert Louis Stevenson*. Yale University Press, 1995.

Stevenson, Robert Louis, and James D. Hart. *From Scotland to Silverado: Comprising The Amateur Emigrant: "From the Clyde to Sandy Hook" and "Across the Plains", The Silverado Squatters and Four Essays on California*. Belknap Press of Harvard University Press, 1968.

Stevenson, Robert Louis, and M Grant Kellermeyer. *Dr Jekyll & Mr Hyde, The Body Snatcher, and Other Horrors: The Best Horror and Ghost Stories of Robert Louis Stevenson*. Independently Published, 2019.

Strauss, Neil. "Inside The World's Longest-Running, Most Successful Free Love Commune." *Maxim*, 17 June 2018, www.maxim.com/maxim-man/how-to-free-love-commune-neil-strauss-2018-6.

Swearingen, Roger G., and Robert Louis Stevenson. *The Prose Writings of Robert Louis Stevenson: a Guide*. Archon Books, 1980.

Tarrant, John. *Bring Me the Rhinoceros: and Other Zen Koans That Will Save Your Life*. Shambhala, 2008.

Tavris, Carol, and Elliot Aronson. *Mistakes Were Made (but Not by Me): Why We Justify Foolish Beliefs, Bad Decisions, and Hurtful Acts*. Mariner Books, 2015.

Terry, R. C. *Robert Louis Stevenson: Interviews and Recollections*. Macmillan, 1996.

"The Reid Technique." *John E. Reid & Associates, Inc.*, 2019, www.reid.com/educational_info/critictechnique.html.

Turing, Alan M. "I.-Computing Machinery and Intelligence." *OUP Academic*, Oxford University Press, 1 Oct. 1950, academic.oup.com/mind/article/LIX/236/433/986238.

"Understanding PTSD and PTSD Treatment." *About Face Booklet*, National Center for PTSD, May 2019, https://www.ptsd.va.gov/publications/print/understandingptsd_booklet.pdf.

Walker, Franklin. *The Seacoast of Bohemia*. Peregrine Smith, 1973.

Wallach, Izhar, et al. "AtomNet: A Deep Convolutional Neural Network for Bioactivity Prediction in Structure-Based Drug Discovery." *ArXiv.org*, 10 Oct. 2015, arxiv.org/abs/1510.02855.

"Welcome to Lafayette Morehouse (Operated More University 1977-1997)." *Lafayette Morehouse: About Us*, 2019, www.lafayettemorehouse.com/about.html.

Wolchover, Natalie. "Artificial Intelligence Will Do What We Ask. That's a Problem." *Quanta Magazine*, 30 Jan. 2020, www.quantamagazine.org/artificial-intelligence-will-do-what-we-ask-thats-a-problem-20200130/.

Zin, Phyo Kyaw, et al. "Cheminformatics-Based Enumeration and Analysis of Large Libraries of Macrolide Scaffolds." *SpringerLink*, Springer International Publishing, 12 Nov. 2018, link.springer.com/article/10.1186/s13321-018-0307-6.